KILL THE NEXT ONE

KILL THE NEXT ONE

FEDERICO AXAT

TRANSLATED BY DAVID FRYE

MULHOLLAND BOOKS

Little, Brown and Company
New York Boston London

Mulholland Books / Little, Brown and Company
Hachette Book Group
1290 Avenue of the Americas, New York, NY 10104
mulhollandbooks.com

First English language edition: December 2016
Originally published as *La última salida* by Planeta de Libros, March 2016

Mulholland Books is an imprint of Little, Brown and Company, a division of Hachette Book Group, Inc. The Mulholland Books name and logo are trademarks of Hachette Book Group, Inc.

ISBN 978-0-316-35421-9
LCCN 2016941642

10 9 8 7 6 5 4 3 2 1

LSC-C

Printed in the United States of America

To my parents,
Luz L. Di Pirro and
Raúl E. Axat

PART I

1

TED MCKAY was about to put a bullet through his brain when the doorbell rang. Insistently.

He paused. He couldn't press the trigger when he had someone waiting at the front door.

Leave, whoever you are.

Again, the doorbell. Then a man's voice.

"Open up! I know you can hear me!"

The voice reached him in his study with amazing clarity. It was so clear that for an instant Ted wondered if he had really heard it.

He looked around, as if to find something in the empty study that might prove that someone had really shouted. He saw his account books, the Monet reproduction, the desk, and finally the letter in which he had explained it all to Holly.

"Please open up!"

Ted still held the Browning inches from his head; its weight was beginning to tire his arm. His plan wouldn't work if the guy at the door heard him shoot and called the police. Holly was at Disney World with the girls, and he didn't want her to get this news so far from home. No way.

The bell stopped ringing. Now, pounding at the door.

"Come on! I won't leave till you let me in!"

The pistol began to shake. Ted lowered his arm, rested the gun in his lap. He ran the fingers of his left hand through his hair and again cursed the stranger. Somebody selling magazines? Door-to-door salesmen weren't welcome in this neighborhood, especially not when they acted as obnoxious as this guy.

For a few seconds the shouts and the knocking stopped. Ted began to raise the gun back to his temple, slowly, very slowly.

He was just starting to think the guy must have gotten tired and taken off when a renewed barrage of shouts and banging proved him wrong. But Ted wasn't going to open the door—not him. He'd wait. Sooner or later the asshole would have to give up, wouldn't he?

Then his eye was drawn to something lying on the desk: a piece of paper folded double, like the note he'd left for Holly, except this one didn't have his wife's name written on it. Had he been so dumb that he'd forgotten to toss a draft of his note? While the guy at the door continued shouting, he consoled himself with the thought that some good, at least, had come from the unexpected interruption. He unfolded the note and read.

What he saw there chilled his blood. It was his own handwriting. But he had no memory of writing these words.

Open the door
It's your only way out

Had he written it in a context he couldn't recall? While playing some game with Cindy or Nadine, maybe? He could find no explanation for the note—not in this crazy situation, with a crazy guy about to pound the front door down. But of course there must have been some rational explanation.

Kid yourself all you want.

The Browning in his right hand weighed a ton.

"Open up now, Ted!"

He jerked his head up, alert. Had he just heard his own name? Ted had never been close with his neighbors, but he thought he could at least recognize their voices. This guy didn't sound like any of them. He stood up and left the pistol on the desk. He knew he'd have no choice but to see what it was all about. Thinking it over for a second, he decided it wasn't the end of the world. He'd get rid of the asshole, whoever he was, and get back to his study and end his life, once and for all. He'd been planning this for weeks, and he wasn't going to back out at the last moment because of some jerk selling magazines or some such crap.

He stood up with determination. A small jar sat on the corner of the desk, filled with old pens, paper clips, half-used erasers—all sorts of junk. Ted quickly upended the jar and found the key he had dropped inside it just two minutes earlier. Picking it up, he looked it over quizzically, an object he had thought he'd never see again. By now he was supposed to be sprawled back across his recliner, with gunshot residue on his fingers, floating toward the light.

When you've decided to take your own life—it doesn't matter whether you have any doubts about your decision—those final minutes will test your will. Ted had just learned this lesson, and he loathed the idea of having to go through it all over again.

He went to the door to his study feeling truly annoyed, put the key in the lock, turned it, and opened the door. He felt another twinge at seeing the note he had taped to the front of the door, just above eye level. It was a warning for Holly. "Honey, I left a copy of the key to the study on top of the fridge. Don't let the kids in. I love you." It seemed cruel, but Ted had thought it all through. He didn't want one of his girls to find him lying behind the desk with a hole through his head. On the other hand, dying in his study made perfect sense. He had seriously weighed the pros and cons of jumping in the river or traveling far away and throwing himself under the wheels of a train somewhere, but he knew the uncertainty would be harder on them. Especially on Holly. She would need to see him with her own eyes, need to be sure. Need to feel...the *impact*. She was young and beautiful and could make a new life for herself. She'd move on.

A salvo of knocking.

"Coming!" Ted yelled.

The knocking stopped.

Open the door. It's your only way out.

He could see the stranger's silhouette through the tall, narrow window beside the door. He crossed the living room with slow, almost defiant steps. Once more he examined everything, much as he had studied the key a few moments ago. He saw the immense flat-screen TV, the table with seats for fifteen guests, the porcelain vases. In his own way, he had taken his leave of all these worldly objects. And yet here he was again, good old Teddy, wandering through his own house like a ghost.

He stopped short. Could this be his own version of "the light"?

For a second he felt a wild urge to run back to his study and check whether his body lay sprawled behind the desk. He reached out and ran his fingers over the back of the sofa. He felt the leather, smooth and cool to his touch, too real to be a figment of his imagination, he thought. But how could he be certain?

He threw the door open. As soon as he saw the young man at the threshold, he knew how he'd survived as a door-to-door salesman despite his bad manners. He was maybe twenty-five, impeccably dressed in white trousers, a snakeskin belt, and a polo shirt with bright, colorful horizontal stripes. He looked more like a golfer than a salesman, but the beat-up leather briefcase in his right hand clashed with his preppy clothes. His hair was blond and shoulder-length, his eyes were sky blue, and his smile was rakish. Ted could easily see Holly, or any of the women in the neighborhood, buying whatever junk the guy had to offer.

"Whatever it is, I'm not interested," Ted said.

The smile grew broader.

"Oh, I'm afraid I'm not here to sell you anything," the guy said, as if the very idea were beyond ridiculous.

Ted glanced over the stranger's shoulder. No car was parked along the curb out front, or anywhere along Sullivan Boulevard. It wasn't as hot out as it had been lately, but walking any distance under the afternoon sun should have left some traces on this shameless dude's face. Besides, why park so far away?

"Don't be scared," the young man said, as if he could read Ted's mind. "My partner dropped me off in front here. Not to raise suspicions in the neighborhood."

The mention of an accomplice didn't faze Ted. Getting killed in a robbery would be even more dignified than shooting himself.

"I'm busy. I need you to go."

Ted started to close the door but the man reached in and stopped him. It wasn't necessarily a hostile move. He had an imploring gleam in his eye.

"My name is Justin Lynch, Mr. McKay. If you'll just..."

"How do you know my name?"

"If you'll just let me come in and talk to you for ten minutes, I'll explain everything."

There was a moment of suspense. Ted had no intention of letting the guy in—that much was clear. But he had to admit to feeling kind of curious about why he was there. In the end, reason won.

"Sorry. This isn't a good time."

"You're wrong. It's the per—"

Ted slammed the door. Lynch's last words reached him, muffled by the door, but perfectly audible. "It's the perfect time." Ted remained facing the door, listening, as if he knew there'd be more to follow.

And so there was. Lynch spoke even louder to make himself heard.

"I know what you're about to do with the nine millimeter you left in your study. I'll promise you one thing: I won't try to talk you out of it."

Ted opened the door.

2

TED HAD planned his suicide with consummate care. This was no impulsive, last-minute decision, plagued with loose ends. He wouldn't be one of those pathetic guys who botch the job in a pitiful cry for attention. Or so he had thought. Because if he had been all that careful, how had Lynch found out? The stranger with the broad smile and the perfect good looks had been right on target about the caliber of Ted's pistol and where he had left it. Venturing that Ted was about to take his own life wasn't totally off the wall, perhaps, but if it was a guess it was a very lucky one. Yet Lynch had tossed it off without a trace of hesitation.

They sat on either side of the table. Ted felt an old, familiar sensation: the shiver of an adrenaline surge, followed by that old mental sharpness and total concentration on beating his opponent. He hadn't played in a chess tournament in years, but the feeling was unmistakable. And pleasant.

"So Travis asked you to spy on me," he stated.

Lynch, who had set his leather briefcase on the table and seemed about to open it, held off, a look of consternation on his face.

"Your business partner has nothing to do with this, Ted. Mind if I call you Ted?"

Ted shrugged.

"I don't see any photos of your kids, Nadine and Cindy," Lynch said, his gazed fixed on the contents of his briefcase. He seemed to be looking for something.

Indeed, there were no family photos. Ted had removed them all from the living room. A piece of advice: if you're going to kill yourself, move any photographs of loved ones out of the way first. It's simpler to plan when your family isn't looking over your shoulder.

"Never mention my daughters."

Lynch displayed his stunning smile. He raised his hands.

"I was just trying to win your trust, a bit of chitchat. I've seen their photos before, and I know they're both with their mother in Florida now. They went down to visit their grandparents, didn't they?"

It sounded like a line from a gangster movie: *We know where your family is; don't be a wise guy*. There was something genuine about Lynch's attitude, though, as if he really were trying to be friendly.

"I let you into my house. I think there's already a certain amount of trust between us."

"I'm glad."

"Tell me what you know about my family."

Lynch sat with his hands on top of his briefcase. He made a dismissive gesture with one of them.

"Oh, not too much, I'm afraid. We don't like to meddle any more than we have to. I know they get back on Friday, which gives us three days to finish our business. More than enough time."

"Our business?"

"Of course!"

Lynch pulled two thin folders from the briefcase and set them to one side. He pushed the briefcase away.

"Ted, have you ever considered doing a hit job?"

Talk about getting straight to the point!

"Are you with the police? If you are, you should have identified yourself."

Ted stood up. He was sure the folders were filled with lurid photographs. They'd been watching him as a murder suspect and the suicide plan had been the decisive piece of evidence to prove his guilt. That's why Lynch had insisted on getting into the house. Was he an FBI agent?

"I'm not with the police, Ted. Please sit."

"I want you out of my house—now." Ted pointed to the door as if Lynch didn't know the way out.

"Do you really want me to leave before we can talk over how we know about your suicide?"

The guy was good. Ted *did* want to know.

"You have five minutes to explain."

Ted didn't sit down.

"Fair enough," Lynch said. "I'll explain it to you now. I work for some people who'd like to learn how a man such as yourself comes to know people such as the ones I have here." He placed a hand on the folders. "If you'll allow me, I'm going to open one of these folders and we'll take a peek in it. You'll get it right away. You're a smart man."

Lynch opened the folder and placed it in the center of the table and turned to face Ted, who remained standing with his hands on his hips.

The first page was a copy of a police file. Stapled in one corner were photos, front and profile, of a man perhaps in his thirties. His skin was tanned and his hair neatly combed and gelled. He peered defiantly into the lens, his chin raised slightly and his light-blue eyes open wide. According to the caption, his name was Edward Blaine.

"Blaine has had a few minor brushes with the law in his time: petty larceny, assault," Lynch said as he turned over the page. "This time he's accused of killing his girlfriend."

Ted had been right about one thing: the folders were full of lurid photos. The one staring at him now was of a woman who had been brutally murdered, lying in the narrow space between a bed and a dresser; there were at least seven stab wounds on her naked torso.

"Her name was Amanda Herdman. She and Blaine saw each other off and on—nothing too formal. He got cheap drugs for her, and every now and then they'd try something heavier. But from what his friends and her friends say, their relationship was an endless cycle of quarreling and making up. When she turned up dead in her apartment, the police started with Blaine. The guy admitted he'd fought with Herdman in a fit of jealousy, but of course he hadn't stabbed her. You want the punch line? They couldn't prove anything. Had to let him go."

At some point Ted had sat down. He couldn't take his eyes off the photographs. Lynch flipped the page. There were some close-ups: Amanda's swollen eyes, deep cuts to her chest, bruises everywhere.

"Innocent?" Ted asked, confused.

"The bastard was careful not to hit her with his fists. Naturally, no murder weapon was ever found. His prints were all over the house, but there were none on the body."

"But he practically confessed when he admitted they'd fought."

"His lawyers argued that he had made his confession under duress, which was more or less true, and they could prove it. The technicality that got him off was the forensic analysis of the time of death. The prosecutor's expert placed the time of death between seven and ten p.m. Multiple witnesses testified to seeing Blaine at a cheap dive, the Black Sombrero Bar, during that time frame. Seems he'd been especially concerned with having as many people as possible see him there; he had more than thirty reliable witnesses. There was even security camera footage from the parking lot."

Ted leafed through the pages. There were a few more photos of Herdman's body and copies of files with passages highlighted.

"You get it now, don't you, Ted?"

Ted was starting to understand.

"How do your people know Blaine killed her?"

"The organization I represent has informants inside the prison system. I'm not talking about criminals; we prefer not to deal with them. Our informants are lawyers, judges, and aides who know when a murder case smells funny. Our business is...*eradicating* any doubt. As for Blaine, the explanation is extremely simple, though for him it was almost certainly a case of dumb luck, nothing more. We hired an expert and asked how they could have made such a huge mistake in calculating the time of death. He told us that the tests they ran depend on the body temperature of the deceased, which they take the moment the corpse is discovered. Core body temperature decreases according to an established—"

Ted stopped him. "I know the method. I've watched *CSI,* too."

Lynch laughed.

"I'll get to the point, then. We figured it out when we visited the scene of the crime—Amanda Herdman's first-floor apartment, which is vacant now. There's an industrial laundry in the basement, directly under her floor. The main ventilation duct from the dryers passes directly beneath the spot where her body was found. It kept the corpse warm so that the heat loss proceeded more slowly than is typical."

"In other words, the guy killed her earlier in the day."

"Exactly. Some six to eight hours earlier. The murder didn't take place at night, but in the middle of the day, before Blaine went to the bar."

"And there was no way to reopen the case?"

"He'd already been tried and found innocent. We don't put the blame on the justice system; we prefer to think that sometimes a bastard slips through the cracks. It happens the other way around, too, sadly. But this isn't about weighing both sides, is it?"

Ted didn't need to hear more.

"And what you want from me is to kill Blaine, isn't it?"

Lynch flashed his perfect teeth.

"Like I said, you're a smart man."

3

HE STOOD looking at the refrigerator. There, held in place on the door by a magnet shaped like an apple, was a photo of Holly that he'd forgotten to remove. The girls had decorated the border with concentric rectangles of glitter. Holly was running from the ocean to the beach, wearing the red bikini that had long been Ted's favorite. She was laughing, her head tilted to one side, her long blond hair aflame with sunlight. The picture had been snapped at the exact moment when one of her legs had disappeared behind her knee, so that her only point of support seemed to violate all the basic laws of balance.

The picture had been on that refrigerator door a long time. Ted stared at it, forgetting why he'd come into the kitchen in the first place. He held the photo by one corner and pulled it down. He could almost hear Holly laughing, and then weeping, interrupted by her heartrending screams at the door to his study...How could he do something like that to her?

He opened a drawer, any drawer, and deposited the photo there among the unfamiliar kitchen tools.

There were two beers left in the fridge. He picked them both up by the neck with one hand and closed the door with a foot. He stood there, resting against the countertop. Lynch was still in the living room; the idea of offering him something to drink had spontaneously popped into Ted's head, but now he regretted it. He needed to think things over on his own for a minute, because the truth was that as soon as the stranger insinuated his plan to him, an inexplicable tingling had run through his body. He was no fan of vigilante justice—not in the strict sense of the term—though he did think the world would be better off without parasites like Blaine. The idea of killing a man didn't motivate him; he wasn't even in favor of the death penalty. Or so he said whenever he was asked. Sometimes, at the shooting range, when the cardboard silhouette was moving toward him and he hit it right between the eyes, he fantasized about taking down one of the "bad guys," one who had committed some despicable crime. He nodded. Lynch might not be a salesman of the sort he had expected, but the guy had managed to push just the right buttons to get Ted to take his proposal seriously.

He kept staring at the apple-shaped refrigerator magnet. Now that Holly's photo was out of sight, he could think clearly. Lynch's ideas were seductive. There was something deep, something decisive about them: the conviction that if Ted killed one of the bad guys, Holly and the girls would see him as a hero, not a coward.

On his way back to the living room, he had the crazy notion that he'd find nobody there. That Lynch had left or, worse still, that Ted had only imagined their meeting.

But Lynch was still there, the two folders on the table in front of him. He stood up to grab the bottle Ted offered him and thanked him with a tilt of the head. He took a long gulp.

Ted sat down again. "How did your people find out?"

"About the suicide?"

Ted nodded.

"The Organization has its methods, Ted. I'm not sure it would be prudent to share them with you."

"I think it's the least I deserve, if you're asking me to kill a man."

Lynch thought it over.

"Does this mean I can count on your acceptance of our offer?"

"It doesn't mean anything. For now, I want you to tell me how your people knew."

"Sounds fair." Lynch took another swig and set the bottle on the table. "We have two ways to pick our candidates. The first gives us the most potential candidates, but it's also proven to be the least effective. A pity, to be sure. There are psychologists committed to our cause who alert us to potential suicides; we—the doctors and the rest of us—allow ourselves a little leeway on the ethics here, since we're aware that what we do violates patient confidentiality. We never force anyone, however. We show up, as I've done at your house, and make our offer. If the candidate doesn't accept, we disappear without a trace. In your case, I have to admit, my entrance was a little more dramatic than usual. I thought that...well, I thought I'd come too late."

"You've been spying on me?"

"Not exactly. When I get to a candidate's house, I usually start by taking a look around the property. In your case, we knew your wife and daughters were traveling, but even so, there might be an unexpected friend or relative. Or a dog that doesn't like visitors. While I was walking the perimeter to make sure everything was in order, I looked through the window of your study and saw what you were about to do."

"I see. So you *were* spying on me."

"My apologies. We try to meddle as little as possible."

"What's your other way of picking people?"

"Oh, right. You see, Ted, a lot of people are so thankful to the Organization that they somehow feel *indebted*. Many of the professionals I've mentioned form part of this group. But in general, they are..."

"People with ties to the victims." Ted pointed at the folders.

Lynch seemed more comfortable dropping hints than stating things baldly. A frown of displeasure flitted across his face.

"Indeed," Lynch admitted, ready to move on. "Now allow me to explain what's in the other folder."

Lynch pushed Blaine's folder aside. He opened the second folder, which was much slimmer. The first page was a color photograph of a man standing on the deck of a boat. He was about forty, wearing a life jacket, holding a fishing rod and an enormous fish.

Ted picked up the photo. "And who is this?"

"Wendell. You may be familiar with his name. He's a well-known businessman."

"Never heard of him."

"It's better that way."

Ted passed the photograph back. There were a couple of typewritten pages in the folder and a few maps with directions. Very little information compared to the first folder.

"Who'd the businessman bump off? His wife?"

Lynch smiled.

"Wendell isn't married. And he hasn't bumped anybody off. He isn't like Blaine. He's like you."

Ted raised his eyebrows.

"He was also going to kill himself," Lynch said. "And like you, he knew how painful and incomprehensible his family would find his suicide. Here's the deal, Ted: You kill Blaine, and in so doing you'll be giving Amanda Herdman's family some peace of mind and a sense of justice. In return, we'll let you join a chain. Wendell is one link; you'll be the next."

Ted pondered for a second. He soon understood.

"After killing Blaine, I'm supposed to kill Wendell?"

"Exactly. He knows all about it; he'll be waiting for you. Likewise, you'll wait here afterwards in your home for the next link in the chain to show up. Think it over, Ted. Think about the difference it will make for your family when they find out a stranger has come into your house and shot you, compared with a suicide—"

"Please stop."

"I know you've thought it through," Lynch said, ignoring Ted's plea. "You figure taking your own life is better than disappearing without a trace. But now we're offering you an even better way out: you get shot by someone else, and you'll be remembered as the victim of a tragedy. Think how much easier it will be for your daughters to get over something like that. I don't know if you're aware of the statistics, but many children, especially if they're young, never recover—"

"That's enough! I get it."

"So, what do you say?"

"I have to think it over some. Wendell is an innocent man."

"Come on, Ted. I've done this dozens of times. You already know the answer. The deal doesn't benefit you alone; you'll be helping Wendell, too. He's waiting at his lakeside home right now for you to carry out his last wish."

"Why don't you guys do it yourselves?"

Lynch didn't bat an eyelash. His smile proved that, as he said, this was hardly the first time he'd gone through the first stage of talking someone into doing the deed. He knew the answers to every question. He was like a telemarketer, just following the script in the playbook.

"We're the good guys in this story, Ted. We believe that whoever kills must be killed. All we do is find people who've outsmarted the system and turn them over to people who are ready to give their lives for a just cause. And we've chosen you. This is your chance. And I'm afraid it's the only way you have left."

Ted looked down at his lap. The note he'd found on the desk was sticking out of his pants pocket. He didn't even remember putting it there. He pulled it out and unfolded it, out of Lynch's reach, as the young man watched him, waiting for a final answer.

It's your only way out, he read.

Lynch had just uttered virtually the same words.

4

EDWARD BLAINE lived alone on a quiet cul-de-sac. His neighbors hated him. His unsociability and his penchant for secrecy had slowly damaged his relations with everyone in the neighborhood, who by now just gritted their teeth and tried to put up with him. Blaine was trash. Even worse, the bastard seemed proud of it, challenging anybody who got in his way, staring them down with his mirrored sunglasses and the smug smile on his face. They'd tried reasoning with him, tried mending fences with him, even tried threatening him. Nothing worked. Like a rebellious child—though already well into his thirties—Blaine seemed set on harassing anybody who came near, anyone who tried to come to any sort of agreement with him. He violated every norm of peaceful social living, from keeping his scraggly lawn unmowed to the way he treated Magnus, the fearsome rottweiler he kept cruelly chained to a post in the yard, where the dog spent long days barking at everyone who passed by. Loud parties with his drinking buddies, the thunderous rumble of his Harley, music cranked up to eleven—all par for the course. Nobody was surprised when he showed up with prostitutes, drunk or high, only to turn the poor women out onto the sidewalk in the middle of the night and let them stumble around half dressed, waiting for a taxi.

When the murder charge against Blaine became public, many of his neighbors popped champagne corks and even volunteered to testify about his unseemly behavior. More than a few even said they were sorry he'd killed the girlfriend at her house, because if he'd done her in at his own place they would have swamped his defense with enough eyewitness accounts to put him behind bars for the rest of his life. Nobody doubted that Blaine was the killer. His neighbors celebrated in advance what they felt was a foregone conclusion: Blaine would face justice and be found guilty of poor Amanda Herdman's murder. A dream come true.

Except that the DA was forced to let him go. A rock solid alibi made it possible. Several witnesses swore to seeing the bum in a bar at the time of the murder, and a number of security cameras proved that Blaine could not possibly have committed the murder. His neighbors didn't agree, of course. They didn't know how the son of a bitch had pulled a fast one on the justice system—maybe he had a twin brother or something—but he had fooled the jury somehow. Now they'd have to cope not just with a creep but with a killer. Many of them seriously considered moving.

Ted thoroughly studied the report Lynch had given him while he sat at a far table in a fast-food joint and ate a burger. Nobody would miss Edward Blaine, he thought. He could walk right into the guy's house through the front door and nobody would notice; his neighbors didn't talk to him. He memorized all the facts he'd need to know, like that the guy kept a duplicate key tucked under a welcome mat. The dog wouldn't be a problem.

As he nibbled at the hamburger, Ted worked out a simple plan. He managed to forget his own problems for a moment, between sips of Coke and handfuls of French fries, and this amazed him. The photos of Amanda Herdman and a few lurid details about Blaine's past and present helped Ted to *truly* want to kill him. He finally understood what Lynch had been saying about the cracks in the system. There was something invigorating about being able to fix this mistake—Ted could feel it.

He hid in the closet of the guest room on the first floor of Blaine's house, making himself comfortable on a pile of boxes that he had taken it upon himself to rearrange. On the underside of the shelf above his head, a Buzz Lightyear sticker glowed in the dark. He imagined the boy who had stuck it there, hiding in the closet and enjoying its glow much as Ted was doing now. He felt a kind of melancholy, now that Buzz had been forgotten by his owner and left there to glow away in solitude.

Blaine got home four hours later. Ted had cased the house before hiding and could picture where Blaine was at every moment. He came in from the garage, talking on his cell phone, yukking it up with some pal. Then he took a shower. There was a very real possibility that Blaine was planning to go out on the town tonight, but that didn't worry Ted: he'd wait. He'd been sitting in the closet for hours, and he could keep sitting there as long as it took. He nodded off a couple of times.

Once more he went over his plan, which would have disillusioned any Hollywood producer. There'd be no confrontation, no vengeful speeches, no warnings of any kind. Ted would wait until Blaine was asleep in bed, and then he'd creep out of the closet and knock him off before the guy even woke up. There was even something merciful about it.

At half past nine—Ted kept track of the time on his cell—Blaine was in the living room watching TV, probably grabbing a quick bite for dinner, occasionally insulting the contestant in some stupid game show. The outlook was unclear. Blaine might go out drinking, in which case the wait could become endless, or he might even have people over. Or maybe he would behave himself and go to bed early. One nontrivial detail could complicate things, though. Ted noticed it even before Blaine did, and he immediately pricked up his ears, listening with all his attention in the darkness that surrounded him, trying to hear past the canned laughter and applause and the game show host's squawking. Magnus was starting to whimper and whine piteously from where he was chained in the front yard. Ted frowned with frustration and shook his head. The sedatives he'd tricked the dog into swallowing hadn't been enough to do the job.

The TV was suddenly put on mute. After a long silence, the front door opened and a moment later closed again. Blaine was talking to someone over the phone, but in such a quiet voice it was impossible to make out what he was saying. He walked around the living room until finally his voice grew clearer and the unexpected happened: he entered the guest room, where Ted was hiding. He turned on the light and shut the door. Ted had left the closet door cracked open. It was too late now to close it without attracting attention. He had Blaine just feet away from him, walking impatiently to the far side of the bed, listening to what the guy on the other end of the line was saying to him.

"I'm telling you, Tony, Magnus is all doped up—he's hardly moving. They did something to him. If it was one of my sumbitch neighbors did it, I'm gonna deal with 'em, you know…What's that? No, no, I haven't done it yet." Blaine stopped talking, sat on the bed with his back to the closet, and then lowered his voice. "You're right, Tony. I'll check on it right now, make sure everything's where it's supposed to be. Sure, yeah. Talk to you in a sec."

He left the room, leaving the light on.

Two separate times, Ted saw Blaine creeping stealthily through the hall. The second time, he thought he caught a glimpse of something shiny in Blaine's right hand. It was only a matter of time before Blaine would check the guest room. Ted reached into the inner pocket of his jacket and pulled out the knife he had planned to stab him with in his sleep. An eye for an eye, he thought.

Some ten minutes later Blaine stood in the doorway, and he was in fact packing a gun. For a second Ted was sure that he'd been spotted, that Blaine had looked straight at the closet and noticed that the door was ajar. But when he came in, he again sat down on the bed with his back to the closet, and he picked up the phone he'd left on the bed.

"Hey, Tony. Everything's cool. Yeah, just wanted you to know. Tomorrow I'll figure out which of my neighbors fucked with Magnus. But I gotta leave it for tomorrow—I'm too wiped out to do it tonight. Two days, no sleep. Sure, of course. Yeah. Told you I would. Don't worry about it. Later, Tony."

He went back out. This time he turned off the light.

Ted kept the knife out. Could it be a trap? Why hadn't Blaine checked the closet? He forced himself to wait half an hour to be sure Blaine was asleep.

He slowly pushed the closet door open. Leaving the guest room, he cut across the living room and headed for the stairs. Little light was filtering in through the windows. Magnus had stopped whimpering and no cars were to be heard on the street. Any misstep or stumble, the slightest noise, could tip off Blaine. He climbed the stairs with great care, stepping as close to the wall as possible to avoid creaks. The wood didn't give him away. The hardest part was over, he thought; the second floor was all carpeted.

Blaine's bedroom was at the end of a narrow hall. Peeking in, Ted saw Blaine's unmistakable form under a white sheet. Light from a streetlamp streamed through the open window, allowing Ted to move through the room without fear of bumping into anything. He tightened his grip on the hilt of the knife and began to bring it up to strike, when—

"Move and I'll blow your fucking head off."

The voice came from behind. The muzzle of a gun pressed into the back of Ted's head. The lights came on, blinding him. When he was able to see again, he realized that the Blaine under the bedsheets was a pile of pillows.

This is your chance. Turn around and throw your knife at him. If he shoots you in the head, you'll be getting what you wanted, right? Your brain won't mind too much if a bullet blows it apart...

In his pants pocket he kept the note from the desk. It's your only way out.

"Drop the knife," Blaine said. "Good. Don't turn around. Raise your hands."

It looked like he would be getting some Hollywood dialogue after all.

Ted didn't feel nervous. Blaine hadn't shot him yet, so he must have had some doubts. Must have been wondering who the guy trying to kill him was. Surely he also knew that the last thing he needed was for a dead body to turn up in his own house, not to mention that a gunshot would wake up the neighbors. Ted was amazed at the number of thoughts lining up to file through his brain, as if this were the most normal situation in the world. He felt like a superhero. And in the midst of this series of rational arguments, he realized that he didn't want to die at this guy's hands. There was something unseemly about having Blaine do him in; now that he was being held with a gun to his back, defenseless, he finally understood. It was one thing to agree to Lynch's conditions and let himself be killed by a stranger, perhaps easing his family's grief to some degree. But by Blaine? Maybe it was just his survival instinct kicking in. Maybe.

"You saw me, didn't you?" Ted asked in a steady voice. "When you came into the room to talk on the phone—you saw me."

"Who sent you?"

"Why do you think anybody sent me?"

"If nobody sent you, tell me so, and your life ends right now. Tell me who sent you and you'll live a little longer. One way or the other, you're not leaving this room alive."

"Not such a good deal on my end."

Ted started turning around, very slowly.

"I told you not to move!"

Ted stopped.

"Sorry. Just wanted you to see me. You and I know each other."

An instant of doubt.

"I don't recognize your voice."

"I know. As soon as you see my face you'll understand. Believe me."

Ted had him now: he'd swallowed the bait, he was hooked. All Ted had to do now was haul him out of the water. Blaine was intrigued, wondering about Ted's face, thinking it through, trying to work out an unsolvable riddle.

"Okay," said Blaine. "Turn around. Slow! And keep your hands up."

Ted began to twist around, as slowly as he could. He calculated the precise moment when his half-raised arms would be lined up. An easy trick. Blaine was focusing all his attention on Ted's face, which Ted deliberately rotated more slowly than the rest of his body. There was a fraction of a second when Ted allowed his face to be seen and, at the same time, surreptitiously lowered his hidden arm and reached into the jacket pocket where he kept the Browning. Blaine noticed the move only when Ted finished turning around with the gun held chest high and fired, all in a single, fluid, unhesitating motion. It was a difficult shot, with his arm bent and at an uncomfortable height, but even so, he pegged Blaine in the middle of the forehead. The blast shattered the quiet of the night. That bullet was meant for me, Ted thought as Blaine collapsed like a puppet with its strings cut.

From another pocket he pulled out a photo of Amanda Herdman. He placed it on Blaine's chest.

Ted stood there, unable to take his eyes off the body. Blaine didn't die instantly; his body twitched for several seconds before falling still.

A noise in the living room put him back on the alert. He wasn't sure exactly what he had heard—maybe a chair being moved. He put the Browning away and picked up the knife. Walking down the hall to the banister, he carefully leaned over to get an overview of the living room. What he saw gave him such a start, he didn't even reflexively try to hide. A thin black man in a lab coat stood in the center of the room. He was watching Ted as if he'd known that Ted would be leaning over the railing at just that moment. He flashed a creepy smile.

"Hello, Ted," he said in a deep voice. He waved a hand in greeting.

It wasn't too surprising that he knew Ted's name. That seemed to be the new norm among strangers.

Ted headed downstairs without taking his eyes off the man.

"Do you work for them?" he asked when he reached the bottom. He leaned against the banister, the Browning by his side. Something told him this guy wasn't a threat.

Out the windows, nothing moved. It was too soon for the police to arrive. Magnus had definitely noticed that there were strangers in the house, because he was whimpering again from time to time. Could he know that his master had died? Can a dog smell blood at such a distance? Possibly. With apparent effort, the dog turned his whimpering into short barks.

"Who the hell are you?"

The man smiled.

"I'm Roger, Ted."

"Roger what? Just Roger? The other guy at least told me his last name." Ted rubbed his forehead with his free hand. "Listen, I don't know what you're doing here, but the police will be showing up any minute now. There's a dead guy upstairs and a drugged-up rottweiler outside. I'm clearing out."

Roger showed an almost paternal smile.

"Didn't you hear me?" Ted insisted.

"Why don't we sit down and talk it over?"

Ted stared, dumbfounded. What was this guy doing here? Why was he checking up on him like this?

"I can't believe it. You're nuts. Didn't you hear the gun fire?"

"That was Blaine, wasn't it?" Roger recited the words as if they were a line from a computer program.

"Yeah. Who else?"

"You shot him?"

The guy must have heard the shot. Ted didn't reply.

"Lucky thing you had the gun with you," Roger declared.

"Always be prepared. You never know."

By this point Ted didn't even know why he wasn't running away already. There was something about the way the man spoke, a mesmerizing cadence to it.

"You're also wearing gloves," Roger tossed off, pointing at Ted's hands. "A knife and a gun, for emergencies. Did you sedate the dog?"

Ted quietly nodded his head in amazement.

"You wanted him to be killed, didn't you?" Ted grew indignant.

"Did you leave a photo on the corpse this time?"

This time?

"Yes." Ted felt resigned. What sense did it make to wonder whether the man had been watching him or had a crystal ball? "If you don't mind, Roger, I'm going to leave. Is that okay with you? I'd think you'd do the same."

Ted went to the front door. But something was wrong. Through a tiny window in the door he caught sight of a man's form leaving the yard and running across the street at top speed toward a car. The light from a streetlamp shone directly on him, and his striped polo shirt came into full view. It was Lynch.

The car started, revved, and sped off.

Why were they keeping tabs on him?

Ted turned to look at Roger, demanding answers, though he hadn't formulated any questions aloud. Roger shrugged.

5

THE POSSUM had chosen the backyard picnic table as the perfect spot to consume the amputated limb. It waved its tail just enough to activate the motion sensor on the porch light, making the hair-raising spectacle visible from inside the house.

Ted stood on the other side of the patio door. He watched in disbelief as the possum sank its needlelike teeth into the dead flesh, its eyes looking mechanically, almost uninterestedly in every direction, ripping the rosy skin from Holly's leg. Ted could see perfectly well that it was his wife's leg. The toes were swollen and bloody, red as maraschino cherries; the uneven edge where the leg had been cut off below the knee was a tattered skein of tendons and broken bone. But he knew it anyway. No need to see a birthmark or a tattoo. He had massaged that leg, kissed it, pulled stockings off it a million times; he would recognize it anywhere, even in a dream. The fucking possum was gnawing on Holly's leg! Ted beat against the glass pane with his open palms. The possum quickly turned to look, stared for a moment at the figure standing behind the glass, but didn't seem to feel threatened. Its jaws were crudely daubed with reddish purple, like ghastly lipstick. Its curiosity satisfied, it went back to gnawing on the leg. Ted banged on the glass again, but this time the animal didn't even stir.

Then he heard the ocean. The Atlantic was many miles from his house, but that didn't matter. He reached over and flicked on the outdoor lights, which revealed that, indeed, the ocean was right there in his own backyard. The gently rising hill he enjoyed seeing every morning when he sat down to read the business section had been replaced by a roaring, foaming expanse of water. On the beach of sand and geraniums stood Holly, stock-still, like a wax statue. The possum had devoured a good portion of her calf, leaving the shiny rounded end of a bone sticking out. She was wearing the red bikini—Ted's favorite—and held her arms out wide, her body tilting slightly to the left. Her hair floated behind her as if held up by invisible hands. Her expression was joyous despite the phantom leg.

Ted slid the patio door open. The possum withdrew to the farthest corner of the table. Now it really did seem concerned about Ted's presence, though not enough to leave its meal behind. It waited, crouching, baring its teeth, ready to run off if need be. Ted made a brusque movement, but it did no good, so he looked around for something to throw. By the barbecue grill he found a wooden box that he immediately recognized, and though he should have felt surprised because he hadn't seen it since he was a kid, it seemed natural to find it casually lying around at his home now that he was grown.

He went over and picked it up as if it were a relic—and in a sense it was. A chessboard was painted on the box, half on the top and half on the bottom, so that it formed a complete board when open. It was lined inside with green velvet, and each chess piece had its own slot. Ted picked out a bishop and flung it. He missed. How could he have missed the foul creature from less than ten feet away? He grabbed another piece and tried again, this time with much more force than was necessary. Again, he missed. Something about his efforts disconcerted him. The projectiles followed unpredictable arcs and seemed determined to dodge the possum an instant before impact. But Ted didn't give up and kept hurling the pieces, one after another, like a man possessed.

The possum must have noticed that the laws of physics were bending in its favor, for it obnoxiously returned to the center of the table and again tucked into its deluxe meal. Its thick white tail wriggled behind it like a snake. Ted had thrown maybe a hundred objects at it, all without success, when he gave up and dropped the box. Looking at the box where it lay on the ground, he could see all the chessmen still in their proper places.

He watched Holly. He wanted to tell her how he felt, that he had done all he could to get her leg back. What kind of husband was he if he couldn't meet his family's needs? He felt so terrible he nearly broke down crying, but then he realized that he still had a way out. How hadn't he seen it before? His right arm grew heavier, and he felt the grip of the Browning in his hand. He raised the pistol and examined it, fascinated. Then, holding the gun with both hands, he took deliberate, almost poetic aim at the possum, savoring the moments before letting off a shot. The animal had lifted its head as if it sensed that the end was near. The bullet hit it right in the back, and the possum exploded like a balloon filled with blood and entrails. Ted dropped the gun and ran to the table, never taking his eyes off Holly's leg; he picked it up with both hands like a surgeon handling an organ about to be transplanted. Now that he could examine it close-up he saw that the leg ended in a threaded bolt, just as he had imagined. Everything was going to be okay, he thought. He'd just have to bring it to Holly and screw it back on. He'd be the perfect husband.

He ran down the two steps from the porch and looked up. Holly was still there, except that now a gigantic, glowing yellow frame hung between them. The bottom of the frame floated about a foot and a half off the ground, and Ted knew he could easily step over it, but even so, he stopped just before doing so. The ocean behind Holly, some ten yards off, was growing turbulent, and his need to give her back her leg and hug her was unbearable. He lifted his own leg and stepped over the yellow frame. For an instant he had the wild sense that he wouldn't be able to get through, but he did. He knew that so long as he didn't touch it he wouldn't run into problems. Once past the yellow frame, he came up against a second frame, green this time, and he repeated the same actions, and again he looked up and saw Holly in the same position, still ten yards away, waiting for him, and another frame, and another, red, purple—Ted no longer needed to look closely to get past them. He could almost do it with his eyes closed, but not closed, always looking straight ahead, straight at Holly, another yellow frame, then sky blue, "Almost there, love," ten yards to go, a frame as black as night, "Holly..." Ted wasn't walking anymore; he was running, jumping through the frames that came in constant succession, one after another, like a competitive athlete leaping hurdles, never stopping, Holly, never stopping, Holly...

And the last frame swallowed him whole, then spit him out with a shout somewhere else.

He was on the sofa.

Ted sat up with a jolt. He anxiously felt for his leg. It was there. Had he dreamt that he was missing a leg? He was starting to forget. He scrutinized the dark room, and then he saw the wrinkled T-shirt and the uncomfortable jacket he was wearing. He stood up and, not really knowing why, walked over to the patio door that opened onto the backyard. He stood there awhile, examining the small hill that melted away into the night. When he came near the glass, the motion sensor turned on the lights and lit up the picnic table and chairs. Ted was assailed by the bizarre vision of a woman's leg. Had he dreamt that Holly was missing a leg? He smiled and made a note of it so he'd remember to tell her when they talked this afternoon. He wondered what time it was; must not be seven yet, because the sun hadn't risen, he thought. He looked instinctively at his wrist, but his watch wasn't there.

As he opened the door, a memory hit him like an arrow, piercing the merciful blanket of forgetfulness that his mind kept trying to spread. He turned sharply and checked under the grill. The chess box wasn't there anymore, but his memory of it was too detailed. Though he'd just had a nightmare in which Holly was missing a leg, it was the detail of the chess box that made his blood run cold.

6

IF HE was putting off his departure from this world, better to keep up his usual routine, and that included a session with Laura Hill, his therapist. In a way, he was happy, because his relationship with her had improved over time; what had started as a series of visits ordered by his doctor had become an almost pleasant experience. Ted would never have agreed to see a therapist if Dr. Carmichael hadn't insisted, and the doctor had been very insistent and persuasive. "Anybody faced with this sort of news, Ted, will need to be restrained"—those had been his exact words. Ted had translated this as, "A man with an inoperable tumor will think, sooner or later, of blowing out his brains." And Carmichael had been right.

The tumor wasn't really inoperable, strictly speaking; an operation was about as likely to succeed as he was to make a basket from a hundred feet away. Dr. Carmichael didn't choose that metaphor, because he tried to use his words to kindle a flame of hope, but Ted, analytical and practical, quickly put things in their place. His choices were: he could risk everything on an operation and hope for a miracle, or he could keep going as if nothing had changed. It didn't take Ted long to think it over. It was a decision he had already come to ahead of time, reflexively, long before the headaches began, before Carmichael delivered the results of the tests in the tone that doctors use for giving devastating news. Maybe he'd made his decision decades earlier, when he watched the ending of *One Flew Over the Cuckoo's Nest,* with Mac moving his head like a puppet without a puppet master. Or maybe it was some other time—not that it matters. He would live his final months in dignity. And if he went to that first session with Dr. Hill, it was to make Carmichael believe that everything was going according to plan. Carmichael's plan, that is. Because like any good doctor, Carmichael believed in doing everything in his power to prolong human life to the last possible moment. Whether it meant shooting a basket from a hundred feet away or from a thousand.

Laura Hill looked to be in her twenties. The first time Ted laid eyes on her, he felt pity for this girl just starting out on her career, with her rectangular glasses and her hair drawn back, her affable manners and calm smile. Just playing at therapist, Ted thought. Later on he was amazed to discover that Laura Hill was already fortyish. He didn't know her exact age; she had never told him.

She managed to disarm him with her youthful good looks, her air of innocence, and her frankness with him during that first conversation. Ted was seduced by the challenge of getting past the traps she set for him in each session, for of course it never occurred to her—any more than it did to Carmichael—to speak with him of the suicidal thoughts that were starting to crowd in on his mind.

"Hello, Ted," Laura said. "So the fishing trip with your business partner was canceled, I see."

"That's right. Thanks for finding the time to see me."

"Sorry about the trip." Today Laura wore her auburn hair tied in a bun. "How are you feeling?"

Yesterday I killed a man. I went to his house, hid inside a closet waiting for him to get home, and murdered him. The world won't miss him.

He could almost taste the words. He imagined the transformation in Laura Hill's expression if he were to tell her any such thing. The truth was, he himself hadn't even gotten used to the idea that he'd killed another human being. Much less the fact that he'd enjoyed it.

"I had another nightmare last night," Ted said. He often talked about his nightmares, basically because he thought they were nonsense and because he could leave out anything he thought might be revealing. "There was something new."

Flanking the lone window in her office was a desk that Laura rarely used during these sessions. Today she sat in the armchair, facing Ted. A small coffee table stood between them, nothing on it but a plastic cup filled with water. Ted never drank from it.

"Tell me about your dream."

"I was in the living room, looking out at the porch. A possum was perched on the table, eating one of Holly's legs. Holly wasn't there, just her leg, but I knew it was hers. I ran outside and looked for something to throw at it and scare it off, and that was when I noticed a box lying on the ground. I recognized it right away. It was my old chess box."

If she had been one of those therapists who write down every important detail in a notebook, Laura couldn't have helped noting this point, given the serious tone of Ted's voice. But she never took notes. She had a prodigious memory.

"I threw the pieces at the animal, but I could never hit it," Ted went on. "They'd veer off inexplicably. And there seemed to be no end of chessmen. Then I noticed Holly in the yard, and I think she had the ocean behind her. Isn't it funny, what the human mind comes up with?"

Ted left out the detail of blowing away the possum with the Browning. It seemed too close to what he would have done to his own head if it hadn't been for Lynch. That was the sort of detail he preferred to keep to himself.

"You didn't kill the possum?" Laura asked. It wasn't the first time she'd displayed an alarming sixth sense.

"No."

She nodded.

"When was the last time you dreamed about anything related to chess?"

"Never."

She paused thoughtfully, searching for the proper words.

"Ted, we have to talk about what happened during that period in your life. You have to tell me why a boy with such a talent for chess would give it up so abruptly. You never played again?"

"Not seriously. I taught my daughters, and I've played a few games with them, but now they play each other."

"Tell me why you gave it up."

It wasn't the first time she'd tried to get him talking about this. Ted had put up a little resistance before, and she hadn't insisted, but talking about that period didn't really bother him much. He settled back in the chair and started in.

"My father taught me to play. By the time I was seven, I could beat him easily. He took me to meet an old man who had retired to his hometown, Windsor Locks, who'd been a pretty well-known chess player in his time." Ted paused. Thinking about his mentor, possibly the only adult he had ever respected and admired in his life, made him feel a mixture of nostalgia and grief. "His name was Miller; I think I've mentioned him before. The first time I saw him I thought he was the oldest man I had ever met: his hair was white, long in back, and his face was all wrinkled. We didn't talk much that time. We sat down at a chessboard he kept in his garage, where he taught the neighborhood kids, and we played a game. My father watched. We made a few moves, not more than twenty, and then Miller led my father off and they talked by themselves. I sat there, waiting. I thought Miller was telling him I was no good, and then I'd go home with my dad and that would be it. Instead it was eight years, until I turned fifteen, that I saw him two or three times a week."

"You two had the horseshoe ritual, didn't you?"

Ted couldn't remember mentioning the horseshoe. More disturbing evidence of his therapist's astonishing mental archive.

"Right. Miller became my coach. We spent hours practicing variations on simultaneous boards."

Laura wrinkled her mouth.

"I'm afraid my knowledge of chess doesn't extend that far."

"There are a certain number of openings in chess, many of them named after the players who popularized them, and then there are what they call variations, which are different ways of continuing the game from those openings. Let's say there's a main road and several branching side roads. They've all been studied, and they're part of what you study in chess. Chess isn't just a game of logic; it's also a game of memory. Miller and I re-created famous games, analyzing each move. Remember, I was a little kid, and though I liked chess, I was also very restless. Miller had to find ways of keeping me involved. He told me stories about chess players, about famous games. So one day he told me the story of the nineteen twenty-seven world championship match in Buenos Aires between a Cuban, José Raúl Capablanca, and a Russian, Alexander Alekhine. Miller was fascinated by the games in that match, and he passed his enthusiasm on to me. Capablanca was the world champion, and everybody thought he was unbeatable, a revolutionary genius. Alekhine, the challenger, was a studious type, a meticulous player that few thought capable of winning. Am I boring you?"

"Not at all. I love seeing how that youthful enthusiasm still moves you today. Go on, please. I want to know how the story of the exceptional genius versus the methodical challenger turns out. Am I very ignorant not to know?"

Ted laughed.

"No, of course not. We're talking about a chess match from nineteen twenty-seven! The thing is, back then there weren't any clear rules for running a world chess championship. They agreed that whoever won six games would be the next champion. But it's very common for chess games to end in a draw, so they had to play lots of games to get to six wins. In the end, they played thirty-four. Over the course of seventy-three days!"

"Who won?"

"To everyone's surprise, it was Alekhine, the challenger. Relations between the two players had always been terrible; afterwards, they became even worse. Alekhine and Capablanca never agreed to terms for a rematch of the world championship, and fifteen years later Capablanca died. But the outcome had surprised everyone, and this is where the horseshoe comes in. It seems that when Alekhine got to Buenos Aires, he found a horseshoe lying in the street. He was a very superstitious man, and he knew that horseshoes are considered good luck. So he told his wife, who had accompanied him to the match, about it, and he decided to keep the object as a good luck charm. He bought a newspaper and wrapped it carefully. He told his wife, 'It was waiting for me.'"

Ted had a faraway stare. He'd let himself get carried away. Miller had told him that story a thousand times, dressing it up with a million realistic details. The old man even kept an album with newspaper clippings from that time, some of them from Argentine newspapers that he had gotten ahold of and had translated in his tiny, beautiful handwriting.

"Miller had a horseshoe hanging on his wall," Ted said, staring off into space, as if he were really seeing it there. "He said it was the very same horseshoe Alekhine had found in Buenos Aires. Said he'd bought it at an auction. When I first started playing in state championship tournaments, we'd take down the horseshoe, wrap it in newspaper, and bring it with us. My father usually drove us, but even he didn't know about the horseshoe. It was our secret, Miller's and mine, and nobody else's. I did pretty well in those tournaments. When we got back, we'd hang it up on the wall of Miller's garage again, like a ritual."

"You speak of Miller with a great deal of pride. He must have been a very important person for you."

"You bet. During those years my father would drive me to his house, a little more than an hour from ours. I'd spend three hours with Miller, and the time would fly. My father was a salesman, so he'd take advantage of these trips and work the area. Things weren't easy at home; my mother's dementia was getting worse, and I couldn't stand their arguments. Windsor Locks was a form of escape, in more ways than one."

"What became of Miller?"

"Miller must have been maybe seventy when I met him, maybe a couple years younger. So eight years later, he was closing in on eighty. I was fifteen, and chess was the only thing that calmed my rebellious spirit. When I wasn't at Miller's garage, I'd become an impulsive young troublemaker. I don't know how much longer I could have kept going like that, because I had really turned into two different people. I was an intolerant teenager who hated his parents and hardly spoke to his father, a problem kid at school, a back talker. But I was also the boy who still loved spending an afternoon with Miller, listening to his stories and analyzing games."

Ted paused. He hadn't even told Holly this much about Miller, much less revealed the story he was about to tell. He cleared his throat.

"The day Miller died, I was there with him. Once or twice a month we played each other, and by the end we were pretty closely matched. It was his turn. He always sat the same way when he was thinking, with his elbows on the table and his chin propped on his fists. I usually sat with my hands under the table, leaning forward. That's how we were sitting when Miller suddenly slumped across the board. His arms splayed out and his head fell like a lead weight, scattering chess pieces everywhere. I jumped up, startled and scared. Miller was a widower; he had a son who visited now and then, but at the time it was just the two of us at home. I was so agitated, I couldn't even get myself to go over and shake him to see if he'd react, find out what had happened. I know it wouldn't have changed anything, because Miller had died of a massive stroke. I stood paralyzed for the longest time by the table, breathing rapidly...At last I ran from the garage to find help. I could have gone to any of the neighbors' houses, but for some ridiculous reason I thought I should go find my father. His Mustang wasn't in the driveway, which didn't surprise me, so I ran off in whatever direction. I got to the corner, turned right arbitrarily, never stopped running...And as luck would have it, I caught sight of his car in the distance, two hundred yards away, parked in front of some house. My father had to be there, selling his encyclopedias or correspondence courses or whatever it was he was selling at the time. You can guess the rest of it, can't you, Laura?"

"I think so."

"I ran into the house and figured out right away that my father hadn't been driving me to visit Miller all those years so I could perfect my chess game or to get away from my mother. Not only that, anyway. The woman who lived there had been his first girlfriend; my father tried to explain it to me later."

"What did you see in that house, Ted?"

They were in the bedroom. I didn't see them. But I could hear them. I sat in the living room in silence, in a chair facing the TV, which was off. I listened to them laughing. I was thinking about Miller, collapsed in his garage, and I had a horrible thought—I remember it perfectly. I was hoping he was dead, because otherwise I still would never be able to go back to that town. Also because it would be my father's fault. And at that moment all I wanted to do was hate him."

The jangle of the telephone startled them both. Nobody ever interrupted Laura in the middle of a session.

"Excuse me, Ted. I have to take this." She stood up and walked to the desk.

Ted nodded.

Laura picked up the receiver and listened. For a brief moment Ted noticed the tension in her face, until she suddenly relaxed and smiled.

"Yes, of course. No problem. You have my okay."

She hung up.

"My son's in the Boy Scouts," she explained to Ted. "He forgot to give me a form to sign, authorizing him to go on one of their camping trips, and they were nice enough to call."

Laura sat down again.

"I'm sorry about the interruption, Ted," she apologized again.

"Don't worry about it. There's not much more to tell. I never talked about it with my father again. He kept on getting away from the house as often as he could, and I stayed at home, hating him intensely and struggling with my mother. They got divorced, and I gave up chess forever."

7

TED KNELT behind the bushes. He'd just tramped through nearly a mile of mosquito-infested woodland. He shook his head and concentrated on what stood across the way.

A whistled melody mingled with the trilling of songbirds. He saw a lake and a boat with a single occupant: Wendell was calmly awaiting his fate, a fishing rod in hand, at peace with himself.

Ted squashed a mosquito with a silent clap of his hands and sat down with his back to the lake to study his surroundings. Then he saw it, glittering in the sunbeams that filtered through the pines: the unmistakable shape of a horseshoe. He was a few yards away and didn't even stand up to get it; he crawled over and picked it up with both hands, amazed at how exactly it looked like the one Miller had kept on the wall of his garage. (Deep down, he knew that it *was* Miller's horseshoe.)

What was it doing here? He gazed at it for a long time and then stuffed it in his pocket.

The path led to Wendell's weekend home, a modernist pile of concrete blocks with huge windows. A wooden deck on one side stretched past the lakeshore, turning into a narrow jetty that projected a few yards into the lake itself. Ted weighed his options. Once Wendell decided he was done fishing, he would undoubtedly dock at the jetty and cross the deck to his house. Ted's most reasonable course of action seemed to be to wait inside for him. At least the wait would be more comfortable there, without all these mosquitoes. He snatched at another and looked at his closed fist with some satisfaction. When he opened his hand, it was empty.

He walked along the private path unimpeded. The closer he came to the modernist home, the larger it loomed. The sporty black car parked in front turned out to be a Lamborghini convertible. Ted couldn't resist the temptation to go over and take a look. It was his dream car; he was beginning to sympathize with Wendell. When he leaned over to check out the interior, his jacket opened under the weight of the Browning, reminding him of the gravity of what he intended to do. He closed the jacket but didn't button up—the heat was unbearable, yet it felt safer to have the gun where he could easily reach it. He stood up just as a red light flashed in the car window. At first he thought it was one of the dashboard lights, but after shifting his head slightly he realized it was a reflection in the car window. He turned around and studied a lamp high on a pole partially hidden in the trees. A security camera atop the pole pointed directly at the spot where he was standing. A tiny red light blinked on and off. Ted felt a chill. The detailed report on the house in Lynch's folder mentioned nothing about a security system, and Lynch hadn't warned him of it. It seemed unlikely that *they* could have missed a detail like this.

As the red LED continued to blink, Ted wondered if anyone was watching the camera feed. Maybe it was a closed-circuit system, in which case Lynch wouldn't have thought it worth mentioning. Lynch and his people would be sure to get rid of the recordings, of course. Ted turned from the security camera with a sense of relief.

He went to the front door. Unlocked, naturally. A handmade rug, perhaps Indian, drew him inside. The place was just as he had imagined it: spacious, with balconies and overhead walkways, all stainless steel, glass, and gleaming white. Like the reception area of a corporate headquarters, not a weekend getaway home. Two staircases with polished wooden steps seemed to float in midair. There were a number of thin, round columns. Ted slowly made his way to the right, toward a large, dark glass table that seemed never to have been used. He immediately saw that the best place for him to wait for Wendell was just past the hallway that presumably led to the kitchen.

He was heading there when he was struck by a distinctive sense of being watched. He stopped and looked around. He saw no cameras inside, but he figured there must have been some. Far across the great room was an enormous flat-screen TV, some leather easy chairs, and a fireplace with photos on the mantel. Ted continued to scrutinize the area, distrustful. When the feeling of being watched passed, he moved on to his hiding place, though he couldn't quite rid himself of his unease. Something wasn't right. What was it?

Apart from intending to murder a man?

Yes.

He shook his head. No.

To kill *another* man.

Once inside the kitchen he drew the Browning from his jacket pocket. The heft of it in his hand reassured him somewhat. A wide picture window provided a panoramic view of the lake, perfect for keeping track of Wendell's movements. He thought he could see the exact spot where the boat had been a short while earlier, but there was no trace of it now. Worried, he looked behind the line of trees but saw nothing there, either. Then he heard it: the distant roar of an outboard motor. Wendell was on his way home.

Ted paced back and forth, tapping his forehead with the butt of the gun. How much time did he have? Not much—that was for sure. Though getting it over with quickly was best for him, a series of intense sensations swept through his body as the time of the deed drew near. He felt unsure of himself. What if Wendell wasn't expecting him? What if, as with the security camera, things weren't exactly as Lynch had said? He halted and, in a smooth, rapid motion, aimed the gun at a wall calendar. The calendar was illustrated with a photo of a scuba diver exploring a coral reef. He aimed at the number 15 in the center. *Come on...Steady...* The barrel trembled slightly, even when he held the gun with both hands to steady it.

"Come on," he muttered.

The rumble from the outboard was getting louder. Wendell would be docking any minute now, and then walking across the deck, from where he'd probably be able to see into the kitchen through the picture window. But Ted needed to calm down. He wouldn't move until his nerves were still. He had stopped sweating in the air-conditioned house, but now his temples and palms were becoming damp again. He flexed his fingers one at a time and adopted the shooting stance he had so often assumed at the range. He closed his eyes.

Wendell needs this bullet as much as you do.

He opened his eyes and stepped back from the window. He returned to the hallway when he heard the motor choke and fall silent. He'd give Wendell two minutes to get to the front door. Ted checked the gun, made sure the safety was off. Once Wendell closed the door behind him, Ted would leave the kitchen, gun raised, take two or three steps forward to minimize his odds of missing, and fire. If Wendell shouted at him not to do it, he'd stop.

"Come on, Wendell. Open the door," Ted said under his breath.

More than a minute passed before Ted heard footsteps on the wooden deck.

Come on, Wendell...

The door opened and closed.

Three, two, one.

Ted strode from the kitchen, went halfway around the table, and raised the weapon.

Wendell stood by the doorway, his back to Ted. He turned his head when he heard steps. His expression totally changed, perhaps in his surprise, but he said nothing. A perfect circle appeared on his forehead, and he collapsed.

Ted was so used to wearing hearing protectors on the practice range that he clenched his teeth at the gun blast. He slowly walked to the body. Wendell lay on the rug, arms splayed, a look of surprise frozen on his face. Though he seemed to be taking a pleasant nap, Ted knew that the shot had been perfect and the bullet had ricocheted inside his skull, scrambling his brains almost painlessly.

Ted was about to leave when a cell phone started ringing in Wendell's coat. Ted's own phone had the same irritating ringtone, a fact that sort of rattled him. He knelt and removed the iPhone from Wendell's front coat pocket. The name on the screen was Lolly. Ted nearly cried out in horror. That was the name he had briefly given Holly when their relationship was getting off the ground. The coincidence was too much. And that wasn't the worst of it. Wendell wasn't supposed to have a wife or a girlfriend. Lynch had assured him that the guy would be leaving no one behind!

The phone stopped ringing.

Who was Lolly? Why hadn't Lynch mentioned her?

The answer came as if by magic. Ted felt a single short vibration in the palm of his hand. It was a text from Lolly.

We're almost there. Time to quit your fishing for the day ☺

"We"?

Ted dropped the phone as if it had given him an electric shock. It landed on Wendell's chest.

"Who is Lolly? Think. Think. Think."

Wendell had been about to have a private party, and the guests would be arriving at any moment. Without a second thought, Ted grabbed the phone and replied.

Party canceled. Too busy here. So sorry.

Another message.

Very funny. You know how much I hate to chat while I'm driving. See you in two minutes, love.

Love...

So Wendell did have a girlfriend. Didn't seem like the sort of detail Lynch could have missed.

The pool of blood on the rug was forming a red halo around Wendell's head.

"Shit."

Lolly had texted that she'd be there in two minutes.

Lolly Holly

She might have been speaking figuratively, or...Ted stuck Wendell's cell phone in his own jacket, and then the Browning. Either way, he'd have to hurry. He needed to hide the body, giving him a head start before the woman notified the police, and then clear out of there as fast as he could. If he could manage this part, the situation would be basically unchanged as far as he was concerned. He was angry that he hadn't been told about the girlfriend, though perhaps this was exactly why Lynch had kept her a secret. He must not lose sight of the fact that Wendell himself had wanted to die, just as he did. Wendell certainly must have given a lot of thought to how it would affect his loved ones, just as Ted had thought about how his own absence would affect...

Lolly Holly

Stop it! He had to concentrate on the question of where to dump the body. Inside or out? It was hard to decide without knowing how much time he had to work with. He glanced around, looking for an answer in the air. Then he stopped in his tracks as if someone had prodded him with the muzzle of a gun, though of course no one was behind him.

He realized what was out of place. He'd overlooked a detail that didn't square with what he knew about the man who lay dead at his feet. The fireplace chimney in the vast great room was covered with photos. He ran across the room, swerving around chairs and jumping down the steps that separated the room into different levels. He stopped a dozen feet from the fireplace: he didn't want to see the pictures close-up. What he could see from here was enough: Wendell with a woman, in each other's arms, on a boat; Wendell on horseback (Ted felt the horseshoe he had slipped into his pocket); in other pictures two girls, about the same age as his own. Ted felt dizzy. He grabbed a column to steady himself. The room was spinning.

We're almost there.

Wendell had daughters? Lynch had lied to him!

That's when he heard the car. For some ten seconds he looked from the photos to the body, from the body to the front door. He stood, paralyzed, unable to process what was happening to him. Finally he returned to the foyer, quietly drew the curtains, and peeked out. A minivan drove slowly up the dirt driveway and parked behind the Lamborghini. Everything was happening too fast. Move! But Ted couldn't move. Three minivan doors opened simultaneously. Lolly stepped from the driver's side. On the passenger side, two little girls wearing floral dresses and carrying pink backpacks jumped out. The girls ran at top speed for the front door. *Daddy! We're home!*

Ted rubbed his eyes. His mind must have been playing tricks on him.

8

WHEN TED made the decision to take his own life—an idea that took hold of him with chilling speed—he knew he'd have to turn to someone he could trust to put certain matters in order. Someone who would keep things confidential. Someone who wasn't part of his everyday circle of friends. Arthur Robichaud's name came to mind immediately.

Ted hadn't seen Robichaud in years, and though they had spent three years at the same high school they'd had hardly any contact since graduation. It was perfect. Besides, Ted knew that the lawyers in Robichaud's practice were the best in the city. Once Ted went to see him, moreover, he realized that they had an even closer bond than the confidentiality agreement between lawyer and client. Perhaps there was some involuntary urge in a guy like Robichaud, who had made his way through public school almost unnoticed, ignored by the popular girls and boys, begging for a spot at a lunchroom table with tiny groups of two or three kids, or sitting off on his own sometimes, convincing himself that he'd be able to make it through a painful time of pranks and marginalization. No matter how things turned out in later life, no matter how his career flourished or how many hours he spent at the gym tuning his flabby body, nothing changed the crucial fact that a loser like Robichaud would always have a primitive instinct to act submissive before the Ted McKays of the world. A need to be noticed, to be accepted by the group, would always lurk in the Arthur Robichauds like a latent virus from the days when they groveled in the school yard for one second of attention.

Ted showed up at his home to see him again after the unpleasant incident at Wendell's place.

Robichaud himself greeted Ted at the door. He wore an elegant polo shirt and held a martini.

"Ted, you came!"

Farther back in the room, several people turned to gaze at the newcomer. The guests were scattered around the living room, some at a bar, others in armchairs. Most were couples. Ted had completely forgotten it was Robichaud's birthday party, though the lawyer had mentioned it to him at least a dozen times over the past few weeks. Why waste time thinking about something that will happen after you're dead?

"I need to talk with you, Arthur. Alone. It's important."

There was no need to add that he hadn't come to celebrate. His face was eloquent enough.

"Sure, come on in."

Ted hesitated a moment. The guests had already guessed that he wasn't there to party and had fallen silent, hanging on any detail that might reveal why he had come. Well dressed, each with a glass in hand, they could have been straight out of a liquor ad. They reeked of privilege. And Ted detested them. When he got a better look at them, he was surprised to recognize many of his old high school classmates. Jesus, it was practically a class reunion!

He walked in and did his best to smile. Robichaud escorted him through the room, unable to hide his childish pride. Today he turned thirty-seven, the same age as Ted. His head had long since seen the last of his hair, he was still pudgy, and he hid his weak chin behind a goatee that made him look like Wooly Willy. He had dropped the Coke-bottle glasses he'd worn in high school, but it made no difference now, because he had apparently reverted to his schoolboy persona, watching Ted with the almost worshipful admiration of those years. Ted McKay himself, here on his birthday!

After some general words of welcome, they went to an office at the other end of the house. Along the way Robichaud introduced Ted to his wife, who had apparently heard his name before, judging from her nervous smile. Ted shook her hand distractedly, forgetting her name the moment he heard it.

"What's up, Ted? You look worried," the lawyer said.

They sat in two leather chairs by a wall of packed bookshelves. The office wasn't very large, but it was tastefully, even sumptuously, decorated. Ted kept his eyes fixed on the window behind his old schoolmate, which offered a partial view of a backyard and kids running around in it. Closer to the house stood a tree with a tire swing. *Doesn't match the interior decor, Arthur.*

"Ted? You okay?"

He couldn't take his eyes off the tire swing. Because it looked out of place?

"I'm fine. I need your help."

The lawyer shifted in his seat. For an instant his primitive instinct for submission reappeared.

"Whatever you need, Ted."

"I need your services again, but this time it's not about drawing up a will. It's more complicated. From this moment on, you're my lawyer, and anything I tell you falls under attorney-client privilege."

Robichaud didn't flinch, Ted was glad to see. Better to deal with the grown lawyer than the nervous schoolkid.

"I'm listening."

"I just killed a man."

For a few seconds, the only sound audible was the chatter of guests in the living room, which was muffled by the closed office door. Robichaud made an involuntary gesture with his index finger along the bridge of his nose. But he had no glasses to adjust.

"You were in an accident, Ted?"

"Not exactly. Look, Arthur, I don't intend to explain every detail of what happened to you—not now. All I can say is, forty-eight hours from now, everything will become clear."

Robichaud wrinkled his forehead.

Ted was losing him. The lawyer was looking at him as if he were insane. Ted leaned over and put a hand on Robichaud's knee. Robichaud stared at it with the same expression of incredulity.

"Arthur," Ted said, "I know it sounds crazy. You have to trust me."

"Ted, I can't advise you if you don't tell me what's going on."

Ted shook his head. He'd come here planning to let out as little information as possible, but now he realized he wouldn't be able to get Robichaud's help unless he told him something solid. How far could he trust him? He hadn't had time to gauge the risks properly. He hadn't had time to do anything, really. Since he fled headlong from Wendell's house, his thoughts had all been a jumble. He couldn't stop thinking about the guy's daughters, watching them skip happily up to the door with their pink backpacks and their blond ponytails. Though Ted had run out a side door before witnessing the girls' discovery of their father's corpse on the carpet in the reception hall, he had taken it upon himself to re-create the scene in his mind over and over again, like a film on an endless loop. Later, when he was running through the woods as if pursued by bloodhounds, the show in his head had morphed slightly. It was no longer Wendell's girls finding the body with the perfect round hole between the eyebrows, but Cindy and Nadine, his own daughters. And the face wasn't Wendell's but his own. Was he going to make his daughters confront that sort of horror? Had it taken killing a man to make him realize how much it would harm them?

"You okay, Ted?"

It was the second time he'd asked the question in less than a minute.

Ted was holding his head in his hands and staring down at the floor. He couldn't remember how long he'd been in that position. Robichaud was watching him from the other chair with genuine worry.

"I'm fine, Arthur. I need to ask you for something."

"Tell me."

"I need to find a man. His name is Justin Lynch. He's about twenty-something, and he's probably a lawyer or something of the sort."

"Is this man connected with the *incident,* or..."

"He's connected, but I can't tell you how."

"Have you tried searching online? It sounds dumb, but you can find more things on the Internet than you might expect."

"I couldn't find anything," Ted lied. "Maybe you'll have better luck. I'm sure you can get your hands on some investigators who can help."

"Of course. Tomorrow, first thing, I'll get my team to work on it."

Ted sat still for a moment.

"I need you to do it now, Arthur."

He said it with authority. Deliberately. He was aware that his tone would set some deep mechanisms in motion and make Arthur try to please him. The lawyer attempted a halfhearted defense, pointing out the obvious: it was his birthday, his house was full of guests planning to spend the afternoon with him. But Ted didn't even have to insist. Arthur himself declared that he'd make a few phone calls on the spot, call in some favors, and try to find something about Lynch. If Lynch was a young lawyer or detective, Arthur would soon track him down.

"You don't know how grateful I am," Ted said. Again he placed his hand on his old schoolmate's knee.

"Don't worry about it."

The office door opened.

"Are you going to be much longer?" Robichaud's wife asked. In the middle of the question she shot Ted a withering look.

"No, dear, just a few more minutes."

Her face disappeared and the door closed. The reproachful expression never left.

"Norma's a good woman," Robichaud said apologetically.

Ted waved it off.

"Let's do something," Robichaud said. "I'll make some calls now. If this Justin Lynch is a lawyer with any local ties, I'll soon find out. I'll also consult some private investigators and my own partners; some of them are here at the party. Do you know if that's his real name?"

"No."

"You're not making this easy for me, Ted."

"I know."

Robichaud scratched his head.

"Tomorrow you'll have to be a little more forthcoming with me. Was it self-defense? At least tell me that much."

"Sorry. I promise, tomorrow I'll explain everything."

Robichaud nodded.

"Go out there, have a drink with everybody else," Robichaud said. "I'll take care of the calls—and of Norma. She'll be back soon to lecture me." He quickly added, "But don't worry. I can manage her."

Ted didn't like the idea of leaving the office. He wasn't in a mood to socialize, and he would rather be there when Arthur made the calls. But he understood that the man needed a little privacy, and Ted decided not to pressure him.

9

TED'S INITIAL intention was to retreat into the farthest corner of the Robichauds' living room and kill time by pretending to look out the window. But his plan fell apart as soon as he left Arthur's office. Norma came up, offered him a cold beer with a forced smile, and escorted him over to two couples in conversation around a coffee table. Fortunately, they were sitting far from the people Ted recognized. He vaguely wondered why she had picked these people in particular.

The women were practically having a private conversation between themselves, and a brief silence was their way of welcoming the new arrival. The men, whose participation in the conversation seemed limited to nodding and occasionally agreeing, looked up and readily greeted Ted—who remained standing, having no intention of taking a seat. At this point Ted recognized one of the men as another former classmate, now sporting a thick black beard. His sky-blue eyes gave him away, not only because Ted vaguely recalled seeing him in the high school corridor, but because he glimpsed a flash of submission in them, just as he had in Robichaud's eyes earlier. God. Was anybody at this party not an old classmate? Ted felt a twinge of envy for this club of outsiders who still enjoyed celebrating together, when his old high school friends hadn't gotten together in years.

"The temperature of the floor saved him," said one of the women. The wife of the guy with the beard and the sky-blue eyes. Her words immediately attracted Ted's attention. He brought the beer can to his lips and moved a baby step closer.

"I don't follow," said the other woman.

"You explain it, Bobby."

Bobby Pendergast! Ted suddenly remembered his name, like an arrow from the past. The guy had always been a sort of mini genius who knew the answers to everything. He had transferred to a school for the gifted in his junior year, Ted recalled.

"You're Pendergast," Ted said, motivated more by his pride at remembering than by anything else.

All four faces turned to look at him, slightly shocked. Bobby nodded in silence. *You got no answers for that one, eh, Bobby?* Ted decided to sit in the only empty chair around the table. With the chatter of the other guests in the background, the silence wasn't too awkward.

"Ted McKay," he said, offering his hand.

Bobby took care of the introductions.

"This is Lance Firestar." Ted was sure he'd never heard the name before. Not one you'd forget. He shook the thin redheaded man's freckled hand. Then he shook hands with the women. "This is Teresa, and this is Tricia."

Tricia's hand was limp as a sponge, and for some reason—you didn't have to be Bobby Pendergast to figure this one out—Ted's mind went straight to Wendell's corpse. Had it been removed yet from the living room rug?

"Ted and I went to school together," Bobby said.

Ted didn't want the conversation to get sidetracked.

"A second ago, you were talking about that police case. I didn't mean to eavesdrop, but I couldn't help hearing."

Tricia wrinkled her brow for a moment. Then she recalled.

"Oh, of course! The guy got off scot-free, and now the family has a theory, how he might have pulled it off, though it's too late now. I can't believe you haven't heard about it, Teresa."

"I haven't turned on the TV."

"You never hear anything. But anyway, he got off. I think he's a *Hispanic*."

She uttered the word "Hispanic" with disdain. When she remembered that someone she had just met had joined the conversation, she blushed, but not much. Ted wanted to keep listening, so he looked serious and nodded with resignation, as if he and everyone else around the table weren't also the descendants of immigrants in search of opportunity.

"How did he fool them all?" Teresa asked.

Ted had a knot in his stomach. Lynch had told him these findings were the result of an investigation carried out by the organization he worked for. If he'd lied about that, why not lie about everything? Ted was afraid of what might come next.

"I already told you: the temperature of the floor," Tricia whispered, as if she were giving away a secret. "There's a commercial laundry in the basement."

Ted's heart sank.

"I don't get it," Teresa said.

Her husband shook his head and rolled his eyes, as if the fact that his wife didn't understand something didn't surprise him in the least.

"Don't you make faces," Teresa said without glancing at him. Lance raised his hands in surrender.

"They use the temperature of the corpse to calculate the time of death," Bobby said in his professorial voice.

"The guy had a perfect alibi," Tricia jumped in. "At the time when the experts decided the poor girl was getting murdered, he was sitting at a bar. And he had tons of witnesses to prove it. That's why they let him off."

Ted was following the conversation as if it were taking place in some other dimension. His worst fears had just been confirmed. How deep did Lynch's duplicity go? He asked himself this over and over again as Bobby Pendergast relayed the rest of the story.

"According to an expert hired by the girl's family to throw light on the crime, the apartment floor was heated by a ventilation duct from the commercial dryers. Therefore the body lost heat much more slowly than normal, on account of which the forensic scientists calculated the ETD incorrectly."

"Talk normal, Bobby!"

"Sorry, dear. They estimated the time of death wrong."

"Do any of you remember the guy's name?" Ted interrupted.

The Pendergasts looked at each other.

"Ramirez," Tricia said without hesitation.

"No, not Ramirez," Bobby said. "And he's not Latino. You're getting it mixed up with another news story, love. The guy's name was Blaine. Edward Blaine."

"You're wrong."

"I don't think so."

"It's Ramirez, Bobby, and I'll prove it to you as soon as we get home. Don't argue with me when you know I'm right."

Bobby lowered his eyes and nodded.

Edward Blaine.

Why had Lynch taken credit for an investigation that was public knowledge? Maybe he and his Organization had taken steps to forward the information to the family, but that was wild speculation, and Ted was tired of accepting the least plausible explanations to justify what had happened over the past twenty-four hours. The truth was much simpler: Lynch had tricked him.

Who have you killed?

Ted sat back in the chair and looked out the picture window a few feet away. Why was Arthur taking so long?

10

THE SCENE outside was more interesting than the conversation between the Pendergasts and the Firestars, which had devolved into unpleasant sniping about their new neighbors. Ted thought it would be too impolite of him to get up and walk over to the window, but he did turn away crossly and gaze out. Arthur had a large, well-tended yard with a set of monkey bars, a slide, and a merry-go-round, which at the moment was the center of attention. A boy who looked a lot like Norma was working the wheel at its center, spinning it faster and faster; two girls held on to their seats with all their might, laughing and screaming for him to stop, please, stop it! Ted could just hear their distant, childish voices. Other, even smaller children were waiting their turns for the merry-go-round, jumping up and down and cheering for the powerful conductor who, with his strong arms and methodical concentration, was whirling the contraption around at the speed of light. One of the girls on board was begging Timothy to stop, but her giddy laughter made it clear that stopping was the last thing she wanted. Timothy had a different future in store than his father, who at his age had been timid and shy around everyone.

The girls' turn on the merry-go-round ended. They staggered off, reeling with dizziness, to Timothy's delight. He stayed on to continue working the central wheel, pretending not to be dizzy, waiting for the next two victims of boyish brawn and centrifugal force. He was born to play

Lord of the Merry-Go-Round. A boy and a girl, smaller than the previous pair of kids, took the two open spaces, one on either side of Timothy. He gave them instructions, though Ted couldn't hear him very well from so far away. The children stopped smiling as they heard the long list of warnings, as if they were about to take their first trip on a dangerous roller coaster.

From where Ted sat, he could also see the tree with the tire swing that had caught his attention when he was in the office. Compared with the rest of the yard, this old rubber tire looked even more out of place than it had before. He couldn't say he really knew the woman of the house, but from the little he had seen of her, such as when she fussed over the guests, including him, she seemed concerned about appearances above all. And that tire swing, visible from every window in the living room, seemed like an odd letter of introduction for a house that oozed perfection. At the moment, the tire swayed gently back and forth. A few feet from the tree, two women sat on a bench. Maybe they were there to supervise the children, but they seemed much more interested in their own lively conversation. Ted saw them in profile, because they had turned to face each other. A girl no more than a year old, in a white dress with red polka dots, toddled around them, falling and standing up again.

Ted alternated his attention between the swinging tire and the toddler who was learning to walk. She was holding on to the bench or clutching at the air, lurching forward in clumsy steps that always ended with her sitting on the grass. She laughed to herself and babbled to her mother, whether or not the woman was listening. The tire seemed to be swinging more vigorously than before. How could that be? Nobody had touched it.

The toddler had homed in on a tiny flower, studying it for the longest time, kneeling next to it, moving her lips, perhaps asking whether she could pick it, finally picking it carefully, grasping its slender stem with chubby fingers. She gave it to her mother, who accepted it with hardly a glance. If the flower had been a lit stick of dynamite, the woman would have taken it with exactly the same smile. *Thank you, sweetie!* The toddler, apparently satisfied by this minimal encouragement, smoothed her dress and set off on a new trek.

The tire was definitely moving in a much wider arc than before. It would have taken quite a gust of wind to make it swing like that, and even from inside the house Ted could see that the wind was barely blowing. There was something dangling from the tire, something that hadn't been there before. At first he thought it was a snake, but then the face of the possum peeked through the hole in the center of the tire. Its tail hung below. The possum stared straight at Ted, who jumped involuntarily. Tricia Pendergast noticed and frowned. Ted pretended it had been his cell phone: he took it out, looked at it, put it back in his pocket. He focused his attention on the tire. His eyes met those of the vile vermin.

Bits and pieces of his dream came back to him as the possum gnawed the tire with its sharp little teeth, never taking its eyes off the window. Off Ted.

The toddler wandered dangerously near the animal, holding her little arms straight out in front of her, ready for a stumble that never came. Ted sprang to his feet and in two strides was at the window. He stopped, aware that the conversation in the room had halted and that several faces had turned to look at him. The possum climbed to the top of the tire, holding on with its front paws; its claws were terrifyingly long. For a second, the little girl seemed to see it: she had stopped six feet away, and then took a couple of ungainly steps, apparently unconvinced. *Come on, come on—get back to your mother*. Pests like that were so dangerous: they carried all sorts of diseases, and they could be aggressive. The toddler might mistake it for a cat or some other harmless animal and try to go over and pet it. At last, after a moment's hesitation, the little girl gathered her courage and hurtled toward the tire. *My God!*

Ted banged on the glass with the palm of his hand.

"Watch out!" he shouted.

Everyone fell silent and turned to look. The quickest guest ran to the window; two or three of them stood behind Ted. Some remained where they were, expectant, looking in every direction without understanding. Norma raced in from the kitchen and asked what had happened. Outside, neither the two women talking on the bench nor any of the kids had heard Ted's warning. Especially not the little girl, who was stumbling forward those last few steps. Ted struggled with the window, which was made to slide open but was latched at top and bottom.

"What's wrong?" asked a man at another window.

"That baby girl!" Ted replied without looking away. "There's a huge possum sitting on the tire!"

His panic spread to the others. The women who had remained in their chairs unfroze and ran over, some of them screaming. How horrible! How was it possible?

"I can't see it!" one woman shouted.

There aren't many other tire swings out there, lady.

Other hands began banging on the windows, finally getting the attention of the chatty mothers, who looked toward the house with worried expressions. The spectacle they saw inside must have been startling, with dozens of faces desperate to get their attention. Had something happened in there? Neither seemed to understand. Fortunately, the noise also got the little girl to stop; her outstretched hand was just a foot or two from the swinging tire.

Ted finally got the window open.

"The baby!" he shouted. "There's a possum in the tire!"

Maternal instinct sprang into action. One of the mothers jumped from the bench and ran to the child.

"Rose!"

A bunch of men who had seconds ago been sitting around the living room were now outside and racing over. The one in front wielded a broom. The mother caught Rose by the waist and picked her up, swung about, and ran from the tire as if it were a bomb set to explode.

Now all three picture windows were open and everybody looked on in silence at what was happening outside. The possum was hiding inside the tire, where there was no place for it to go. Ted wondered if a broom would be enough to stop it if it jumped down and tried to run away.

"Hey guys!" one of the extemporary hunters shouted to the kids standing by the merry-go-round. "Get up on it—all of you!"

There were eight kids. The merry-go-round had only four seats, but they all squeezed on board. Smart move. The possum might feel threatened by being shooed off and try to bite somebody on the ankle. The two women got the same idea and climbed onto the bench, bringing Rose with them. Now only the four men remained on the grass, marching forward in diamond formation, armed with a broom.

"Hey Steve," said Broom Guy, "go find something more convincing, like a shovel or whatever."

The man bringing up the rear scurried off. The remaining triumvirate marched on. The kids on the merry-go-round, the women on the bench, the guests at the windows—all followed the action with bated breath. Broom Guy came to a halt about ten feet back from the tire swing, went into a sort of crouch, and, brandishing the broom by the bristle end, jabbed the handle as far as it would reach.

"Wait for Steve to get back!" yelled a woman at a window.

The man shook his head no. The tire had stopped moving.

The tip of the broom handle gently pushed the tire, which wobbled in circles. Steve got back just then. He hadn't found a shovel, but he had brought a baseball bat. Everyone approved of the new weapon. Broom Guy gave instructions, telling Steve to circle around to the other side while he poked the broom handle into the tire to get the critter to leave.

That's what they did, circling the tire, sticking the handle in here, then there. The possum might be running around inside the cavity of the tire, in which case they'd never get it to leave. Slowly they drew closer, step by step, until they could see inside.

No possum.

Broom Guy lifted the tire with both hands, displaying it to the audience at the windows like a magician showing an empty top hat that a dove had settled into seconds before. All eyes turned from the tire to Ted. All at the same time. The kids, still standing on the merry-go-round, looked unbelievingly at the stranger who seemed to be responsible for the commotion. So did the adults. The guests standing around him in the living room silently moved away, as if his ravings might be contagious.

Ted was barely conscious of their reactions. He was unable to take his eyes off the swing. The possum had been there; there was no way it could have escaped without being seen. He had only glanced away for one split second to unlatch the window, but by then other people were watching. He turned around. The room had gone totally quiet. Everyone was staring at him, perhaps expecting an explanation. Lance and Teresa looked at him disapprovingly; Bobby Pendergast seemed disappointed. Norma stared daggers at him. Arthur Robichaud, who had left his office at some point, perhaps attracted by the uproar, was the first to approach him, putting a hand on his shoulder. Ted didn't react.

"We were lucky with Lynch," Arthur said. At first Ted had no idea what he was talking about. "He's a lawyer, works on his own."

He handed Ted an index card with something written on it.

"My contacts got me his office address and phone number. Hope it helps. Call me later and let me know how it turned out. Maybe you should go now."

Ted had to agree.

11

THE BUILDING where Lynch had his office was a decaying brick box in an aging suburb on the outskirts of town, surrounded by parking lots, abandoned buildings, dangerous backstreets, rusting car frames, and swirling trash. It was 7 p.m. and there were no signs of life. The only window with a light on behind it was on the seventh floor; Lynch's office was on the fifth. Ted pulled out his cell and called the number on the index card, and for the second time he listened to the weary voice of an older woman announcing that the working hours of the law firm were from 8 a.m. to 4 p.m., Monday through Friday, and that he could leave a message after the tone. Ted hung up without a word. He hadn't harbored much hope of finding the guy this late, but he'd had to give it a try anyway. Maybe Lynch would turn out to be the sort who liked working late.

While the last red wounds of sunset faded on the horizon behind that mass of architectural brutality, Ted made a plan that would have to wait for the following day. On his way home he managed to avoid thinking about anything at all. As soon as he arrived, however, he realized that something was off, and he immediately went on the alert. The front door was slightly ajar; inside, everything was a mess. In the welter of scattered books, ripped seat cushions, and file boxes turned upside down he saw a blatant malice that infuriated him. The intruders hadn't come searching for anything in particular, but had gone out of their way to leave the biggest trail of destruction they could. Knickknacks shattered against the floor, cracks in the TV screen where it had been smashed, food stains on the walls...Ted rubbed his temples, not daring to cross this minefield of objects from his daily life.

He went robotically to his study. The search had been even more exhaustive and destructive here: not a single book was left on the shelves, the computer was a piece of space junk, the desk drawers were everywhere. The Monet reproduction, curiously, remained untouched. Ted went over and took it down, as he had done so often before, and contemplated the safe, thinking that such a silly hiding place might fool somebody in a hurry, but not the perpetrators of this atrocity. A perfect quarter-inch hole through the center of the lock confirmed his suspicions. He pulled the handle and the safe swung open. The little bit of money he had set aside for emergencies had disappeared, but not Lynch's two file folders, which still lay where he had left them, in a neat and provoking pile. When Ted opened the file on Wendell, he saw that only a few pages remained. All the rest were gone.

The false information.

Who did you kill?

"They must have missed something," Ted said aloud. He was almost certain there weren't any hidden microphones, but part of him wanted to be heard.

Tomorrow I'll settle accounts with Lynch.

He didn't care if Lynch was only a hired hand for *them,* just a bit player. Ted had anticipated this possibility and felt that it was more than likely; otherwise, why had the handsome lawyer given his real name? Why not provide a false identity? Ted had thought of a fairly simple reason. The Organization must have foreseen that he might try to find out something about a man who came knocking at his door with such a proposal. What better disguise than a real name? If Ted had taken the initiative to look up Lynch *beforehand,* through Robichaud or any other way, he would have found him easily enough, and that would have lent credibility to the rest of the story.

Walking back down the hall to the living room, Ted stopped for a moment in front of the stairs. He frowned, knowing that going up to check on his and his girls' bedrooms would be hard, but he'd have to do it to find out whether the destruction continued up there. He went to the sofa and impatiently swept aside everything piled on top of it: a pizza box, knickknacks, a lamp, two pillows. He flopped down, exhausted, mentally reviewing the list of things he had to do, to which he now added cleaning and straightening up the entire house. His wife would have enough to contend with after he died; the least he could do for her was see to it that she had a clean and orderly place to do it in.

He smiled at how stupid that sounded. He pulled out his phone and swiped a finger across the screen to turn it on. He had last spoken with Holly on Tuesday morning, holding back his tears and faking a casual tone. He had told her he was going fishing in Travis's boat for a few days, until she and the girls got back. Holly briefly scolded him about it, since the reason Ted hadn't gone to Disney with them was because he had to be at a series of urgent meetings (pure fiction, of course). He replied that one lunch with his client had been enough to close the deal, though everyone had thought it would take them all week to hammer it out. Holly was sorry, but, she said, this way she'd be able to spend more time with her boyfriend in Florida. Cindy must have overheard, because she immediately shouted that her mommy didn't have a boyfriend in Florida, and she demanded to speak with her daddy. Ted talked with her, and then with Nadine, who, after the requisite complaints about the behavior of her sister *who doesn't help Mommy at all,* gave him a detailed report on everything they'd done that day, which Ted listened to with pleasure.

Holly was a phone call away. He ran down his contact list until he got to her name, and stopped. The screen began to fade and almost grow dark, but not so his desire to talk with her. He lifted his thumb and gave two quick taps.

Holly's voice was like a breath of air for a drowning man.

"What happened to your fishing trip?"

"The girls canceled on us at the last minute."

Holly laughed.

"I'm not surprised. They must have seen your photographs."

A pause. Ted hadn't turned on the lights, and the daylight filtering from outside was growing faint in the living room. The shadowy chaos around him found its proper counterbalance in Holly's voice.

God, how I miss you.

"Hi, sweet."

"Hi, Ted. Today it was sweltering. The girls won't tell you this, but they're starting to get tired of this blazing heat."

He could hear Cindy in the background.

"Liar!"

"I'm sure they just miss their daddy," Ted said, and immediately regretted it.

"I doubt that's it. The girls hardly even mention you."

In the background: "She's lying, Daddy!"

"Travis and I decided to come back this afternoon," Ted said, returning to the fishing trip. "I didn't think I could take another night of listening to my business partner's snores in a fifty-square-foot cabin."

"Listen, we're about to eat dinner. The girls didn't want to go out; they asked me to order room service, like in the movies. The truth is, they don't want to leave the air-conditioning."

"Mommy!"

It was Nadine.

"What?"

There was a short conversation between mother and daughters, and then Holly came back on.

"Ted, the food's here. We'll talk later, okay?"

"Enjoy those burgers." Ted didn't have to ask. He *knew* his girls had ordered hamburgers.

"Bye, Ted. Girls, say good-bye to your father."

"Bye, Daddy!"

Ted said good-bye, but nobody heard him. The arm holding the cell phone dropped to the sofa. Once more he hadn't been able to say a proper farewell to Holly, tell her how much he loved her, if only so that she'd remember it later, when she found his body slumped in his office with a bullet in the forehead. He wondered if fate was trying to send him some sort of message.

The room was totally dark.

12

A FEW hours of sleep disturbed by nightmares was all he managed. He showered downstairs, put on the same clothes he had worn the day before, and at five in the morning was scrounging in the kitchen for something to eat. Jack Wilson's voice was the backdrop to his normal morning ritual, but today Ted doubted that the Channel 4 newscaster would make good company. He figured that Wendell's murder would be the lead story today, and he was especially afraid that the weeping family would be the main focus of coverage during these early hours. He pressed the remote control button with resignation. When the TV came on, he remembered the cracked screen, which placed a gray splotch the size of a football across the newscaster's face. It was easy to see from her low-cut dress that she wasn't Jack Wilson. Underneath her image, beyond range of the gray splotch, a running caption stated that the voice speaking was that of the first police officer on the scene at the lakeside home.

"...was patrolling the area when the call came in from dispatch. I've lived in the area all my life, and I know the best ways down to the lake, so I was here in under ten minutes..."

Ted was distracted: something in the living room had shifted. From the corner of his eye he'd seen a dark shape disappear behind a piece of furniture lying on its side.

"Officer, is it true that there may be security camera footage of the murderer?"

A floor lamp toppled noisily. Ted cringed.

Fucking animal!

"Well, with an investigation in progress, all I'm at liberty to confirm is that the owner did have a security camera system installed, but I can't guarantee anything."

The rolling caption changed to "Murderer caught on security cameras."

Ted had walked up to the screen almost without realizing it, partly mesmerized by the story, partly wrapped up in what was going on in the living room, where the possum was managing to keep out of sight, though its progress through the piles of debris was plain to hear.

The newscaster was speaking.

"...from Officer Garnet, who we heard just moments ago, on the discovery of Wendell's body by his wife and two daughters. They survived, we are told, thanks to the family's bulletproof car. The motive for this tragic crime remains at this time unknown..."

Ted feared the worst.

"A family, torn apart: the lives of his wife, Holly, and his daughters, Nadine and Cindy, will never be the same. Later in the hour: more on this breaking story, with live coverage from your on-the-ground Channel 4 news team." Pause. "In other news, Channel 4 Weather tells us to slather on the sunscreen: today's going to be a scorcher, as the heat wave..."

Holly, Nadine, Cindy.

13

NINA WAS coming in to work fifteen minutes late this morning. She had brought doughnuts and was hoping Lynch would be more interested in them than in his secretary's punctuality. She'd been working here for six months and still couldn't predict how he'd react to anything. Lynch was a mystery to her. Her friends assured her that sooner or later he'd try hitting on her, but he hadn't made a move yet, which threw Nina. She'd tried low-cut blouses, seductive poses, subtly suggestive comments—but nothing. Lynch was fifteen years her elder, but he looked nice, and if Nina needed anything at this point in her life, it was a man with his feet on the ground.

She opened the office door and bent to pick up the doughnut box that she had set on the floor. When she stood, she noticed the dark shadow on her right spreading, rushing toward her, taking on the form of a man. In less than a second he was on top of her, waving a gun that looked enormous to Nina.

"Come in," Ted ordered. "Leave the box and your handbag on the desk. Good. Don't turn around yet. Do what I tell you and you won't get hurt."

Nina couldn't remember ever being so scared in her life. She was afraid to see the man's face. She knew what that meant.

"Don't kill me," she begged.

"Where's Lynch?"

"I...I don't know."

"You can turn around."

"I'd rather not."

Ted wasn't happy at all with this situation. He'd been expecting Lynch, and instead this girl had turned up, his secretary, no doubt, and he'd been forced to move quickly, acting on instinct. What was he doing? Threatening defenseless secretaries with a pistol? The girl was scared to death and she had nothing to do with it.

"I'll put the gun away," he said in a calmer voice. "Don't scream and you have my word I won't hurt you. All I want is to talk to your boss. It's a matter of life or death."

His words seemed to have the right effect on the girl, who kept her hands in the air and whimpered.

"What's your name?"

"Nina."

"I apologize for this situation, Nina. You can turn around now. Trust me. I don't care if you see my face. Your boss and I know each other."

Nina turned around, slowly. She wasn't crying, but she'd been about to. She looked Ted up and down, confirming that the gun really was out of sight.

"Sorry for the rude introduction. That was very tactless of me."

She nodded. The fear hadn't left her face.

"No need to worry. Is this your desk?"

"Yes."

"You sit there. I'll take this chair, and we'll both wait here for Lynch. Is that okay with you?"

Nina walked around the desk, very slowly. She sat down.

"Hands on top of the desk, please."

She complied.

"Have you been working for Lynch long?"

"No. I started a few months ago."

"I see." Ted nodded. "Is anyone in the office next door?"

Nina hesitated.

"Tell me the truth, Nina."

"The other suites on this floor are vacant."

"Better."

"You gave me your word before..."

"I won't hurt you. I should have introduced myself differently to you—I can see that now. I wasn't expecting you to come in then. I don't know why, but it didn't occur to me that Lynch would have a secretary. That was stupid of me."

Nina didn't reply. "You can have a doughnut if you want," she finally said, pointing at the box with her chin.

Ted couldn't help laughing.

"No thanks. So Lynch usually gets here at nine?"

Nina couldn't remember having said that, but maybe she had. The last few minutes were registered in her brain as a chaotic whirlwind of events and emotions.

"Yes," she replied curtly.

Ted leaned all the way back in the chair, sticking his hands in the pockets of the sports jacket he had chosen, the better to hide the gun. He felt the pistol butt and closed his eyes for a moment. He asked himself the same question he'd asked a little while before: *What was he doing?*

14

LYNCH SAW the Dunkin' Donuts box on Nina's desk, went over, and lifted the top with his index finger. He looked at the contents with a slight frown. He was wondering if the girl had gone to the bathroom when he heard a noise in his office. Was she up to something in there? He hoped not, because otherwise he might be forced to hold an uncomfortable discussion about limits with her. He opened the door and found her sitting at his desk, stiff as a board, eyes wide-open. She wasn't dressed provocatively, and her pale face made it clear that she wasn't up to some game of seduction. Lynch saw Nina's eyes turn toward a corner of the office, where a man stood.

"What's going on in here?" Lynch asked.

Ted stared closely at him. He couldn't get over it. Amazing. It really was Lynch, but he looked years older than the young man who'd visited him at home. His forehead was thinly lined and his hair was going gray. He hadn't lost his handsome looks; age had been good to him. But the youthful patina was entirely gone. Ted raised his hand and held it over his eyes for an instant. When he removed it, nothing changed.

"He's got a gun," Nina said.

"But I'm not planning to draw it, so long as we can talk like civilized people."

"Has he hurt you?" Lynch asked his secretary.

"No."

"Sit down," Ted ordered.

Lynch walked around the desk and sank heavily into the chair next to Nina's.

"Did you see the news this morning?" Ted asked as he went to the door and locked it, deliberately turning his back on his two hostages.

Lynch smirked. "Are you asking me or her?"

"From now on, all my questions are for you. The girl is collateral damage."

"Why not let her go, and we'll work it out between us?"

"Maybe. We'll see."

Ted leaned against the office door.

"I haven't seen the news," Lynch said.

"Wendell's dead." Ted studied the lawyer's expression but saw no trace of surprise. "Murdered."

"Why can't we talk this over like civilized gentlemen?" Lynch said while glancing to his right, where Nina sat.

"Don't even think of it."

"She'll keep quiet," Lynch pointed out. "Won't you, Nina?"

The girl had missed part of the dialogue but she vigorously nodded.

"I won't say a word."

"Now that you see that Ted and I already know each other," Lynch went on, "there's no reason for you to call the police or anything. Meanwhile, Ted and I have a bit of pending business to clear up."

Ted thought it over. It was true that he couldn't discuss Wendell's death openly with the girl here. He couldn't confess to a murder in front of a perfect stranger.

"Get out, go home," Ted suddenly said to her.

Nina sprang from her chair, ran around the desk, and stopped when she came to Ted, who still blocked the door. Nina clutched her purse and looked at him beseechingly. Ted kept his eyes on Lynch, who understood what he was thinking.

"Nina, not a word about this, to anyone," Lynch said. "Ted and I really do have to settle some affairs."

Ted stepped aside. Nina ran out and didn't even bother to close the door behind her. Ted shut it for her.

"Now you're going to tell me the whole truth, Lynch. You set a trap for me, you miserable little bastard."

"I admit that I concealed some information, but believe me, it was necessary."

Ted bounded forward. Leaning with both arms on the desk, he brought his face close to Lynch's.

"'It was necessary,' he says! You neglected to mention that Wendell was married and had two daughters. Ever since I found out, I haven't been able to stop thinking of them as my own family."

"If I'd told you he had a wife and kids, you never would have done the job," Lynch said coldly.

Ted stuck his hand in the pocket of his jacket. He pulled out the Browning.

"And you, Lynch? Do you have a wife and kids? Be careful how you answer, because I can blow your head off any second."

"Please, Ted, put the gun down and allow me to explain."

"You already did explain it to me, you son of a bitch." Ted scratched his head. "It's all so confusing..."

"What are you talking about?"

Ted lowered the gun. He put it back in his pocket. He pulled up a chair that was by the filing cabinets and collapsed into it.

"Tell me what you have to tell me, Lynch. Stop playing games, okay?"

The lawyer nodded.

"I gave you my real name, Ted. I knew you'd come see me sooner or later. It's time to be honest with you." Lynch settled back in his chair and dropped a devastating tidbit. "Wendell didn't want to commit suicide."

As soon as Lynch uttered those words, something stirred inside the filing cabinet. To be more precise, in the bottom drawer. Ted instinctively turned to look. The sound was gone. Lynch showed no sign of having heard it.

"Wendell and I met in college," Lynch said, "and we became best friends. Those were the years when the Organization was being formed, and Wendell soon became involved; he became the cornerstone of it. But Wendell wasn't interested in dealing out justice, Ted. Wendell is a stone-cold fucking killer. He's been offing people for years."

Ted wrinkled his forehead. Lynch kept talking.

"I learned of Wendell's unofficial activities fairly recently, almost by accident. In a way, I suppose I always suspected, but I didn't want to see it."

"Why didn't you turn him in?"

"Did you see the way he lives? He has a lot of power, lots of connections, the best lawyers. He's gotten into scrapes before and he always comes out on top. Not to mention I couldn't pin anything specific on him."

"It wasn't just his wife and daughters you forgot to mention. You also left out the security cameras."

"I'm sorry."

"You're sorry," Ted said morosely. "You realize you're dealing with a man who's got nothing to lose, don't you?"

"You'll understand everything. You'll see."

"And Blaine? The information you gave me about him was pure bullshit. Everybody knew the guy was guilty. If Wendell was your target, why send me to kill Blaine?"

The sound in the file drawer again. Louder than before. Like a fist pounding on the metal box from the inside. Ted jumped.

"What was that?"

"What was what?"

Ted's heart was pounding.

"Can I show you something?" Lynch asked. "I've got it right here, in the desk drawer."

Ted pulled out the Browning again and pointed it at Lynch.

"Open it slowly."

"Of course."

Lynch opened the middle drawer.

"It's that folder," he said.

"Pull it out."

Lynch put it on the desk, within Ted's reach.

Ted sat back down. The folder looked like the ones Lynch had given him at his home. He was about to open it when Lynch asked him not to.

"Before you open it, let me explain something to you. As I just told you, I only learned fairly recently about Wendell's activities, the murders. He was my friend a long time ago, but the harm he was causing was too great." He paused. "Open the folder."

Ted put away the Browning.

"Tell me what's in it." He didn't dare touch it.

"Holly's been deceiving you for a long time," Lynch said without further ado. "That folder contains irrefutable evidence. Photographs, telephone records, hotel receipts."

Ted frowned contemptuously. It couldn't be true. He reached out to open the folder, but at the last second he stopped. Something in his face changed.

"Holly asked you for a divorce," Lynch went on. "Things have been bad between you two for years."

"That's goddamn bullshit."

"Think about it for a second..."

Ted again pictured Holly at Wendell's house, the girls running to the front door with their smiling faces and pink backpacks. A string of experiences he'd been through with her over the past several months flooded into his head. It was true that, in general, he was the one who had been acting evasive, distant, excusing himself with work, and so on. Ted didn't want to open the folder.

"I investigated Wendell," Lynch said, "and accidentally found out about Holly's cheating. It's a long story."

The banging in the file drawer started up again.

"Stop it!" Ted screamed at the metal drawer.

Lynch stared at him with a look of horror on his face. Ted jumped up and ran to the file cabinet. He gave it a good kick.

"Quiet!"

He returned to the desk and, overcome by a sudden attack of rage, swept the folder away. It fell next to the filing cabinet; a few pages spilled out, including one of the photos. Ted screamed and dropped to his knees next to the partially covered photograph, looking at it dumbstruck. It had been taken from outside a restaurant. Through the window, he saw Holly in profile, bent slightly forward over the table, smiling with her mouth open, about to try a bite that someone on the other side of the table was offering her. Only part of the man's arm was visible. Ted stood up. He stepped back, not taking his eyes off the photo, and slammed into the cabinet. A series of bangs rumbled inside.

Ted bent down and opened the drawer. He stifled a scream, covering his mouth with both hands.

"What is it?" Lynch asked.

The possum peeked over the edge of the drawer; sniffed at the air in the office, just as it had done the day before on the tire swing at Robichaud's house; and climbed up until its front paws were in the air. It pivoted and fell to the floor with a thud.

Ted ran stumbling from the office, forgetting about the gun, which was trembling like an extension of his arm. He ran along the corridor, lunging at each door in turn, only to smash into it and back away. Where was the fucking elevator? Holding his head in his hands, he reached the end of the corridor and rushed down a narrow, nasty staircase, the steps growing narrower and narrower as he went down. Twice he nearly fell. The first floor was almost dark: no lights were on, and he saw trampled piles of mail in front of many of the office doors. He picked a door, forced it open, and was swallowed by an empty office that stank of disuse. A massive old filing cabinet, which even its owners had not bothered to move, one of its drawers missing, greeted him with a blank expression of surprise. Ted hugged it and slumped down softly by its side. He was staring at the open door, knowing that the possum would come in at any moment...

PART II

15

TED MCKAY was about to put a bullet through his brain when the doorbell rang. Insistently.

He opened his eyes. The natural light flowing in through the window of his study blinded him. Soon enough he heard the knocking at the door, and with it the voice of the visitor who should have been a stranger to him.

He stood up and immediately felt something weighing down his left pants pocket. He fingered the lump in the pocket: no mistaking this semicircular form. It was the horseshoe. Ted tried to take it all in. Unbelievable. The study, which in his memory had been ransacked and turned upside down, was now back to normal. The desk was neat and orderly, the books sitting on their proper shelves, the computer on the side table. As Lynch shouted for him to open the door (Ted knew it to be Lynch), the most Ted could do was lift a finger and touch the computer's on button, as if doing so would provide definitive proof that all this was really happening. The machine whirred to life with the usual hums and flickering LEDs. Ted, half terrified and half annoyed, quickly turned it back off by pressing the button and holding it down. He could hear Nadine warning him: *That's not how you turn it off, Daddy. You should go to shut down from the start button. Mommy taught me.* Ted shivered. The letter to Holly lay on the desk.

"Open up, please!"

Ted fumbled for the keys in the small jar while the shouting continued. He was waiting for the demand that he knew was about to come.

"Open up now, Ted!"

Why am I not surprised that you know me by name, Lynch?

He opened the study door. He read his note to Holly: "Honey, I left a copy of the key to the study on top of the fridge. Don't let the kids in. I love you." It was as if somebody else had written it. Ted couldn't get the photograph from the restaurant out of his head: Holly, leaning across the table to taste the bite of food her lover was offering her. How could he possibly remember something that hadn't happened yet?

"Coming!" Ted shouted.

Reaching the living room, he recognized the silhouette in the window. This time, too, he gazed at everything with unusual interest—not because he had said farewell to all these objects expecting never to see them again, but because his last memory was of seeing them smashed and broken.

When he opened the door, there was Lynch—the friendly version of Lynch—with his fabulous smile, the polo shirt with the brightly colored horizontal stripes, and the briefcase that seemed out of place.

"Whatever you're selling, I'm not interested," Ted said, paraphrasing his other self.

"Oh, I'm afraid I'm not here to sell you anything."

As the dialogue continued, Ted noticed that Lynch showed no sign of having had this conversation before; he was acting too natural. Again Ted closed the door in Lynch's face, but this time he didn't stand around to hear Lynch telling him he knew what he was about to do with the gun he'd left on the desk. He ran to the kitchen, to the fridge, and there was the photo of Holly at the beach, running in that particular frozen posture, surrounded by the frame that Cindy and Nadine had decorated with glitter. He stood there for a moment, relieved. He ran a finger over his wife's printed body, as if he needed to feel the slick surface of the photographic paper and assure himself that it was really there.

He stuck his hand in his pocket. The horseshoe was real, too. He clutched it without taking it out. But then his fingertips felt a piece of paper. In disbelief, he pulled out the tattered note, written in his own handwriting: Open the door. It's your only way out.

He went back to the living room and let his persistent visitor come in. Lynch was still standing there, smiling under the midday sun.

16

TED WAS in a crouch. He held his head in both hands, rocking slowly back and forth, staring at the photo of Holly on the beach, which he had set on the floor inches from his feet. He needed to understand.

It's the tumor...

Dr. Carmichael had told him that his headaches might return, that he might even get dizzy spells or hallucinations. Hadn't he said that?

Yes, Dr. Carmichael had told him he might experience hallucinations. But hallucinating a gnome running through the backyard, or a rainbow in the bathroom, or some such psychological shit—that was one thing. Going through all this stuff now, though: that was a completely different matter.

He forced himself to stand. When he got to his feet, the weight of the horseshoe reminded him that at least one thing had changed. He pulled it from his pocket and took a good long look at it. The memory of picking it up on Wendell's private drive was vivid; he could see every detail of the house. He also had the note, wrinkled up enough to show that he'd been carrying it in his pocket for a while.

He stooped down for an instant and placed the horseshoe next to the photo; later he would decide whether to leave it there or carry it with him. The priority now was to talk to Holly. He had agreed with her that they wouldn't speak again until Friday, when she would be back to sign the divorce papers. How had he forgotten that little detail? He had told her he would need a few days for the lawyers to make all the arrangements, and she had told him she'd go visit her parents with the girls, just as Ted had anticipated. They'd had one last, amicable conversation in the living room, and had said an amicable good-bye, as if for one fleeting moment the old Holly and Ted had been reborn from the ashes.

But that illusion had lasted only as long as a quick hug and a lukewarm smile. The events of the last few months had demolished everything; there was nothing to rebuild. Ted accepted some of the blame. Almost all of it, actually. He'd let himself get wrapped up in his work without realizing how distant he'd become, as he would later tell Laura Hill. He'd again become the Ted of his teenage years, the rebel, the misunderstood kid, the person he'd finally overcome thanks to his feelings for his family. The headaches had begun, the constant bad moods. Even the girls had started looking at him warily. "It's the fear, Laura. There's nothing worse than realizing your own kid is afraid of you. It's as if someone else has taken over." That was when he had turned to Carmichael. His headaches had gone from once-daily torments to three or four times a day, and they were growing more intense. Ted feared the worst: a malignant tumor. On the other hand, it was a relief to be able to attribute his shitty behavior to a clump of malevolent cells.

The news, far from upsetting him, helped Ted see his fate clearly. Laura helped him, he had to admit. She helped him shake off some certainties he had lived with for too long. His relationship with his daughters improved, and with Holly, too. And that was when she asked him for the divorce. "I've wanted to have a civilized discussion with you about it for a long time." Their conversation was polite. She told him she preferred it this way, that they deserved to end up on good terms, the same way they started. Ted agreed.

Now he understood his wife's motives much better.

"Hello, Ted," Holly's voice said on the other end of the line.

"Hello..."

Honey.

He felt a pang in his chest. At his feet was the photo of Holly, smiling at the beach, in the red bikini. Ted's favorite.

"Are you okay?" she asked.

"Yes. Sorry I called you on your cell."

"Don't worry about it. Is there a problem with the papers?"

"No. The papers are almost ready."

Silence.

"Holly, are you at your parents' house?"

Or at your lover's?

"I don't owe you any explanations."

"You have my daughters, so I think you do."

As soon as the words were out of his mouth he wanted to take them back.

"Sorry."

"What do you want, Ted? I'm busy."

Ted felt very confused. If Holly really had been cheating on him, then she might be in genuine danger. Wendell could be a dangerous man.

You don't know Wendell.

"Take care of yourself, Holly."

"I always do. What are you talking about? Is there something I ought to know?"

Ted knew he had to make up something to excuse his phone call.

"I've been getting some strange calls at home, and they have me worried."

"Strange calls? What sort of calls? Have you reported them to the police?"

"I don't think that's necessary. They mentioned your name—that's why I'm worried."

"My name?" Now Holly did seem to be paying attention.

"I don't want to worry you, but you can see why I needed to call you, right?"

"Yes. Yes, I do."

"Just…take care."

"I will. Thanks."

Ted couldn't help smiling at this minimal display of gratitude.

"Bye, Holly."

"See you on Friday, Ted."

17

"I ALMOST killed myself today," Ted said in a neutral tone.

He was sitting on the usual couch in Laura Hill's office, staring at the plastic water cup in the middle of the coffee table. He looked up.

"You don't seem very concerned," he told his therapist with a thin smile.

"You're still here," she replied, returning his smile.

"It's been a crazy morning. I don't know where to start."

"We have time."

Ted had been talking to Laura for several minutes, but he'd been so agitated that he hadn't noticed how she looked.

"You've let your hair down," he observed.

Laura blushed and tossed her head, making her hair swish against her cheeks. It was a shade lighter than before.

"I got it done yesterday. I decided to change styles."

In his recent hallucinations, Laura hadn't gone to the hair salon. Apparently tumors didn't bother with cosmetic details.

It wasn't a hallucination! Lynch came to see you this morning.

Ted's smile disappeared. If he needed any more proof that these last few days really happened, he had it in his pocket. He'd found the horseshoe near Wendell's house, a place he remembered perfectly well even though he'd never been there in his life.

"What happened this morning, Ted?"

“I was in my study at home, holding my Browning to my head, when suddenly someone started knocking frantically at the front door. That was when I came to and saw where I was, what I was about to do.”

Laura’s expression was indecipherable.

“You didn’t remember picking up the gun?”

“Worse. I didn’t remember any of the past few days. And I still don’t. Just bits and pieces, all jumbled together, partly because I have...well, it’s a little hard to explain. I have *other* memories. It’s as if the tumor has scrambled everything.”

“Go on about what happened this morning. You’re in your study. You hear those noises at the front door. What happens next?”

“There’s a letter to Holly lying on the desk, written in my handwriting. I had also left her a note on the door to my study telling her to keep the girls away. Apparently I had it all planned out. It’s like, as I discover these details, bits of information from the past are unveiled in my brain.”

“Do you really think you were going to press the trigger?”

Ted put his head down and rubbed his temples. Laura reached over and squeezed his shoulder.

“Ted, stay with me. Look at me. That’s right. Who was knocking on your door?”

“A man named Lynch,” Ted said. “I thought he was trying to sell something and I tried to get rid of him, but he said he knew what I was about to do in my study; he said something about my gun, I don’t remember what, but it was pretty specific. The craziest thing was, I remember going through the whole situation once before. I knew everything Lynch was about to tell me, what he was going to propose. It was like watching a movie you already know by heart.”

“And do you believe you actually have lived through the same experience before?”

“No,” Ted said. “It’s the tumor, Laura. Dr. Carmichael said that a tumor like mine can cause hallucinations. It can put pressure on parts of your brain, and that can cause—”

"Hold on, Ted. We can consult with Dr. Carmichael later if we have to. What I want to know is whether there is any chance that you met Lynch some other time. In the past, perhaps, when he was younger."

"Funny you should ask that."

"Why?"

"Because in the fantasy I was telling you about, I saw Lynch again a few days later, and the guy seemed to have gotten older—like, ten or fifteen years older. Just like that." Ted snapped his fingers. "Like in a dream, when people instantaneously change how they look."

Ted remembered something. He shook his head and laughed.

"What is it?" Laura asked.

"I remember being here with you," Ted said, looking around at the walls. "Your hair was like before. My tumor didn't have any way of knowing you'd gotten it done. But God...I remember insignificant details. Do you think that's possible? Imagining something like that?"

"What were we talking about? In the session, I mean."

Ted put his hands on his pockets. He felt the semicircular shape of the horseshoe.

"About why I gave up chess," Ted said.

Laura seemed surprised.

"What do you have in your pocket?"

Ted pulled out the horseshoe. He held it in both hands and studied it for a long time, with the expression of someone who was trying to work out a complicated problem. Laura spoke softly to him.

"Miller gave you that before you quit chess, didn't he?"

Ted looked up at once. Laura smiled gently.

"I have a good memory—what can you do?" said Laura. "When you told me about Miller and the horseshoe, I knew it was important for you somehow. I didn't know you still kept it."

"Oh, this isn't the same horseshoe Miller gave me. But it looks a lot like it. I found it...I don't remember exactly where. I can't remember," Ted lied.

Next to Wendell's lake!

"You told me earlier that this man, Lynch, proposed something to you. What was it?"

"Jesus, it's so crazy...He said he was part of a secret organization that recruits people like me to settle accounts, to deliver justice. To deal with murderers who got off on technicalities or whatever. In exchange, they'd let me join a sort of suicide circle, though that's not what he called it."

"And that way your family and others wouldn't suffer the consequences of your committing suicide," Laura reflected, with some amazement.

"Exactly."

"I can't say it isn't brilliant. And chilling. Was it the first time you'd heard of such a thing?"

"Of course."

"Who did they want you to kill? To deal with, I mean."

"Some guy named Edward Blaine. He murdered his girlfriend and got off scot-free."

"Oh, right. I heard about it on TV. The woman's sister is asking for a retrial because of the mistakes the detectives made."

Ted remembered Tricia Pendergast explaining the case at Arthur Robichaud's house.

"Apparently there was a commercial laundry under the apartment, and the heat from the dryer vents kept the body warm."

"What did you do in your fantasy, Ted?"

"'Fantasy.' It sounds so ridiculous."

"I know."

"Laura, do you think these memories really come from my past?"

"I guess it's possible that some elements in them do. But let's focus on what you can remember. What did you feel about Blaine?"

"That I had to kill him. Today I thought it was the most ridiculous idea in the world, but in that other reality, killing Blaine seemed perfectly reasonable. As reasonable as committing suicide. So I went to his house;

I remember every detail of the inside of his house, and I'm sure I've never been there. I hid in a closet and waited for the guy to fall asleep. Then I went to his bedroom and killed him."

"You killed him. In cold blood?"

"No. Blaine noticed I was there, and he made it kind of hard for me. But I did kill him."

"What happened next?"

"Well, after that, it starts to sound more like a dream. I went to the house of the other guy I was supposed to kill. His name was Wendell, and he was supposed to be waiting for me. After all, he supposedly belonged to the suicide circle. He lived in an enormous house, way off by itself in the middle of the woods, with a private lake. Supposedly Wendell was unmarried and had no kids. At least that's what Lynch had told me. And yet, just a few minutes later, a woman shows up with two girls."

"Though Wendell wasn't supposed to have any kids."

"So I thought. Lynch hid that bit of information from me because he knew that I'd never agree otherwise."

"How do you know that?"

"Lynch told me so afterwards."

"So you saw him again."

"Exactly. When I suspected he had tricked me, I turned to an old high school classmate, Arthur Robichaud, a lawyer. I hadn't seen him in years. At school he was a shy kid who hardly hung out with anybody; I was one of the bullies who used to make fun of him and play jokes on him. The sort of thing that stays with you your whole life long, I guess. The thing is, I went to his house and it turned out it was his birthday. I saw other classmates there, all losers like Arthur, but I hardly recognized them."

"Wait a second," Laura broke in. "You must have several lawyers working for you at your company. Why didn't you use them?"

"Arthur had helped me draw up my will," Ted said. As soon as he said it, he realized it didn't square with what he'd said earlier. In his fantasy, he had taken it for granted that they hadn't seen each other in years, and that was how Robichaud had acted, too. But...

"Did Robichaud help you find Lynch?"

"What's behind all this, Laura?" Ted clasped his head again. "It's like I'm in a waking dream. Now that I think about it, at the birthday party at Robichaud's house...there was also an animal, a possum, that kept appearing."

Laura sat up straight, alert.

"A possum?"

"Yes. I saw it several times. The first time was on the picnic table on the porch in back of the house; I barely remember that one. Then I saw it at Arthur's house, hiding in an old tire swing. And again at Lynch's office, when I finally went to see him."

"At his office?"

"It crawled out of a filing cabinet." Ted shook his head and laughed. "My God, such a stupid dream. I just wish it felt like it was only a dream."

"Let's pretend that's exactly what it was, Ted. Tell me what happened when you went to Lynch's office."

"Lynch had aged. He was my age, or a little older. I had to threaten him, and he admitted that Wendell did indeed have a wife and two daughters, and also something much worse."

"What?"

"That Wendell didn't really want to commit suicide. Wendell belonged to the Organization"—Ted's eyes fixed on the water cup—"but he had gone...off track."

"He was killing people on his own?"

Ted was astonished. Laura's guess sounded crazy, yet it was correct.

"Yes. He had to be stopped."

"And why you?"

It was time to come to the heart of the matter. If there was any point of contact between his delirium and reality, Ted was afraid it was Holly's cheating. The rest might be nothing but the grisly packaging his unconscious had wrapped her deception in to disguise that devastating reality.

"Lynch trailed Wendell and discovered that he had a lover..."

Ted left the words hanging in midair. He clasped the horseshoe with both hands; without being fully aware of it, he was pulling on either end, as if he were trying to pull it straight.

"Holly, right?"

Ted silently nodded.

"Would you like some water, Ted?"

"No thanks."

"Did you talk with Holly today?"

"Yes. It was a pretty friendly chat, in the end. I didn't tell her any of this."

"I think we'd better stop here for today."

Ted seemed not to hear her.

"What is all this, Laura? Is it possible that I knew about it? About Holly, I mean. Now that I think of it, there were some signs, and maybe..."

"That's enough. Leave it for now."

"Okay."

"I want us to meet every day, Ted."

"Perfect."

"Try to get some rest."

Ted stood up. Laura did the same.

"Ted?"

He looked at her.

"Don't leave home, understood?"

"Understood," Ted said. And then he remembered something. A detail from that other, outlandish reality. "Your son is a Boy Scout, isn't he?"

"Yes."

"In that fantasy, he had some sort of problem with an authorization form for a camping trip. Somebody told you about it in a phone call in the middle of our session."

Laura smiled. She pointed at the phone, which of course hadn't rung once since Ted had started going there.

"Fortunately, nothing has happened," Laura said.

Ted went to the door. He was still holding on tight to the horseshoe.

"Carmichael was right about therapy helping me," he said, more to himself than to his therapist.

18

TED WAS looking at the precise spot where he had found the horseshoe. He was on the dirt path that led to Wendell's home. He caught sight of the house itself in the distance, through a gap in the foliage, and he raised his head to get a better look. He had been there before—he was sure of it. He knew that if he got any closer, if he went in and walked around the luxury home, his memories would commingle with reality and he wouldn't be able to distinguish between the two.

He had promised Laura that he'd stay home, but his need to know had been too pressing. He closed his eyes and, taking several deep breaths, conjured up every detail he could recall: the private jetty, the vast great room with the panoramic lakeside view, the play area behind the house. And yet this was supposedly the first time he'd set foot here.

Of course you've been here! You killed Wendell. When you found out he was Holly's lover, you went off your rocker and murdered him. Simple as that. Then you joined the loony club so you wouldn't have to deal with the truth.

If that were true, he would soon find out. Just five hundred feet to Wendell's lake house. He had left the Browning at home on purpose; in his right hand he held the horseshoe, which he might be able to use to defend himself in a fight, but for now he held it mainly to keep his courage up.

The Lamborghini was parked in the same old spot, leading him to think that Wendell must be out on the lake, peacefully fishing. Not so. Ted stood on the shore by the jetty and scrutinized the lake, expecting to see the orange life jacket. No trace of Wendell. Maybe he's sailing around the other end of the lake, Ted thought. He looked around and saw one of the many security cameras. He gave it a smile.

The front door was locked—another difference from his prior visit. Ted went to one of the windows. It was tinted, and he had to put his hands around his face to be able to see in at all. He didn't mind if Wendell saw him standing there; in fact, he hoped he would. He was entranced by the sight of the rug in the foyer where Wendell had fallen and bled out. Yet it showed not a trace of blood. This was the type of detail that exasperated him. He could accept the fact of having been at the lake house before without remembering his visit, but where had he gotten that image of Wendell lying dead on the rug?

He circled the house, looking for another way in. He could have just knocked or rung the doorbell, but he wanted to poke around a bit before confronting Wendell. If Lynch was telling the truth, Wendell was a dangerous killer, and Ted had no difficulty picturing what the guy would do if he came across his lover's husband, alone and unarmed. For a second Ted regretted leaving the Browning behind, though he had carefully thought through his decision not to bring it. He was no killer.

Wendell wasn't at the other end of the lake, either; his boat was tied up at the jetty. Ted ran around back and tried the door to the huge garage, large enough for several cars. No luck there. He was thinking that he might try breaking a window with the horseshoe when his eyes turned to the play area on the gentle hill behind the house. A pretty pink child-sized castle made of solid wood, which must have cost a fortune, stood there. A white gravel path bordered by stones led to it. Ted walked up the hill, his eyes focused on the castle. It was maybe seven feet high, with towers on each corner and Disney princesses painted on the walls. Belle,

Tiana, Ariel—Ted knew them all. He couldn't resist the temptation to peek through an open window. A small plastic table and two little chairs were arrayed inside.

"Who are you?" someone called out behind him.

Ted had been looking through the castle window when he heard the voice. It was Wendell. He'd never heard him speak before, yet there was something astonishingly familiar about his voice. That fact seemed very revealing somehow. Ted raised his hands as a sign that he meant no harm, and he slowly backed away from the window.

"I'm Ted," he said as he turned around. There was no real need to say it, since, after all, Wendell would recognize him as soon as he saw him. Unless he had already recognized him and was just playing games.

But Wendell arched his eyebrows, disconcerted. He stood at the forest's edge, dressed in the clothes Ted remembered: jeans, blue flannel shirt, orange life jacket. Why was he wearing a life jacket in the woods?

"What are you doing on my property? Are you alone?" The disconcerted look was apparently not an act. There was something in his voice.

Why do you look so familiar to me?

"Yes, I'm alone."

Again, the disconcerted look on Wendell's face. He kept checking his perimeter.

"Did Lynch send you?"

Ted smiled. At last they were getting somewhere.

"Look, Ted," Wendell said, "I don't know who the hell you are. If Lynch sent you to kill me, he's an idiot. You couldn't hurt a fly."

A gun appeared as if by magic in Wendell's right hand. Ted had been concentrating on his face, and when he looked down, there was the weapon.

"Holly is my wife," Ted said to defend himself.

Wendell's face immediately changed. He rubbed his chin with his free hand.

"Interesting...Come on in."

Ted pointed at the castle.

"Here?"

"Of course. I'm not going to let you into my house. And this"—he indicated the gun—"is just for insurance. If we come to an understanding, you'll walk out of here. I don't want to ruin my daughters' castle."

The castle had a double door big enough for a small girl to walk through without ducking, but Ted practically had to crawl in on his knees. The floor was rubberized. Besides the plastic table and chairs, there was a shelf with a tea set. Wendell followed Ted inside. They each took a chair, like a couple of invading giants. The air inside was several degrees warmer. It wasn't circulating. Wendell placed his automatic on the table.

"This is ridiculous," Ted said.

"So Holly is your wife," Wendell remarked in the same tone of amazement as before. "And Lynch sent you to kill me. Let me guess. He told you your wife and I were lovers. Right?"

"He told me a couple other things, too."

"So I see."

Wendell reflected for a few moments.

"You're going to tell me everything Lynch told you about me."

"That's not going to happen."

"Funny," Wendell said. "For a second there, I forgot I was the one with the gun."

Ted sighed. He felt a pounding in his head. He'd gone to the lakeside home to make sure Wendell wasn't dead, but now that he had him sitting there, he wasn't sure what to do next. The only thing he was clear about was that he needed to find out whether the guy was dangerous, for Holly's sake.

"Lynch told me about the Organization, straightening out the mistakes the system makes, dealing justice. He told me you had lost your way, that you had started acting on your own, outside the rules. He asked me to kill you."

Wendell shook his head. His face was slowly twisted by rage.

"The fucking asshole," Wendell said to himself.

"Why?"

"There *is* no Organization, Ted," Wendell said angrily. "I've known Lynch since college, and it was just a stupid idea he had. We were pretty close back then, but that was more than twenty years ago. We saw each other once in a while over the years, but our friendship slowly faded. Then, a few months ago, he tried to blackmail me over something from the past. It doesn't matter what. It was a stupid move on his part, because it was easy to find something on him. He's smart, but he didn't know how to cover his own ass. Understand?"

"No."

"Lynch is your wife's lover, not me."

"What?"

"I hired two guys to find something on him," Wendell explained. "They discovered he was going out with a married woman, and they took a ton of pictures. I sent him the photos and told him: next time he tried blackmailing me, things would get a lot uglier. That was the last I heard of him."

"Describe the photos to me."

"Why?"

"Please."

"I don't know. I didn't look at them too closely."

"Was there one inside a restaurant?"

"Yes. It was a sequence shot from outside, through a window. They were sitting at a table, across from each other, and he was giving her a bite to taste."

Ted remembered the photograph, but he'd seen only part of the scene. If Wendell was telling the truth, the man with Holly in that photo was Lynch himself.

"Don't you get it?" Wendell asked. "Lynch went and found you, and he drew you in with that nonsense about the Organization to kill two birds with one stone."

It made sense, but Ted didn't want to believe him blindly. Believing Lynch blindly hadn't worked out so well.

"Why would he want you dead?" Ted asked, settling back in the tiny, uncomfortable chair.

"Apart from the fact that I might reveal his love affair? Let me spell it out for you. Justin Lynch was jealous of me from the moment we met, and his jealousy only grew more intense and more blatant over the years. His resentment ate away at our friendship and finally destroyed it. Look at where I live. Look at my car. Look at my family. My company brings in hundreds of millions a year. Did you see where he works? A grimy office in a shitty building, where he takes on little dipshit cases—women with two-timing husbands, crap like that. Nobody can say I didn't help him out at first—but for every right choice I made, he made two wrong ones. You don't think that's motive enough for murder? But the coward didn't even dare to do it himself. So he turned to you and dug up his bullshit idea of the Organization."

Ted thought it over. There were some key questions that he still hadn't come close to answering. How had Lynch known about his suicide? There was no way Lynch could have dreamt up the suicide circle on the spot. He must have known about the suicide beforehand. But how? And if he had known, why not let Ted go through with it and clear the way for Holly and himself?

You didn't want to commit suicide.

"What are you thinking?" Wendell asked.

"I'm so confused."

"It's all pretty simple, believe me. Justin would never dare to stand in front of me and pull the trigger. He doesn't have the balls. He needed somebody to do it for him, and there you were. I'm surprised he thought you would be capable; he obviously doesn't know how to pick people."

Ted felt foolishly offended. In his fantasy, he had killed Blaine and Wendell like a professional hit man. He had even drugged Blaine's dog!

Unfortunately, in this reality, the only things Ted had shot were the silhouettes at the shooting range. Wendell was right: he couldn't kill another person.

There was just one flaw in Wendell's theory. If they really didn't know each other, how could Ted possibly remember being here at his house before?

You don't remember it. This is the first time you've been here.

Once more the same infuriating thought. He wanted to cling to what he had felt when he got here, walking down the dirt road to the house, when he'd been able to summon up every detail of the mansion before he even got there. That thought had been real. He had to cling to it. He suddenly thought of the horseshoe; if he could clench it in his fist, he thought, he might erase all his doubts. He reached into his pocket.

Wendell went on the alert. He grabbed his gun, fast as lightning.

But Ted soon realized that Wendell hadn't been reacting to his attempt to get his horseshoe. While aiming the gun at him, Wendell was looking out one of the windows in the castle.

"I thought you came alone!" Wendell accused him without taking his eyes off the window.

"I did."

"Then you were followed."

Ted couldn't tell who Wendell was talking about from where he sat. He leaned forward slightly to look out—and froze. A black man in a white lab coat was walking along the side of the house. It was Roger, the strange fellow Ted remembered from his visit to Blaine's.

"Do you know that guy?" Wendell was still pointing the gun at Ted. "What's he doing at my house?"

"I'm not sure if I do."

"You're not sure?"

Roger walked nonchalantly, hands in his pockets. When he reached the corner of the house, he turned and walked toward the lake, away from them.

"I think he's leaving," Ted said.

"Where's he going? There's nothing here for two miles in either direction. What's that guy doing here?"

19

THE SIGHT of Roger haunting Wendell's property was the second direct connection between his "fantasy" (Ted didn't like the term, but who cares?) and the present. The other connection was the horseshoe. And the note from the desk.

Wendell practically shoved him out of the castle.

"Do you know the guy or not?"

"Yeah, I guess I met him somewhere."

Wendell sighed and rolled his eyes, as if he might find a clue to Ted's behavior in the sky. He grabbed Ted by his jacket collar.

"Concentrate!" Wendell stuck his face in Ted's and stared him in the eye. "Do you think that guy followed you, or is he searching for you blindly?"

"Blindly, I think."

Wendell let him go. Rubbing his chin, he shot a glance at the side of the castle, and then turned to stare at the white gravel in the play area.

"Come with me."

Together they walked into the woods.

"Where are we going?"

"I want to show you something I've got in my car. But best not to let the guy see us."

They went far enough in to stay hidden, circling the house until they came out on the private road. By then Roger must have been on the far side of the house, so there was no way he could see them. They went to the car's luggage compartment, which opened automatically before they touched it.

An elaborately organized set of file boxes were arranged inside the compartment. Wendell picked one and lifted the lid. He drew out a folder and pushed it at Ted.

"What's that?"

"Let's move," Wendell urged him, shaking the folder. "There's a guy circling my house. We don't have a lot of time."

Ted took the folder. It was identical to the ones Lynch had given him. He opened it. The first thing he saw was the photo at the restaurant. Wendell hadn't been lying. In the photo he could clearly see that Lynch was the man offering Holly a taste of something on his fork. There was no doubt that it was a recent photo, as seen by Holly's lighter hair and shorter cut. Ted flipped to the next photo. The pair of them walking on a busy sidewalk—holding hands! In the third...

Wendell snatched the folder from his hands.

"You don't need to see more."

Ted stood with his hands open, holding an imaginary folder, unable to react.

"Convinced? There is no Organization; it's much simpler than that. Lynch has been pulling the wool over your eyes. He wanted to get rid of you by incriminating you in *my* murder. We'll deal with Lynch when the time comes. But not yet."

Ted didn't say anything. Wendell shook him to bring him back to reality.

"Listen to me. Walk that way. Cut through the woods and you'll get to the highway. It's roundabout, but I don't want the guy to see you. Do you know what his name is?"

"Roger," Ted muttered. "I think it's Roger."

"Okay. I'll deal with our friend Roger." Wendell drew the pistol.

Ted's eyes went wide.

"What are you going to do to him?"

"He's on my property." Wendell smiled. "Don't worry. I'll just give him a scare. Call you later."

Ted walked toward the trees. He took a last glance over his shoulder to see Wendell walking away. He realized that Wendell had said he would call him, but he hadn't given Wendell his phone number. The idea made him laugh out loud. Something told him that Wendell wouldn't find this a problem.

20

THERE WAS only a wood-paneled wall now in the living room where the patio door used to be. And though Ted could see only a tiny window from inside the room, he knew that the wall was painted pink outside and decorated with pictures of Disney princesses.

He almost had to feel his way forward in the dark. It was nighttime and the square of light guided him; all he could hear was the hypnotic *swoosh* of waves breaking in the yard. He reached the window and had to stoop to look out, just as at Wendell's house.

Foamy tongues of ocean spray lapped against the hill in back. The white ripples racing across the vast expanse of water shone bright in the moonlight. Ted reached through the open window and waved his hand until the motion sensor finally noticed and the single porch light clicked on. No sign of the possum, or of Holly. The wooden chess box still lay at the foot of the barbecue grill, however.

Ted stretched his arm out as far as he could, his fingers grazing the lid of the wooden box, but when he tried to grab it he only succeeded in pushing it an inch or two farther away. He knelt and adjusted his position, extending his whole shoulder through the window until the window frame dug into his neck and ribs. Then he tried again, groping blindly this time since his face was pressed against the wall and he could see only the living room darkness. His probing fingers found a corner of the box, scratched at it, and managed to drag it a little closer. He hadn't stopped to wonder why he was so interested in this chess box, but holding it and opening it had become an urgent need. The box must have been closer now, yet his fingertips seemed to find it at the same spot each time he felt. The wild illusion that the box was moving farther away, that it was floating on that vast sea, took shape in his head. And each time he touched it, he pictured his arm as an incredibly long, elastic limb jutting from the castle window and stretching all the way to the box. No matter how he tried, how he stretched, the box was always a little too far away, and all he could do was barely touch it.

He slapped it forcefully, again and again, like a crazed swimmer practicing the breaststroke, his fingers transformed into claws, grabbing again and again for the corner of the box, always unable to grasp it. He felt impotent. The window frame was biting into his sore body, and his cheek had fallen asleep.

Exhausted, he let his arm drop, and it immediately returned to its normal size. He dangled from the window for a while, his body on one side and his arm on the other, getting his breath back. He peeked out again. There was the chess box, still by the grill, in the same place as ever, its cover untouched.

A noise made Ted look up. A dark object was protruding from the ocean, a dripping-wet shell that Ted soon recognized: his father's red Mustang, from when Ted was a boy. The back of the car emerged slowly, a decrepit, algae-covered jalopy, but still recognizable. It stopped when it was still half underwater. Then the trunk opened as if by magic and Ted felt a visceral fear. He didn't want to see what it held.

Roger walked over from around the house. When he got to the Mustang's trunk he held out his arm as if inviting someone to dance, and a hand reached out and grasped his. Holly climbed from the trunk with some difficulty. Naturally, she was missing one leg. She was wearing the bikini Ted liked, the one in the photo on the fridge, except the red seemed faded, lackluster. Her skin was pale and soapy; her haggard face had lost any trace of humanity. It was possible that she wouldn't have been able to move normally even with her missing limb. Roger helped her.

They reached the porch and climbed the steps with some difficulty. At that exact moment, Holly seemed to notice the pink wall facing her. A wan smile formed on her lips as she recognized each of the princesses in turn, but her happiness vanished when she came to the window. When she saw Ted she glared at him accusingly, reproachfully, so that he felt an urge to go hide. This was, of course, a decision that was not his to make. Holly condemned him with a prolonged glare, and then moved on to the grill, still aided by Roger, who showed no interest in Ted, only in his task as an escort.

Holly pointed out the chess box to Roger. He bent over and carefully picked it up in both hands. He solemnly handed it to Holly, who held it to her bosom like a newborn child. She hugged it hard, jealously, while she shot another warning glance at Ted: *The box is mine!* She turned around and walked away slowly, still under Roger's attentive care. Ted felt a pang of grief at seeing her gaunt, scraggly body, so different from the vigorous, muscular body he remembered.

Holly and Roger returned to the ocean and she climbed back into the trunk of the Mustang, which stood in the same spot, like a tin monster with gaping jaws. Before the trunk lid closed, Holly turned to Ted to direct one last, heartless glare at him.

And then Ted had no choice but to hide. And wake up.

21

"IN THE girls' castle?" Laura asked, thrown for a loop.

"Yes," Ted said, surprised that this should be the detail that got his therapist's attention. "I went there. I don't really know why. I guess because the castle caught my eye and I thought how much my own daughters would have liked one like that. Wendell showed up and told me to go inside with him. Why do you find that so interesting?"

Laura laughed.

"I don't know. I guess it makes sense that he didn't ask you inside his house until he was sure what you were doing there."

"Of course."

"Can you describe the castle to me?"

Ted wrinkled his forehead.

"Is it important?"

"I find it interesting that you went over to the castle in the first place. From what you're telling me, it was kind of far from the house."

"Yes. About fifty yards, I'd say. There's a play area right at the edge of the woods. The castle is an attention grabber: it's girly pink and covered with pictures of Disney princesses, one after another. It's got four towers, one on each corner, with pointed roofs, eaves for the windows—all sorts of fine detail."

"You mentioned just now that your own daughters would have loved a castle like that, and you were thinking about them as you walked toward it. Why do you think they don't have such a castle?"

"Well, my girls have had lots of things. I haven't done badly at all."

"But nothing like the castle? Why not?"

Their sessions didn't normally go in this direction. Ted felt disoriented.

"Let me put it another way," Laura said. "You live well, and I'm sure you've bought Cindy and Nadine all sorts of toys. Yet when you saw this castle, what you thought was, they've never had anything like this."

"I don't see what's so important about that. I just saw the castle and I thought about them. I miss them, and I guess my going to the castle was a way of getting closer to them, imagining what they would say if they saw it. Stuff like that. I think that's perfectly reasonable."

Laura remained silent.

"I don't know, Laura. I thought we'd talk about the other part, about Lynch and Holly." Ted shook his head. "I need you to help me understand."

"Yes, you're right. Let's talk about them." Laura put on one of her devastating smiles. "So, Wendell told you the Organization was just a crazy idea he and Lynch had dreamt up at college, and their friendship had become strained over time."

"Correct. Lynch had apparently tried to blackmail him about something—I don't really know what—and so Wendell had him investigated, and that's how he found out about Holly."

"And you believed him? From what you've told me, Wendell doesn't seem like a very trustworthy person."

"I didn't have to believe him. When we left the castle he took me to look at the photos. They left no doubt."

"He let you into his house?"

"No. He kept them in his car."

Laura was silent. At last she asked, "How do you feel about it, Ted?"

"I'm not angry, if that's what you mean. It's my fault our marriage fell apart. Last night I had another dream about her."

For the next two minutes Ted described his dream about the back porch. When he mentioned the pink castle, Laura became immediately interested; the sparkle in her eyes showed that she was now sure she was right. There was something particularly important about that castle. The only detail from the dream that Ted hid was the part about the man who helped Holly rise out of the sea. He wasn't ready to mention Roger. Not yet.

"Interesting that the chess box turned up," Laura noted. "That box is closely tied to your past. You were telling me that Holly picked the box up and watched you distrustfully, like she was protecting it."

"Yes. And it felt terrible."

"What exactly did you feel?"

"It was like the chess box belonged to her and she had caught me trying to take it for myself. Holly has never even seen it. It's been years since I last saw it myself. But yeah, I guess it does represent my past, who I used to be, once upon a time, and I suppose Holly became distrustful when she saw that it meant so much to me. It's just old dreams, though. Today's reality is quite different, I'm afraid."

He'd been so wrapped up in the conversation that he hadn't looked around the office until this very moment. It was a bright day, and the morning sun entered brazenly through the window, throwing a large rectangle of light across the center of the room. Laura hadn't closed the curtains today. Ted stared out the window. The sunbeams refracting from the glass blinded him. When he looked away, he saw a black square superimposed on Laura's face, slowly fading.

"And? You were about to tell me about the chess box."

Ted nodded.

"It belonged to my grandfather Edwin. A rectangular case, about this big." Ted gave its dimensions by placing his hands as if he were actually holding the box on his lap. "Tropical wood, dark, highly polished. There was half a chessboard made of inlaid wood on either side. It opened up like a book, and then you had a full chessboard."

Ted conjured up these details in a pleasant reverie.

"The pieces were stored inside it," he went on. "Each piece had its own slot cut in the thick felt liner, so it fit snugly with just a light press. One of the slots had been widened for some reason, I remember. It was for one of the white pawns. I knew I had to open the case in a certain way so that the white pieces would be on the bottom. I always took that pawn out first. The second pawn on the right."

"Your face lights up when you talk to me about chess."

"Sure. I guess that's because I associate it with my early childhood, when I was happy. When Miller died, I completely stopped playing and homelife became torture, with my mother getting sicker and sicker and my father abusing her all the time. He left to live with his lover. I stayed at home with my mother, just when her illness was getting worse. I was alone, and it's a difficult age. The change was brutal."

"Your father abandoned you?"

"Practically. He tried to keep in touch at first, but I refused to see him. I was a rebellious teenager, angry with the world. The worst of it was that I had a mother at home who didn't give a shit whether I was angry or not. She was in her own world. For different reasons, my mother had also rebelled; I always felt that my father's cheating made her give up, that she let her illness take over and control her life. Those years were horrible. Later she had to be committed."

Ted paused. He smiled enigmatically.

"You're good at your job, Laura," he said in a friendly tone. "You know which buttons to press to get a guy talking."

She smiled, too.

"Where was the chess box all those years?"

"I know it was put away somewhere in my house at first. I remember once, when I was coming home from school, I found a pile of junk out on the front lawn by the street. The chess box was there. A lot of that stuff was still good, but my mother had gotten it into her head that she had to get rid of it. She did things like that all the time, saying there were insects brooding inside or whatever. I recovered the box and hid it in my room where she wouldn't find it. No doubt she came across it later on, because it's never been seen again."

"You just said your mother was committed."

"Correct. Shortly before my eighteenth birthday. I dropped the bad boy attitude, stopped playing the chronic nonconformist, and enrolled at the university. Away from home, I had a chance to recover from those awful years, to do well in my studies, even make peace with my mother. Visiting her at the residence home was completely different. They kept her under control there and made sure she took her medicine."

"Can you remember dreaming about the chess box before?"

"No, I really don't. But with regard to that, it isn't the first time I've had the same dream, or almost the same. I think something must have happened on the back porch of my house, something I can't recall."

Ted spoke in an enigmatic tone. He wasn't just thinking about a recurrent dream; there was something deeper.

"What makes you think that?"

"There's a hole in my memory, Laura. It's as if my mind had filled it with a series of repeating memories, bits and scraps of the present—I don't know." Ted held his head in his hands. He felt powerless. "Something happened on the back porch of my house, and I think it had something to do with Wendell. I've been to his house before, I'm sure of it. I need..."

"Calm down, Ted. I'm going to help you put your memories in order."

Ted felt a chill. He raised his eyes and looked at Laura in amazement.

"What, Ted? What did I say?"

"Put my memories in order," Ted repeated. "That's exactly what I was thinking I need. Do you think the tumor..."

Laura checked her watch.

"I think that's enough for one day."

22

TED WAITED for Wendell in the vast parking lot. Until some forty years ago this had been a prosperous factory, churning out thousands of typewriters. All that remained was an empty shell of a building.

Wendell stopped cold when he saw him. "What are you doing here?"

Ted shrugged. "I need to talk to you."

"How did you find me?"

"You're the owner, aren't you?"

In fact, Wendell had bought the factory through a front man. He had raised the perimeter wall a couple of yards higher, ringed it with barbed wire on top, and padlocked the gates. The factory was in the middle of nowhere, yet broken bottles lay scattered through the parking lot and the walls were covered in graffiti.

"What are you doing here, Ted?" Wendell asked in resignation. He stood by the door of his convertible.

"I just said. I have to talk to you."

Wendell looked in every direction.

"Is the guy in the lab coat with you?"

"I'm here alone."

Wendell nodded and walked to a corner of the building.

"Follow me."

After a few seconds of indecision, Ted did so. Rounding the corner, he saw Wendell bending over the lock on a metal door, fingering a large ring that held more than twenty keys. When he tried one and the lock didn't turn, he kicked at the door and cursed under his breath, a gesture that reminded Ted of his father, who used to kick the garage door like this when Ted was young. At last Wendell found the right key and went in, leaving the door ajar behind him.

Ted looked in. At first he saw only a dark rectangle against which he could barely make out Wendell's face. As his eyes grew accustomed to the dark, he discovered that they were in a utility closet not much larger than a washroom. It held a worktable full of stuff, shelves along the walls stocked with bottles, paint cans, and other junk, all covered in dust. Before Ted even entered, the smell of solvents and stuffiness, of being closed up for too long, almost bowled him over. He wrinkled his nose. Wendell flipped a switch and a single naked lightbulb came on.

"Come in," he ordered.

What's with this guy and his obsession with picking ridiculous, uncomfortable places to talk? There's hardly room to stand in this closet!

"Are you going to close the door?" Ted asked.

In answer, Wendell leaned over and grabbed the doorknob. The rectangle of natural light narrowed and finally disappeared. It took a few seconds for the dim lightbulb to lend form to the interior of the room.

In addition to the penetrating odor of solvent, there was the uncomfortable heat to deal with now. Wendell was wearing a leather jacket, so he must have been broiling.

"What do you want to know, Ted?" He barely moved his lips; his expression appeared carved in stone.

They stood a foot and a half apart. Ted propped himself against a shelf, afraid he might faint.

"I'll get to the point. I know you lied to me, and I want to know why. Yesterday, at your house, you pretended you didn't know me. But you and I have seen each other before."

"Oh, really? Where?"

"You know I don't have the answer to that question. You pretended not to know me so you could get your own way."

"Sorry, but you're wrong."

"I'm not," Ted said. The truth was, he had nothing concrete to back up his accusations, but to test Wendell he would have to take some risks. Sometimes in chess you develop an attack without knowing whether it will give you a concrete advantage or lead to your own demise; the important thing is not to let your opponent know that you're unsure. "Things are starting to come back to me."

Wendell's face transformed; his uncertainty showed.

"I'm listening." Wendell took a step back and ran into a shelf that wasn't altogether steady. The stuff on it wobbled but didn't fall.

"I know I've been at your house before," Ted tried.

Wendell's expression remained vigilant.

"And I know something happened on my back porch," he went on.

This time Wendell's reaction was obvious: a grimace of displeasure, lips tight, nostrils flared. And a second later, an explosive reaction: a fist smashing into the worktable.

"Fuck it, Ted! You're screwing everything up."

"Come off it, Wendell. I'm sick of playing games. I'm being open with you; there's a hole in my memory. It's like certain events have gotten all jumbled up."

Wendell shook his head.

"Who told you that? Dr. Hill?"

Now it was Ted's turn to be surprised.

"You know her?"

"Ted, please, can we let things stay the way they are? Your best bet would be to open that door and leave. Believe me, this is all for your own good. I've done nothing but protect you the whole time."

They stared at each other for quite a while.

"You want me to tell you what I think?" Ted asked, his voice trembling.

Wendell spread his palms and looked at the ceiling, as if there'd be no point in saying no.

"I think the Organization does exist," he went on, "and that I belonged to it. I think Lynch recruited me, a long time ago, when I was younger—"

"Enough with the stupid Organization!" Wendell's cry resounded in the tiny room. "I already told you, it was an idea Lynch came up with at college for a stupid short story he did for his creative writing class. It has nothing to do with us."

Ted examined one of the walls, where a board was hung with tools. He could pick any one of them and overcome Wendell, forcing him to tell everything he knew.

"Going to stick a screwdriver in my neck?"

Ted snorted.

"Tell me what you know, Wendell. Stop playing games. Tell me what you're supposedly protecting me from."

Wendell shook his head.

"I can see you won't give up. You wouldn't be here if you were a quitter." Wendell paused. "Remember the guy at my house yesterday?"

"Roger."

"They're keeping a close eye on you, Ted—him and that doctor, Laura Hill—and you've been dumb enough to talk to her, tell her everything. But I don't blame you. They tricked you into doing it."

"Wait a second. I'm not following you. Who are 'they'? And how do you know Laura?"

"Laura Hill and Carmichael are the public face."

"Carmichael?"

"Exactly. Look, Ted, your amnesia, or whatever's wrong with you, has been a blessing. You're right: we have met, you've come to my house a million times. Lynch, too. Everything went more or less okay until that idiot Lynch got mixed up with Holly. That's where the problems started."

Wendell jerked his thumb to point behind him. Ted was so engrossed in what he was saying that he didn't pay enough attention to the gesture.

"What did we and Lynch do?"

"It had nothing to do with that stupid Organization. Stop thinking about it. The poor guy had lots of stupid ideas, believe me. Getting mixed up with your wife wasn't the only one."

"You said he *'had.'* Past tense."

"Lynch is dead to me."

Ted nodded.

"Look, Ted, you have some information here in your head"—Wendell leaned forward and pointed at Ted's forehead—"that could get you into trouble. Get me into trouble, too, I won't deny it. Things were fine, there was nothing to worry about. But then Holly cheated on you with Lynch, you found out...and that made you...well, lose a screw."

Ted decided to go along with it.

"At one point I think I was planning to kill myself," Ted said, "but not on account of Holly's affair. I have a brain tumor, Wendell. You say I've got a screw loose—it's the fucking tumor."

If Wendell was surprised to learn of the tumor, he did a good job of hiding it.

"Laura Hill is searching for that information inside your brain," Wendell went on, almost in a whisper. "She's been doing that in every session. And they're afraid you'll discover it on your own. That's why they're keeping an eye on you."

"So why don't you tell me what it is? Wouldn't that be more logical, if knowing it will protect me from them?"

"I didn't say I knew it."

A staring contest. At last Wendell spoke.

"It's better this way, Ted. And follow my advice: Don't talk to Laura Hill. Don't trust her for a second. Know what she'll do the moment she guesses you suspect her? She'll lock you up with the raving loonies in Lavender Memorial. She has the power to do it, I'm telling you.

You've taken a risk by trailing me here. Most likely you've already gone too far."

"How come you know so much about her?"

"Because the secret you have in your head, Ted, could destroy me and Lynch, too. We've done our best to keep you from getting this far. And we've failed."

Ted felt his forehead. His headaches had been real, he reflected. He was about to say something when the unmistakable sound of squealing brakes stopped him. The surprised looks on both of their faces made it clear that neither of them was expecting a visitor. Wendell opened the door a crack and sunlight flooded in. They ran from the room, protecting their eyes with their forearms, but Wendell didn't head for the front of the building, where they could hear at least two car doors slamming almost in unison. A couple of yards away was a hatch, an exterior access to the basement. Wendell searched the crowded key ring for the right key. If the visitors decided to come around the building instead of going straight in, they would run into Ted and Wendell there by the hatch. But they didn't, and in less than a minute, Ted and Wendell were running down a rickety staircase, plunging once more into a world of shadows.

23

THE BASEMENT was a graveyard for typewriters, some sitting on tables or shelves, covered in dust and cobwebs but still intact, others piled in corners, in various stages of decomposition. There were also lathes, balances, and other ancient machinery. The long, narrow windows near the ceiling were so dirty they let in almost no light.

They practically had to feel their way through the maze of junk, occasionally tripping over some piece of scrap, pushing cobwebs aside and sneezing from the dust. Ignoring Wendell's complaints, Ted climbed on top of a table by the wall to reach one of the windows. He wiped the glass with his sleeve as best he could, which wasn't much, until he could peer through the smudged glass and see two human figures outside walking parallel to the building. They wore lab coats, and one of them, the leader, was black.

"It's Roger," Ted muttered.

"What did I tell you?" Wendell tugged at his arm. "Get down from there and don't do that again."

After an endless trek through that futuristic landscape of outlandish shapes and filthy corridors, air thick with dust, they reached a wooden staircase.

Wendell climbed it first. He found the correct key in record time and opened the door, but before crossing the threshold he turned and stopped Ted with an outstretched arm.

"You'd better stay here. I have to take care of some business out back. Then I'll deal with your pals."

Ted recalled Wendell's gesture in the toolroom when mentioning Lynch's name: he had pointed his thumb back toward the interior of the factory.

"Don't look out the windows," Wendell reminded him before closing the door behind him.

Ted heard the latch click shut. He didn't bother trying the knob or calling out to Wendell and demanding to be let out; he turned around and started slowly back down the stairs, holding on to the rails. Something attracted his attention and he stopped halfway down.

In one corner of the basement, a tower of junk collapsed with a deafening clang of metal crashing into the cement floor. Ted wasn't mistaken: something had been moving in the shadows.

As he descended to the bottom of the stairs, he never took his eyes off the spot where the pile had collapsed. Reaching the floor, he took a few steps forward, afraid of what might happen at any moment. He came across what appeared to be an antique lathe and didn't dare lean over to see what was behind it. He waited, frightened and resigned, until the inevitable happened: the possum stuck its pointed head around one side of the machine, sniffed the air, yawned, and dragged its thickset body toward Ted.

The animal's eyes wandered around the basement; its tail snaked behind it.

Ted stepped back and ran into the table that he had used a short time before to peek outside. The possum observed him from below, patiently.

What?

Ted turned around and got onto the table. Through the window he saw Roger and the other man, not where they had been before but much closer. They were talking to each other; they seemed to be waiting for something. Then Wendell's unmistakable form joined them. Everyone shook hands and they had a short conversation. Wendell pointed at the building and made a gesture with his hand.

Roger and his partner nodded.

Ted collapsed. Sitting on the table, his legs pressed against his chest, he grabbed his head and screamed with all his might. The possum settled back to watch him attentively. Ted couldn't take it anymore. He closed his eyes.

He saw his study. He felt the weight of the Browning. The knocking at the door.

He opened his eyes.

Again the basement shadowland. The possum.

He stuck his hand in his pocket. He pulled out the horseshoe and contemplated it, clasping it tightly in both hands.

The door opened. There was Roger, with a second nurse as backup. He held a syringe. The possum moved aside to let him through.

PART III

24

AT THE Boston-area psychiatric hospital Lavender Memorial, the forty most dangerous patients were confined to the modern C wing of the annex. They brought Ted McKay there, propped in a wheelchair, head lolling to one side, a trail of saliva dribbling from the corner of his mouth. Roger Connors, head nurse, pushed the wheelchair, flanked by one of his trusted assistants, a tall, wiry, stern-faced woman named Alex McManus. The rooms were at the far end, and to reach them they had to pass through a guarded door. When the security officer on duty saw them approaching, he raised an eyebrow and held up an arm to stop them.

"And who is this?"

"Theodore McKay," Roger replied.

The officer set down the newspaper he had been reading and glanced at the security monitors overhead, a norm he was supposed to follow every time he left the guard room. He approached the newcomers and observed them through the door.

"I haven't seen any admission papers, Roger," he said rather uneasily. He'd been working at the hospital for less than a year, and protocol was always followed, without exception.

"Dr. Hill is speaking with Marcus now."

Marcus Grant was the head of C wing.

The officer didn't know what to say. In all the time he'd worked the day shift there, he had seen only a handful of admissions, and in every one of those cases he had been notified days in advance.

"Can't buzz you through without papers. Sorry."

"We'll wait."

The officer nodded, uncomfortable with the situation, and looked more closely at Ted, whose head still lay to one side, his eyelids half open, the dribble of spit dangling two inches below his chin. He was wearing the regulation gray uniform and had restraints on his hands and feet. For a brief moment his pupils seemed to focus on the officer's eyes, but the tranquilizer he had been given was clearly not going to release him from this trance for several hours to come.

"What's that guy's deal?" he asked.

A number of the patients in this wing were murderers, rapists, or both; several had gotten some buzz in the media. The name Theodore McKay didn't ring any bells.

"Can we at least take him to his room?" asked McManus, visibly upset. It was the first time she had spoken. Roger, who kept his grip on the wheelchair, shot her a disapproving glance.

"He's one of Dr. Hill's patients," Roger explained.

"That's going to have to stay out there," the officer said, pointing at the horseshoe that Ted clutched in both hands.

"We'll see."

25

MARCUS GRANT was the director of C wing, fifty years old and a likely candidate for rising someday to the position of general director of the hospital. That was his motivation to work hard, day after day. He was a bachelor, childless, and showed no signs of planning to have children in the future. Making it to the top rung at Lavender Memorial had, sadly, become his only realistic aspiration. He hadn't completely given up on the possibility of meeting a woman worth marrying, but it was a dream he saw slipping farther and farther away with the passage of time.

He'd had lasting relationships with the wrong women. Take his current relationship, with Carmen, for example. A woman one year younger than him, divorced, with two sons in their twenties off at college, Carmen was bright and cheerful, a free spirit. Middle age, the empty nest, a house with the mortgage paid off, an undemanding job as a hairstylist—all that and maybe more had made her ready, willing, and able to enjoy every moment, to "try new things."

But Marcus had no genuine interest in her, beyond sex and random moments of relaxation. Carmen was superficial, had no ambitions, and, worst of all, couldn't understand why work held such an important spot in Marcus's life.

"You work too hard, honey! You should do what I did at the beauty shop: I got organized, and now I even have time on my hands."

A relationship with no future.

"May I come in?" Laura Hill asked, poking her head through the doorway to Marcus's office.

Marcus was yanked from his troubles, and his face lit up.

"What a pleasant surprise! Come on in."

Marcus stood up and walked around his desk. He meant to greet Laura with a kiss on the cheek, but she placed herself in such a way that all he could do was pull out a chair for her to sit on. It wasn't an uncomfortable moment—Marcus was always a gentleman—but it was a clear signal on her part.

"Have you already had lunch?" Laura asked.

Marcus was about to sit down again.

"Not yet," he said, hopes raised. "You want to go get something?"

"No. I'm going to skip lunch. It's that...what I have to tell you can't wait."

Marcus nodded, dejected, and sat down. That's how it always went with Laura. She dangled the carrot and then quickly withdrew it. She could do this to him a hundred times, and each time Marcus would take the bait. Or maybe it was him. Maybe he was just imagining carrots the whole time.

Lately the tension between them had been building somewhat. Marcus's interest in Laura was unmistakable, even though he'd never talked to her directly about it. She didn't seem to have the same feelings for him.

When his romance with Carmen went on the rocks, Marcus subtly began trying to get closer to Dr. Hill, dropping comments on how things were going badly with his girlfriend, things like that, and one fine day Laura started giving him hints (carrots): a smile, a swish of the hips, a hand on his back that lingered a beat longer than usual. He tried to take things a little bit further a couple of times, suggesting that they go out for dinner or meet after working hours, but she came up with one excuse after another, without ever categorically turning him down. Marcus had come to think that Laura acted like this only because she was trying to forget her ex-husband.

But there was another angle on it, one that Marcus chose not to see, which was that Laura had been cashing in on her good relationship with him. She had moved up the ranks at the hospital and had gotten Marcus to intercede on her behalf more than once with Dr. McMills, the general director of the hospital.

Laura looked him right in the eye.

"I need a tremendous favor from you, Marcus."

She'd asked him for favors before, but never a *tremendous* favor.

"If there's anything I can do."

"I need to get a patient admitted to C wing," she said, going straight to the point.

Marcus relaxed.

"That won't be a problem. We have five rooms available. I'll send Sarah the paperwork right now so that she can—"

"I need it done *now*."

Laura turned her Medusa glare on him.

"What do you mean by 'now'?"

The process of admitting a new patient normally took several days. Marcus could do his part in record time, but even so...

"My head nurse is in the wing right now, with the patient. I need you to authorize his admission."

Don't slip up, Marcus. Don't give her the wrong answer.

Or she'll turn you into stone...

"Laura, are you out of your mind? What do you mean they're in the wing now?"

"In the admissions room. Your security people won't let them in, even though my people told them they were there on my behalf."

"Of course they didn't let them in!" Marcus stood up. "I can't believe it. The fact that they are there at all puts me in a bad light. Please get them off my wing immediately."

Marcus strode over to the sole window in his second-floor office and gazed down at the hospital courtyard, empty now but for an orderly raking the fallen leaves. He massaged his temples. He didn't want to turn around, because he knew that if he looked at her he'd give in. What she was asking of him was insane, a potential career ender. He heard Laura stand up and smelled the sweet fragrance of her perfume, and then heard her voice whispering into his ear.

"Look at me, Marcus. Let me explain."

He turned around.

There it was again, that deep gaze, the soft touch of her fingers on the back of his hand, the thumb circling in a barely perceptible caress.

"I know how much I'm asking of you," Laura said, her voice very low. "I wouldn't have turned to you if I didn't think you were my only hope."

"Laura, please," he said, scuttling to the other side of the room to put his desk between them. She followed him with her eyes but didn't move any closer, remaining by the window with a forlorn expression that almost forced Marcus to return and comfort her. She'd gone from seductive flirt to helpless maiden in the blink of an eye.

"I'm sorry you don't trust me."

"Trust you! At least tell me who the patient is. Why do you need to get him admitted on such short notice?"

"He's a special patient."

"I don't understand. Someone you know?"

"No." Laura sat back down. "I can't tell you the whole case, at least not yet. It would take too long, and as I said, Roger is with him now in C wing. It is very important for his treatment that he be admitted immediately. He might have a breakdown otherwise."

"My God, Laura." Marcus also sat. With his elbows on the desk, he closed his eyes, clutched his head, and shook it back and forth.

When he looked up, he caught sight of a smile on Laura's lips that quickly disappeared.

"What's so funny, Laura?"

"The gesture you just made—never mind. It's personal."

"Like your patient."

"Exactly."

Marcus's resolve was growing stronger.

"If this patient of yours can't stay in the general wing—and I have no reason to doubt your professional opinion—then I'm sure Sarah will understand. Let's go talk to her now and explain the situation. I'll give you my full support, but that's as far as I'll go."

Laura paused to size him up.

"Sarah will never authorize an admission to C wing until it has been evaluated by the medical board. You know that perfectly well."

"I don't know what to tell you. My hands are tied."

"I'll tell you what we'll do," she said gravely. "Give me the admission form with your signature. I'll fill it out and bring it to C wing in person. If anyone complains, I'll tell them I lifted it from your office."

Marcus was flabbergasted.

"Why would you do something like that?"

"You know how I feel about my practice, Marcus. I don't give a damn about bureaucratic bullshit or getting ahead in this crappy hospital. All I care about are my patients. This one in particular. If I don't get him into C wing today, I might as well flush all the progress we've made down the drain, and I'm determined not to do that."

"If he's going to be on my wing, I'll need you to tell me about him."

"I will. Give me a couple of hours and I'll tell you all you want."

"When will you speak to Sarah?"

"As soon as I can. Where are the admission forms?"

They left the office together. Marcus's secretary was on her lunch break, luckily for them.

"Here you go," he said, handing her a form he had pulled from one of the filing cabinets. "You saw where I got it from."

She nodded. She set it on the desk.

"I need you to sign it, Marcus."

"What? You just said you were going to forge my signature!"

"No, that's what I'll tell them later, when I have to make excuses for the form. Right now I have to be sure nobody down there gets suspicious. I couldn't even try to fake your signature. Make your mark. That'll be good enough."

Marcus had fallen for it once more.

"A handwriting expert could—"

"Marcus, I told you: I'll say I forged it! It's my ass on the line here. I'll give you all the details later, if you want them so badly, and I'll say I stole the form. You're so worried about not screwing up your job, you've turned into a little bureaucrat."

Ouch.

"I'll sign." Marcus grabbed a pen off his secretary's desk.

He handed her the form, now with his signature on it.

"I knew I could count on you," Laura said with another hint of a smile. She moved closer, until her face was less than a foot from his. Was she going to give him a kiss? Her pupils moved feverishly, exploring his face.

She did not kiss him.

26

LAURA HILL handed the form to the guard in an obvious rush. He started to tell her she needed to take it to the administrative offices first; before he finished his sentence, she had already told him she'd do it later, but for now the main thing was to get her patient to his room. The guard said no more.

Laura, Roger, and Nurse McManus set off for the patients' rooms. To get there they had to pass through two more security checks and the common room, where several patients watched them with interest. There they met Robert Scott, head nurse of C wing, who was friendly with Roger. He greeted them formally and informed them without delay that the room was ready; he was aware of the situation and would ask no questions. As far as he was concerned, if Dr. Hill and Director Grant had agreed between themselves to break a few rules, he had no reason to get involved.

These were modern rooms. One wall of each was entirely made of glass. The doors could be opened remotely or by punching in a code. Scott slid his ID card into the slot and entered the combination. The door yielded with a soft suction sound. Laura rolled the wheelchair inside; Roger and McManus grabbed Ted under his arms and laid him on the bed. The horseshoe slipped from his lap and clattered across the tile floor. Laura bent down, picked it up, and, after thinking it over for a second, put it back in Ted's hands. The effects of the sedative were wearing off, and he was able to close his fingers around one end of the iron object.

"Leave me alone with him for a moment."

Roger and McManus looked at each other uneasily. At last they consented. Ted was manacled hand and foot and could barely lift a finger.

The pair rejoined Scott in the corridor. Scott was staring intently through the glass wall of the patient's room. If anything happened to the doctor, it would be his responsibility, and the fact was, he knew nothing about this guy, who might be pretending and might try strangling the doctor at his first chance. There were patients on the wing who would do that and worse if you let down your guard just a little.

On the other side of the glass wall, Laura moved close to Ted.

"We'll talk tomorrow," she said. "Try to rest. You'll be perfectly fine here."

Ted's eyes were still half closed and unfocused. When Laura turned to leave, he shifted his gaze slightly to watch her walk out of the room.

McManus returned later and, with another nurse's help, dressed Ted in a new set of grays. At some point Ted flipped onto his side. The bed was relatively comfortable.

He awoke several times during the night, confused. From the bed he could see the darkened corridor and across it to the room opposite his. In it, a man of about fifty stood, staring back at him, his face twisted into a grimace of hatred.

27

"HEY, ANYBODY! I need you here, right fucking now!"

Ted banged on the glass again with the palms of his hands. He remembered Lynch knocking on his own door almost as vehemently.

He turned around. The horseshoe lay on the bed; he had fallen asleep holding it, like a kid with his favorite teddy bear. He knew he couldn't use it to break the glass, which must have been bulletproof, but he could make more noise with it than by slapping the glass or screaming. He went to get it and was just about to start banging it against the glass when the man in the room across the hall, who had been sitting on his bed the whole time with his face buried in a book, looked up a little and spoke.

"Not a good idea," he said calmly. His voice was dampened by the two glass walls between them.

"So now you can talk," Ted said. The first thing he'd tried to do before he started in with all this bullshit was get his neighbor's attention, but the man had chosen to ignore him.

"They'll be here in fifteen minutes," the man replied in the same distant-sounding voice.

The vision of the man—standing behind the glass with that expression of utter hatred—that Ted had had the night before assailed him like a ghastly reminder of a bad dream. The contrast with his serenity now and with the incipient smile on his face was extreme. He was handsome, tanned, with close-cropped hair that was beginning to gray, as was his neatly trimmed beard. He seemed like the most harmless and trustworthy guy in the world.

"Fifteen minutes, huh? How do you know?"

The man held the book in one hand and stretched out his free arm. The sleeve of his gray shirt drew back to reveal a watch.

"I can tell time."

"Very funny."

"Seven is wash time. I was hoping to finish this chapter before they come, but I wasn't counting on your effusive morning conversation." He set the book aside. "My name is Mike Dawson."

"Wash time's at seven? I have to pee! There isn't even a toilet in this fucking bedroom."

Mike laughed.

"What's so funny?"

"You call it a bedroom, like them. The real rooms are on the other side of the building. They bring us here when we misbehave."

A silence fell. A short, bald man watched Ted timidly from another of the glassed-in cells. When Ted noticed him, the man withdrew.

"I'm Ted."

"Welcome to Lavender, Ted. And don't worry. I didn't misbehave. It's just that I tend to get agitated at night."

"Weren't you here when they brought me?"

"No. When I got here, you were already in bed."

"Do you know Dr. Hill?"

Dawson thought it over before he answered.

"Yes, but she doesn't come around here much. She spends most of her time in the main building."

"She'll have to come today, I assure you."

"If you say so."

Ted considered the horseshoe and, after a second's hesitation, tossed it back on the bed.

"What's that?"

"Nothing. A souvenir."

"Those can come in handy around here. But I'll give you a piece of advice: don't show it off too much. As soon as the guys on the other side figure out it's important to you, it'll be important to them, too. That's how things work around here. If you lose it, you'll never get it back, because, believe me, if there's anything *those guys* know, it's how to find hiding places."

Mike Dawson pointed a finger at his temple and twirled it in a circle.

"I'll keep that in mind. Not that it matters. I don't plan on getting to know the guys on the other side. I'll get out of here today."

Mike stood up. He stretched by his bed, arms and legs wide, spine arching back. He yawned and stepped over to the glass. The bulb threw more light on his face, and now he looked more like the man Ted remembered seeing in his dreams that night.

"Nobody decides when he's going to leave here, Ted," he said, quite serious.

28

TWO NURSES showed up at seven on the dot. The doors opened and the patients left with them in silence, to the astonishment of Ted, who banged on the glass and demanded an explanation that never came. His fellow inmates watched him with interest, including the little bald man, who was the only one wearing shackles on his hands and feet. Dawson nodded good-bye to Ted.

Ted remained alone and in silence. Maybe screaming and banging on the glass was just what they wanted him to do. He sat on the bed and fished the horseshoe out of the wrinkled sheets. He waited for an eternity, holding his full bladder and his urge to shout.

A nurse showed up after Ted had fallen back into bed.

"Good morning."

Ted sat up.

"Who are you?"

"Alex McManus. I'll be in charge of you during your stay on C wing. Now I have to ask you a question, Ted: Will there be any need for these?"

She held up a set of shackles.

"Where is Dr. Hill?"

"She'll be by later to talk to you. She asked me to tell you so."

"When is 'later'?"

"I wouldn't know."

Ted went up to the glass. He spoke in a whisper.

"Something's wrong here, Alex. It's Alex, right? I don't know what's up. They tracked me down and brought me here without my consent. My wife and daughters get back from a trip today. I have to get out of here."

McManus stooped and set the shackles on the floor. She punched in a code on the panel by the door, and then unlocked the door using a key that was chained to her waist. A voice called out from the other end of the corridor and McManus gestured in that direction. The door opened.

"Dr. Hill will talk to you today, probably this afternoon."

Ted began saying, "It needs to be before—"

"Hold on," McManus interrupted. "Don't try and question anything I tell you. It'll make things worse, and it won't do you any good. We'll go to the baths now. Then I'll take you to join the others. In a few hours Dr. Hill will come and see you, and you can ask her all the questions you like. Don't waste your breath on me."

Ted nodded.

They walked together to the end of the corridor. They came to a locked door, which McManus unlocked, openly turning her back on Ted. They reached the common room. There was a TV, turned off; several tables; and a few shelves with books and labeled boxes. A couple of houseplants and the natural light streaming through four large windows made the place fairly cozy.

"Where is everybody?"

McManus gave him a funny look.

"Having breakfast."

Ted was looking at one of the bookshelves.

"I forgot something in the room," he suddenly said, clearly anxious.

"Don't worry. It'll still be there when you get back."

Ted remembered Mike Dawson's words about how easily things disappeared at Lavender.

They came to the showers. A man in a green uniform met them and handed Ted a towel and a change of clothes. McManus sat on a wooden bench where she could keep an eye on Ted over the low wall of the shower stalls.

"Do you really have to follow me everywhere?"

McManus shrugged.

Ted calmly undressed, neatly folded his clothes, and placed them on a wooden bench next to the pile of clean clothes. He picked a shower stall and turned on the water. The temperature was perfect.

"Does Roger work with you?" Ted asked as the warm water coursed over his face.

"Yeah. He'll come by later, I guess."

"He's been watching me for days."

McManus said nothing. Ted began soaping up. He talked without looking at the nurse.

"You didn't know that, did you?"

"Know what?"

"That he'd been trailing me. I caught him doing it twice. I think he's also been to my house."

Once more, no answer.

"That alone is due cause for suing him," Ted went on. "My lawyers would love it. I know my rights, and I know that drugging me and hauling me here in the middle of the night is a flagrant violation. If I agree to wait and talk to Dr. Hill, it's because I want her to tell me to my face why she's done what she's done." He paused a beat. "Aren't you going to say anything?"

"I don't know what to tell you, man. All they told me was to watch you for your first few hours here, nothing else. Nothing personal. We do this with all the patients."

"I'm not a patient."

"Have it your way. This is what we do with everyone who's admitted to the wing. Some of them don't adapt well to change. New faces mean a change in the world they're used to. Now we're going to go have breakfast, and you can meet your new wing mates."

There was a curious shampoo dispenser on the wall. It was a hemisphere embedded in the wall itself, hard to disassemble or hurt anyone with. Ted pressed it and a thin stream of pink shampoo poured out.

"I already had the pleasure of meeting the guy in the room across from mine," Ted said as he massaged the foam into his hair.

"Who's that?"

"Dawson."

"Oh. He's been here for more than a decade. If you hit it off with Dawson, you shouldn't have trouble with any of the others."

"You keep talking as if I were going to stay here."

Ted turned off the water. He walked quickly to the bench and wrapped himself in the towel.

"You're convinced they're going to keep me locked up in here, aren't you?"

"I told you already: I don't know anything about you."

"Good enough."

Ted dressed in silence. When he was done, he sat on the bench. McManus was twenty feet away, on another bench against the wall.

"You ready?" the nurse said at last.

"What do we do with this?" Ted pointed at the dirty clothes.

McManus, in turn, pointed at an empty laundry basket.

When they came out of the showers, Ted asked McManus to take him by his room to pick up the horseshoe.

29

WHEN HE entered the common room, all conversation stopped. People's faces expressed surprise and also mistrust. The host of an entertainment program was the only one who ignored the tension and continued asking humorous questions on the television.

Robert Scott, head nurse of C wing, introduced Ted to the other patients. He told them all that he didn't want any problems, and he left. McManus kept watch from an adjoining room, through a window with wire mesh glass. There was another nurse with her.

There were three well-differentiated groups in the commons. One, the largest, gathered around the TV. The other two sat at the tables, one playing chess, the other playing cards. The only patient keeping to himself was Mike Dawson, who sat in the wide window nook and read his book. When he saw Ted he waved hello, and then directly immersed himself again in his reading, as if Ted weren't there. Ted went to the center of the room. He was tempted to join the group of chess players, but he was unsure if it was a good idea.

As the others turned their attention away from him, the noise level went back up. The cardplayers chattered nonstop; the TV viewers spoke in bursts, shouting answers to questions or getting into arguments. Ted went to the bookshelves and began examining the books while subtly keeping his attention trained on the chess players and the kibitzers around them. He was about ten feet away and could study the board for a few seconds. The game had just begun. It didn't follow any standard opening, he was unsurprised to see. As he pretended to read the titles of the novels, he played out the game in his head. Black won.

One of the cardplayers, a tall, jumpy fellow, was the first to notice Ted's fascination with the books. He pointed a trembling finger at Ted, and the others at the table turned to look, staring at him for several moments, laughing and sneering at him, before going back to their game.

Some twenty minutes later, the little guy Ted had seen from his room, whose name turned out to be Lester, came in from the garden with another inmate. He wasn't shackled, and when he noticed Ted in the commons, he went crazy.

"He stole my gear!" he yelled at the top of his voice.

When Ted turned around, Lester rushed across the room at him. Mike Dawson jumped up from the window nook to intercept him. The nurses in the small adjoining room stirred. Several of the patients laughed and encouraged the impending fight. Lester repeated his accusation over and over again, wriggling frantically but unable to move any closer to Ted. Mike had planted himself between him and Ted, and that was enough to stop him.

"Nobody stole anything from you, Lester," Mike said calmly. "Get out of here."

"I'm gonna kill him! He's got my gear!" Lester's head was red, the veins stood out on his neck, and he waved his arms and danced his feet like a boxer.

The nurse with McManus turned and left the little room, trudging wearily into the commons. She raised her hands to quiet everyone. She was huge, like a Viking, able to restrain Lester with one hand no matter how frenzied the little guy became. But it was Dawson who kept the situation under control.

"Calm down," he insisted.

"He came last night," Lester said, pacing like a caged animal. "I saw him. He stole my gear and now I don't have any way to communicate."

Ted remained by the books, aware of all the eyes on him. Perhaps it was the word "stole" that made him unconsciously put his hand in his pocket and touch the horseshoe. Lester noticed it and exploded.

"He's got it there, in his pocket! Check it out!"

The nurse shook her head no. Mike took a step toward Lester, putting a finger on his chest and chewing him out.

"Nobody's got your gear," he said severely. "So let me read now, if you don't want any problems."

The intimidation worked. Lester kept wriggling, but only on account of his nerves. His voice broke.

"But, Mike, I can't send in my reports if I don't have my gear. They need my report. You know that."

"I don't give a shit. Let the *Millennium Falcon* come and get it if they need it so bad. As for you, back in the garden. I don't want to see you around here anymore. Is that clear?"

Lester nodded. No trace of his boundless rage remained. He left, dejected.

Mike gestured to the nurse and smiled. *You don't owe me anything for this favor...* Then he winked at Ted and went back to his nook to resume reading.

Ted went over to the table where the chess game was almost done and was becoming less interesting. The guy playing white, clearly at a disadvantage, stared at the position of the pieces as if he might be able to move them by telekinesis. His opponent relaxed and awaited his turn, looking from the board to his tiny audience and back. Ted's presence seemed to put him out, but he didn't say anything.

"Come on, Sketch. I ain't got all day! I'll tell Scott to get us some of them double clocks, so I'll be able to knock you guys off faster."

Sketch, still immersed in the game, pretended not to hear. He'd have zero chance against a player with any skill, Ted thought, though he might have some hope if he moved his knight from f5 to h6.

One of the three kibitzers piped up.

"You got him now, right, Lolo?" He hit the palm of his hand with his other fist. "They're gonna squash you like a fly, Sketch."

"Shut up," said another onlooker. "You don't even know how the pieces move. This is chess, you know?"

Everybody laughed except the butt of the joke and Sketch, who, still concentrating on the board, at last lifted his hand from his lap to make a move. His fingers touched the knight on f5. He had two squares where he might move it: h6, which would give him a sliver of hope, or h4, which would sink him.

He went for h4.

"You're no match for me, Sketch!" Lolo said as he moved a pawn one space dangerously closer to getting crowned. "Let's see how you wriggle out of this."

Sketch sank again into thought.

Ted moved on. It would be forever before Laura came to see him.

He was walking toward the door when he noticed that Dawson had set his book down and was now staring at him. Unsure whether it was a smart thing to do, Ted walked over to his nook, perhaps to thank Dawson for restraining Lester.

"You knew, didn't you?" Dawson surprised him. "About the knight to h4."

For a second, Ted didn't know what he was talking about. When he figured it out, he shrugged.

"I played a little chess when I was younger."

"Me too. Nothing professional," Dawson admitted. "Maybe you and I should play a game someday."

He was testing him.

"Sure." Ted started to walk on.

"Hold up."

Dawson studied him.

"Let me go with you. Lester's still out there."

Just then Ted became aware of the silence that had once more fallen on the common room. Everyone but the TV host seemed to be eavesdropping on his exchange with Mike Dawson. He remembered McManus's words earlier this morning in the showers. *If you hit it off with Dawson, you shouldn't have trouble with any of the others.*

The garden was extensive, with flower beds, leafy trees, and paths running through it, which at this time of day only a few solitary patients were enjoying. Lester had joined a small group on a corner of the basketball court, some sitting on a bench and others standing. They immediately turned to look at the two men.

"So you don't know why you're here?" Mike asked.

Ted looked at him in disbelief. In the morning sunlight he still seemed the sanest person in the world. If he hadn't seen Dawson glaring at him with that deranged look the night before, he would have had a hard time understanding what he was doing at Lavender.

Just like you, and here you are.

They walked over to one of the more isolated benches, under a huge pine tree.

"Well?" Mike insisted after they sat down.

"It's not that I don't know," Ted said with a certain resignation. "Dr. Hill has been treating me for the past few weeks. I've got...an inoperable tumor, and my doctor thought the therapy would help me cope with it. To be fair, he was right. I thought talking to Dr. Hill wouldn't do me any good—but it did. Some good. Now she's taken it too far."

Lester and the others were playing on the basketball court now. The ball hammered against the cement with each bounce.

"Dr. Hill had you committed against your will?"

"Yeah."

Mike reached into his pocket and pulled out a pack of cigarettes. He offered one to Ted, who turned it down.

"I didn't use to smoke, either," Mike said, flicking a gilded lighter. He took a long drag. Then, studying the cigarette in his fingers, he added something cryptic: "Sometimes I think I do it just to set myself apart from the guy I used to be, out there."

Ted was still looking at the lighter. Mike noticed and said, "Things get better the more you can get them to trust you. My days are pretty peaceful here now. It's the nights that torture me."

"Why are you here?"

"They didn't tell you?"

Ted shook his head.

Mike looked down, visibly moved even before he opened his mouth.

"I killed my best friend's family."

The ball continued to pound in the distance.

"I was very sick," Mike went on. Now he was slumping, shrunken, forearms resting on his knees, staring at the ground. "If there were some sort of mass jailbreak here, or if they let me go for some crazy reason, I'd refuse to leave." He bitterly added, "My friend's daughter survived. Hanging myself from that tree wouldn't be fair to her. Too easy."

Ted kept silent.

"You know what? Being crazy doesn't change things all that much," Mike went on. "It doesn't let you off the hook, I mean. Instead of going to prison, they lock you up somewhere like this. But a part of you is always responsible—responsible for not stopping the other part. Because part of you *knows*. Knows it *all*."

Now it was Wendell Ted remembered, in the closet at the abandoned factory...

You have some information here, in your head, that could get you into trouble.

Mike paused thoughtfully, now staring up at the sky, apparently recalling the details of a past that wouldn't leave him in peace. He touched his temple and turned his wide-eyed, eerie stare on Ted.

"The mind is a magic box. Full of tricks. It always figures out a way to warn you. To give you a way out, too. A door..."

Open the door. It's your only way out.

Ted thought of the pine tree shading their view and pictured Mike Dawson's body hanging from a branch, swinging to the rhythm of a gentle breeze.

"I guess you're right."

Mike smiled. Again the friendly, supportive expression.

"Maybe it's like you say, and tomorrow you won't be here. Or maybe you will be, and we'll be sitting on this bench again then. We all have to open that door sooner or later."

30

LAURA WAS waiting for him in an assessment room. Ted stood outside the room, his hands in restraints, until McManus found the right key to let him in.

"It's open," said a voice from inside the room. Ted recognized it immediately.

Laura Hill smiled faintly. Roger, sitting next to her, was by contrast the very image of seriousness, his eyes wide and cold.

"Dr. Hill. At last," Ted said.

"You can still call me Laura."

"Laura—of course. Thanks for putting me up here in the Hilton last night. Very generous of you."

McManus led him to the table where Dr. Hill sat, but before he took a seat Ted displayed the chain that bound his wrists.

"Please have a seat, Ted," said Laura. She made no mention of the restraints.

He examined the room, not that there was much to see: depressing drab-green wall tiles, the Formica-topped table where they sat, six fluorescent tubes that erased every shadow, and a window of darkened glass behind which no doubt a video camera was running. While seeing the reflection in this window, Ted noticed McManus signal something with a shake of her head and then leave.

"How do you feel, Ted?"

"No, no, no. None of this 'How do you feel, Ted?' business. I feel like an ass. I want to know what I'm doing here. And I want to hear it now."

Laura looked down for a few seconds, straightened out the file folder that lay before her, and cleared her throat.

"I'll explain it in a second, believe me, but there are a few things I have to know first. Roger and I only want to help you, and—"

"Yeah, yeah, cut the crap. What do you want me to tell you?"

Laura took a breath.

"Yesterday you told Roger we were going to lock you up at Lavender Memorial, and you said you already knew everything. What were you referring to?"

"I don't think that needs much explanation, does it? I meant this." Ted again displayed his shackled hands.

"Who told you?"

"What difference does it make who told me? It was true."

"Was it Wendell?"

Silence.

Ted recalled his conversation with Wendell in the toolroom at the abandoned factory.

She'll lock you up with the raving loonies in Lavender Memorial. She has the power to do it, I'm telling you.

"That's enough, Laura. Your turn to talk."

Laura and Roger exchanged a glance that Ted was unable to interpret. She nodded and opened the folder in front of her. She turned it around so he could see, just as Lynch had done in Ted's living room. This time, however, it wasn't a criminal file but MRIs of Ted's brain. He immediately recognized the images that Carmichael had shown him in his office; his name was printed in the corner of each picture.

"Do you recognize them?"

"Of course. There's the tumor." Ted pointed to an area slightly darker than the rest of the image.

"You don't have a tumor, Ted."

Why doesn't that surprise you?

She turned around and gestured toward the dark window. Moments later the door opened.

"Hello, Ted."

There stood Carmichael, hands in his pockets, looking sad or contrite, as if he had bad news.

Carmichael's mixed up in this, too.

"I'm afraid Dr. Hill is telling the truth," he said, still standing in the doorway.

He came in slowly, went around the table, and sat down. Now it was Ted against three.

"I've asked Carmichael to come to Lavender and tell you himself," Laura explained.

Carmichael nodded gravely.

"There never was a mass," Carmichael calmly stated. "When the first images came, I told you that your brain was perfectly healthy and something else must be causing your headaches, and that we'd track down the cause together, just as we'd done with every illness you've had over the years. You got all upset, and it was only when I told you we'd redo the MRIs that you started to calm down. I figured that would gain me a little more time, because there wasn't a trace of a tumor in your brain, and I knew we'd get the same results next time."

Ted looked at them, unfazed.

"You don't remember any of this?" Laura asked.

"You switched the test results. How do I know those images are of my brain?"

"I'm sorry," Carmichael apologized.

"And what about the headaches? The periods of confusion?" For the first time Ted betrayed signs of desperation. "Maybe it's a small tumor, or it's lodged in a part of the brain where the MRI can't pick it up. I've read up on the subject. Don't try to pull one over on me."

"We will continue moving forward with the treatment to help you to—"

"Help me? You don't get it, Laura. The last few sessions, it was a miracle I even went to see you. If things had gone according to plan, I'd be in my study at home right now with a bullet in my brain." Ted laughed. "This is absurd. If it wasn't for that fucking Lynch, I would have done it."

He made a pistol with his fingers and put it to his temple. He made a gunshot sound.

The doctors looked at each other.

"What's going on?" Ted had lost patience. "Stop treating me like I'm crazy!"

He sprang to his feet, his chair falling over backward. Nobody blinked. They just watched him as he paced in a circle.

"I can't believe it," Ted was muttering to himself. He walked with his hands on his stomach, staring at the linoleum floor.

"Do you have the horseshoe?" Laura asked.

Ted suddenly stopped short, frantically feeling his pants pockets. There was the hard horseshoe shape. He pulled it from his pocket and held it in his fingers, viewing it as a powerful talisman.

"Remember, you told me about it, right?" Laura went on. "About Miller, your chess teacher. About the match between Capablanca and Alekhine in Buenos Aires..."

At some point Roger came over to Ted and led him back to his chair. Ted didn't seem fully conscious. His eyes were still fixed on the horseshoe.

"I found it by Wendell's house," Ted said, astonished, hypnotized by this bent piece of iron.

"Ted, look at me," Laura said.

He looked up.

"The rules here are strict, and a blunt metal object like your horseshoe is definitely a violation. But I'll allow you to keep it. And when you feel confused, I want you to concentrate on it, to think about Miller, about playing chess, okay?"

"About the good times," he murmured.

"Exactly," said Laura, pleased. "About the good times."

No trace of his angry outburst remained. Ted lowered his gaze again, turning away from the horseshoe, which lay in his lap and which he still felt between his fingers.

"Was it because of Holly?" he said. "She...was having an affair with Lynch—not Wendell but Lynch. I've seen the photos. They were at a restaurant."

"Don't think about that now, Ted. I don't know why you decided to try killing yourself. But we'll figure it out."

Ted was like a child being scolded. Then his expression changed, as if he had remembered something. He looked at Laura, and there was genuine terror in his eyes.

"Are Holly and the girls all right?"

"They're fine. At her parents' house, in Florida."

"They were supposed to be back on Friday. What day is it?"

Laura didn't answer. She closed the folder on the table. Dr. Carmichael excused himself, saying he had things to take care of, nodding to Ted on his way out, declaring he'd be back to visit, telling him to stay strong, he was in good hands.

The horror hadn't left Ted's eyes.

"What are all these memories, Laura?"

"We'll deal with that later, though I'm afraid I don't have all the answers. I don't want to overburden you now. It's important for you to take in everything I've told you. We'll see each other the day after tomorrow, and we'll keep talking. Next visit it'll just be you and me, like old times."

Laura smiled compassionately.

"Did Holly have me locked up here? I'm not stupid: I know she had to give her consent. Does she know? Know what I was about to do in my study?"

"She doesn't."

"Better."

"But you do understand you have to stay here a few days, right?"

"I guess so."

No, you don't believe it, but play along. Everything's happening just as Wendell predicted. He's the only one who's been honest with you—the only one who's shown you real evidence.

"You'll spend the night in the maximum security room, but tomorrow I'll tell them to give you a regular room, where you'll be a lot more comfortable. McManus told me that you hit it off with Dawson, which is excellent news. He tends to be very choosy."

"I don't know if 'hit it off' is the right term. We talked in the garden. He told me why he's here—that's all."

"He's said more to you in one day than most people hear from him in a lifetime."

Ted shrugged. The last thing he cared to do was hit it off with a homicidal maniac.

31

IT WAS late. Talk had long since ceased on the maximum security corridor. Ted rested on his bunk, hands behind his head, staring at the ceiling. His anxiety to get out of Lavender was gone. He didn't know whether Laura had been entirely frank with him—probably not—but he had too many unknowns to process. Had he really made up having a brain tumor? Two fragmented realities coexisted in his mind: in one of them, he had murdered Wendell; in the other, not only had he not killed him, he had talked with him—*in a pink castle!* He clearly had issues; why deny it?

And don't forget Blaine. You hid in his house and waited for him. He discovered you, but with one swift move you knocked him off.

He had to get some sleep and digest these things calmly. He felt the comforting weight of the horseshoe on his chest. He closed his eyes, ready to let sleep carry him away...but he suddenly opened them again. He sat on the edge of his bed. The horseshoe flipped off his chest and landed on the floor with a prolonged metallic clatter that sounded, in the quiet, like the tolling of a bell. Somebody at the other end of the corridor shushed him. Ted went to the glass wall. Lester was watching him from the room next to Mike Dawson's.

"Don't you ever sleep, Lester? Go to bed!" he snapped, to the bald inmate's surprise. "Mike, are you awake?"

Again somebody hushed him.

"Shut up, fool!" someone shouted down the dark corridor.

In Mike's room, a faint light came on by the bed. Mike got up. It looked as though he hadn't been able to get to sleep yet.

"You should lower your voice," he suggested.

Ted nodded.

"Were you asleep?"

Mike shook his head.

"I have insomnia, so the answer is no. What's up?"

"I have to ask you something."

"Shoot."

"That chess set in the commons...it looks pretty new, especially the roll-up board."

"They brought it here maybe six months ago," Mike said. "There had been another one a couple years ago, but I don't know what happened to it."

Six months!

That was even before his first visit to Carmichael.

Ted was convinced that the chess set had been put there especially for him. What better than a chess set to make him feel at home? He looked at the horseshoe, still lying on the floor.

"Did Dr. Hill bring it?" Ted asked.

"No idea. Is that what you were wondering? I guess it was too important to leave it for the morning."

Mike lay down again and turned off the light.

Ted did likewise after a moment, but now he had reached a conclusion. That chess set had been put there for him. *Six months ago.*

32

THE NEXT morning McManus took him to his new room. It was on the second floor of C wing. To reach it they walked along a carpeted hallway, quite unlike the cold, glass-lined corridor in the maximum security zone. Ted wore the gray pants and jacket he had been issued, but he was no longer in restraints; things were starting to improve. From a side door, Sketch—Ted recognized him from the chess game the day before—watched with an undecipherable expression.

"Let me give you one piece of advice," McManus said before they reached the end of the hall. "Take this as an opportunity. Don't do anything stupid. You seem like an intelligent man."

The recommendation sounded sincere. Ted solemnly nodded. When they entered the room, he understood what the nurse meant a little better. Compared with the bare bunk he had spent the last two nights on, this was a room at the Hilton. He remembered his joke to Laura and smiled.

The room was large. Sun streamed in luxuriously through a huge window. There were two beds, each with a desk and a small shelf; everything was arranged symmetrically, except for an inner door that led to a bathroom. The half belonging to Mike Dawson, his new roommate, was crammed with books, clippings fixed to the walls, photos—everything necessary to make a room acceptably homey. McManus explained that Mike hadn't shared the room with anyone in years.

On the bare mattress sat a cardboard box with Ted's name written in black marker.

"Great! They already brought your stuff."

My stuff?

McManus left and Ted remained alone. He went over to the window, following the imaginary dividing line that separated Dawson's settled and colorful world from his, barren but for a cardboard box that held who knew what. A square of sunlight was all that knit their distinct universes together. He squinted against the sun's glare until he could make out the basketball court and the paths through the garden. For a while he followed the erratic tracks of patients out for a stroll.

He stepped away and looked at his new roommate's belongings. The newspaper clippings taped to a poster board over the desk attracted his attention. He took a step in that direction, but he stopped. He chose to go instead to the bathroom door.

"Mike?"

"What?" The voice came from the other side.

"It's Ted. I need a pen or something to cut the tape on the box they left for me here. Mind if I take one from your desk?"

Silence.

"Mike?"

"Of course you can take a goddamn pen. Let me shit and read my book in peace."

"Sorry."

No response.

Maybe Dawson wasn't as awful as everyone said. Ted went to the desk. This time he couldn't help glancing at one of the articles. The headline read,

ANDREA GREEN WINS SPECIAL MENTION AT VENICE BIENNALE

He grabbed a pen and moved along. If Mike had come out of the bathroom at that moment, the relations between them, which apparently had gotten off to a good start, would of course have been ruined. He broke the tape on the cardboard box with the tip of the pen and opened the flaps. The box contained a pile of neatly folded clothes, books, a number of sealed plastic bags, a table lamp that he immediately recognized, and...a pink tentacle that wriggled and disappeared.

Ted gave a start. He dropped the flaps and stumbled back until he hit Mike's bed and sat on it abruptly. He couldn't take his eyes off the box. Something was moving inside it; not only had he seen it, but the noise of it knocking about the objects in the box was unmistakable. And Ted knew why. That was no tentacle: it was the pink tail of the possum.

His breathing became labored. Impossible. Seeing the possum had to be something out of a bad dream...

Are you certain? At Arthur Robichaud's house, too?

Just then Mike came out of the bathroom. He saw right off that there was something the matter.

"What's in the box?" he asked, heading in that direction. He was about to touch the box, but at the last moment he thought better of it. "A rat?"

"No," Ted said. The box had stopped moving.

Mike opened a flap with a quick motion and kept his distance. Gingerly drawing closer, he reached in and pulled out the lamp, then a plastic bag, then another one...

"There's nothing in here." He turned around with a look of surprise.

"I saw its tail. The box was moving."

Mike looked at Ted with one eyebrow raised.

Ted stood up, shaking his head.

"I swear, there was—"

Mike stopped him with an upraised hand.

"What did you see?"

"Nothing."

"What did you see?"

Ted thought it over.

"I thought I saw a possum, but maybe I imagined it."

"Was this the first time you saw it?"

The question caught Ted by surprise.

"What do you mean?"

"It's a simple question."

"Yes," Ted finally said.

Mike rubbed his chin.

"A possum," he pondered.

"What's wrong? Have you seen it, too? Before, I mean."

"No, but after lunch you're going to tell me all about this possum."

His mysterious expression vanished. He picked up the book he had thrown on his bed when he came out of the bathroom and lay down to read without saying another word.

33

TED TOOK the lunch tray—breaded fish and peas—and went to sit at the farthest table. The dining hall on C wing wasn't very spacious, so he still couldn't get all the quiet he was seeking. Four inmates at the next table over watched him closely and tried to start up a conversation that sounded friendly enough. He told them he didn't feel like talking, and they went along. The fact was, he needed to think. He realized he had accepted his stay at Lavender rather quickly, and that made him a little angry, as if he knew deep down that he really did need to be locked up. But what if it were true? His mind was a meaningless jigsaw puzzle. He'd tried to kill himself over a tumor he never really had. He might have even killed two people! Was that why they'd locked him up on C wing? Was he a murderer, like Dawson? Too many questions not to give in to the idea of his being locked up. He didn't even have the strength to fight for his right to see Holly, or the girls. He missed them, of course, especially Cindy and Nadine; thinking about them was more painful than anything...but what would he say to them? How could he explain to Holly? If he didn't have a tumor in his head, what was behind his behavior?

He ate in silence, alone with his thoughts, staring vacantly out a window. Somebody at the next table tried speaking to him again, but he didn't hear. The incident in the room troubled him. When would it end? He had seen the possum in the box and hadn't taken his eyes off it until Mike had turned his attention to him. After that, it was gone.

The same thing had happened at Robichaud's house when the pest had hidden inside the tire swing. Every time he'd seen the sickening animal he had thought it was real, only to convince himself later that he had simply dreamt it, or worse, hallucinated it. What was he supposed to think now?

He sighed. He looked resignedly at what remained of his fish, and then at the broken knife.

He was about to leave when Lester arrived out of nowhere and sat down next to him. He didn't seem as disturbed as before.

"I know you didn't have anything to do with my gear," he said in a conciliatory tone. "I found it."

"I don't give a damn."

Lester had Gollum eyes, large and cunning, and the more Ted looked at them, the bigger they seemed to get. What would happen if he stuck a broken piece of knife in one of those bug eyes?

"I listened to you last night, talking to Dawson," Lester went on. "You were asking him about the chess set."

Ted had been getting up. He sat back down and nodded.

"I could hear you from my room," the little man went on. "You were asking him when they'd brought us the chess set. And he told you six months ago."

That was in fact what Mike had said. Could he have been lying?

"Is it true?"

Lester rubbed his chin. He made some mental calculations.

"Yes, it's true. But I know who brought it."

"Who?"

"Well, actually..."

"Who?!"

Ted grabbed Lester by his shirt collar and pulled him close. Some of the patients turned to watch. Robert Scott, the head nurse, looked up from one of the other tables and kept his eyes on them until Ted gestured to let him know they were just having a friendly conversation.

"Who was it, Lester?" Ted asked again.

The little man must have seen something in Ted's eyes, because there was nothing left of the effusive behavior he had flaunted the day before.

"It was Dr. Hill. She and the black male nurse came in one day and gave it to Scott. I saw them."

Ted studied his face for a long time.

"I don't believe you. Where were you when this happened?"

"In the hallway. They gave it to him right there, where everybody could see. Well, not everybody, because it was just me there, but they didn't even pay attention. Dr. Hill doesn't come around here often, and when she does she's always with that nurse—Roger, I think his name is. She gave Scott the chess set, except at first I didn't know it was a chess set. I followed him to the commons and saw him put it on the shelf with the other games."

"And that was six months ago."

Lester nodded vigorously and added, "I suspected, too."

"What did you suspect?"

"I heard the other thing you asked Dawson yesterday. Asking him how they could have known they were going to bring you here six months in advance."

"That's none of your business."

"Of course it is. They know lots of things. They have tiny cameras and microphones."

Ted shook his head. It made no sense to continue talking to this lunatic. He made his second attempt to get up, but this time Lester clasped his arm. He could have easily pulled away, but when he saw Lester's woebegone expression, he let the man unburden himself.

"Do you think they've got the chessmen bugged?"

"No, Lester, there aren't any microphones in those chess pieces."

Lester's face twisted into a grimace of baffled horror.

"And how can you be so sure?"

There was no sense in continuing the conversation.

34

MIKE WAS waiting for him on the bench under the pine tree. This time he wasn't smoking or reading; he followed Ted with his gaze until he'd sat down next to him.

"Problems with Lester, huh? If he bothers you again—"

"I can take care of myself," Ted broke it. "I have a few tricks up my sleeve, too."

"Yeah, so I hear."

The basketball court sat empty. Under the afternoon sun, the patches of peeling blue paint that remained on the court looked like puddles of water. Mike pointed at one of the hoops. An overweight inmate was holding the pole and spinning around it.

"That's Espósito. He's seen them, too."

For a second, Ted had no idea what his roommate was talking about. He looked around, thinking he meant that the man had seen some particular people.

"Seen who?"

"The animals," Mike said solemnly, looking at Espósito, still spinning around the basketball pole, at top speed now. His expression was almost identical to the one Timothy Robichaud had worn when he was spinning his supersonic merry-go-round.

"What animal did you see?" Mike asked.

"I told you: a possum. But I'm sure it was a dream. I lay down on the bed, closed my eyes for a second, and..."

"You and I both know that was no dream, Ted. Are you sure it was a possum?"

"Or something just like it. Have you seen it?"

"Not the possum. I've seen a rat, and a locust. Our buddy Espósito, spinning like a top over there, has seen two of the big ones: a hyena and a lynx. A couple of the guys who were here before had seen a few more, but nobody else has seen the possum."

Mike kept looking toward the basketball court, as if he were mulling over an unsolvable problem.

"Mike, you realize these animals don't exist, right?"

"Don't look at me like that. I know the animals are in here." He rapped on his head. "But that doesn't mean they don't exist."

Ted clicked his tongue. He was about to get up and leave when Mike lightly touched him on the knee.

"Wait."

"I want to forget the fucking possum, Mike—seriously. I have to get my thoughts in order. I talked with Dr. Hill yesterday and everything is getting more and more mixed up. The last thing I need now is to add more confusion."

"I understand. Let me tell you something. Dr. McMills is the general director of the hospital, and she's been in charge of my case from the beginning. A few years after I was committed, I told her about the animals. She laughed, and we talk about them from time to time, though she never asks many questions. She's a brilliant woman, and she treated lots of patients before she became the director, and there's one thing I'm sure of: she knows the animals are real. I haven't seen them for two or three years now."

"When did you start seeing them...exactly? Was it when..."

"When I killed them? Yes."

So who did you kill, Ted? Wendell? Blaine? Both?

"I started seeing the locust almost all the time," Mike said. "It was a lot bigger than a normal locust, and bolder, because it would walk right up to me with this attitude. I had the weird sensation that it might suddenly jump straight into my mouth. Just thinking about it made me want to puke. At first I tried to pay no attention to it, but much later I realized that the locust appeared whenever I was about to *go off my path*. It was like a sort of...guardian. The rat, too, but it was more frightening."

Ted felt a shiver. He was also afraid of the possum.

"Look at the basketball court," Mike went on. "There's two sides to it, well-defined, separated by the line across the center. Same with the real world and the world of insanity, Ted. You're either sane or you're not; there's no middle ground. You play on one team or on the other, and if you're locked up in here and you're lucky, if the medicine works and the doctors get your diagnosis and your treatment right, maybe you'll be lucky enough to get traded from one team to the other, at least for a while. What you can't do is play on both teams. Understand?"

"I don't think this is insanity."

"Well, you should, because it is. It's like another dimension, if it helps to look at it that way. A world with its own rules. Like dreams. Don't you ever have dreams?"

"You think the animals belong to that other world."

"Not exactly. You see that circle in the middle of the court? That's the intermediate zone. That's why I like the analogy; it didn't just occur to me right now. I often sit here and think about these things. That circle is the door that joins the two worlds, where you're not supposed to be, because, like I said, you can't play on both teams at once. But there are some people, like you, like me, like Espósito, who stay there longer than they should, in the *doorway,* and of course that can't be good." Mike paused before adding, in an ominous tone, "The circle is dangerous, because both worlds coexist there."

Espósito had stopped spinning around the pole and was now pacing back and forth, enjoying the effects of dizziness. With his arms spread wide and his face turned to the sky, he was gliding like a chubby airplane.

"The animals are there to scare us out of the circle, Ted," Mike said, and again he sounded like the sanest man on earth.

"Why just some of us?"

"I don't know."

"Mike, I don't want you to take this badly, but you're telling me that circle is bad. Let's say that's true. But what could be worse than being completely insane?"

"Let me ask you something, Ted. When have you seen the possum?"

"A few times."

"Tell me one."

"It was in a dream. I was in my living room at home and something attracted my attention in the backyard. I looked out the patio door and my wife was there in her swimming suit, standing still in an impossible position. She was also missing a leg. The possum was on the table we keep on the back porch, gnawing on my wife's amputated leg."

Ted shivered when he recalled it.

"That's a pretty fucked-up dream," Mike admitted. "Have you seen your wife since then?"

"What's that supposed to mean?"

"Maybe it's not the best example."

Ted lost patience and grabbed Mike by the arm.

"Why are you asking me if I've seen my wife since then? Is there something you know?"

Mike didn't lose his cool. He waited until Ted let go of his arm and then spoke in measured tones.

"Look, it's not like I'm an expert on the subject or anything. All I know is my own experience and what I've found out from being here. Before Espósito there was another guy. Ricci was his name. He got out five years ago." Mike gestured with his head up at the sky. "He was the first guy who talked to me about the animals and the circle, only he didn't talk about them like that. I didn't believe a word he said, like you now with me, but then I thought about the locust, which for some reason my mind had forgotten, and lots of things started to make sense. You know? When all that stuff happened with my friend..." Mike's face darkened for a moment. "When I did...what I did, everything was all jumbled in my mind. Even months later, it was hard for me to distinguish between what had been real and what hadn't. The evidence was right in front of me, but I refused to see it. One piece of evidence indicated that I had killed my friend's housekeeper, a lovely woman named Rosalía who I had known for quite a while and who had a little boy. It breaks my heart whenever I think of her. The police found the body in her room and they knew it had been from my killing spree. I convinced myself that it was true. It made sense. But I suddenly remembered something from that time, a memory that had been buried and cropped up from nowhere. I was on the porch of my house, drinking a beer by myself, when the fucking locust showed up from out of nowhere and landed on my knee. I almost died of fright. I swept it off with my hand and it landed by the door. Then it went inside the house, moving calmly, and I knew I was supposed to follow it. Can you believe that shit? There I was, following a locust into my own house because I was sure the little fucker wanted to show me something." Mike laughed and shook his head. "So we reached an empty bedroom, and there it stopped. When I remembered all this, I thought it was from a dream, just like with you. The door to the room didn't look like it normally did: it had a peephole, so of course I looked in. And there I saw something that made my hair stand on end: it was a little boy I knew, stabbing Rosalía savagely with a knife. I couldn't stop watching, just like in a dream, where time stretches and stretches."

Mike stopped talking. This couldn't have been an act.

Ted finished the story. "The woman had been stabbed."

Mike nodded.

"My memories from that time have never been clear, and I can't deny there's a chance I might have killed her...But something tells me it wasn't me. Not her."

"So you mean that what happened with the locust, there at your house..."

Ted left the sentence unfinished. His thoughts went back to Holly, rapturous in their backyard, with her leg cut off.

"A moment ago you were asking me what could be worse than losing your mind," Mike said, "and there's your answer. When you go crazy, everything is up here, in your head. But when you're in the circle, where both worlds coexist..."

Ted quickly thought it over.

"You mean when I dream that my wife is missing a leg, then she magically..."

"When you put it that way, it sounds stupid. What I recommend is, if you see the possum again, get away from it. As I told you, the animals prowl around the circle, the border between both worlds."

They sat in silence for a while. At some point Espósito had left, and Lester, Lolo, Sketch, and a few others had taken his place.

"Ever since I first saw you, I knew you could see them, too," said Mike, more to himself than to Ted. "It was weird."

35

LAURA WAS waiting for him in the assessment room. She had a notebook and a laptop.

"Are these necessary?" Ted asked, displaying his restraints. He had just walked in.

"I'm afraid so."

Ted plopped heavily into his chair. McManus, who had escorted him from his room, quietly left.

"Have you thought about what we said, Ted? Are you convinced now that the tumor doesn't exist? Tell me the truth."

"I haven't thought much about the tumor."

Laura took off her glasses and scratched the tip of her nose as if to rid herself of an irritating itch.

"McManus told me that you've done a good job of fitting in with some of the other patients."

Ted remained silent.

"Is there anything you want to tell me, Ted?"

"Actually, there is. There's a chess set in the common room. Did you bring it here?"

Laura's smile quivered. For a moment the truth could be seen in her eyes.

"I thought it would help you feel at home," she admitted. "You could play with some of your boys."

Ted shook his head. He looked up at the ceiling for a minute.

"You brought it here six months ago," he said calmly.

Laura opened her mouth.

"Don't deny it. I know the truth. What I want to know now is how you knew six months ago that I'd end up here."

"Calm down, Ted."

"I am calm. Perfectly calm. Just tell me why you brought that chess set before you'd even met me. Was it Carmichael? Did he tell you? Is this all part of his plan? Tell me the fucking truth, just this once."

Laura leaned over the table to get as close to him as the situation allowed. The look in her eyes said everything. He was horror-struck.

"You and I met seven months ago," Laura said softly. "You've been in the hospital all this time."

Ted studied her in turn, searching in vain for the gesture that would give her away. He couldn't detect it. He stood up and strode away as well as he could with his fettered legs.

"I know this is a lot to process, but I was going to let you know today."

"I came here three days ago," Ted insisted.

"Come back. Sit down. Let me show you something. This is why I brought my laptop." Laura opened it and waited for it to power up. She put her glasses back on and found a folder on the desktop. In the meantime, Ted sat back down and waited. The only way to allay his anxiety was to take the horseshoe from his pocket and hold it tightly in his lap.

"Today is Thursday, April eighteenth, two thousand and thirteen," Laura said without looking away from the screen and while remaining out of Ted's reach. "You were admitted here on September twentieth of last year. Well, not here but to B wing, where I serve as director. I took on your case personally."

She angled the screen so they could both see it. It showed a video taken by a security camera in the corner of a room very similar to the one Ted had occupied in the isolation ward, except that this one didn't have a glass wall. Sitting on the bunk was Ted, shackled hand and foot, rocking rhythmically back and forth, gesticulating in the air and nodding now and then. He was wearing a blue shirt and blue pants. The date was displayed in a box at a corner of the screen. It could have been faked, of course, but why couldn't Ted remember anything about this?

"This is the state you were in when you arrived, Ted, and I'm afraid your condition didn't improve much at first."

Ted couldn't take his eyes off the screen.

"Who am I talking to?" he muttered, referring to his alter ego on the screen.

"Who knows? Lynch, perhaps?"

Ted looked away, and then imploringly at Dr. Hill.

"I don't remember this at all."

"I know. Let me show you one more thing. Soon you'll understand."

Laura closed the video. A window displayed a long list of files. She selected one and a new video occupied the screen. This time Ted recognized the place: it was Laura's private office. There was the desk, her bookshelf, the coffee table with the glass of water he never touched. Ted was wearing the blue uniform and was shackled. Suddenly he heard his voice and was startled. This video had sound.

"Thanks for finding the time to see me, Laura," said Ted in the video. "The fishing trip with my business partner was canceled."

"Sorry about the trip," she replied. "I'm glad to see you."

"Last night I had a nightmare."

After a brief conversation, Laura asked him to tell her about the dream.

"I was in the living room, looking at the porch through the patio window. There was a possum perched on the table, eating one of Holly's legs. Holly wasn't there, just her leg, but I knew it was hers..."

The date in the corner indicated that it was filmed in September 2012. Laura pressed the space bar and the video stopped. She closed it and selected another file from the same folder. All that had changed was Laura's clothing: now she was wearing a red sweater that Ted vaguely recalled.

"Thanks for finding the time to see me, Laura," said Ted in the video. "The fishing trip with my business partner was canceled."

The Ted who was watching the video opened his eyes as wide as they could go. He looked desperately at the corner of the screen and confirmed what he had feared: the video was taken in January 2013. Four months after the previous video.

"Last night I had a nightmare," Ted said in the video, and he began describing the same details.

"Enough," said the Ted of flesh and bones.

Laura paused the video.

"That is my office in B wing. We've had sessions every other day for the past seven months. For the first three months, our sessions revolved around what I have called the first cycle. Your mind created a paranoid delusion, and everything was confined to that: to your meeting with Lynch, his proposal to join the suicide club, kill Blaine first and enter the circle, in which you would have to kill Wendell as a part of the deal."

Ted couldn't remember revealing all those details to Laura, but clearly he'd done so. He had stopped handling the horseshoe, which now lay almost forgotten in his lap.

"Do you feel all right, Ted?"

He nodded.

"Okay. In this first cycle, you killed Blaine, and later you went to Wendell's house. You murdered him in his lakeside house, but then you discovered that Lynch had tricked you with regard to your family. So you decided to track him down, and to do that you turned to Robichaud, your old acquaintance from high school. Do you remember all this, Ted?"

"Yes."

"Lynch was a virtually unknown lawyer, but you found him and confronted him in his office. He told you that Wendell really did belong to the Organization and that he was a dangerous man who therefore had to die. That was how you found out that he had used you, and things got out of hand..."

"Laura, this is crazy. I don't know if I want you to be telling me that I was in a fucking five-by-ten-foot cell imagining all this stuff. Did I really kill one of those people? Is that why I'm here?"

"Let me continue, Ted."

"No! Tell me. Have I killed anyone?"

"No," Laura said.

Ted nodded.

"So none of that was real?" he asked hopefully.

"I'm afraid it's a little more complicated than that."

Ted couldn't imagine how anything could get more complicated.

"For the first three months," Laura went on, "it was impossible to get you off the first cycle. It would take a week, or sometimes just two days, and then it was as if you had been reset to the initial moment, in your office, about to shoot yourself. The first time it happened I didn't know how to react, and I'm afraid I didn't react well. But with every repetition I got a little better, could ask you more precise questions, and so I gradually filled in all the details. The first cycle repeated more than fifteen times; some of those times you were more talkative than others. Then, one day, this happened."

Laura searched for another video. It was from their session of December 19. She fast-forwarded a few minutes in and hit play. The Ted of the video spoke.

"The guy showed up at my front door. I'd never seen him before in my life, but even so, I knew his name was Lynch. Even stranger, I remember going through the whole situation once before. I knew everything the guy was about to tell me—"

Laura stopped the video.

"You exited the cycle," she said, "and believe me, at first I didn't know why, and I didn't know whether it would last. As it turned out, it didn't. When you reset again, you went all the way back to the start of the first cycle, once more to the very beginning."

"My God, Laura, what the hell was going on?"

Laura tried a gentle, hopeful smile.

"Something serious was happening to you when Dr. Carmichael asked you to come see me. Most likely you had tried to kill yourself, but not because of a tumor. I really don't know what your reasons were. You've blocked those memories and replaced them with others, which you relive over and over again."

"I have to recover those memories."

"I think we've made significant advances. During the second cycle you were conscious of the earlier cycle, so things were different. You were aware of how you'd been tricked, so when you went to Wendell's house you talked to him instead of shooting him point-blank. Do you remember where?"

"Of course. It was in his daughters' pink castle."

Laura nodded thoughtfully.

"That detail always leaped out at me. Wendell revealed to you there that he and Lynch had met at college and that the famous Organization never existed, that it was just part of Lynch's ploy to get Wendell out of the way."

"Wendell showed me the photos," Ted said, recalling this particular point in great detail. "Holly and Lynch were together at a restaurant. That memory must be real."

Laura nodded.

"Probably. Each cycle represents a distorted view of reality. An adaptation to make reality..."

"Less painful." Ted finished the sentence.

"I'm afraid so."

Ted shook his head.

"There's one thing I don't get. If Holly cheated on me with that guy, I wouldn't blame her at all. Things weren't going well between us. The more I think about it, the more certain I am that the photo can't be why I invented all this—" He suddenly stopped short.

"What's wrong?"

"Have you talked to her, Laura? You must have talked to Holly in all this time. All these...seven months. Did she confirm it? The affair, I mean."

"I'd rather we left that for later. I want you to understand that, while I'm pretty sure you've finally broken free and the cycles won't repeat, we can't risk it. We should approach this fact slowly, stepping on solid ground. That's why these first days are so important. I don't want to stuff you full of too much information at once. It's important for you to think over what we talk about here. In later sessions we'll explore the days that came before."

"Can I see them?" Ted unexpectedly asked. "I miss them."

"I imagine you do, Ted. I'm a mother and I know how you feel."

"It's that...if so much time has passed..."

"You have no need to worry, I assure you."

Ted nodded. Just then one piece of the puzzle fell into place. For the first time, he thought about Roger.

"Roger, the nurse—I've seen him several times. At Blaine's house and also at Wendell's."

"So you told me, and it had me worried at first. I didn't know if it was a good thing or a bad thing. No part of your routine in B wing ever interfered with your delusion, except for Roger. Because of his strong connection to you, I guess. His role was like McManus's here. For a few days I asked another nurse to take care of you, but I didn't notice any changes. I guessed that Roger was one more element that your mind put to use to construct these memories."

"Those memories are so real, Laura," Ted said, almost in disbelief. "This is so hard."

"Most of these memories have an important component of truth, Ted. You have simply transformed them, reordering them to suit your mind."

"The second time I met Wendell, he told me that you guys wanted to lock me up in here."

"And that was our lucky break."

"I don't understand."

"Let me explain." Laura shut the laptop and pushed it aside. "You only managed to reach the second cycle a few times. You almost always went back to the first and started over again. It was frustrating. We had no idea what it was that caused you to move on to the second cycle, until one day I stumbled across it. The key was something from your past, Ted. I realized you only went into the second cycle after we'd been dealing with topics related to your past, to your childhood, especially your chess lessons with Miller. It was as if something in that past were pushing you to move forward, to emerge from that first cycle of killings and enter the second, where you no longer became a killer, where your marriage was unhappy but you accepted it. Do you see?"

Ted thought about Miller. It certainly did make him happy to recall his old chess teacher.

"I encouraged you to tell me about Miller," Laura went on, "and one day you told me about the horseshoe he kept in the garage where he coached you, and how you'd used it as a good luck charm in tournaments. You also told me about the world championship match between Alekhine and Capablanca in Buenos Aires. You told it with such passion...and then I thought, if I could only get you to cling to that past, maybe you could emerge from these cycles once and for all."

Ted took the horseshoe from his lap and held it above the desk so that Laura could see it, too.

"The importance of chess," Laura explained, "was there from the start, but I wasn't able to see it. It was always present in the dreams you told me."

"I found this horseshoe at Wendell's house."

"No. Roger gave it to you. And you incorporated it into your fantasy, because it was too important for you to set it aside. And it worked. All that remained was to see what came next, how you'd get out of the second cycle. Then one day, when Roger went to get you from your room to take you to dinner, you told him you knew all about it, that we were trying to trick you and you knew we were going to have you committed to Lavender Memorial."

Ted couldn't help smiling.

"It's funny, if you think about it."

Laura smiled, too.

"Roger told me right away, and we saw our chance to connect your fantasy with reality. I had to call in some favors; the director of this wing is my friend, and I was able to clear a few hurdles without too many explanations. We brought you here and the two worlds came together."

The two worlds.

That sounded too much like Mike Dawson's bizarre theories.

"The horseshoe was the key, Ted, and I suggest you keep it with you at all times."

"What comes next?"

"You've escaped from a dangerous spiral of repression and denial, but you still have a long ways to go. We need to recover those last days of your life, find out what really happened, what you've chosen to forget."

Ted remained silent for a moment and then said, "I'd like to see where I've been staying all this time, and also your office."

Laura was surprised.

"You mean the videos?"

"No. In person."

"I don't know if that would be such a good idea."

"I have to see it with my own eyes."

36

MARCUS HAD broken up with Carmen. He told her over the phone and she told him that she understood, but not to worry: if he wanted he could call her anytime and they could get together and have a little fun; he shouldn't get angry about it or take things so seriously. Life was meant to be enjoyed. In short, she didn't give a shit.

Marcus had DVR'd two episodes of *Breaking Bad,* his favorite series. It was late morning, and he made some microwave popcorn, grabbed a beer from the fridge, and walked to the movie room, smiling from ear to ear.

He dimmed the lights all the way and activated the screen. A comforting hum accompanied the descent of the silvery rectangle. It had just reached the floor when his cell began to ring.

His annoyance vanished when he saw that it was Laura.

"What a surprise!"

"Hello, Marcus."

The short silence that followed worried him.

"Anything wrong at Lavender?"

"No. I wanted...Are you busy with anything now?"

"Nothing at all."

"Want to have lunch?"

Marcus had to wait a second to tone down his boundless enthusiasm.

"Of course."

"I need to discuss a few issues regarding Ted McKay's case with you, and then I need you to join me in a little crusade."

"Count on it. You've got me intrigued."

"Great. That means you won't skip out on our date."

Date.

"Can I pick you up in an hour?" he asked.

"Sounds perfect."

When he hung up, Marcus sat for ten minutes staring at the blank screen.

37

MARCUS DROVE to her house beset by a whirlwind of thoughts.

She asked you to lunch! She used the word "date."

"But she said it ironically," he replied, looking himself in the eye in the rearview mirror. "You realize that, don't you?"

What she knows is that she likes you. If she called you, it's because you haven't approached her lately. Didn't she let you know her marriage was over once and for all?

That was true.

He got to her house before noon. Laura didn't invite him in, saying they'd better leave right away because there was somewhere she had to be at two, so they should go ahead and eat as soon as possible. She gave him a peck on the cheek and walked to the car, leaving Marcus on her doorstep. He was glad he hadn't bought flowers or anything stupid like that. Even his clothes—white woolen trousers, sky-blue linen shirt, his everlasting derby—were too formal compared with her jeans and plaid blouse. Laura had her hair up in a bun and was wearing less makeup than usual.

You wanted a sign? There's your sign. There's nothing romantic about this date, pal. She just needs to talk to you about McKay and for you to go who knows where with her.

They had lunch at Romanelli's, a restaurant with a balcony overlooking the Charles River, on the road to Newtonville. They both ordered the tuna salad.

"So McKay is making progress?" Marcus said. He had tried starting conversations on various subjects in the car on the way, but nothing had worked. Laura wanted to talk about the case that was obsessing her.

"Yes! I have so much to tell you. I'm almost certain he's gotten past the cycles. It's a matter of time before he begins to remember. I am convinced."

"Have you shown him the video from...the office of..."

Marcus had forgotten the guy's name.

"From Lynch's office? Not yet. It's not the right moment. I've shown him the videos from his room at Lavender, and also the videos from a couple of our sessions. It was hard on him, and I swear, for a moment I thought we'd be back to square one. But no, he seems to have absorbed it pretty well."

"I'm glad. Eat, Laura. You haven't touched your salad."

She looked at her plate as if she hadn't known it was there. She speared a bite of tuna and slowly brought it to her mouth.

"Don't get angry if I tell you this, Laura, but I think you're getting too involved with this patient."

She laughed and shrugged.

"I knew you'd say that," she said breezily. "I'm thinking I could write a book about it."

Marcus looked skeptical.

"Really?"

Laura became serious. She looked both ways and leaned forward slightly.

"Can I make a confession?"

Marcus tensed up.

Here it comes.

"The reason I didn't ask you to come in wasn't because we have so little time. I mean, it's true, we don't have much time, but I could have let you in for a minute; believe me, I meant to. After I called you, I thought I should start cleaning up the living room, where I had Ted's file scattered everywhere. Photos, documents, newspaper clippings." Laura laughed again like a mischievous girl.

"You still could have let me in."

"I know—we're friends. But it really is a disaster area. Walter's going to be with his father all day, and I guess I let myself get carried away, you know. I took advantage of having the house to myself."

"Want to tell me what you're up to?"

"Of course! That's why we're here."

Laura had a few more bites of her salad and washed them down with two sips of her Pellegrino. She seemed anxious to start telling her story.

"Ted was a chess prodigy. He gave up the game as a teenager, but I'm afraid there are modes of thinking that a chess player never loses." Laura paused. She didn't seem completely satisfied with her explanation. "I've watched a number of documentaries in recent months, even read a few biographies. Yesterday I saw one of the documentaries about Bobby Fischer again. I imagine you know who he was, right?"

"Of course. You were a baby, but in nineteen seventy-two there was a huge media storm when he played for the world championship with that Russian."

"Spassky."

"Right—I'd forgotten the name. It was a tremendous event, middle of the Cold War, Soviet Union versus America. I didn't watch the games, but I do remember the press coverage. Fischer became sort of a national hero. Whatever happened to him?"

"I'll give you the short version. It's an incredible story. By nineteen seventy-two, when Fischer played for the championship, he was already showing signs of paranoia. He was twenty-nine years old, and up until then he had been considered an eccentric genius, but the pathology became more and more blatant. He made excessive demands before he would agree to play, he skipped one of the games, and he constantly complained about the most bizarre things. He claimed the TV cameras were emitting some sort of radiation to harm him, and he even demanded that they be removed, claiming that the Russians were using some type of technology to make him lose his concentration. The match went on for weeks. Fischer won, of course, and became world champion. And then...he vanished."

"Vanished?"

"He didn't play again for twenty years! He fell off the map. He secluded himself in various places and made no public appearances. There were even doubts about whether he was dead or alive. Bear in mind that he was at the top of his game, and also at the top of his fame. As you say, he was a national hero here. Chess was his life, he'd always been obsessed with it, he'd hardly done anything else. And once he became world champion, he quit—just like that."

"I didn't know. And you say he came back to it twenty years later."

"Precisely, but only because a millionaire paid for a rematch with Spassky, which was held in Yugoslavia in 1992. He won again. It was a brief comeback. He showed no interest in defending his title as world champion, and when he refused to play a match under conditions set by the world chess organization, he forfeited the championship. By then he had become a virulent anti-Semite and in radio interviews he occasionally made horrible remarks against Jews and the United States. When they announced that the rematch would take place in Yugoslavia, the U.S. government sent him a letter telling him that playing there would violate the trade embargo, and if he went through with his plan he might end up in prison. He didn't care. He announced at a press conference that he would play anyway, and he literally spat on the feds' notification. He had gone downhill. His hatred of Jews and Americans had become his obsession."

"How sad. So, did he go to prison?"

"The government revoked his passport, and he was arrested once in Japan on that account during a stay there. He had nowhere to turn. It was Iceland, where he had played that first championship match with Spassky, that sort of took pity on him and granted him citizenship. The images of him when he was transferred to Reykjavík make an impression on you. He died there in two thousand and eight."

"He never got treatment? From what you say, he was suffering from acute psychosis."

"I don't know. The interesting thing is, he isn't the only brilliant chess master who has had severe paranoia. There have been several cases. Not caused by playing chess, of course, but it does appear that these individuals' mental structure isn't the ideal sort for coping with such an illness." Laura added with a nervous laugh, "Chess is a little paranoia-provoking in itself. You constantly have to be anticipating threats that might never materialize, and the possible variations are virtually infinite. Brilliant chess minds analyze those variations, the possible moves, one after another, each one leading to limitless ramifications. Apply that same structure off the chessboard and the result is catastrophic."

"I'm not sure I completely understand. Do you think something of the sort has happened to McKay?"

"The recurrent characteristic in players like Fischer is that they stop playing from one day to the next. Others retire but they keep playing as amateurs—exhibition games and such. But the ones who show signs of schizophrenic or paranoid behaviors simply quit. And what I suspect is, in their cases a sort of transference is occurring. The mind continues to calculate variations; it just can't suddenly stop cold—that's all it has ever done! These prodigies started playing when they were young children, and when they no longer have the game to play, they take the game off the chessboard. The odd thing in Ted's case is that he quit as a teenager. He lived a normal life for twenty years, until the process suddenly started up."

"Maybe it was latent in him, and when reality led him into using the same logic, it reactivated his old thought structures. Whatever problem he had, that must be what set the mechanism in motion."

"Quite likely. Ted has gone through two well-differentiated cycles over the past few months, one inside the other, and each cycle has repeated several times. Maybe 'cycles' is the wrong word. Call them 'variations,' perhaps."

"Have you found any documented cases of this?"

"Only theories with little scientific evidence to back them up." Laura looked at her half-eaten salad. She had been talking with such enthusiasm, she had once more forgotten about it.

"And you think the horseshoe is what shook him out of the cycles, like it's an anchor in reality or something."

"Exactly. When he left the first cycle, he conceived the second—a new variation. Closer to reality this time, though it, too, was unreal. In the first cycle, for example, Ted wasn't aware of his wife's cheating. In the second, he realized that things weren't going well between them."

Laura looked at her watch.

"Should we be going?" Marcus asked.

"They're expecting us in half an hour, but it's not far."

"Who's expecting us?"

"You'll see. So far I've been staying pretty far ahead of Ted in what he knows, and I still know a few things he hasn't found out yet. But there are lots of details I can't understand, and one of them is the role Edward Blaine plays in all this."

"You don't think he simply used the information he heard about that case on the TV news? I mean, it was a famous case, and then his mind used that information to concoct the profile of the person he was supposed to kill."

Laura nodded.

"Yes, that's exactly what I thought. But today, as I was reading through the transcriptions of our sessions, there was something that jumped out at me. Something that might help us figure out if it's just what you suggest or if there's a more complicated connection."

"Such as what? Don't leave me hanging!"

Laura stood up.

"Come on. I'll explain it along the way."

38

IT WAS perfectly reasonable to assume that Ted, like everybody else, had learned the details of the Blaine case from newspaper and television reports. Amanda Herdman's murder was front-page news for weeks. The victim's sister, a publicity seeker named Melissa Hengeller, had gotten a journalist at the *Boston Star* to publish her account; it had quickly spread from there. It contained the ingredients of an attractive story: a grisly murder (at first police said that the murder weapon was a hammer) and what seemed like an unexpected twist, with the not guilty verdict for Blaine. After the verdict, Hengeller hired an expert to investigate her sister's death, gather new data, and comb through the existing evidence. What he found was hair-raising. There was no actual science behind his hypothesis that the laundry heat vent located directly under Amanda's apartment had kept her corpse warm enough to cause an error in the estimated time of death, but the discovery was certainly a surprising turn in the case. The revelation led to cross fire between Hengeller's expert; the lawyers for the defense, who were now defending his acquittal; and the prosecutors, who wanted only to cover their asses. Public opinion was divided, though most believed the sister's version of events.

Blaine's house had been put up for sale, and Laura had made an appointment with the real estate agent to see it. She had called him that very morning, on a hunch, and the fellow had told her it was her lucky day: he was in the area and would be glad to show her the house that afternoon. Laura agreed, suspecting that he was lying about being in the area.

"Hey there! Jonathan Howard." The agent introduced himself with a smile that matched his likeness on the sign staked in the front yard.

Laura shook hands with him.

"Hello. Laura Hill, and this is Marcus, my husband." She turned to give Marcus a bare hint of a mischievous smile.

"Wonderful!" Howard gushed as they walked to the property. "This house is quite the find, as you'll see. Do you...do you two have kids?"

"Yes, one," Laura immediately answered.

"Marvelous. Are you from around here?"

"No. But we've heard the history of the house," said Marcus, playing bad cop.

Howard's face fell for a fraction of a second, but his smile instantly resurfaced.

"Oh, that. Yes, the guy had to leave. But he didn't live here long, and anyway, he was only a renter. Fortunately, though, people are very understanding, and it's drawing a lot of interest now. After all, it's not like the, um, the unfortunate incident took place here, is it?"

Laura defused the situation.

"Of course not. That's what I keep telling him."

Howard was right about one thing: it was a beautiful house. That much was easy to see even with the house completely empty, and it was difficult to imagine a despicable character like Blaine living here. For a moment Laura performed the mental exercise of picturing the place with her own furniture. They did a quick run-through of the house, and one of the first things Laura and Marcus verified was that there was, indeed, a guest room on the first floor. Did that confirm Ted's story of having been there? Possibly.

They came to the master bedroom, on the second floor, and Laura turned her attention to the agent, who walked across the room toward a huge closet and asked them to follow him. He undoubtedly thought the closet would be an important selling point with Laura, because he went overboard here, showing it off with melodramatic gestures, asking her to imagine her shoes on the shelves, her dresses and other clothes in the various compartments, her jewelry in a jewel box under the mirror. Her eyes grew wider with every comment, though for different reasons than Howard supposed. Ted had told Laura in one of their sessions that he had hidden in the first-floor guest room because there wasn't anywhere to hide in the master bedroom, yet here was this gigantic walk-in closet, a perfect hiding place in which to wait for Blaine. This proved what she already suspected: Ted had never entered this bedroom.

"Mind if I take some pictures?" she excitedly asked, pulling her phone from her bag. "I want to see my sister's face when she gets a load of this."

"Please do!" Howard urged her.

Marcus, ready to get out of the closet, gave her a quizzical look.

When they were downstairs again, Laura dragged Marcus to the guest room.

"Can I talk with my husband alone for a minute?"

"Of course!"

Howard went outside.

Marcus looked at her.

"What's with taking pictures, Laura? And what are we supposed to be talking about?"

She crossed the room, opened the closet door, and knelt to see the underside of the shelf. She froze.

"What is it?" Marcus went over and knelt next to her.

There was Buzz Lightyear. The *Toy Story* sticker that Ted had described during his sessions. The one that glowed in the dark.

"Close the door," Laura said.

Marcus complied. They both knelt against the back wall of the closet, like a couple of kids playing hide-and-seek. Marcus hardly had time to wonder what the real estate agent would think if he came in right then and found them in there.

With the space totally dark, Buzz's outline glowed softly. Laura opened the closet door.

"I can't understand it," she said as she walked out.

Marcus stood up and went after her.

"What can't you understand?"

"That sticker. It's just the way Ted described," Laura said, perplexed. "Until I saw that, I was convinced that the Blaine episode was a product of his paranoia, that he had never been to this house. The details of the upstairs bedroom contradict his story, but that sticker...It proves he really was here, shut inside this closet."

"You told me he murdered Blaine in his story. Obviously, that never happened."

Laura thought it over, pacing back and forth in the empty room.

"In the first cycle he killed him, in the second he didn't."

"Maybe he meant to kill him," Marcus hazarded.

"This makes no sense," she said softly. "Ted's being in this house is a piece that doesn't fit with anything else—"

A knock on the door made them start.

"Mr. and Mrs. Hill! Is everything all right? I'm sure we can negotiate a lower price if you're interested in the house. I can talk to..."

Laura opened the door. She glared at the agent, pretending to be upset.

"My husband isn't convinced," she growled. "Apparently his is the only opinion that counts around here."

She walked around the agent and stormed to the front door.

"I'm so sorry," Marcus said. And he was completely sincere.

"If there's anything you're unsure about, we can fix it. The sellers are willing, I'm sure."

Marcus put his hand on the agent's shoulder.

"I'm sorry for wasting your time. I really am."

39

IT WAS his first night in the room he would be sharing with Dawson. Ted was grateful to be alone at this moment. Lying on the bed, he contemplated the gray forms in this unknown territory, especially the two desks, one on either side of the single window. The photo of Holly and him with the girls stood out on his desk. It had been taken three Christmases ago, when their marriage was still working. Though the moon threw only enough light for him to see the frame, Ted could recall every detail in the photo and even conjure up the moment when it was taken. They were all smiling except Nadine, who was pointing to one side with a touch of horror. The camera had been set on automatic; Ted had programmed it and run to take his place, and just then Nadine had noticed the neighbors' cat, which often visited them in search of a bite to eat, running off with one of the fish fillets Holly had fried up for dinner. Nobody but Nadine had noticed it, and her shock at seeing the cat's sudden raid was captured for all time. Ted had kept the photo in his study ever since.

"And now you've ended up here," he told the photograph.

He continued looking around incredulously, unable to believe where he was. But unlike over the previous days, when he had felt an utter lack of belonging, now he felt he was in the right place. The videos Laura had shown him in the assessment room had affected him deeply, he had to admit. He had fallen into a trap set by his own mind; he couldn't blame himself. But now he was making progress, wasn't he? That's why Laura had shown him the videos...

Maybe she had already played them for you three dozen times before this.

He again addressed the photo. "No. She was showing them to me for the first time."

He had to have something to hold on to.

Accepting that he was in the right place was an important step. And now he felt it. He felt he needed Lavender if he wanted to continue getting better, if he wanted to understand why his mind had concocted those alternate realities.

The cycles.

What lurked behind them?

To think that his daughters hadn't seen him in months—that was another idea that would take some getting used to. How had the idea of ending his own life crossed his mind? *Leaving them behind...*It was inconceivable. Now he saw that clearly.

"Whatever has happened to Daddy, he'll overcome it and get better," he said, leaning slightly forward, looking straight at the photo. "For your sakes."

He smiled.

But an instant later the smile vanished, as if by magic. He jumped from the bed in terror. A valve was opened...He ran out the door and into the corridor. The lights were out and all was silent. Ted felt an urge to yell for McManus at the top of his lungs, but then he remembered that McManus wasn't on duty that night. He reached the end of the hall, where the nurse on duty was watching TV. Ted hadn't met this one before, or he thought not, and indeed she seemed pretty startled to see him standing there. She grabbed the walkie-talkie from the desk and pressed the button, ready to speak.

"No, no," Ted reassured her, exhibiting his empty palms. "There's nothing wrong. I just need to talk to Dr. Hill. It's important."

The nurse put the radio down, but she still regarded Ted with mistrust.

"You can talk to her tomorrow," she said. "For now, back to bed."

"It can't wait. She told me so. She told me I could call her if I needed to talk with her. She told me that—she really did."

There was a mixture of entreaty and horror in Ted's eyes that the nurse had rarely seen in all her years at Lavender Memorial.

40

LAURA'S LIVING room really was a mess; she hadn't been making it up. Marcus was astonished to see files scattered all across the carpet, newspaper clippings, a half-finished cup of coffee. She smiled, amused.

"Told you so. Walter's with his father. And when Walter is with his father..." She made a gesture that took in the entire room.

"But why on the floor?"

She laughed.

"Childhood habits. My sister and I shared a room. We only had one desk and she had claimed it for studying, so I studied on the floor. I liked it. I kept it up at college."

Laura piled up some documents and carried them to the living room table.

"This case has you obsessed."

"Cup of coffee?"

"Sure."

Minutes later they were drinking their coffee and eating doughnuts at the table. Laura was deep in thought.

"Laura, tell me how it is that the patient constructed Blaine's murder. That's the part I understand the least of anything you've told me."

"Until I saw that sticker at Blaine's house I was sure Ted's dream about murdering him had no basis at all in reality," Laura explained. She riffled through the folders she had piled up on the table. "Look at how many newspaper clippings I have about the case, all from the period before Ted was admitted. The logical supposition was that his mind was parroting a case that was in the news."

"But how did he incorporate it into his delusion?"

"He thought he had joined a suicide club, an organization for people who wanted to commit suicide, which had recruited him. Their aim was to ease the grief of their loved ones by making their suicides look like murder. Each member would kill the next one on the list. The price of joining the chain was to take revenge for an unjust death—a sort of vengeance."

Marcus wrinkled his nose.

"That's pretty complicated. But fascinating."

"Definitely. There are three characteristic elements that link the first cycle to what really took place. The first is the suicide. I'm certain that Ted intended to take his own life at some point; he may have even attempted suicide. Then there's his family's grief. He stressed that point so often, it shows how his thinking about the consequences of his suicide have affected him. The third element, the most puzzling, is his visit to Blaine's house. That's the one that doesn't fit."

"I was just about to say, if the man from that organization—what's his name?"

"Lynch."

"If Lynch had simply suggested camouflaging the suicide as a murder, everything would make sense. But why ask Ted to kill somebody else?"

"I don't know. And now that we know Ted really did go to Blaine's house, and possibly hid there as he said he did, in his first cycle...I don't know what to think. He clearly had to have gone there for some reason."

"From what you've told me, these cycles are altered versions of real events that took place before he was admitted."

"Exactly. Each event has a basis in reality. Including his visit to Blaine's house, as we now know."

"What if Ted really meant to kill Blaine, like an avenger? What if he waited at his house, hiding just like he told you, and in the end couldn't kill him?"

Laura thought it over. They drank the last drops of coffee.

"That doesn't make much sense. It would change everything." Laura scratched the tip of her nose. "I thought I had it all more or less figured out, until now."

"Maybe we're blowing this sticker all out of proportion. Ted saw it at some point, maybe a long time ago, and the detail was etched in his memory. Do we know anything about the former owners of the house?"

"If I had only thought of asking the real estate agent," Laura said with regret. "I could call and ask, but I doubt he'd feel much like cooperating after our little scene. But I have the feeling the answer is right in front of our noses."

Marcus remained silent. Laura stared at the ceiling.

"I'm compiling a document with every detail Ted has told me in all our sessions. I guided my questions in different directions each time, so it all forms a sort of jigsaw puzzle. I just finished the first cycle. Would you be interested in reading it?"

"Of course. A fresh set of eyes might be just what you need."

Laura looked at him with a curious intensity.

"What is it?" he asked.

She continued gazing at him in the same enigmatic way.

"What?" he repeated. "Do I have a piece of doughnut on my lips?"

He put the back of his hand to his mouth.

"No, silly." Laura softly pushed his hand away. "It really helps me to talk this over with you. That's all."

"I'm glad."

He moved a little closer. He didn't find the situation uncomfortable. He lowered his voice a little.

"Let's let it rest till tomorrow. Maybe we'll see things a little more clearly then. It might be simpler than it appears: Ted found out his wife was having an affair with the guy and he lost control. How is the guy doing?"

"Lynch is still in a coma. His prognosis isn't all that encouraging."

"Does Ted know?"

"No. He still believes Wendell did it."

"Wendell." Marcus smiled. "Funny, in its own way."

"Don't laugh," she scolded him with feigned anger. "I'm really worried about how he'll react when he finds out. That's the last door we still have to open. And the most dangerous one."

"Do you plan to transfer him back to your wing?"

"Not for now. As long as he keeps improving I don't want to go backwards. Besides, he seems to fit in well with some of the patients, including Dawson."

Marcus took a sharp breath and frowned.

"What a roommate."

"Marcus?"

"Yes?"

"I'm glad you came. Really."

Laura's hand rested on his. Marcus looked at it, unsure what to do next.

If there was a moment when he might have leaned forward and kissed her, it was lost when the phone rang. Laura ran to answer it, and when she returned she had a completely different look on her face. Talking to her ex-husband instantly put her in a bad mood, as Marcus well knew. She didn't even have to tell him who had called.

"Walter will be here in a few minutes," she said in annoyance, shaking her head.

Marcus stood up. He assumed the comment was a request for him to leave. Laura was talking more to herself than to him.

"He's supposed to be the father, and I can't get him to spend one whole fucking day with his son. I almost have to beg him. Today he was supposed to take him to play, then they were going to spend the rest of the afternoon in the park with his cousins. Now he calls to tell me something came up at work. On a Sunday!"

"Take it easy, Laura."

"I just don't get it. I really don't. It's *one day*. What could be more important than seeing your own son?"

Marcus was about to suggest that he stay and organize something to do with little Walter, but he told himself that would be moving too fast. He tried to calm Laura down, to take her mind off things with silly comments, even tried to get back to Ted's case, but nothing worked.

"Sometimes I think he does it on purpose. He knows it drives me crazy when he shows no interest in Walter. He knows that perfectly well. He seems to enjoy calling me to tell me that something came up unexpectedly. The bastard."

41

WALTER WAS an intelligent, sensitive, rather shy boy. On weekends Laura would prepare a bubble bath for him, give him some of his favorite bath toys, and sit by the side of the tub to talk with him. The rubber duckies of a few years ago had given way to battleships, spaceships, and Transformers, and several months ago Walter had told her, very seriously, that he could no longer be naked when he was around her, but had to wear his bathing suit. Laura replied, just as solemnly, that she agreed.

While she massaged the shampoo into his hair, careful not to let the foam get in his eyes, Walter enthusiastically told her about everything he had done with his father that day. In his telling, all of Scott's contributions were the deeds of a mighty hero. It was too bad, he said, that Daddy always had those unexpected things that made him have to leave for work. Laura clamped her mouth shut as she listened. Walter's admiring tone in talking about his father was moving yet sad; he didn't care how often his father let him down, canceled plans, skipped the school play, or went back on his promises. Walter always understood. Laura had confronted Scott more than once over these issues, and the fact that Walter was always so understanding served as his trump card whenever a conflict arose between them: "Hey, I talked it over with Walt and he understood completely." Laura told him that the fact that a seven-year-old boy idolized his father and accepted all his stupid excuses gave him no right to go on acting like an irresponsible idiot. But this was a path they'd been down many times, and nothing ever changed. Scott would spread his arms, look up at the sky, and say something like "Don't start pulling all that psychology crap on me. The kid's smart. He understands how things are." At the end of these conversations, Laura always had the same thought: *Fuck it: you're the one who married him. Next time, don't fall for the rebel on the motorcycle.*

There won't be a next time.

"Mommy, the water's getting cold."

"Time to get out, then."

Walter pulled the plug and the two of them watched the foamy water circle down the drain. Laura turned on the shower to let her boy rinse off. When he was done, she wrapped him in a towel, dried his hair, and hugged him.

"I'm very proud of you," she said.

"What for?"

For not complaining about that father of yours.

"For everything."

One hour later, Walter was asleep. She had just gotten drawn into a Robin Cook novel when her cell phone began to ring. She instinctively looked at her watch; she knew it was after ten. She ran to the kitchen table and picked up immediately. The call was from the hospital. The nurse on duty in C wing told her wearily that one of her patients wanted to talk to her, and it said in his file that...

"Yes, yes, put him on, please."

"Laura," Ted muttered. "They're dead, aren't they? Holly, Cindy, Nadine—they're all dead."

"Ted, what happened?"

"I figured it out. I was in my room and the truth just hit me. I understood everything like that. They're dead."

"Your wife and daughters are not dead," Laura reassured him. "Are you listening to me, Ted? Would I lie about something like this?"

"I don't know."

"I'd never lie about this."

"But then—"

"They're fine."

Silence for several seconds.

"Ted?"

"I need to see them."

"Can we talk about this tomorrow?"

"No. I need to see them."

"Ted, I'll promise you this: Tomorrow, first thing, I'll talk to Holly. I'll tell her you're better, that you want to see her and the girls, and I'll see what she says."

More silence.

"Why wouldn't they want to see me?"

Laura was sorry she'd had that glass of wine. Between the alcohol and her exhaustion, she wasn't handling the situation as well as she would have liked.

"She wants you to be completely better before you see the girls," Laura said. "All this time—you remember the videos I showed you, right?"

"Yes."

"You're making progress. You need to be strong. I'll explain things to Holly and see what she says. I'll try to convince her it would be good for you to see the girls. I'm sure they're itching to see you. But you understand how important it is to them for you to get better?"

When no answer came, Laura insisted, "You do understand, don't you, Ted?"

"Sorry I called you at home. But I was convinced that..."

"Don't mention it. And don't worry. I'll talk with Holly tomorrow and then you and I will see what she says. Sound good?"

"Thanks, Laura."

They hung up. Laura stayed in the kitchen for a while, thinking. She had known this moment would come sooner or later.

42

THE PATIO door was back; the pink castle hadn't taken its place this time. Other than the vast expanse of water, which Ted had now almost grown used to, everything looked normal. The chess box wasn't even lying by the grill. Ted recalled how, in his last dream, he had watched Holly emerge from the water with Roger, pick up the box, and give him a look of resentment before returning to the depths of the sea. Now he stood facing the glass door, as he had the last time, and reached out to unlatch it. He did so without conviction, knowing that due to some caprice of his dreams he wouldn't be able to go beyond the ridiculous limit of his own living room. But the door easily slid open. The motion sensor switched on the back porch light, and Ted stopped to look around. The sea was calm, no waves, no salt in the breeze. On the contrary, the only odor he could detect was that of damp woodlands.

"Still don't get it?"

The voice made him jump. He turned to his right. The porch went out pretty far in that direction. Sitting on a folding beach chair was Roger, with his white lab coat and his incandescent smile.

"Get what?"

The nurse turned away to look at the sea, his face a dark mask that blended with the night. He didn't answer.

"Get what?" Ted repeated.

The only reply was a slow, sweeping gesture that took in all the boundless ocean.

Still don't get it?

The porch light clicked off. Ted was about to wave his arm to reactivate it when a thin gray patch on the ocean attracted his attention. At first he thought it was an enormous ship, but as his eyes got used to the dark he understood. What he saw wasn't a boat, wasn't anything floating on the water. It was *the other shore.*

Still don't get it?

That's why there were no waves this time, no sea breeze. This wasn't the ocean: it was a lake. As he mulled this over, he noticed that the long porch was actually a jetty. A jetty that he'd seen before, of course. He was at Wendell's house. He walked to the end of the jetty and looked down. Tied up there was the boat he had seen the fellow sitting in the first time.

Previously, he had seen the waves crashing onto the lawn—he was sure.

"Last time, I..." He turned to Roger.

But Roger wasn't there—only his empty chair. Ted approached it slowly, turning for the first time to look at Wendell's ultramodern home. He looked at the patio door, responsible for transporting him from his own living room to the home of this man he knew so little about. When he reached the beach chair he saw something lying on it. At first he thought it was the nurse's white coat, left behind when Roger had been teletransported off somewhere. But that wasn't it: it was Holly's red bikini. Ted knelt to pick it up, and he found the cloth damp, as if his ex-wife had just taken it off and left it there.

Ex-wife.

His heart pounding, he looked for her in the lake. He pictured her swimming naked.

But Holly wasn't there. Only her bikini. He collapsed onto the chair and squeezed the cloth into a ball between his hands. He held it in front of his face and buried his nose in it, seeking the familiar scent of his wife.

Ex-wife.

Still don't get it?

He sat like this for a long time, enjoying the howling of the wind through the trees, the chirping of the crickets. There was something familiar and reassuring about these woods. After a while he stood up, went to the end of the wooden esplanade, and walked down the gently sloping yard to the lakeshore. He walked around the property. Around front he found the black Lamborghini, as silent as a large, sleeping beast.

Then he thought he noticed movement in a window of the house. Just a swift-moving hint of shadow, caught by the corner of his eye. Maybe Roger was still around...

He went to the front door, not completely convinced he wanted to run into the nurse, and when he tested the handle the heavy door swung open.

And then he saw himself. The Ted waiting for him inside the house was standing in the middle of the Indian rug, aiming the Browning at his head. For a brief instant they stared into each other's eyes. One of them let out a gasp of surprise when the gun went off and the bullet pegged Ted in the middle of his forehead. He fell heavily onto the rug. Curiously, though the impact of the bullet had knocked him down, he had only felt a slight sting on his forehead. When he tried to touch it, he realized that his arms were two lax tentacles beside his body. The flowing blood blinded his right eye, but even so, he could see the other Ted pacing from side to side.

His chest vibrated. The other Ted noticed, bent over him, and looked inside his jacket until he found his cell. When he pulled it out, for a fraction of a second the screen remained in view and he could make out Holly's face.

The other Ted suddenly looked at him.

"Who's Holly? Could this mess up my plans, Wendell?"

He felt the damp roll of Holly's bikini in his hand. He tried to squeeze it, as if that might help him keep his grasp on reality, on his memories. But his fingers didn't respond. All they could do was feel...

The other Ted was in a frenzy, visibly worried. He was reading the text messages coming in on the phone, and his face was transformed.

We're almost there. Time to quit your fishing for the day.

Outside, a familiar engine sound announced the arrival of the minivan. The other Ted went to the window and looked out.

"Shit!"

Seconds later the vehicle stopped. Ted, lying sprawled on the rug, opened his eyes as wide as he could, but he couldn't quite see the door through which he had entered. He did see the other Ted race across the room to the kitchen and slip out a side door. By now he could hear Cindy's and Nadine's unmistakable voices on the other side of the door. He didn't want them to enter, didn't want them to find him lying here with a bullet in his forehead. There was a moment of suspense.

"What's that piece of paper on the door?" Cindy asked.

"It's a note," her sister answered. "It has Mommy's name on it."

Ted followed their conversation clearly through the door, sprawled on the floor with a bullet in his brain.

"What does it say, Mommy? We want to know, too."

A pause.

"Why are you crying, Mommy?"

43

TED WAS sitting on the usual bench. He'd finished his breakfast quickly and was alone now. Mike was one of the first patients to come outside and join him. He saw that Ted was in a bad mood.

"Looks like I'll have to start sharing my favorite bench." Mike carried his book with him.

Ted didn't answer. He focused his gaze on the basketball court.

"You aren't going to tell me life is like a box of chocolates, are you?" Mike said as he sat down next to Ted. "Don't feel like talking?" He opened his book and began to read.

After a while he felt a tap on his knee. Mike followed the direction of Ted's gaze to the Lavender garden door, where Roger stood waving for him to come.

"What is it?" Mike couldn't understand his roommate's reaction.

"Can't you see him?"

"See who? There's nobody there, Ted," Mike joked. But when he saw Ted's expression darken, he decided it wasn't the best time to make fun of him. "Of course I can see him! It's that male nurse from B wing who's always hanging out with your doctor. Roger something."

Ted pulled himself together.

"You feeling okay, buddy?"

"Yeah, yeah." Ted stood up. "See you later."

He walked over to Roger. Last night's dream had profoundly disturbed him.

Still don't get it?

Laura was waiting for them in the assessment room. Ted entered with his head down, almost dragging his feet. She had been expecting a man anxious for news from his family, but today Ted wasn't that man.

Roger gestured to attract her attention.

"You're sure you don't want..." He held up the restraints.

Laura shook her head. She had decided it was time to start doing without them.

"Want me to stick around?" Roger offered.

"It won't be necessary."

The nurse seemed unconvinced, but at last he withdrew. Ted sat on his usual chair.

"Ted, look at me. Should we talk later?"

"No, no. I need to talk to you today more than ever. I'm trying to put my thoughts in order."

"Did you take your medicine today?"

"Of course. Not like your friends give me any choice," he joked.

Laura smiled.

"I was wondering if they had given you some sort of sedative. I don't see anything in your file."

"No sedatives."

"I thought you'd be eager to talk with Holly, and perhaps..."

A hopeful smile lit up Ted's face when he heard her name. He couldn't help it.

"Were you able to reach her?"

"Yes. Holly specifically asked me to tell you that she won't keep the girls from seeing their father; she knows how much you love them, and how much they love you. Cindy and Nadine miss you, but they understand that you are recovering in a hospital."

"Maybe you were right yesterday: maybe it's better to wait awhile. I only wanted to be sure they were okay."

"It would be best to wait a few days, I think. You're making good progress—giant steps. What changed your mind, Ted?"

"I had the same dream last night, on the porch of my house, but this time something else happened. I could go out past the porch to the ocean, only it wasn't the ocean: it was a lake."

Laura looked in her purse for her portable recorder. Ted had never left his house before in his dreams. This might mean...

She felt a growing excitement. She set the recorder on the table and asked him to tell her about the dream, in as much detail as he could. Ted began talking. Nothing had vanished when he awoke; it was all there in his mind, as vivid as a movie he had just finished watching.

The only detail he left out, because he thought it was irrelevant and because it was particularly painful to him, was finding Holly's damp bikini on the beach chair.

When he finished, Laura turned off the recorder and put it back in her purse. She picked up her notebook to take some notes.

"Laura, all this time that you've been talking to Holly, to Dr. Carmichael, and, I imagine, to other people with connections to me, have you been able to locate Wendell?"

Laura gulped. The question took her by surprise.

"Ted, the dream you had last night should help you see the truth."

"I don't understand."

"There's no easy way to put this. Wendell is you."

44

LAURA KNEW from the start that Wendell wasn't a real person but a projection of Ted that he had generated. Holly had confirmed that the lake house was theirs, that they used to spend almost every weekend at the lake, but that lately—since their marriage had started to go bad—it was mainly Ted who went there, by himself. He was the one who liked fishing; the one who owned the black Lamborghini, which he treated like another child; the one who had assembled the Disney princess castle that he had described so often during their sessions.

It was Ted himself who had met Lynch at college; they were pretty tight during their university years, and for some time thereafter. Later they started seeing less of each other, though they never completely lost contact. Holly assured Laura that when she and Lynch began going together, her marriage with Ted had already fallen apart and they had agreed it was time for them to end it. If they hadn't done so yet, it was because they were waiting for the right time to tell their daughters.

Holly and Lynch were very discreet, though they made one single mistake: the dinner at the restaurant where they were caught on camera. They wanted to enjoy a normal night out, without skulking around, and they decided to drive separately to Beverly, ten miles away. They were foolish enough to take a seat by the window, because they wanted to feel completely free. They joked about it each time someone walked by and noticed them, Holly told Laura with regret. Neither she nor Lynch noticed the private detective who had tailed them from Boston.

Holly maintained that Ted had stopped loving her long before she gave up on him. Ted had always been reserved, a bit of a recluse, except with Holly; in recent months, however, he had even begun to act distant and undemonstrative with her. As much as Ted tried to hide it, his withdrawal became obvious. Sex became less and less frequent until it basically disappeared. He stopped seeking it, and for months it fell on Holly to take the initiative. She believed that his faltering desire could be revived, like throwing a miraculous piece of firewood onto a sputtering bonfire at the last moment. But it distressed her to have to beg for a few moments of mechanical frenzy.

She tried to deceive herself and believe Ted's nightly excuses—too much work, the girls hadn't fallen asleep yet—but the moment came when she saw it, she *felt* it. He didn't desire her. It was as if her blindfold had fallen off. Ted traveled out of state once a month, sometimes twice, to visit his most important clients, the ones he needed to see *in person* as president of the company. These were their seven-figure clients, he always told Holly, the ones that really mattered, the ones he had to inform directly about the state of their investments. Ted would go away for at least three days, or often for a whole week, and come back in a better mood, bearing presents for the girls, acting nice again; Captain Erection would even deign to visit them for a night or two after his return.

But all too soon things would be back to normal. He became unsociable and moody again, and he'd take the first opportunity to run off to the lake and go fishing. Holly didn't know if there was another woman, or several women; all she knew was that her husband was happiest when he was farthest from home.

It wasn't exactly pride that Holly felt, but an obligation to verify the truth of her husband's travels. She called his company, spoke to Ted's secretary, to his business partner; everything checked out. Either he had planned everything very meticulously or he wasn't cheating. Of course, who needed a whole week for a business trip? Ted told her he took advantage of the trips to go fishing, and she corroborated this point, too, with a fishing club out of Denver. Clearly, if Ted was cheating on her, he was much more careful about it than she herself would be a few weeks later when she sat down with her lover at a window seat in a restaurant in full view of the world.

At last Holly threw in the towel. In the end, it made no substantial difference whether Ted was cheating or not. There was something else now: she had started to fall out of love with him, almost without realizing it. After a few weeks she began to welcome her husband's apathy, tacitly inviting it. She came to hope there was another woman, because that would make everything so much easier.

One day Justin Lynch dropped by to visit them. Ted wasn't home, nor were the girls. Holly got along well with Justin, so she asked him to come in. They shared a glass of wine, talked, and in just two hours Holly told him everything. Everything. Justin had no idea they were having so many problems with their marriage. Much less, he assured her, did he know whether Ted had a lover. His friend had never told him anything along those lines; Ted was very reserved, Justin said apologetically. But the chemistry between Justin and Holly was evident, and he quickly became her closest confidant.

When her situation had grown unbearable, Holly decided to talk to Ted and tell him the obvious. Divorce was best. He agreed from the beginning. By then Ted had started suffering terrible headaches; his body was protesting. Holly and Justin continued seeing each other, always as confidants, but their mutual attraction grew until it was unbearable. The more they got to know each other, the more they liked being together. The preliminary divorce agreement between Holly and Ted was all it took for them to give free rein to their affair. The fact that they suspected Ted might also have a lover was a lie they told themselves to lessen their sense of guilt.

Holly never knew that Ted, convinced that he had a malignant tumor taking over his brain, had begun seeing Dr. Carmichael around this time. Much less did she know that the idea of ending his life was slowly but surely taking shape in his mind.

Another thing she learned only later was that a private detective was following her and had photographed her at the restaurant. Ted had never confronted her, or Lynch, either; instead, he kept the photos in an envelope inside his wall safe, and went on with his life as if nothing had happened, remaining in that transitional limbo until they decided how to manage the matter of their divorce as it concerned the girls and their nearest family. In fact, those were paradoxically the days when they got along best.

Holly found the photos only later, much later, she would tell Laura afterward. She didn't have access to the safe and had had to force it open. But that was a month after the fact! For a whole month, Ted had continued living with her without breathing a word, as if it didn't matter to him.

Why did Ted wait a month? A month before he went to see Lynch at his office, after almost everyone but Lynch had left his building, and beat him with a brass lamp. Someone on the floor below heard the beating and the screams and called the police, who found Ted sitting in the lobby of the building with the lamp in his lap and his friend's blood all over him. When the officer who found him asked for his name, he said he didn't know, but a short while later he said that his name was Wendell. They took him in and discovered that his real name was Theodore McKay.

The beating put Lynch in the hospital, in a coma. The doctors were optimistic for the first few days; they performed an emergency operation to repair a damaged artery and hoped that, in combination with osmotherapy to reduce fluid pressure on the brain, the inflammation would be relieved and he would awaken. But that didn't happen.

Holly visited every week. Justin had few close relatives; it was devastating to find him always alone, lying on that hospital bed, waiting for a miracle that might never arrive. Holly couldn't say she had fallen in love with him, but she was sure she had been heading in that direction. And she felt responsible, of course. Why hadn't she been more careful? At Laura's recommendation, she tried therapy, and it really did help her. Nobody could have guessed that Ted, a peaceful person, open to dialogue, could have kept his discovery of her infidelity a secret for an entire month, only to explode like Mount Vesuvius.

Ted, for his part, went into a catatonic state. He was admitted to Lavender Memorial. Dr. Laura Hill took his case and immediately contacted Dr. Carmichael, who had been treating Ted up until then.

45

TED LISTENED to Laura without interrupting her. When she told him about the beating he had given Lynch, he seemed slightly surprised, but that was all.

"Is he still in a coma?"

"I'm afraid so."

"There's no doubt I did it, is there?"

Laura shook her head.

"There's got to be an explanation," Ted said. "Why would I beat a friend and put him in a coma? Believe me, his having a consensual relationship with my wife wouldn't be enough of an excuse. I've never done anything like that. Maybe he really pissed me off, I don't deny it, but not so much that I'd want to kill him. There's got to be more to it than that."

"The answer is inside your head, and in Lynch's, but for the time being he can't tell us anything."

"My God."

"You clearly weren't well when you acted as you did. The same is true of the days leading up to it. Holly says that for an entire month you held on to the photos from the restaurant, keeping them secret, which she says wasn't like you. She's sure you normally would have said something to her about it."

He nodded.

There had to be something else. It was hard to speculate about Lynch, the friend who Ted couldn't remember at all. Maybe Lynch knew something about Ted that could hurt Holly...

Laura saw that he was worried. "What are you thinking?"

"Did Holly tell you anything about Lynch? Any suspicions? I imagine that if she had an affair with him, it was because she thought he was a good man, but sometimes, you know, we get mixed up with the wrong person."

"I know what you mean. Look, I'll be honest with you. Holly told me that Lynch is a calm sort of guy, nice, considerate. Though he and Holly began to have feelings for each other, he was the one who refused to go any further until you and she had come to a verbal agreement about the divorce. Lynch wanted to talk to you and explain everything. Of course, that doesn't mean there wasn't something else; it's just what Holly thinks of him."

"Holly is a very intuitive person. If that's what she said, it's most likely true."

"I think the same as you, though," Laura said. She searched for something in a folder full of plastic envelopes. "Something must have made you react to Lynch like that. Maybe something you discovered when you followed him. I haven't talked to the private detective who worked for you, but Holly did, and the guy says that all he did was tail them and give you the photos."

"The detective's name is Peterson, isn't it?"

"You remember him?"

"Wendell told me about him. God, all this time I've been talking about someone who doesn't exist. How is that possible?"

"Your friendship with Lynch, your relationship with Holly, the lakeshore house—they're all part of Wendell. Your mind has compartmentalized that information, and now it belongs to him. In a sense, you could say that you don't have access to it. You seem to have a locked room inside your head now."

Open the door.

Laura spoke measuredly. It was as if with each word she was testing Ted's capacity to continue assimilating information.

"What do you have there?" Ted asked. Laura had pulled a photograph from the folder. It was small and had been taken years ago.

It showed a young Ted and Lynch at a college dorm party, smiling next to a poster of Uma Thurman in *Pulp Fiction*. For Ted, the poster immediately brought back memories. It had hung in the hallway outside his dorm room. Uma had dark hair and was smoking provocatively. The Ted in the photo was handsome, thin, with hair down to his shoulders. He wore a bandanna like Axl Rose and had a plastic cup in his hand. At his side, Lynch wore the same jovial smile as when he rang the doorbell at Ted's house in the imagined vision. His good looks were magnetic.

"I remember that poster perfectly. But not Lynch. Looks like we were close."

Laura nodded. She returned the photo to the folder.

"In my dream, there was something new about the lakeside house," Ted said. "A feeling of familiarity to the place. Also, when I woke up today I realized something: I couldn't recall Wendell's face. I wasn't sure what color his eyes were; his features were blurry in my mind. Was he thin? Did he wear glasses? I couldn't quite tell."

"As for Wendell, there's something I want to ask you," Laura said. "Does his name mean anything to you?"

Ted thought about it.

"If you mean did I ever know anybody with that name, the answer is no. At least not so far as I can remember. Which, under the circumstances, isn't very far."

Laura nodded.

"I can't believe I put a man into a coma," Ted said, holding his head and shaking it over and over.

"Don't think about it, Ted. I'm convinced that part of your psychosis began before the incident with Lynch. Long before. I gave it a lot of thought before I revealed to you that Wendell doesn't exist, that he's really a part of you in disguise."

"Are you afraid I might go back into one of those cycles?"

"I doubt it. We've come too far."

"Too far?"

"Exactly. Think about the first cycle. In it, you were going to take your life because of a brain tumor. In turn, you had to kill Wendell, the part of you that knew the truth about Holly's affair, and also the part that was responsible for beating Lynch. In a certain sense, it constituted a perfect cycle. My theory is that you had planned to kill yourself after your encounter with Lynch, but your judgment was clouded and you didn't do it. Then your mind devised this cycle, repeating it over and over, in which you killed Wendell and everything he represented."

"I see where you're going," Ted said. "In that cycle, I didn't even have any problems with Holly."

"It was the perfect suicide."

"And Blaine? Where does he come in?"

This was the only question Laura had feared, the one she had no answer for since her discovery of the Buzz Lightyear sticker. She didn't want to mention that just yet, so she merely gave him the answer she would have given only two days earlier.

"You had to find a way to justify murdering Wendell, and your mind conceived of this brilliant plan of suicidal people killing each other. Think: What's the best way to dissuade a man from taking his own life? By appealing to his awareness of how hard his suicide will be on his family. That's the key. I'm sure that these same questions were in your head while you were weighing the idea. You see, Ted, why I say the first cycle was the perfect suicide? In it, you even solved the problem of how it would affect your loved ones. Everything worked perfectly. And the Blaine case was all over the news in the days before you were admitted to Lavender; I collected tons of newspaper articles about it. Most likely you used it to construct the cycle. And bear in mind another important factor: Lynch was a stranger to you. Only Wendell knew him."

"Why did our sessions form part of the cycle? Why weren't they like the rest of my life at Lavender, which I have no recollection of?"

"Well, at first they didn't enter into it. It was only when we began to explore your past that our sessions started bursting into the cycles, breaking them open. Do you have the horseshoe?"

Ted nodded. He could feel the weight of it in his pocket.

"That was when the first cracks appeared in the first cycle. Memories of your girls running up the path to the lakeside house, for example. That was your unconscious trying to find a way to shatter that idyllic ending, to unmask Wendell."

Ted nodded in amazement. He understood.

"That's why I didn't kill him in the second cycle," he said, recalling it.

"Exactly. In the second cycle, you were already aware that Wendell and Lynch actually knew each other, that they'd been college roommates. That was *your* life history, Ted! All you were doing was discovering your own ties to Lynch. But Wendell didn't want to be unmasked, because that would mean outing that part of yourself, so he tried getting you angry at Lynch, among other things, by showing you the photo at the restaurant. Remember, in the second cycle you also knew about your problems with Holly. In each cycle, you came closer to reality."

"That's why Wendell was trying to set me against you and Roger. God, I'm still thinking of the guy as if he really existed."

Look, Ted, there's some information up here, in your head—Wendell bent over and pointed his index finger at Ted's forehead—*that's bad news for you. For me, too—I won't deny it.*

"Now I understand why Holly doesn't want to see me," Ted said.

"Actually, Holly does want to see you."

"Really?"

"She understands that you would never have hurt Lynch under normal circumstances. She's confident that the treatment you're getting here will turn you back into the person you always were."

"So you were able to talk to her?"

Laura nodded.

"I talked with her today, first thing, just as I promised you. Now that we've made all this progress, I honestly think it might be a good idea for you to see the girls. Holly has said she's ready to bring them with her whenever we ask."

A mixture of happiness and anxiety rushed over Ted, but his memories of happier times with his daughters prevailed—a collage of images of Nadine and Cindy, of hugs, of good night kisses, of bedtime stories. The tears soon came. He was crying for the first time since he arrived at Lavender seven months earlier.

46

MARCUS WAS instructing his secretary not to let anyone interrupt him—he had to go over the expense reports and forward them to the general director—when Laura appeared in the hallway. In an instant his priorities changed.

"What a pleasant surprise!" he said when he saw her.

His secretary, who knew him better than his own mother did, peered over the round rims of her glasses at him, her expression a mix of reproach and pity.

"Are you busy now?" Laura asked as she walked into his office.

He followed her. "No more than usual. You look happy. Did something happen?"

"Is it that obvious?"

"Just a little."

"I'm pleased," she admitted. "I talked with Ted about what he did to Lynch, about Wendell, about everything. He had a revealing dream last night in which he almost discovered it by himself. I felt it was the right moment, and I wasn't wrong."

"I'm so glad." Marcus pushed aside the papers cluttering his desk.

"You're really not busy?"

"Not at all," he said, lowering his voice.

"I think I'm getting very near the bottom of it all, Marcus."

"I'm happy for you."

"You're part of the story now. You can't get away from me." She winked at him.

Marcus laughed.

"I don't know if that's a good thing or a bad thing. But when you write your book about it, do me a favor and leave out our little deal to get McKay transferred to my wing."

"Speaking of which, I never thanked you enough for that. I drag you into my crazy schemes and you're always there for me. Thank you."

"As I said, I'm glad I was able to help."

"Well, I didn't come just to tell you that, or to interrupt you while you're preparing the expense reports." Laura pointed to the documents Marcus had piled to one side. "Want to come over to my house tomorrow for dinner?"

"Of course."

"Terrific. Is seven okay?"

"I'll be there tomorrow at seven."

"I'll ask my sister to come pick up Walter. He loves spending the night with his older cousins, and they love to spoil him."

Marcus didn't react right away. Was this a date?

Laura stood up. "So I'll see you tomorrow," she announced. "I'll let you get on with your work..."

He gave her one last smile before closing the door. Back in the lobby, Laura stifled a laugh. Dropping the invitation on him like that had been a little mean of her, she knew. Marcus had been expecting another request for a favor at work, not an invitation to dinner at her house.

Claudia caught the mischievous look on Laura's face and glared at her with her watchdog eyes. Dr. Hill immediately composed herself and nodded good-bye to the secretary.

47

WALTER SAT on the living room sofa with his backpack and a bag of carefully chosen toys, waiting. Though his aunt wasn't coming for him until six, he had insisted on being ready way in advance. *In case Aunt Deedee gets here early*. The fact was, Walter never slept over at anyone's house, not even his father's (since the jerk had never bothered to fix up a bedroom for his son), except at the house of Aunt Deedee and her daughters, Grace and Michelle, his cousins.

Laura came downstairs and saw him sitting there, quiet and eager, clutching his backpack and bag, ready to bolt from the house as soon as the doorbell rang. Her heart melted. He was sitting in the same spot where he usually waited for his father, whose habit of canceling his plans at the last minute was clearly undermining Walter's self-esteem. Another reason to despise her ex, Laura thought.

"Will she come, Mommy?"

She sat next to him and stroked his cheek.

"Of course she will."

Walter nodded, relieved. Just then he seemed to notice the dress his mother was wearing and the makeup she had put on. He looked her up and down.

"Is Marcus your boyfriend?"

Laura thought the question was hilarious, but when she saw Walter's serious expression she maintained her composure. She smiled gently.

"Marcus is my friend. We work together and have lots in common."

He nodded.

"You're wearing a dress."

"Do you like it?"

"Yes." Walter thought over what he should say before he went on. "Daddy has girlfriends. Marcus could be your boyfriend. Grace has a boyfriend, too, but that's a secret. Aunt Deedee doesn't know about him."

"For now, Mommy doesn't have any boyfriends. If that changes, I'll let you know, okay?"

Walter seemed to approve.

Deedee arrived at that moment. Walter jumped up and, still clutching his things, ran to the front door. He surprised his aunt before she could ring the bell.

"How's my favorite nephew?"

Deedee gave Walter a bear hug.

"I thought you weren't coming. Are my cousins here?"

"They stayed home to wait for you. I had to run a few errands first."

Still hugging Walter, Deedee glanced over his shoulder. When she saw how Laura was dressed, she mimed a "Wow" that her big sister didn't miss.

"Jessica Rabbit wants her dress back," Deedee said.

Laura frowned.

"Who's Jessica Rabbit?" Walter asked.

"Nobody," Laura said. "Your aunt is acting smart."

"Yeah, she's very smart," Walter said, the sarcastic banter of the two sisters going right over his head.

"Well, Walt, time for us to skedaddle. Michelle has been asking about you all day long."

"Bye, Mommy!" Walter couldn't stop smiling. He went over to Laura and she crouched down to give him a kiss.

Deedee took advantage of his turned back and pointed at Laura's dress and gave it a thumbs-up.

"Say hi to the girls for me," Laura said. "Have a great time!"

"You too!" Deedee replied as they went out the door.

Laura stood in the front yard and waved good-bye. She lingered there for a minute or more after the car vanished down Embers Lane.

Back inside, she checked to see how the dinner was doing. She had decided to make a roast with beets and potatoes, a dish she found easy to slap together. The only disadvantage was the three hours plus that it had to remain in the oven, but it was almost done.

Marcus was punctual. He gave her the bottle of wine he had insisted on bringing, and he praised her dress. He looked very elegant himself, in dress pants, a linen sports coat, and a modern gray hat that Laura didn't think she had seen before.

"It smells wonderful!"

"I'm warning you: cooking isn't my strong point, though I do have my specialties. Come on. Let's have a glass of wine while things finish cooking."

The table was set, but instead of sitting there, they went to the living room sofa and made small talk for a while: about Walter, about the hospital. The conversation drifted naturally toward film, in which they already knew they had similar interests, and then a seemingly harmless comment by Marcus led them to a subject he would rather have avoided: his recently defunct relationship with Carmen. Anyway, his interest in Laura had long been obvious, and she was a very perceptive and intelligent woman. Not talking about the elephant in the room wouldn't have made it invisible.

Dinner was relaxed. The roast was exquisite, and Marcus allowed himself to relish the moment. He wasn't going to tell Laura that he thought about her constantly while she was raising a forkful of roast beet to her mouth.

"I read your draft account of the first cycle," he said, referring to a document Laura had emailed him.

Laura instantly perked up. "What did you think of it?"

"I read it yesterday, in one sitting," Marcus said. It was incredible how talking about his field of knowledge immediately gave him back his confidence. "I found it extremely interesting. Now I have a better understanding of your—"

"Obsession."

Marcus laughed.

"I was going to say your dedication and enthusiasm. But it's true, the case has got you a little obsessed. First, let me tell you that I agree with your manner of presenting it. From the patient's point of view. It's spot-on correct. Each cycle was real for Ted; substituting them for an outsider's account of his first months in the hospital is a very useful way of presenting things from his perspective. In fact, I think your presentation was what brought one interesting fact to mind for me."

Laura's eyes widened.

"What is it? Wait a second, wait a second—help me carry all this to the kitchen. We'll have some coffee and you'll tell me all about it. I know myself. I won't be able to stop."

This was exactly what Marcus had feared.

"Sounds perfect."

They made two trips to the kitchen in silence, crossing paths in the middle, in an everyday ritual of mutual trust. Marcus pictured doing this day after day, and he felt a shiver; that's how foolish he was.

When the coffee was ready they went back to the living room.

"I agree with you that the first cycle is perfect, a closed cycle," Marcus said. "Wendell represents everything that Ted hates about himself, and dissociating himself from Wendell in order to kill him seems reasonable. Now that we've seen the sticker in Blaine's house, it's logical to assume that every sequence in the cycle has a basis in reality."

"That's true," Laura agreed.

"Let me run through them and see if we're on the same page about the moment when each of them diverged from reality, because that's where we might find the most interesting points for analysis."

Laura listened intently, hands clasped around her coffee cup.

"Let's start with the suicide itself," Marcus said. "The part where the young Lynch interrupts and makes his eloquent proposal. That's easy enough: Ted wanted to kill himself at some point, for reasons we don't know, and when he was about to do it, something or someone interrupted him. Maybe Lynch himself, though for a completely different reason than Ted recalls."

"I don't think it was Lynch, but I do agree that Ted had reached the point of trying to take his own life."

"The next event is Blaine's murder. Ted went to his house, hid in the closet, and saw the sticker. He clearly didn't go there to kill Blaine, but he must have been there, since we've seen the sticker with our own eyes. That's the piece that doesn't fit."

"I've been thinking it over, and I believe we have to discard the possibility that Ted saw the sticker farther back in the past—for example, when other people were living there. In that case, how could he have learned that Blaine later lived in the same house? That makes no sense."

"Good point. There was no way to tie the sticker to the articles about Blaine in the papers. Therefore we can conclude that Ted was in the house recently, hiding in that closet. From that point, reality diverges, and we don't know in what direction. Do you rule out the possibility that he meant to kill Blaine?"

"I don't rule anything out. What Ted did to Lynch with the lamp was different. There was no planning involved."

"You're right. Let's keep going. The next episode is his visit to the lawyer, Robichaud, his childhood friend. You've talked to him, haven't you?"

"Yes. But he didn't tell me much more than what I wrote in the draft. Ted went to him to draw up a will. He told Robichaud he wanted a lawyer who didn't belong to his usual circle, which was very reasonable under the circumstances."

"In any case, the collection of figures from his past at Robichaud's house, all those schoolmates he had never seen again, shows how he felt about those years, his regrets about how he had behaved with some of them. It was a smart move on your part to emphasize his past, especially his chess playing, to bring him back to reality."

"Thanks. Chess was there all along, in every one of his dreams, like a hook I could reel him in with. I wish I'd seen it earlier."

"It wouldn't have changed much. It might not even have worked."

"Possibly."

"Continuing the timeline, we come to his visit to Lynch's office," Marcus said. "And that's what I wanted to get to. The key is establishing exactly where the line between reality and Ted's paranoia goes. We know he went to the office and met Lynch's secretary, Nina, there. Now, she says she came in late that day—isn't that right?"

"It is."

"But what if she's lying? What if, as in all the other sequences in the first cycle, this first part really happened?"

Laura thought about it.

"Do you think the police checked out her story?"

Laura shook her head. The detective in charge of the brief investigation, a young man named Carl Brater who met with Laura twice after Ted was admitted to Lavender, seemed to focus solely on the question of who had committed the assault. There was no doubt that Ted had beaten Lynch nearly to death. The police found him at the scene of the crime, holding the bloody lamp; his prints were everywhere. Why look into whether his secretary had lied about some insignificant detail?

"What I mean," Marcus said, "is that if every sequence in the first cycle has roots in reality, as the sticker should lead us to believe, then it's possible that Ted really did see Nina that day. Otherwise, why include her? She doesn't fit any pattern, at least none that I can see. Seeing his childhood friends at Robichaud's house is another matter."

Laura had never paid much attention to Ted's meeting with Nina, focusing instead on his later conversation with Lynch. She realized now that she'd been wrong to neglect this angle. Why even mention the secretary if she'd come in late that day? What purpose could there be? She remembered something her father, an avid fan of detective stories, used to say: when a detail seems to play no role in the story, focus on it, because it is undoubtedly significant. Nina's presence seemed to be one such detail.

"According to Ted's own version," Marcus added, "he let her go when he started talking to Lynch, and Lynch was the one who asked her not to call the police. Why not suppose that this was where Ted's delirium begins?"

Laura was experiencing the nervous tension she always felt when she was on the verge of glimpsing some revelatory truth. Marcus's words made perfect sense. She sprang to her feet.

"What is it?"

"Just a second, please."

She returned a minute later carrying a blue folder.

"It's a copy of the police report," Laura announced. "I told Brater it might be important for the treatment and he gave it to me."

"A bit careless on his part."

"I can be persuasive when the situation demands it," she said, giving her hair a quick flip before sitting down. She opened the folder. "Nina's address ought to be here, along with her testimony."

Marcus stared openly at her, taking advantage of how absorbed she was in the document. Laura stopped when she came across the photos of Lynch's office: a few wide-angle shots, a close-up of the body on the floor, another of the bronze lamp used in beating the lawyer, the wound to his head, the blows to his face...They were photocopies, so the quality was abysmal. One picture in particular grabbed Laura's attention. She sat looking at it. Marcus leaned over but didn't see anything special about it. It was the reception area, where Nina's desk stood.

"There," Laura said, pointing to a corner of the desk.

It was the box from Dunkin' Donuts.

"Those are the doughnuts Nina brought to the office that day," Laura said. "She even offered one to Ted."

"Of course! Another detail that should have alerted us. This shows that Nina was with Ted! And no doubt she was there when Lynch arrived."

Laura stood up again, visibly losing her cool.

"I can't believe it. Why didn't she say anything?"

"Well, if things happened as we think they did, she left before Ted beat Lynch. It was a personal matter between friends."

"But he had a gun!"

"If Lynch asked her not to tell the police, perhaps she was just following his instructions. And the next day, when the police told her that her boss was in a coma and that they had caught the guy who did it, she may have convinced herself that it made no sense to tell them that she'd been there. What did she say in her statement?"

"That she'd asked for the day off to take care of some personal stuff. I doubt that Brater checked out her story." Laura looked through the sheets in the file. "Here it is. What she said, to be exact, was that she had an appointment with the eye doctor. I have her phone number and address. Tomorrow I'll go see her early in the morning before heading to the hospital."

"Want me to go with you?"

"No need." Laura sat down, very close to Marcus this time. "Can you imagine what this means? If Nina was able to hear any of their conversation—the real conversation—then we might find out why Ted beat Lynch like that. You're a genius, Marcus!"

Laura put her hands on Marcus's cheeks, unable to hide her euphoria. Yet after a brief but intense look into his eyes, she put her hands down and withdrew.

The rest of their dinner party went on in more or less the same way. They talked about the case and how her visit to Nina might go the next day. Marcus kept struggling with the inner voice telling him that time was running short, that he needed to do something, that this opportunity was slipping away and that it would get harder and harder for him to reveal his feelings. Even Laura seemed a bit disconcerted. There were several uncomfortable silences, and subtle looks of incomprehension, and nothing seemed to give Marcus the confidence he needed to make the leap into the unknown.

Finally she said she was feeling sort of tired and she wanted to go see Nina nice and early the next morning so she would find her at home. Marcus said he was a little tired, too; he asked her to call him the next day and tell him how things went with Lynch's secretary. She said she would. They walked in silence to the front door.

He stopped at the front closet, took out the hat he'd bought specially to impress her, and put it on very slowly, as if he were pondering some important question (which in fact he was). This was his last chance.

"I had a great time," he said.

He didn't move. Laura waited as long as she could. At last she went to him, put her hand on his shoulder, and kissed him on the cheek.

"I really enjoyed it, too. I'll call you tomorrow."

Marcus walked across the darkened lawn, turning twice to wave goodbye to Laura, brooding over his regret and reproaching himself with every step he took toward the car. She was in shadow now, a look of disappointment sketched on her invisible face.

48

LAURA SUPPOSED that Nina wouldn't be going to work on a Saturday, but she didn't want to risk missing her, so at half past seven that morning she rang the doorbell at the young woman's modest apartment on Merrimack. Laura had hardly slept, in part because her dinner with Marcus hadn't gone in the direction she had expected but mainly because she was sure that Lynch's secretary would have something to tell her. Something revealing.

A sleepy face peeked out a window and disappeared. A second later a grumpy, disheveled Nina cracked the door open just wide enough to bark at Laura.

"Who is it?"

"Nina Jones?"

"Who are *you?*" the young woman said.

"Dr. Laura Hill. Ted McKay is my patient."

She expected to see a reaction from the woman. Nina's eyes, two slits held tight against the early morning sun, opened slightly.

"I don't know anybody named—"

"The man who left your former boss in a coma," Laura added. She waved the folder in her left hand. "Your declaration to Detective Brater indicates that you did know McKay. And he has confirmed it to me. May I come in?"

The door opened.

"It isn't even eight yet," Nina greeted her. She was wearing a baggy T-shirt and shorts. She turned around and went to a table covered with empty bottles, plastic cups, and disposable plates. Laura followed her. They sat down.

"What'd you say your name was?"

"Laura."

The young woman nodded. "Any news about Mr. Lynch?"

"Still in a coma. The prognosis isn't very promising."

"I'm sorry. I'm really sorry." Nina sat in her chair like a young girl, holding her knees to her chest. "I didn't work for him very long, barely got to know him. He was very reserved, and a little odd, but he was a good person. Didn't the guy who beat him go to prison?"

"Ted McKay is at Lavender Memorial Hospital, in the maximum security wing."

Nina nodded. She seemed truly surprised.

"I know you were there on that day, Nina. I understand why you felt no need to tell it to Detective Brater, and I don't think there's any need to tell him now, but it might be important for you to talk to me."

Nina denied it without much conviction. Laura had come prepared to use as much persuasion as necessary, to threaten turning her over to the police if necessary, but she found a defenseless, terrified young woman and she knew immediately that threats would be the wrong approach for her. Nina felt the burden of having misled the police, and apparently that was enough. Laura went on.

"The police report has photographs that show the Dunkin' Donuts box you brought in that morning. Besides, Ted has made a lot of progress lately, and he remembers some of what happened that day: how he waited for you by the door to the office and how he forced you to let him in. You waited for Lynch with him and he threatened you with a pistol."

That was enough. Nina was ready to break.

"Don't worry," Laura reassured her. "Like I said, I'm not with the police. I'm a doctor, and whatever you say will be held in confidence. Your account may be vital for curing Ted McKay. Help me understand why he did it. He and Lynch were college buddies—did you know that?"

"No."

"Nina, I need you to tell me what happened that day."

"You already practically said it all."

"Not what happened when Lynch got to the office. I need you to remember every detail."

Nina rubbed her face and sighed.

"Can I make myself some coffee? I didn't sleep well."

Laura nodded.

"Would you like some?"

"Actually, I would. I didn't sleep well, either."

While the water was heating, Nina ran to the bathroom, brushed her teeth, and combed her hair. When she returned, now fully awake, she looked like a different person. She poured the coffee and set the cups on a corner of the table. She quickly cleared the bottles and plastic cups.

"Sorry about the mess. It was my roommate's birthday."

"Don't sweat it. Have you found work?"

"Yes, another secretarial job. For another attorney."

"I'm glad." Laura got straight to the point. "Nina, please tell me what happened that day."

"First off, I want to say that if I didn't tell the police I was there that morning, it was because that's what Lynch asked me to do, and also because the detective told me they'd already caught the guy. And the truth is, he didn't seem very interested in what I had to say."

"I understand."

"What did you say the guy's name was?"

"Ted McKay. You'd never seen him at the office before?"

"No, never. He was hiding in the shadows, waiting for me. He had a gun, and he was off his rocker. He really gave me a scare. He told me he wasn't going to hurt me, asked me about the other offices, and told me we were going to wait for Lynch because he needed to talk with him. We were there for a while, several minutes—I don't know how long. What I do know is that McKay changed during that time: he said he was sorry he had scared me, he promised nothing would happen to me. At first I didn't even want to see his face."

"What do you mean by he 'changed'?"

"I mean, for a moment he seemed lost, sorry he'd shown up like that. Now that you tell me the guy's crazy, I understand it all a lot better. He even told me I could have a doughnut."

"Ted would never have hurt you."

Nina wasn't so sure.

"Maybe not. Anyway, he didn't. We waited for Lynch in his office. When Lynch walked in, he saw me sitting at his desk and knew something was wrong. But when he saw McKay standing by one of his filing cabinets, his face was transformed. Like he turned to stone. Like he'd seen a ghost. By then I had started to relax a little, but when I saw his reaction I was more scared than ever. Lynch couldn't stop staring at McKay..."

Nina drank half her cup of coffee. She put it down on the saucer and went on.

"Suddenly Lynch looked at me as if he'd forgotten I was sitting there. He told me him and Ted were friends, so not to worry. At the time I didn't think it was true—I thought he was just saying that to get me to chill. He asked McKay to let me go, but at first McKay wouldn't agree. Actually, more like he couldn't hear Lynch. Lynch was trying to calm him down, slowly moving closer with his arms out, telling him everything was going to be all right, that he shouldn't do anything he'd regret, and that he and some girl named Holly were going to tell him about it sooner or later—they were just waiting for the right time."

Laura couldn't hide her surprise.

"That's right," Nina added. "I got it right away, too. Lynch and McKay's wife were having an affair, and McKay had just found out. I can't remember if he was any more specific about it, but at the moment nothing could have been clearer. That's what you think, too, isn't it?"

Actually, what Laura felt was disappointment, because the truth was that she had been hoping Ted's motive for going to the office wasn't to confront Lynch over the affair with Holly. Ted had known about it for weeks. Why such an explosive reaction at this point?

"But McKay told Lynch he hadn't come there to talk about that," Nina said.

That's it!

The young woman finished her coffee in one quick gulp and went on.

"Lynch was very nervous. I'd never seen him like that. He asked McKay to let me go, said I didn't have anything to do with it, and McKay agreed. He told me if I called the police it would just make things worse. I would have done it anyway, but Lynch also asked me not to. I hadn't known him very long, but I could tell he was asking me sincerely—it wasn't just an act to make McKay think the opposite. I don't know if they were mixed up in some sort of dirty business or what, and frankly I don't want to find out. But Lynch asked me not to tell the police, so I didn't. I—I had no way of knowing what would happen next."

"You did what Lynch asked you. If you had called the police, no doubt Lynch would be dead."

"That's what McKay told me! If the police showed up, he'd shoot Lynch on the spot."

"Nina, are you sure Ted said his visit had nothing to do with his wife's affair?"

"I'm sure. When I left the office, I went to my desk to get my handbag. At that moment I heard McKay on the other side of the door. He was furious."

"What did he say?"

"He said, 'You trailed me to Blaine's house. I saw you.' I remember the name perfectly because my old boyfriend had a book with that title and it stuck in my memory."

49

THAT SATURDAY Ted played chess for the first time. He didn't lose a single game, of course, not even when he held back and left openings for his opponents. None of them had a strategic understanding of the game; they knew only the basic moves and a few simple tactics, so Ted beat them almost without trying. He started out cautiously, afraid that his superior skill might generate some sort of resentment among them, but the effect was the exact opposite. Sketch himself, practically unbeatable in C wing, displayed wonder and respect. Between games, Ted spoke to them of his time as a child chess prodigy, about the tournaments, and he told them he could teach them if they wanted. They all agreed, including Lester, who could be pretty reasonable when he wasn't a prisoner of his extraterrestrial hallucinations.

The following day, in the showers, Sketch revealed that the patients in B wing also played chess. C wing had competed against them once and had gotten thrashed. The big guy, soaped up and smiling from ear to ear, told Ted that if they had another tournament and C wing had him on their side, they'd easily win. Sketch got an erection fantasizing about that possibility.

Ted quickly fit in at Lavender. He was beginning to get to know the three well-defined groups. In addition to the Chessmen, there were the Lunatics: older, worn down by years of medication and imprisonment. Some of them had severe problems and spent most of their time in front of the TV, or they simply isolated themselves in some nook where they stared vacantly. The third group was the Walkers, who preferred to be outdoors, either on the basketball court or anywhere in the enormous yard, walking, normally in pairs.

Mike didn't belong to any of these groups; he seemed above them all. Ted was starting to wonder why he had been drawn to Mike in the first place. The guy had never shared his room with anyone, for example, and now...

Mike said hello. He was on his usual bench, reading a tattered book—not the one he'd been reading earlier that morning.

"You're a reading machine."

Mike dog-eared the page he was on and set the book aside. He never used a bookmark.

"It's the only way to get out of here," he reflected.

Ted sat down beside him. Several patients observed them closely, paying attention to the ritual by which they were getting to know each other, but none of them joined in.

"No games with your chess buddies today?" Mike asked in a serious tone. Ted was getting used to his dry sense of humor.

"Not today. Chess has the ability to transport you, focus your mind completely on the game, and I need to focus on other things."

"Still thinking about your friend?"

"Yeah." Ted reached into his pocket for the photo of himself and Lynch by the Uma Thurman poster. "I remember all of this—the dorm, the room, the damn poster—but not him."

"That valve will open sooner or later, I promise. I've been through it. Almost everybody here has. Your brain keeps that valve closed because it can't stand the pressure. When it heals and is ready for it, it opens it up again. It'll happen from one moment to the next."

"It sort of terrifies me. What could justify beating a friend and putting him in a coma?" Ted shook his head. "When I was in high school, I liked to get into trouble. I was a mixed-up kid, I guess. Over time, I put that temperament behind me. I'm a peaceful person. I can't understand what could have happened."

"Maybe your wife can throw some light on it. Is her visit still on for tomorrow?"

"Yes. Her and the girls. It's silly, but I'm nervous about it. Do you have kids?"

Mike shook his head, gazing vacantly.

"I had a godson."

They remained silent for a few minutes.

"But you get my point, don't you?" Ted insisted. "How can my own family make me nervous? My girls! I want to see them more than anything in the world."

"It isn't easy for us to be seen like this—locked up."

"Exactly. I'm supposed to be out there, with them, watching them grow up. Protecting them."

"It'll all go fine. You'll see."

Maybe the time had come to let himself be seen as vulnerable for once in his fucking life, Ted thought.

"Hey, Mike, about that possum..."

Mike looked at him. "Did you see it again?"

"No."

"Look, Ted, what I just said is true. Your head will heal, and it will open that door when the moment comes. You'll remember your friend, and also the reason why you beat him like that. All these 'cycles' you told me about are your mind's attempt to create an illusion to protect you. Like the backdrops they use in plays. But backdrops come down, sooner or later, and you see what's behind them. The possum might take you behind the curtain before you're ready to see it. And that could be dangerous."

50

MARCUS HAD hardly slept, torturing himself all night over every detail of his date with Laura and regretting every lost opportunity. At lunchtime he had no choice but to go to the cafeteria, but he picked a small table for four that most people avoided because it was right next to the kitchen door. To make it clear that he didn't want to be disturbed, he brought along a thick pathology manual that he had no intention of reading. He propped the manual next to the salad plate he planned to scarf down in record time.

Laura, who rarely ate lunch at the same time as the others, walked into the cafeteria just then, looking everywhere. When she saw Marcus, she waved to him and hurried over.

"I need to talk to you."

Marcus realized from the excitement in her face that this wasn't a personal issue.

Better.

"Can I get you something to eat?"

"No, no, I'm fine. I don't have time. This morning I went to see Nina..."

Nina? Marcus hid his confusion for a few seconds while he placed the name: Lynch's secretary.

"Oh, really? Did she tell you anything?"

"Yes." Laura couldn't hide her enthusiasm. "It was easy after I showed her the picture we found of the Dunkin' Donuts box. It happened exactly the way Ted told it in the first cycle. She was there until they let her leave. But get a load of what happened next."

Laura was leaning across the table, her face just inches from his. Marcus had time to glance around and notice that some of his colleagues were watching them.

"What happened?"

"Before she left, she heard through the door that Ted was telling Lynch he knew he had tailed him to Blaine's house."

Marcus tried to fit this piece into the puzzle. He recognized that the case was gradually drawing him into its web, too. This simple statement could be telling them a couple of things. First, that Lynch also knew Blaine. Second, that Ted's visit to Blaine's house seemed to be what had led to the confrontation between the two friends and the subsequent attack.

"What do you think?" Laura asked.

"Well, there's no doubt about it now: Ted really did go to Blaine's house. And if you want to know my opinion, I doubt he went there with friendly intentions. I'm not saying he went to kill the guy, but to beat him up, at least."

"I think we're getting close, Marcus. Ted's motive for visiting Blaine that night must be the key to it all. Ted was planning to commit suicide, but first he wanted to settle accounts with Blaine. Over what? Lynch followed him there, maybe because he suspected something might happen, and he messed up Ted's plans. Does that sound about right?"

"Pretty much. The thing is to figure out what the connection was between Ted and Blaine."

"I think we're getting very close."

I only wish.

"Isn't his family coming to see him in the next few days?"

"Tomorrow. I'm a little nervous."

"Everything will be fine."

Laura nodded. Such an emotional encounter could be tremendously productive or cause a serious regression. She stood up.

"What are you going to do with all this, Laura?"

"I think the time has come to use it in our next session. Lay all my cards on the table."

Marcus nodded approvingly.

"Laura..."

"Yes?"

"I had a great time last night," Marcus said. It was as close as he could get to admitting how embarrassed he was at his cowardice.

Her reply came in the form of a pitying smile, enough to push Marcus over the edge into an abyss of gloom.

51

TED WAS waiting by himself in a small, tastefully decorated break room. Laura had given him the privilege of meeting with his family there instead of in the C wing visitation area, a cold and horrid room that looked every bit like a seven-year-old girl's image of a prison. Ted had asked, begged her to let him meet his daughters somewhere else, and she had agreed almost immediately. Laura informed him that she would need special permission to get him out of the wing, and it could take a little while to obtain it, but she had a room in mind that might do. Three guards would be watching the room from outside: one by the door and two at the window.

It was nice to look out an unbarred window, Ted thought, feeling about as nervous as he had ever been in his life. He was wearing blue linen trousers and a white shirt that hung loose on him; he'd lost some weight in recent months. His thinner frame wasn't the only sign of the passage of time: getting dressed up, even to this trivial degree, now irritated him. He sat on a love seat, laced his fingers, got up, and paced the room, walking around the table and sitting down again, now on one of the wooden chairs. He stood up again. There was a mini refrigerator in the corner and a few coffee cups on a shelf above it. He went over and unthinkingly began to align the cup handles. Laura had gone out a few minutes before to look for Holly and the girls.

The door opened.

Laura came in alone, her hands behind her back. She was hiding something.

"I'm sorry, Ted. Your daughters can't come. You were right: you did kill them. That's why you're locked up here. But at least someone came to see you..."

She rapidly held out her hands. One was empty. From the other hung a furry bag, which soon sprouted a snout and a naked tail and began twisting around. The possum was trying to break free, but Laura was holding it in her extended arm, steady as a statue. Then the possum screeched, a high-pitched sound like a child's shriek. Dr. Hill trembled and folded up into herself. A different Dr. Hill stood in her place, bright and happy.

"Ready for your visitors?"

The girls' voices were the prelude to the joyful shouts that assailed him and pushed him back onto the sofa.

"Daddyyyyyy!" the girls sang in perfect harmony.

Cindy and Nadine clung to Ted's body. He wrapped them in his arms. He was never letting them go.

Nadine was the first to pull away, worried that the drawing she had brought was getting wrinkled. She was the less demonstrative, quieter, and more rational of the two—the same temperament as Ted. Cindy was the living image of Holly: open-minded and theatrical, she almost always played the leader.

"My picture!" Nadine said.

"It isn't *your* picture. Daddy, we made you a picture. Why are you crying?"

Ted's eyes really were wet. He wiped them with his palm.

"Because I missed you two so much."

Cindy hugged him again.

"And we missed you!"

Nadine hesitated to join the hug. She looked at the drawing in her hands, and in the end she waited. Ted smiled at her over her sister's shoulder. There was a special connection between him and Nadine; they could say a lot with just a glance.

"We made you a picture," Cindy said when she let her father go. "Give it to him now, Nadine. Look: We're all on the beach. Here's Mommy, this is us—"

"You don't have to explain it," Nadine broke in.

Ted was looking at the drawing. It showed the four of them standing in front of the ocean. Ted held his fishing rod, Holly wore the red bikini, and each girl had a dolphin float. That was strange, because they had only one rubber dolphin; they had bought it the year before, and it soon became the source of constant fighting. Ted had suggested buying a second one, but Holly had insisted that the girls learn to share it, and of course she had been right.

"I love it. Thank you."

"Where are you going to keep it?"

"I have a really nice room here. I'll hang it on my wall so I can look at it every day."

"When are you coming back home?" Cindy didn't like beating around the bush. Another quality she'd inherited from her mother.

"I don't know, but I'm sure I'll be back soon."

Cindy didn't give up.

"Mommy says this isn't like the hospital Granddad was in. Is this where they make your head get better?"

Ted smiled.

"That's right. Daddy has headaches and dizzy spells, and here I'm getting all better. I already feel better."

Cindy gave a sigh of relief.

"Nadine said you'd have tubes coming out of your head."

"Did not!"

Ted hugged Nadine and pulled her close. He didn't want her to feel excluded.

"I'm glad you're asking questions," Ted said. "When you have head problems, you can't always solve them with an operation like the one Granddad had when he got his hip fixed. You have to take medicine—and do a lot of talking."

"Talking?"

"That's right. They call it therapy sessions."

"Like on that TV show Mommy likes!"

"Yes! Except here we do the sessions in person, not over the Internet like on Mommy's program."

"And if we tell Dr. Hill to do it over the Internet, could you come home?"

Ted laughed.

"It isn't as easy as on TV. The main thing is, I'll be home with you soon."

They both danced with excitement, and Ted seared their expressions—the need displayed on their faces to have their father at home with them—into his memory. Had he really tried to commit suicide? What had he been thinking? He found it harder and harder to understand the Ted who had assaulted his friend, the suicidal Ted who had planned to leave two seven-year-old girls alone with their mother.

He wasn't *that* Ted anymore—he was sure of it. He'd get out of Lavender and back to his business and his life. If he was lucky, Lynch would come out of his coma and Ted could beg him for forgiveness.

They spent more than half an hour together. They talked about school, about the dolls their mommy had bought them (Ariel and Alex), and about a new friend they'd made in their grandparents' neighborhood, a girl two years older than them. Her name was Haley, and since she had a sister in high school, she knew tons of stuff. She knew how to put on makeup, and she was teaching them! But that was a secret; Mommy couldn't find out. Ted promised not to tell. He almost cried when he realized that some things hadn't changed, and probably never would. Holly had always been put in the bad cop role.

And speaking of Holly, why hadn't she come in with the girls?

52

LAURA LED the girls away, promising them that they'd get to see their father again before they left. Then Holly came in, avoiding his gaze; her hair was cut shorter and tinted several shades darker than usual.

"Hi, Holly." Ted remained on the love seat. When he saw that she wasn't coming any closer, he stood up and went to the table.

"Hi, Ted. I'm glad to see you're doing better." Holly gave him a frail smile. She took one of the chairs. She was carrying her handbag, which she set on the table with excessive care.

"Have you spoken with Dr. Hill?" Ted sat down, leaving an empty chair between them.

"Yes, a few times, over the months. Today, too. She tells me you've made a lot of progress recently."

"It's true. Up until a few weeks ago—well, I don't really have any memories of that time. My mind has been a bit lost. But with Dr. Hill's help, I'm starting to remember."

Holly nodded.

"She told me it might help if we talked a little, you and I." Holly rubbed her forehead. "I don't want to play the victim, but it's been so hard for me. The girls ask about you all the time, and I didn't know what to tell them."

"I can imagine. I know it's my fault. I'm responsible for the bad decisions I've made. That's why I'm here. But I'm going to get out, Holly, and I'll be a proper father to the girls. Have you had any money problems?"

"No, no." Holly frowned, as if money were the last thing on earth that mattered. "Travis has been taking care of everything."

Holly watched Ted, waiting for his reaction.

"Oh, yeah. I remember Travis," he said.

She nodded.

They were silent for a while. But someone had to say it, and Ted figured it was his responsibility.

"How is Lynch doing?"

"I can't believe you don't remember Justin. You've never called him by his last name."

Ted shrugged.

"His condition is unchanged."

"You don't know how sorry I feel. I...I don't know what happened that day. My mind has erased it completely."

"Yes, that is what the doctor told me."

"I want you to know that as far as I am concerned, you and he—"

"Drop it, Ted. Please. The fact of the matter is, I don't need your permission."

"Sorry."

"Dr. Hill asked me to talk with you—about how things were going with us. Do you remember?"

Ted lowered his head.

"Pretty bad," he whispered. "I...was sort of distant."

"At least you can remember that." Holly didn't use a scolding tone, but Ted knew her, and he knew she was angry. "Ted, you would shut yourself in your study, you went to the lake house all the time, you constantly avoided me. When I managed to talk to you it was a monologue on my part, and a short one, because you know I always liked getting straight to the point. My presence was an annoyance to you. I saw it, you saw it, even the girls were starting to see it."

"Unfortunately, I do remember that part."

"I'm going to be honest with you, because that's what this is all about.

At the time I thought you had another woman. I thought your business trips, your long stays at the lake house, were all about some affair. It made perfect sense. And you know what? I even wished it were true, as ridiculous as that sounds. I knew you didn't love me anymore."

"Holly, I—"

"Let me finish, please. At first I made a few calls to your office, when you were off on one of your trips, and I talked with Travis or with your secretary. I'd get bits of information and check it against what you were telling me. Places, times, clients—it all added up. What didn't add up was what *I* was doing. It wasn't my style. I didn't want to spy on you like a private eye, the way you did to me later on..."

Holly paused.

"I didn't know what to do, Ted. When I tried talking with you, it was like you didn't give a shit. I knew I'd have to ask you for a divorce. I was getting used to the idea, gathering my courage to do it. That was around the time I talked to Justin. Not like I thought he'd know whether you were seeing another woman, or that he'd tell me if he did know. I talked to him because he knows you almost as well as I do, or maybe better, and I wanted to confirm what I was thinking: that you'd changed. Something had happened to you, and I didn't know what. I needed to verify it somehow, because it was either that or, well, or I was..."

"Going crazy." Ted finished her sentence with a smile. "Don't worry. It's not that bad."

Holly nodded but didn't smile.

"I talked to Justin, and he told me you and he almost never saw each other anymore, that you had pushed him away, just as you were pushing me away. We met a few more times, for no other purpose than to talk about you and what was happening to you, and that's how our relationship began. It wasn't the ideal situation—of course not. By the time we were aware that things were getting serious, you and I were hardly even on speaking terms, and you were even beginning to be distant toward the girls. I finally got up my courage and we talked. I asked you for a divorce."

"I do remember that. It was in the living room. After that, things weren't quite so tense."

"What I didn't know at the time was that you were seeing a doctor, or that you had asked a former schoolmate to draw up a will for you. Much less that you were keeping those photos of Justin and me in your safe. You had them there for more than a month, Ted! You knew all about it, and you didn't say anything to me, not even when I asked you for the divorce."

Ted spread his arms.

"I don't know why I didn't say anything, Holly. I really don't."

She nodded.

"I want to believe you."

"I don't know why I assaulted Lynch—Justin, I mean—but I swear it had nothing to do with you. With your relationship. That much I know. I want you to be happy, Holly—you and the girls."

Once more Holly nodded.

"Dr. Hill has kept me updated all along. I know it hasn't been easy for you. She told me you were living in...a sort of hallucination. Something like that."

"Something like that. It's horrible. It's as if someone had taken my last memories from before I was brought here and scrambled them all up. It's the closest thing to being in a dream you can imagine. There's a name: Wendell. Does it mean anything to you?"

"No. Dr. Hill also asked me, and I didn't know what to tell her. Who is Wendell?"

"Part of me, apparently. It's as if my mind had a storage room where some of my memories got put away, and I don't have the key to it. The storage room is Wendell. I've seen that man dozens of times, and it turns out, he's me. I know it sounds absurd. At first I was trapped in these cycles that repeated endlessly, but thanks to Dr. Hill I've been finding my way out of them. I feel I'm getting close to the truth, and pretty soon, once and for all, I'll unmask Wendell."

Ted was aware of how Holly was looking at him: as if he were crazy, of course. How else was she going to look at him? And of course he had no intention of telling her about the possum, or about what he'd seen through the patio door...

"What's wrong, Ted?"

He barely heard her. He jumped out of his chair and went to the sofa. He grabbed Cindy and Nadine's picture. The beach. The red bathing suit. A coincidence?

"Why did they draw us on the beach?" Ted asked.

Holly wrinkled her forehead.

"I don't know. Does it matter? I told them it would be a nice idea to bring you a picture, and they went up to their room to make you one. I guess our vacation was a happy memory, and that's why they picked it."

Ted sat down again without taking his eyes off the picture. Was there some other detail that might tell him something? Not at first. The fishing rod, the inflatable dolphins—no other revealing details. He ran his finger over the folding chairs, sunbathers, a few palm trees—nothing out of place. No crouching possums, no pink castles. Nothing to remind him of the visions he'd had.

"Do you feel all right, Ted? What's the big deal about the beach?"

"It's nothing. I had a dream a few days ago—that's all. It's a coincidence. In it, you were also wearing your red bikini..."

Holly didn't seem completely comfortable with the fact that her former husband was dreaming of her in a bikini.

Ted set the drawing aside.

They spent a few more minutes together, talking about banal family matters. Ted couldn't concentrate on the conversation. When the girls came back to tell him good-bye, he managed to forget about the drawing on the table. He gave them each a hug and promised he'd get out of Lavender soon so he could be with them.

A promise he never should have made, of course.

53

CINDY AND Nadine's drawing was the only thing on the cork bulletin board above Ted's desk. It was held up with four pieces of tape. Mike, walking down the corridor toward the yard, caught Ted looking at it and went over. He cleared his throat.

"They don't allow thumbtacks in here," he said. "If you're wondering why we have bulletin boards, you're not the first."

Ted turned around with a dull smile. Thumbtacks were the last thing he was thinking about.

"I need to see what's behind the backdrop, Mike."

It took Mike a few seconds to understand.

"The visit from your family got to you, didn't it?"

"That's not it. I mean, that's not the only thing. I need to find out the truth, get out of here, and be with my kids."

Mike agreed.

"How can I find the fucking possum, Mike?"

54

THURSDAY AFTERNOON. It had rained that morning, and a thick layer of clouds threatened more rain at any moment. It felt like a late fall day in the middle of spring.

Almost all the patients were in the common room. Sketch and Lolo were battling it out on the chessboard, now under Ted's supervision. He wasn't seen as a rival but as some sort of invincible force or font of wisdom. After each game, Ted could reproduce it from beginning to end without a single error and analyze each move, to the delight of his companions. They were fascinated by the possibility of defeating the guys from B wing in their next tournament. Lester, who was completely over his hostile feelings, also joined the team.

Mike walked in at some point and asked Ted to come outside with him. He was with Espósito, the pudgy inmate who said he could see animals and hardly ever talked. Ted asked no questions. The others tried to join the group, but Mike stopped them, first with a threatening glare and then with a direct warning not to even think of going outside. It surprised Ted to see how much terror the man could elicit when he showed his implacable, authoritarian side. Sketch, Lolo, and Lester silently nodded and returned to the chess table. Ted got his coat from one of the hooks and went out with Mike. Espósito followed them like a giant balloon bobbing along at ground level.

Other than the three of them, only two patients were roaming the yard. Mike called to them and they came over; he told them to go inside, and they obeyed without a word. Mike looked toward the building to make sure nobody was watching them at the windows. It wasn't that they were going to do anything suspect, he explained to Ted, but he still didn't want a whole gang of spectators glued to the glass. They headed for his usual bench, and Ted assumed they would sit there, as they'd done so many times before. He knew that this operation had something to do with the possum, but he had no idea what exactly they'd do or why the hell they had Espósito with them. As for Espósito, he was taking baby steps, letting his voluminous belly wag to and fro, and constantly throwing fearful glances at Mike. When they reached the bench, Mike asked Ted to grab one end because they were going to move it.

"Quick," Mike said as they lifted it. "Somebody might see what we're doing—not one of our people; maybe somebody from higher up—and then they'll tell a guard, if none of the guards are watching us already, that is. Just follow me and don't stop."

Ted and Mike crossed the yard, heading toward the basketball court. Espósito followed them. Indeed, when they were almost up to the circle in the center of the court, the main door opened and a guard and a nurse came out, waving their arms and yelling.

"Hey! What do you guys think you're doing?"

"Keep moving," Mike said. Just a couple of yards to go…"Good. Drop it here and sit down. You too, Espósito."

All three sat: Mike and Ted on the ends, Espósito in the middle. They had their backs to the building, so they couldn't see the approaching pair until they walked around the bench and stopped in front of it. The nurse was McManus.

"What the fuck are you guys up to?" said the guard.

It was a surreal scene. The three men on the bench remained expressionless, their hands in their pockets and their eyes avoiding McManus and the guard, as if sitting in the center of a basketball court were the most normal thing in the world.

"Well?"

Mike raised a hand to signal peace: *It's okay, I'll explain*. He pointed toward the tree by the bench's former location and slowly shook his head.

"It's terrible over there," he said with consternation. "The wind shakes the tree branches, and it's like it's raining on you. Terrible! Right, guys?"

"Bullshit, Dawson!" the guard said. "I was watching you. You didn't even try sitting."

Mike smiled and nodded: *You got me!* He signaled peace again and tried coming up with another excuse. He bent forward slightly and cupped his hand around his mouth: *Here's a secret for you*.

"These two guys aren't right in the head," he said, touching his own. "I don't know what they were thinking."

"Jesus, Dawson. Come off it. You know you can't go around moving shit wherever you want. Put the bench back where it goes. Right now."

"Listen, Myers, the bench is here already," Mike said. Again there was something menacing in his tone. "We'll sit here for a little while. You know how *we people* get..."

The guard shook his head. McManus spoke for the first time.

"Whatever. I'm going inside." She sounded annoyed.

Myers sighed.

"This better be the last time, Dawson. You know that when you do anything, next thing you know everybody's copying you. I don't want an army of crazy guys moving shit all over."

"Got it, boss. Now if you don't mind, we'd like to bask in the sunlight while it lasts. Who brought the suntan lotion, guys?"

The guard gave up and left. Mike dropped the jokey tone and turned to Ted.

"I hope this is worth it, buddy."

The line dividing the court lay only inches from Ted's feet.

The border between the real world and the world of madness, Mike had said.

"What are we doing here, Mike?"

"You wanted to see it, didn't you?"

Espósito obviously knew what they were talking about, because he shook, ill at ease, slamming lightly into both of his companions.

"Sit still, Espósito."

"Yeah, I do want to see it," Ted said. "But..."

"Here's the line." Mike pointed at the white line. It was almost invisible under the puddled water. "We're more likely to see it if we're by the line. Shit, I forgot my book!"

Ted sat and cringed, unable to say more. For a second he saw it all quite clearly, saw the real Mike—not the menacing man who at times seemed the most rational person in the world, with his books and his off-the-wall theories, but the raving mad inmate with the lifetime membership at Lavender Memorial. Ted looked around and realized how absurd it all was.

"You gotta believe," Espósito suddenly said. It was the first time Ted had heard his voice.

"Shut up, Espósito," Mike ordered.

And they were supposed to see the possum, just like that? Stupidly, Ted found himself peering at the back of the yard, where the trees and the benches were, looking for the nasty animal. He saw nothing.

"Mike, I'm sorry," Ted said, "but we've been here a million times before, even here by the line, and I've never seen anything. What makes you think this time will be different?"

"This big guy we have with us, right here," Mike said, patting Espósito on the back. "Didn't I tell you he's always seeing them? Espósito is like a floodlight, except he doesn't attract insects. Right, Espósito?"

"Been a l-l-long time since I saw one."

Mike laughed out loud.

"That lie's as big as your ass. Anyway, all three of us have seen them. The more of us, the better." Mike bent forward to see Ted and give him one of his withering looks. "Hey. You want to see it or not? 'Cause I'm doing all this for you."

Ted nodded.

"You're right. Sorry."

What the hell? What did he have to lose? If sitting in the middle of a basketball court with a couple of nutcases might help him discover the truth, why not give it a try?

"I'm ready," Ted said with conviction. "Come on, Espósito. Use your Aquaman powers and call them. Tell them to get here."

"That's not how it works," Espósito replied in his high-pitched voice.

Nobody asked him how it did work.

They waited in silence. The scene must have seemed more outlandish from the building. Three men sitting on a bench, with their backs to the hospital, in the center of the basketball court. It could have been a poster for a buddy flick. *Three Men and a Possum,* coming soon to this screen.

Twenty minutes later they were sitting in the same positions, not having said a word. Suddenly Ted smiled. He hadn't seen the possum, but he was thinking about his daughters. They sometimes played Whoever Talks First Loses, almost always at the urging of Nadine, who, tired of her sister's constant suggestions and ramblings, would challenge her to try to hold her tongue longer than she could. Ted wondered which of the three of them would be the first to speak. Not Espósito, who played Whoever Talks First Loses every minute of his life, while Dawson seemed to have sunk into some unfathomable reverie. Only Ted seemed unable to stop thinking about what they were doing. *The stupid thing they're doing.*

He was starting to get cold despite his thick coat. He settled back on the bench and in doing so felt the weight of the horseshoe in his pocket. That was it! At that moment he saw it clearly. The possum would never come near if he had the horseshoe with him. He jumped up and pulled the horseshoe from his pocket for his companions to see. He didn't say anything, but they seemed to understand. He thought of throwing it as far as he could, but he didn't want McManus and the other guy to come back and stir up trouble, so he merely walked to the edge of the court and left it there.

"Cover it up," he heard Espósito say.

"What the hell am I supposed to cover it with?" Ted said as he walked back.

"With your coat," Mike broke in. "Cover it."

Ted sighed. Wonderful. Now he'd be catching a cold. But still, he had to admit that covering up the horseshoe seemed, for some crazy reason, like the most rational thing in the world. He took off his coat and laid it over the horseshoe. This time he made sure nobody was watching from the windows. He rushed back to the bench, rubbing his hands together.

"Move over, Espósito. Let me sit in the middle."

The big guy slid over with no objection. "They're coming," he said at almost the same moment. There was no hesitation in his voice.

Ted paid close attention to everything around him. He didn't feel anything odd. But wasn't he also noticing that *something* was starting to change? And then he saw it. In one of the puddles just past the dividing line, a reflection of something moving caught his eye. Something red.

"Red is my favorite color," Espósito announced out of nowhere. His voice now sounded not only stronger but deeper than normal.

"What?" Ted asked.

Espósito didn't answer.

Again that reflection, unmistakable now. Holly's slender body in the red bikini appeared in the puddle, trembled when a gust of wind rippled the surface, and disappeared. But it had been there—Ted was sure of it. When he raised his head, he froze.

On one corner of the court stood the Disney princess castle. Not a reflection or a translucent apparition. The castle itself. Ted pointed at it.

"We can see it," Mike announced.

"It's my daughters' castle," Ted said in a quavering voice.

He stood up and walked toward it, alone. Halfway there he turned, saw Mike with a worried look on his face and Espósito trying to shrink his enormous body, sinking his head below his shoulders. They looked as though they were riding the most terrifying roller coaster on earth. Yet

Ted felt an urge, almost a need, to return and sit with them in the safety of the bench.

Beyond them, he saw McManus's silhouette through the glass door in the Lavender building. There was no way McManus could fail to see the castle. Ted resumed walking.

The castle was set on the border between the basketball court and the trees. When he reached it, he knelt down to look through one of the side windows. He had no intention of going inside; it didn't even seem like a good idea to touch it. For some reason he was convinced he'd see the possum in there, but he didn't. The castle was completely empty. He walked away, scratching his head. Snow White, Cinderella, Ariel, and Pocahontas were looking at him from one of the sidewalls. *What will you do now?* He walked around the castle. On the front wall he saw Esmeralda and, next to her, Sleeping Beauty; Ted couldn't remember her real name. Then an image hit him. He saw himself walking hand in hand with Cindy around this same castle at a Toys "R" Us, the little girl telling him each princess's story.

Aurora!

Cindy's voice gave him the answer. Sleeping Beauty's name was Aurora. He felt a shiver. This was the first memory he had stolen from Wendell. He continued to walk around the castle.

"That one is Belle," Cindy said.

"From *Beauty and the Beast,*" Ted noted.

"Of course. And that is Pocahontas, and this is Mulan."

There were no princesses around back—just a wall of bricks painted on the plywood. Ted stared at the wall. He took a few steps back, meaning only to get some perspective, when his right foot stepped on something hard. The possum! He jumped involuntarily and moved aside. But it wasn't the possum: it was a butcher knife.

"It isn't at Lavender, Daddy. It's just like the castle."

Ted bent down and picked up the knife. When he touched it, he noticed a red stain on the handle.

Red is my favorite color.

What was this knife doing here? He looked at Mike and Espósito, as if they might be able to give him an answer from afar. Not only did they not answer him: they seemed frozen in the same pose as before. Ted thought of waving at them, trying to get them to wave back, but he didn't bother. He knew they wouldn't. Besides, at that instant he heard the grass rustling a few yards from where he stood, and this time he knew it was the possum, shuffling away with its rambling gait. It didn't seem interested in Ted. It didn't seem interested in anything, sniffing here and there, raising its head from time to time. Ted followed it, not entirely conscious that he was still grasping the knife like some sort of poacher.

He entered the Lavender woods, which he didn't recognize at all, and within minutes he lost all visual contact with his friends. He was walking down a tree-lined dirt path. The possum was leading the way, guiding him.

At the edge of a clearing, the possum moved aside and watched him with as near to a grin as the demonic creature could muster. Its tail snaked behind its stocky body. When Ted had walked on a few yards, he understood why it smiled. In the clearing lay a dead body. Ted *knew* it was dead. It was lying facedown, arms splayed, and wearing a Massachusetts State University varsity hoodie and an MSU baseball cap. Ted recognized the outfit immediately: he had worn the same hoodie and cap a million times, like all his friends at the university. He couldn't see the victim's face, and frankly, he didn't want to see it.

Then he remembered the knife in his hand, and he instinctively looked more closely at the body. He had a partial view of a slash across the neck. Blood stained the grass and darkened the soil.

Who are you?

He began to walk around the body.

He had to move it. Look at the face.

"Ted," said a voice behind him.

He turned.

It was McManus. Behind her stood Mike and Espósito. All three looked worried. Ted turned back to verify what he already knew to be true: there was no dead Mass State student lying in the woods, much less a grinning possum. He put up his hands in a show of surrender. Where had the knife he had found gone?

They started walking back in silence.

"Did you see the possum?" Mike asked.

Ted gave the slightest nod.

"But I'm not too sure I saw what's behind the backdrop, Mike. To be honest, I have no idea what it was I saw."

The image of the dead student was still etched in his mind. *Who was it?*

55

THEY HAD already spent half an hour in the assessment room at Lavender Memorial. Laura cursorily described her visit to see Nina, Lynch's secretary. But for the time being she withheld the young woman's final revelation.

"The police never interrogated her, but she was there with you, Ted, before you went into Lynch's office."

Ted's mind was elsewhere. His family's visit and his weird experience in the hospital yard had disturbed him.

"Does any of this matter?"

"I haven't gotten to the end of the story yet. But first let me say that, yes, it does matter, because it proves that every event in the first cycle is based on some real incident. That can help us reconstruct your final days."

"If that's true, why would I visit a guy like Blaine?"

"That is exactly what I wanted to ask you. When Nina was leaving Lynch's office, she heard you complain that he had followed you to Blaine's place."

This last statement grabbed Ted's attention. He slowly repeated it.

"I don't get what connection I could possibly have to that guy."

"But now we positively know that you and he knew each other. Most likely it was a link no one else knew about, not even Holly. When you found out Lynch had followed you there, you became furious with him."

Laura had an enigmatic look. Every now and then she threw an especially keen glance at him, or so it seemed to Ted.

"Just a second, Laura. What do you mean by 'a link'?"

"Nothing in particular. Let's not get hasty. But I think it's important to find out what it was. Ted, is something wrong?"

He looked down.

"Yes, actually, there is. I have to ask you for a favor. Ever since I saw the girls..."

"Yes?"

Ted seemed broken. Thinking about Cindy and Nadine reminded him of the promise he had made to them before they left.

"Ted, you can tell me anything. I want you to talk to me about what you felt when you saw Holly and the girls. That is something we should deal with here, too."

He said it flat out: "I need to get out, Laura. For a day or two. I need to go to the lake house, see my stuff, be in my own place. I can't connect with a reality that I can't recall. Being here has helped me, don't get me wrong, but I feel it's time for me to get back to the place where it all started."

"Ted, I don't know if this is the right moment. We're making significant progress."

"I know, and I'm really grateful to you. I was able to see my girls, and I owe that to you. But I have to keep recovering my memories, and there are answers at that lake house. I'm sure of it."

"What makes you think that?"

He knew that if he wanted to convince her, he would have no choice but to tell her what he'd seen in the hospital yard.

"I had a very weird dream. It was...a vision, something like that. The first thing I remember is the girls' pink castle. I was walking over to look at it, inspecting it closely, until I discovered a path behind it. My daughter Cindy was with me, I think. Then she left. I followed the path behind the lake house for I don't know how long. But the main thing is how I felt while I was walking. Like I knew for sure that I would find a revelation at the end. The key to everything."

Laura had picked up a notebook and was scribbling furiously.

"Then I found a dead body. It was an MSU alum—it was wearing a Mass State hoodie and cap. There was a puddle of blood under the body. I couldn't see his face."

"When did you have this dream?"

"Yesterday."

Ted wasn't about to tell her that he'd been awake at the time, or that Mike and Espósito had been watching him from the basketball court. If he had any faint hope of getting out of there, he wasn't going to be so stupid as to tell her that an imaginary possum had led him to the body.

"What else?"

"That's all. I don't know what the castle or the dead man mean; it must be something that escapes me. What I know for sure is that there are important answers hidden on that path behind the lake house. The feeling was so strong, I haven't been able to think about anything else."

"Ted, you know that dreams often have that characteristic. In our dreams we're convinced of things that aren't true when we wake."

"I know. But this was different. In a way, it was as if...as if a part of me were talking and giving me the answer I'd been searching for."

Ted knew he was exaggerating. But he needed to sound convincing. When he looked at Laura's expression, he saw that his story had at least awakened her curiosity.

Laura continued taking notes.

"Did what you saw on the path remind you in some way of your time at college?"

"Not exactly. I mean, the hoodie and cap must have been there for a reason. But the fact is, my time at college is a bit blurry. I remember some parts clearly, such as my professors, the poker games, the jobs I held—I don't know, details like that. I find other things impossible to recall. Everything related to Lynch, I guess. To Justin. If he was my roommate and we became friends there, I suppose it makes sense that I can't remember much about the things I did with him."

Laura nodded.

"So, Laura? What do you say about me maybe visiting the lake house?"

Dr. Hill gently shook her head. There was a tinge of sadness in her eyes.

"It's not time yet, Ted. I'm sorry. I'm not ruling out a possible therapeutic outing in the near future. We often do that when we think it will be helpful."

Ted stood up. He had no restraints on his arms or legs. Though of course McManus, in the adjoining room, never took her eyes off him.

"Laura, I understand. And I trust you. The only thing I ask is for you to consider it. If the path doesn't exist, or doesn't lead anywhere, we haven't lost anything."

Ted looked like a schoolboy who had stood up to recite his lessons. Laura watched him over the rims of her reading glasses.

"I promise you, I'll take it into consideration. However, you must know that the decision isn't mine to make. I'm not the director of C wing."

Ted sat down.

"I understand. Knowing that you'll think about it is good enough for me."

"And I will. I promise you."

56

MARCUS HADN'T spoken with Laura since their brief lunch at the hospital cafeteria, and he hadn't been able to get her off his mind since then. When she called him in his office and told him she needed to talk about something to do with Ted McKay, Marcus agreed to see her and immediately made a resolution: he wasn't going to wait one more second to tell her how he felt. He was tired of coming up with excuses. Ted McKay would have to wait. The world would have to wait.

Laura found him sitting in one of the two small armchairs by the window.

"May I?"

"Please."

Laura sat in the other chair. They were at right angles to each other. He was looking out the window, trying to find the right words. No. Actually, he was trying to find his resolve.

"Are you feeling all right, Marcus?"

"You know? Not really. I'm..."

She leaned a bit forward, urging him to go on. In his mind, Marcus rephrased what he was about to say. He took a breath.

"I can't stop thinking about you," he said at last.

She smiled with a mixture of satisfaction and pity.

"The other day, at your house—I wanted so much to kiss you."

Laura rested her hand on his forearm.

"Hold on. Let's do this the right way. Why don't you invite me to your house on Saturday? When you open your front door, it'll be the first time we get together—no need to talk about it."

He nodded.

"It's a date," she said, and stood up.

"I thought you wanted..."

Laura left his office. The door closed and opened again.

"Dr. Grant? May I have a word with you?"

Marcus laughed.

Laura sat in the chair across from his desk, and he went back to his usual seat.

"Your secretary thinks I'm crazy." Laura stifled a giggle.

"Just a bit," Marcus said, and after a short pause he pointed to where they had just been sitting and added, "And thanks, for...you know what. What did you want to talk about?"

Laura's expression changed instantly.

"Ted has remembered some things from his past, and I think it's time to start pressing him a little."

Laura related Ted's dream about the Mass State student. She also mentioned the path behind the pink castle.

"Ted wants to go to the lake house," Laura explained. "He thinks the path could help him remember, or maybe it will lead to some place that's important to him. I've thought it over, and I want to try it, Marcus."

He pondered a moment.

"Are you certain that the time is right?"

"Frankly, no. But so far nothing has been very rational. The other day, his daughters came—you don't know how sweet those girls are. If this is what Ted needs to be able to open that last door, I think I ought to try it. At worst, it won't work and the trip will yield nothing."

"It's up to you, Laura. You know that since I'm the director of this wing, everything that happens inside here is my responsibility. But you are his doctor. Put in the request and I'll authorize it. When do you want him to go there?"

"On Saturday?"

Marcus opened his eyes wide, horror-struck.

Laura laughed.

"I have the day off," she explained. "Walter and his father are going to see Walter's grandparents. It's the perfect day for me. That morning I'll organize Ted's outing, and that afternoon I'll get back in plenty of time to dress up and go out on our date. I know it's my decision, but your opinion matters to me."

"Your instincts have proved crucial to this case. Pinpointing chess as an anchor to his past, the horseshoe trick, moving him to C wing—you deserve credit for everything. I know McKay means a lot to you. If your instincts are telling you this is the right time, go for it."

"Thank you."

"I can put in a word to Bob, my friend on the Boston police force, remember?"

Laura nodded and put a hand over her mouth to keep from laughing.

"Robert Duvall. How could I forget."

Marcus laughed, too.

"The one and only. But if you ever see him, don't even think of calling him by his full name. I'm going to ask him if he can find out anything about this murder, if it turns out to be a real thing. What years did McKay go to the university?"

"He entered in nineteen ninety-three, class of ninety-seven. It would be great to find out if there was a murder there around that time."

"As for his release, I'll authorize it with maximum security precautions. Restraints on hands and feet at all times, an armed guard."

"That sounds fine."

"I already know what you're going to say, but I'd like to go along..."

"You know me too well. I'd rather go with somebody who'll be a familiar face for him."

"I'll see which of the guys is on duty that day. Any of them will be happy to get outside for a while."

"It's a three-hour drive each way," Laura said. She had kept this bit of information for the end.

Marcus noticed the subtle maneuver.

"You're incorrigible, Laura."

"I promise I'll be on time for our date," she said, standing up.

"Send me his release request form and I'll get it done today."

"Thank you so much."

"I'm sure we'll see each other before Saturday, but if not, good luck."

"We won't talk about the case on Saturday," Laura said before she left. "You have my word."

"I don't know if I should believe you."

She smiled.

"And remember what you have to do when you open your front door."

"I won't forget."

PART IV

57

1993

MASSACHUSETTS STATE University had more than twenty thousand enrolled students in 1993. Many undergraduates roomed in doubles or triples at one of fifty campus dorms, their roommates assigned to them by a process that supposedly took the student's personal preferences into account. To that end, new students filled out detailed questionnaires for what the university billed as its state-of-the-art system for matching them with the perfect roommate. The university touted this system as a key selling point in the brochures it sent to prospective applicants.

When Ted McKay met his freshman roommate, his first thought was that the people in the housing office had no fucking clue what they were doing. No other explanation was possible. How could anyone have thought he and Justin Lynch would get along? You could tell by looking at them that they lived in different orbits. In the housing office's favor: both Ted and Justin had won scholarship packages that required them to keep up their GPAs and live in one of three specially designated "university scholar" dorms. Their assigned dorm was Shephard Hall, universally known as the Box for reasons evident to anyone who gave it a second glance. So perhaps it was simply their equally precarious economic situations that threw them together in a double—room 503, the Box. Poverty: the great equalizer! Otherwise, the only thing they appeared to have in common was being fans of Nirvana. But the same could have been said of half the class of '97.

Justin Lynch was an exceptionally handsome young man—tall, rugged, with big blue eyes and a square jaw. His hair was always perfect, Ted noticed during their tense early weeks together, not because Justin spent all his time getting it done at the barbershop but because it seemed to adopt new shapes as it grew, as if it had a life of its own. Lynch didn't go unnoticed on campus for long. Coeds of all ages found their way to the all-male fifth floor of Shephard Hall, where they would hang out in the hallway near room 503 or in the common room. Sometimes they stopped Ted in the hall to ask him all sorts of questions about his roommate. The less daring women just asked Ted for basic information, such as whether Justin already had a girlfriend. Others were more direct, and given the chance they would have marched straight into room 503 to settle their questions themselves.

This Don Juan quality about Justin was what most irritated Ted, who had never been very good at relations with the opposite sex. He wasn't exactly jealous of his new roommate—well, maybe just a little—but there was something else, something deeper. Ted's dislike of womanizers hadn't emerged from nowhere. His father had been one. Mr. Big Shot. Hadn't Ted written as much in the long comment he appended to his housing application? Of course he had. "Please add any additional comments you would like the housing office to take into consideration," the questionnaire had said, and after thinking about who he did and didn't want to room with, Ted had taken off, submitting as his response a mini essay on his present living situation, his family history, his parents' breakup, and the reasons behind it. He explained that his father had kept a lover for years, and that he hated his father for his philandering, for breaking up the home. And that he hated all the other bastards who cheated on their wives and girlfriends. So the obvious question was, why had the housing office forced Ted to share a room with a guy who represented everything he despised? He was outraged. But he was sure of one thing: as soon as the girls started parading through, Ted would have a little chat with his roommate. And it wouldn't be a pleasant chat, for sure. Because the guy said he had a girlfriend back home, and he'd even hung her photo on the wall.

Lynch's impression of Ted wasn't much better. Not so much because of his bad boy attitude, with the leather jacket and the rude manners; as far as Lynch was concerned, Ted's insistence on going against the flow was merely a pathetic display. Ted even had a rusty Datsun with a bumper sticker that said OUTLAW. Jesus. But that wasn't it. What really galled Lynch was that, while he himself took his studies seriously, holding down a work-study job at the library and studying till his eyes ached, Ted, that low-rent Johnny Depp, split his time between dropping in on the odd class, slacking off at his job in the dining hall, and playing marathon poker games on the sixth floor. Mainly poker games on the sixth floor. Lynch would stay up half the night studying and find his roommate sneaking in, reeking of cigarettes, eyes red from smoke. Sometimes Ted would crack open his math or accounting textbook, but half an hour later he'd be passed out, sleeping facedown on the open book, still fully dressed. Lynch knew that Ted had received a particularly stringent scholarship, and he also knew it would be a miracle if Ted survived his midterms. In a way, Lynch was just waiting for the midterms to get rid of this roommate and get himself a new one.

For the first couple of months the roommates' interactions were minimal. They only connected when Nirvana or Pearl Jam came on Lynch's stereo. Apart from brief conversations they had then, always about music, there was no relationship between them. They never talked about their jobs, never shared a table in the dining hall. Even their incipient circles of friends seemed destined never to intersect.

Ted was the first to realize that the housing office people might have been a bunch of fucking geniuses and that he had perhaps judged Lynch too quickly. The parade of Lynch girlfriends he kept expecting to see never materialized. In fact, the one and only girl who entered their room before mid-October was a student Ted had invited over. Not only did Lynch seem uninterested in cheating on his hometown girlfriend, but he appeared deeply embarrassed whenever women he didn't know asked about him. He had a magnetism that any guy would envy; with much less, another college dude could have been making the bed creak every five minutes. (At the time, that was MSU code for sex; the ancient spring mattresses in dorm beds were very comfortable but very creaky.) Lynch didn't make his bed creak once during those first weeks, and God knew he could have—all he wanted. Ted started thinking his roommate must be gay and that the photo on the wall was just some girl he knew. But he heard Lynch on the phone a few times, and it was too much to imagine that he was merely pretending to have those conversations with her. The guy was faithful. He had enough charm to sweep any girl off her feet, but he didn't seem interested in using it. What an odd bird. Ted was becoming intrigued.

When mid-October rolled around, and with it the first exams, Lynch got a B plus and four A minuses. He felt satisfied. But it shocked him to see his rule-breaking roommate's grades: all As, including a couple of A pluses. Impossible. It had to be some sort of scam. He'd been watching Ted, and he knew how little time he spent studying: usually less than an hour a day. Lynch doubted his roommate could have been studying on the job in the dining hall. He never even brought his books! So what was his trick? His trick, as Lynch would discover over the coming months, was that Ted was very smart, and in addition, he had an astounding photographic memory. So Ted excelled in analytic courses and subjects that required lots of memorization. He was an astonishing speed-reader, zipping through dense material three or four times as quickly as other students. And nothing ever slipped his mind.

Lynch knew that Ted had been frequenting illegal off-campus gambling dens, in addition to playing poker upstairs, and was living off his winnings. After things were completely smoothed over between them, Ted admitted that he actually hated playing poker, but it was a popular enough game that he could make the rounds of various gambling circles without attracting too much suspicion. A player who consistently wins more often than he loses will be ejected from any gaming parlor sooner or later. Ted could memorize cards flawlessly and make statistically complicated decisions in a matter of seconds, giving him better than random odds in the game. Dorm games were just penny-ante, but even with small stakes, Ted rounded up enough cash to cover the expenses his scholarship didn't and, more importantly, pay for his mother's hospitalization.

It turned out the housing office people had done their job well after all. Ted and Justin soon became friends.

58

1993

THE LEAD-UP to their friendship was a deepening sense of mutual respect. Ted hadn't really socialized much at college; his poker buddies undoubtedly considered him a friend, but he was always pretending when he was around them, saying and doing what he thought they expected of him and no more. He had learned how to get along in any environment, but he did so by following cool reason, not his emotions. Justin was the first person he felt any real interest in. The sensation was completely new to him; he hadn't cultivated friendships at high school, either.

Justin, for his part, had struck up some promising relationships, but he had gradually let them fall by the wayside and shut himself off in his own world. He was a loner by nature, and having a friend who understood him gave him the assurance he needed to start being himself. This sudden acceptance of his inner self led to changes in his life that became apparent during the course of that first year at college.

One cold afternoon before Christmas, Justin was trying to concentrate on an essay for his creative writing class. Kurt Cobain rasped in the background. Ted had already finished his study session: half an hour of lying on the bed with his calculus, statistics, and God knows what other textbooks, flipping through all the pages at once, like a studious octopus. Watching Ted "study" was enough to make anyone lose heart. Now Ted was about to head for the sixth floor, where the poker games went later and later every night. Ted said the other players were improving; in addition, he knew for a fact that a couple of them had concocted a stratagem to hurt his chances by joining forces and using subtle signals, which he had already deciphered. When your winnings consistently outpaced your losses, you came to expect a backlash sooner or later. He could manage it for the time being, or so he hoped. There was always the option of steering clear of the cheaters' table, or of finding another poker venue, even if it was off campus.

But he had time to kill before the sixth-floor games, so almost as an afterthought he asked Justin a question that he suspected his friend had been waiting for him to ask. Justin always talked about his mother, never his father, and this afternoon Ted saw that he could barely concentrate on his homework: he kept looking out the window, pacing the floor, bouncing a tennis ball off the wall. So Ted went ahead and asked the question he had held off on for so long. He suspected Justin's father was dead or had abandoned him when he was little, but it turned out he was wrong.

Justin's father was alive and kicking, living in Deerfield with Mrs. Lynch and their other son, but Justin felt a deep contempt for him. Another coincidence!

"We hardly speak," said Justin. "Nobody knows why not." He put on his Mass State hoodie and opened the window. An icy breeze chilled the room in a moment. He sat on the sill and lit a cigarette. He did all this mechanically, wrapped in a cloud of smoke and focusing his eyes on the past. "My father doesn't even know why not—can you believe it? I never told him. Maybe someday I will."

Ted sat on his bed. The poker game could wait.

"I'm with you. My father's an idiot, too."

Justin nodded, his face turned to the window, defying the cold.

"He thinks it's my age, that I'm in a rebellious stage and I'll grow out of it. My mother thinks so, too, though I act completely different with her, or at least I try to. The guy is so dumb, it never occurs to him that he might have done anything wrong. When I was little we were inseparable. My father was my idol. I wanted to be just like him. He was perfect."

Justin finished his cigarette and quickly shut the window. He rubbed his hands and stood by the radiator to warm up.

"My father and I are like two peas," he said with resignation. "We look like clones. If I showed you a picture of him from thirty years ago, you'd think it was me, except for the aviator glasses and the bell-bottoms. Anyway, I guess that had something to do with how close we were, or maybe not. I don't know. There was a special connection. It wasn't the same with my brother, for example. Do you have brothers or sisters?"

Ted shook his head.

"Sorry I'm talking your ear off like this. You've got to go."

"Don't worry about it, man. Go ahead—get it out."

"My father's an electrician. His own boss. When I was a kid, I couldn't wait for school vacation to come around so I could go with him in his van. We'd drive all over, buying materials and doing jobs. He used to tell me I was his helper and one day I'd be just like him. That was all I wanted to hear, I swear. Whenever anybody asked me back then what I wanted to be, I said an electrician. No hesitation. Like that."

Justin snapped his fingers.

"There were three or four stores my father shopped at regularly. A couple of them had these salesgirls my father always flirted with. Then they'd joke around with me and tell me I shouldn't tell my mother anything. Of course I never did tell her, ever. When we went to a house to do a job and a woman let us in, it was more of the same. He'd tell me things like, 'Don't say anything to Mommy, Justin, because you know how she is: she'll be sad if she finds out.' He said it didn't mean he didn't love her, that we men liked to flirt with other women—crap like that." Justin shook his head. "I know it sounds kind of stupid now, but I was convinced it was true, Ted. My father would say things like, 'Did you see that salesgirl staring at my biceps? I flexed it on purpose, so she'd notice.' If a good-looking woman came on TV, if my mother wasn't watching, he'd point to her and make faces at me. And I was eight years old! He was like that all the time. Except by the time I turned twelve, he wasn't just flirting. He had occasional flings with several of those women."

Ted was listening as closely as he ever had to another human being. He was thinking about all sorts of things, among them that he was almost certain this was why he and Justin had ended up sharing a room. The housing office people had definitely done a masterful job.

"You know what's worse?"

"What?"

"When I turned sixteen I started acting just like him. Because I was convinced men were supposed to behave like that. I think of myself as a smart guy, Ted. Not so smart as you!" Justin laughed. "But not stupid. And let me tell you, I *never* questioned what my father had taught me. It was as if his words were handed down by the gods, like they were the truth. By then I had realized that my mother, who is no fool, either, had some pretty strong suspicions, maybe more than suspicions, about my father's running around. And I really do love my mother, more than anyone in the world. How was it that I never questioned something that could hurt *her?* "

"Well, you realized it in time. That's the important thing."

"Yeah, I guess so."

Nevermind had stopped playing at some point. Now it was as quiet as it ever got on a Friday night in a student dorm. The noise policy was pretty strict, but on weekends everybody loosened up quite a bit.

"It's funny," Justin reflected. "I've never told anyone about this. The closest I came was mentioning in my college application essay that my relationship with my father was a disaster, but that's as much as I said. I've never told anyone why I despise him."

Ted didn't know what to say. He was deeply moved, or so he thought.

"At first he didn't understand why I wanted to distance myself from him," Justin went on. "Not like he understands it now. It's just that he's come to accept it. But he keeps making these pathetic attempts to get closer, and he almost always does it by trying to talk to me about women. He thinks that's the easiest way for us to connect. It's so sad. Last year I brought my girlfriend home. The first girl I've introduced to my family. Her name is Lila—I think I've mentioned her." He pointed at her photo on the wall. "You can see, Lila isn't exactly...a knockout. The thing is..."

Justin jumped up, his head in his hands.

"God, what's gotten into me? I haven't stopped talking. You must think I'm..."

Ted stood and put a hand on Justin's shoulder.

"Not a problem. Someday I'll make you listen to me griping about *my* father," Ted said, though he had no intention of revealing his own story. "It'll be a hard-fought battle of the idiots, I swear. So what happened with Lila?"

Justin stood frozen in thought.

"After Lila went home," he finally said, "my father came over and told me I could do a lot better than her. He winked at me and smiled. Can you believe it? I met Lila by chance, through a friend, and you know what? One of the first things I imagined after Lila and I were introduced was what my father would say about her. And that was exactly what he did say. That's how well I know the son of a bitch."

"Maybe that's why you fell for her."

"Maybe so. The truth is, Lila and I don't have much in common."

Justin laughed.

"Our conversations have been sort of cold lately. And living so far away—I really don't know." He suddenly stopped. "Don't you have to run upstairs and start ripping off those twits?"

Ted shrugged.

"I'm giving them the day off," he replied. "I made plenty yesterday. You want to go have a couple of beers? I'm buying."

"Sure!"

Ted put on his leather jacket and a cap with earflaps. Justin left room 503, the Box, and Ted followed. It was too early to be certain, but he was starting to think he was developing a genuine friendship with Justin.

A genuine friendship. For the first time in his life.

59

1994

THE HARSH winter of 1994 marked a turning point in Justin Lynch's life. He broke off with Lila in a short phone conversation and his academic efforts took a nosedive. One event didn't cause the other, though both had the same origin. He was starting to realize that the only reason he was at college was because he didn't want to be a fucking electrician like his father. Getting a university education was another means of punishing *him,* of acting in a way that *he* found incomprehensible. Lila was more of the same, though her case was more transparent. He had picked a girlfriend who he knew his father, the Casanova of Deerfield, would never have chosen for himself or for his son. Justin's college career was more of the same. It was all bullshit. His father had become a black hole, pulling everything near him down into a bottomless pit. Whether Justin did things to please his father or to earn his hatred, the universe still revolved around him.

Justin began to consider—a little late in the game, he felt—what he wanted to do with his life. Did he really want to study English lit? Reading was one of the few activities that awoke a glimmer of redemption in him, like a distant glimpse of beauty in this gloom-bedimmed world. What he wasn't so clear about was whether he was willing to submit to the requirements for the major, not to mention the rhythms of university life. And the exams! One way to avoid the issue was by allowing his academic career to slowly founder while he immersed himself in compulsive extracurricular reading: Kafka, Melville, Borges, Lovecraft. The poetry of Sylvia Plath, who grew up in Massachusetts and went to college just down the road from Deerfield, and who suffered from depression for most of her life and ultimately committed suicide, captured his attention almost to the point of obsession. This was, of course, not an optimal reading list for someone who was slipping nearer, day by day, to the mouth of the abyss.

Ted witnessed Justin's slide and was the only one who tried to help him. He did what he could, from keeping an eye on details, such as urging Justin to shave or take a shower, to tackling bigger things, like walking him to his classes and giving him advice. He wasn't having much luck at it.

Justin started keeping a diary of sorts, into which he poured out his thoughts, half-baked poetry, and dense paragraphs brimming with despair. He carried that notebook with him everywhere. At night he would take long walks around campus, lie down somewhere, sometimes even fall asleep on a park bench. His nocturnal habits got him into trouble with campus security. Sometimes Ted, who had to work the sixth floor harder and harder to cover his costs, would come home in the early hours of the morning and find that Justin had not yet returned.

One of those nights Ted lay in bed exhausted, staring at his friend's empty bed. He couldn't remember doing anything meaningful for another person since he was a kid, and tonight he decided he really wanted to do something. Something to shake Justin out of his downward spiral. He got up and dressed. He had a pretty good idea of where his roommate went on his nightly walks, and in less than an hour Ted tracked him down. He found Justin sitting on a bench in an unkempt, poorly lit corner of campus, in back of the library. If it hadn't been for the lit cigarette, Ted probably would have missed him in the dense darkness.

He sat next to Justin without a word and put his hand on his shoulder for a moment.

"I guess I've become predictable," Justin said. A puff of white flew from his mouth. The cold was intense; it would snow at any minute.

And now, for the first time, Ted allowed himself to talk about his father. It wasn't a detailed report—just the minimum necessary to let Justin know that he, too, understood what it was to have a father who shat all over his family. Ted spoke briefly of the trips to Miller's house for chess lessons and the double life his father had led. Justin seemed quite struck—not by the story itself, but by the fact that Ted would open up and talk about such personal matters. Until this moment, Ted's entire life had been an enigma.

"I hate him, too," Ted said, "and I'm not going to try and convince you that life isn't a crock of shit, because it is. And if guys like your father or mine are the guilty ones, well, so are the slackers I sit down to play poker with night after night. And the spoiled frat boys. Pricks. They're all responsible. You know how I know? Because I feel it, too. That emptiness. I feel it, too."

Ted fell silent. They both sat awhile without talking.

"They're responsible for that gaping hole," Ted said, more ominously now. "The question, you know, is what we should do about it."

"I don't know. I'm sick and tired of lying to my mother. I'm thinking about dropping out."

"That's exactly what you shouldn't do. Because then they win. Can't you see? That's what they want—to shove you into the shithole. I know it might be easier to give up. Believe me, I know. But you have to find a way to make things work out for you. I'm going to graduate from this fucking university, I'm going to get married, I'm going to have kids and a big house, maybe even a weekend house. I'm going to be rich!"

Justin smiled.

"I wish I had your confidence, Ted McKay."

"Look, Justin. Sure, I'm good at memorizing the damn textbooks. I have that in my favor. Everybody has his strong points. And don't tell me I don't know yours. You should put them to use, find a way to feed the beast, learn to live with it."

"You make it sound simple."

"It is! Believe me, it is. This darkness is…like an awful parasite that will always be with you. You can't let it eat you alive."

Justin ground out his cigarette under his boot.

"Who was that girl you were telling me about?" Ted asked. "The one in your creative writing class."

"Denise Garrett."

"Right. What's new with her?"

"I don't know. We talk sometimes. But I haven't shown up there much lately."

"Invite her to dinner or a movie. It could be the start of something."

Justin nodded.

"And now let's get moving, because I can't feel my ears anymore," Ted said. "I forgot my hat, damn it."

They walked back to the Box, talking in a more relaxed tone, laughing and rubbing shoulders while never taking their hands from their pockets.

"So I'm a slow learner," Justin said. "At least I'm good-looking."

"Precisely. I was afraid you wouldn't get it."

"Prick."

"But a prick who cares, asshole."

60

1994

THINGS SEEMED to be looking up with the arrival of spring. Justin buckled down with his schoolwork and forced himself to spend a certain number of hours studying every day. He also got a job working two days a week at the library. He still hadn't asked Denise Garrett on a date, but he would do so anytime now. Ted himself was going out with a girl from one of his classes, and seeing them together encouraged Justin, though he had a feeling that Denise was in a relationship already; she hadn't said so directly, but she'd hinted at a boyfriend back home. She behaved strangely with him, especially in the classes they shared, as if Justin's presence made her uncomfortable somehow. Ted told Justin not to worry, that there was a list of girls interested in him as long as his arm.

But Justin didn't feel completely out of the woods yet. He was still reading Sylvia Plath and filling his notebook with apocalyptic notions; he also continued taking his solitary night walks, though at least now he felt as though he had things under control, as though everything else in his life were moving forward. Maybe Ted was right after all. What had Ted told him that freezing night? That he had to feed his inner beast, and if he did, everything would turn out okay. And he was right about it. Of course he was! Ted was a fucking genius.

But then on April 8, 1994, terrible news rocked the campus of Massachusetts State, and the world.

Ted was in the dining hall. Today he was on dishwasher duty, a task he loathed, though it had the advantage of letting him work while wearing headphones and plugged into his new Discman. He'd been doing that for the past hour, steering clear of talking to his fellow workers, with whom he rarely interacted. At some point a group of them congregated in a corner of the huge kitchen. They seemed worked up about something, but Ted couldn't care less. If the supervisor had anything to tell them, he'd come and talk to them directly. Ted was humming along with a Soundgarden album when Justin showed up, looking excited or upset, and grabbed him by the shoulder. Justin never went looking for him at work. Ted took off his headphones and set down the glass he was drying. Justin told him the news that had been making the rounds. News that had just been confirmed.

Kurt Cobain had shot himself to death at his Seattle home.

As might have been expected, several versions of the story circulated during those early hours, but the suicide story was the most common. It was later determined that Kurt had escaped from a detox center and had taken this drastic step after spending several days alone and out of contact. A letter he left behind made a huge impact on MSU students, and on Justin Lynch in particular. That spring Kurt's songs were heard more often in the rooms of the Box than ever before.

A week after the tragic news, Ted went to the movies with Georgia McKenzie, the girl he had started going out with a few weeks earlier. Things were going quite well between them. Georgia was pretty and uninhibited, a middling student who couldn't understand her new boyfriend and who may have fallen in love with him for that very reason. She wasn't the demanding sort, one of those girls who want their boyfriends' lives to revolve around them. Ted and Georgia would get together for a couple of hours on the weekend—bed-creaking included—and would meet on an occasional weekday to kiss and do a bit of studying side by side. That was all.

That Saturday, Ted walked Georgia to the front door of her building, one of three women-only residence halls remaining at MSU. He kissed her with the customary desperate urgency and begged her to let him up to her room. She agreed after a slight and studied resistance. She enjoyed challenges and rule breaking. Sneaking her boyfriend into her room fit both bills. After a brief but intense encounter, Ted took off.

Back in his own dorm room, a shiver ran through his body. Something was wrong. The light in their tiny bathroom had been left on, the door was open...but the key detail was that Justin's notebook lay open on his bed. He thought of Kurt's body lying on the floor in his home. Ted leaned over the bed and saw two pages covered with a long, dense handwritten text. At first it didn't look like a suicide note, mainly because it wasn't addressed to anyone. A rapid scan revealed the word "Boddah" lower on the page, and Ted trembled. Cobain had addressed his suicide note to an imaginary childhood friend named Boddah. Ted reached the bathroom in two strides. He steeled himself to see his friend's body in the bathtub or hanging from the overhead pipes. During that fraction of a second, his mind worked at top speed. Justin was depressive, but suicidal?

The bathroom was empty. Why had Justin left the light on?

He just forgot. It wouldn't be the first time.

What about his notebook?

And what about Boddah?

Before undertaking a search of the entire Box, Ted needed to read those pages. He went back and, still standing, leaned over his roommate's bed, supporting himself with his hands on either side of the notebook, as if he didn't want to touch the paper. He finally did so to turn the page and read to the end of the passage. Though the text was long, he read it all in less than twenty seconds.

It seemed less like a suicide note than an unfinished short story. Its theme did nothing to calm Ted, though. The story was about a man who was on the verge of shooting himself; just before he went through with it, at the precise instant he was about to squeeze the trigger, a stranger named Boddah showed up at his door and said he had a proposal. He was very persuasive, and he seemed to know what the protagonist—whose name was never mentioned—was planning to do. He said he knew other people like him, and if they would work together they might not only help their families bear their grief but make the world a better place. Boddah began to explain to the protagonist that he would be asked to kill a despicable man. Then the story came to an abrupt end.

In a box at the top of the page, Justin had written the title of the story: "A Better World." His handwriting was clumsy and chaotic, with additions and strike-throughs everywhere.

Ted stood thinking for a moment. It might be nothing but a short story—very well written, for that matter—that Justin was working on, inspired by recent events. Or it might be some sort of unfinished warning that Ted couldn't quite understand. He ran from the room. In the corridor he bumped into Irving Prosser, a lumbering, taciturn kid who lived in the room next door. Ted asked him urgently if he had seen Justin. Irving took his time, scratching his head and looking at the ceiling, as if that would kick-start his brain, before answering.

"Have I seen him *lately?*" he asked.

"Of course!"

If he didn't know Irving, Ted would have thought the guy was pulling his leg. But Prosser was simply dumb.

"Lemme think. I saw him leave his room about an hour ago. I was gonna..."

Ted left his neighbor with the sentence unfinished. He ran down the stairs two at a time, asking the same question of everyone he saw along the way. They all knew Justin—that was a definite advantage of having a roommate who was the reincarnation of James Dean. A student just walking into the Box told Ted he had seen Justin near the library. Ted went there next, jogging the whole way, amazed at how worried he felt about somebody he'd known for less than a year. He truly was worried; the emotion was so new to him that it made him feel distinctly different.

He found Justin on his usual bench behind the library, which appeared much less threatening in daylight under the greening trees of spring.

"Ted!" Justin was surprised to see him. He took off his headphones. "What are you doing here?"

Ted sat next to him.

"Did something happen?" Justin asked.

"Nah." At that instant Ted decided that he wouldn't tell Justin what he'd been thinking. Justin seemed to be in a pretty good mood. "I was planning to go up to the sixth floor later, and I wanted to ask you something."

"I'm all ears."

"Last night I played a couple of poker games with some idiots from Delta Tau. It was basically hostile terrain, but I managed to come out on top. Be that as it may, they're having a frat party today and I'm invited."

Justin looked at Ted as if he had just let off a putrid smell.

"A frat party? You?"

Ted laughed.

"I don't have any idea who these Delta Tau guys are," Justin went on. "Do they know you're a freshman? And don't they charge outsiders an arm and a leg to get in to their parties?"

"Look, in a way they'll be paying for it themselves." Ted rapped his knuckles against his pocket to indicate where their money had ended up. "And it's true, I despise those guys. But there'll be alcohol, girls, music—come on, let's both go. We stay there awhile, drink all we want, clear out. What would college life be without crappy parties?"

"You're right. Is that really all you came here for?" Justin paused and smiled. "Sorry, I should be thanking you. It's just that you're getting soft, McKay, worrying about your fellow man like this. Thanks. The party sounds like a great idea. I'll have to go to one sooner or later."

They fell silent. The unmistakable guitarmanship of Nirvana could be heard through the speakers of the headphones dangling from Justin's neck. He reached into his pocket and pressed stop on his Walkman.

"Hey," Ted said. "You left your notebook open on your bed..."

Justin started, immediately grasping the possible implications of this.

"It's really good, Justin," Ted reassured him.

"Oh, God, how embarrassing. It's just a work in progress."

"It's great."

Justin nodded.

"Thanks, Ted."

"I'm serious."

"If you liked it so much, maybe I'll give your name to the main character."

Justin winked at him.

61

Present day

AT NINE in the morning on Saturday, a van left Lavender Memorial for Dover, Vermont. Lee Stillwell was driving, Laura rode in the front passenger seat, and Ted sat alone in the back. Lee, an ordinarily unsociable guard who seemed to spend his days at Lavender counting down to the moment of his planned retirement, now seemed to be in a great mood, even talkative. He had his own reason, of course: he was getting triple pay for working this trip. Besides, he liked to drive, not to mention the fact that Dr. Hill was plenty easy on the eyes when she wasn't wrapped in that nasty hospital coat.

Ted kept quiet almost the whole way there. Trying to hold a conversation through the little window in the Plexiglas wall between the back compartment and the front of the van wasn't exactly easy, even less so when it meant leaning forward and thereby tightening the chain binding him to the metal floor. For Ted the trip seemed endless, with no view of the landscape from his uncomfortable fixed bench. He decided he'd be better off thinking about what might happen when they got there, because it was clear that there would be nothing for him to do in the van except wait. The guard was monopolizing the conversation. Laura turned back several times to look at Ted through the Plexiglas, with both dismay and resignation in her eyes. There was nothing she could have done about the security measures, she seemed to be reminding him every time she looked his way.

They were taking Route 2 west across the state. Traffic was light and the wooded setting lent itself to contemplation and reflection. For any employee at Lavender, where bars, security doors, and security cameras were everywhere, the vast blue sky and the green of the trees were almost overwhelming this morning. Lee Stillwell felt especially entranced; keeping his eyes on the highway, he explained that his lifelong dream had been to buy a house in a hidden spot like this, where he could live out his last days. He'd always lived with that dream, and so had his wife. Now that he was nearing retirement, he could tell that he'd never really been in a position to realize it. The fact profoundly saddened him. He had rarely been able to sock away money, and he'd ultimately been forced to spend what little he had managed to save on one necessity or other. He'd spent the last thirty years sincerely believing he would achieve his dream, but he would never come close.

"Maybe that's all that mattered," he said, tightening his grip on the steering wheel. "Believing I'd make it someday."

After this revelation, he fell silent. He almost seemed about to cry behind his mirrored sunglasses. It was probably the first time he'd said anything like that aloud.

"When you're an old man like me, the truth is, it don't really matter all that much."

"Lee, you're not an old man."

He nodded.

"Old enough to know my dreams aren't coming true, not old enough yet to forget them."

They'd been driving for more than an hour, and for the first time Ted really spoke up.

"I got my dream, my weekend home, and here I am, locked up, because I had nothing better to do one day than go out of my mind."

Lee didn't respond.

"Do you love your wife?" Ted asked.

Lee did not seem very disposed to speaking with Ted. Or maybe he was just thinking about his broken dreams and how he'd failed his wife, Martha.

"Sure do," he answered after a moment. And it was the truth.

"Then you've got everything."

Ted stared at the toes of his shoes, his elbows resting on his knees and his head in his hands. One of his chains dangled in front of his face, swaying to the gentle motion of the van. The other chain was a cold-blooded serpent crouching at his feet. He said no more.

They exited onto I-91 shortly after eleven.

"At least I have my woodworking shop in back of the house." Lee hadn't given up.

"I've seen the chair you made for the director," Laura said. "Very elegant."

"Thanks. I love woodworking. Guess I'll spend more time at that after I retire. Won't be long now."

Lee went on talking about his woodworking hobby, how he found a satisfaction in shaping wood that he couldn't get from his job at the hospital. At that point he apologized to Laura for what he'd said, but immediately afterward said it wasn't the fault of the team at Lavender. It was him; he'd ended up working a job he wasn't excited about, but he hadn't gotten out in time. He'd started working there by accident, planning only to save up a nest egg while looking for something better. Then the months turned into years, and the years into decades. "And then it gets harder and harder to leave. And almost before you know it you're up against retirement, and you haven't done any of the things you'd planned."

Laura listened to him closely. She understood only too well the unhappiness of this man whose life had slipped through his fingers. Laura loved her job and didn't feel as though she were wasting her time at Lavender, not at all, but she certainly recognized the feeling. In fact, something like it had happened to her after the divorce, when for some mysterious reason she had assumed that her love life was over. It was stupid for a woman who had only recently turned forty to think that way, but that's how it was, at first. In the end she understood: time put things into perspective, opening up her heart to new possibilities. She thought of Marcus, whom she would be seeing that night.

The GPS guided them through the intricate final leg of the journey. Lee refused to ask Ted for directions. They left the interstate behind and finally reached a little-traveled dirt road. Two miles farther on they arrived at the lake house. Lee cut the engine and silence overwhelmed them. Nobody got out; Lee sat expressionless behind the wheel as he contemplated the imposing spread. The house obviously exceeded his most ambitious fantasies.

The guard stepped from the van. Instead of his uniform, he wore jeans and a light jacket. He carried his Beretta under his jacket and his Taser was holstered to his belt. He opened the van's double door in back and undid the padlock so Ted could get out.

"What I said before was the truth," Lee said. "I don't love my job, but I'm good at it. Don't get any closer than six feet to Dr. Hill. If you need anything, ask me. I'll be right behind you and I'll have my eyes on you the whole time. I've only had to unholster my Taser twice and I've never fired my gun at work, but I can assure you I practice every week and I can hit this chain at thirty feet. No surprises. Understood?"

Ted nodded. "There won't be any problems," he said.

At that point, Laura got out of the van.

Ted walked around the vehicle. The chains on his feet allowed him some freedom of movement—not enough to run a race, but plenty for walking at a reasonable pace. When he saw the house, he felt a strange sense of familiarity. It looked different from the way he remembered it—more neglected. Holly and the girls had obviously not come up here in all these months. Of course there wasn't a trace of the Lamborghini convertible.

"Holly gave me the keys," Laura said, displaying a ring. "I think it would be a good idea to look around inside, don't you?"

Ted didn't answer. He was staring at everything like a curious child. The trees, the ground covered in pine needles, the surface of the lake rippling under the breeze. The air smelled different. He took in one deep breath after another, feeling that the oxygen had the power to heal him, to bring back his forgotten memories. To turn the clock back.

He saw the pink castle from a distance, at the edge of the woods, and his eyes were glued to it.

Answers.

"Come on, Ted. I want us to take a look around inside the house first."

He nodded and went to the front door. Lee stuck close behind.

Ted entered cautiously, measuring each step he took across the Indian rug. The rug where, according to his memories, Wendell had fallen after he shot him. The memory was so real, yet when he tried to focus on Wendell's face, his mind produced a giant question mark. Ted walked around the first floor, pausing in front of the photographs. He had taken many of them. He went into the hallway leading to the kitchen, saw the calendar, and flipped through its pages to find the scuba diver on the coral reef. It wasn't there—not on any of the months. Only landscapes.

"This is where I waited for him," Ted said. Laura was watching with interest as he examined the calendar. "First I saw him pass by this..."

Ted fell silent.

"There was a window over there," Ted said, pointing at the kitchen wall by the double-doored refrigerator and the counter. "I watched Wendell through the window when he was on the lake."

Laura noticed the confusion on his face. It was as if part of him were still holding on to the possibility that it had all really happened. That Wendell wasn't actually a creation of his own mind.

"Let's go upstairs, Ted. There's something I want you to see."

"What is it, Laura?"

She didn't answer.

He nodded.

They went back to the great room and over to the bottom of one of the staircases.

Unlike the first floor, where the wide picture windows bathed everything in natural light, the upstairs seemed to be plunged into darkness. Lee flipped the switch at the bottom of the stairs, but nothing happened.

"The electricity is shut off, Lee," Laura noted. "I'll go up and open some windows."

She ran lightly up. Ted waited halfway up the stairs, with Lee right behind him.

A moment later, Laura looked down from above and signaled to them to head on up. Ted found himself in a hallway he had no memory of. He took a few steps forward and halted in front of the window Laura had opened. It offered a perfect view of the pink castle. Ted realized that if the castle had been built just a few yards farther off, the foliage would have hidden it entirely. From this window, therefore, it was possible to keep an eye on the girls. He stood there wondering how many times he must have looked out this window to make sure everything was okay.

"Open that door," Laura said.

Ted turned to see. There, indeed, was a closed door across from the window. He opened it.

What he saw surprised but above all deeply saddened him. More evidence of how unreliable his memories were.

It was his study. The desk, the bookshelves, the Monet reproduction concealing the safe. He recognized all the objects in the room, which he didn't even dare to enter.

Laura spoke to him from behind.

"Holly told me there's no study at your home in the city."

Ted took in the study. More than a minute passed.

"This is where I was going to do it, Laura. Sitting in that chair."

"Do you want to go in?"

"Do you think it would do me any good?"

"I don't know. Follow your feelings."

Ted didn't want to enter.

"I'd rather check out the path behind the castle."

"Perfect. Let's go there, then."

They went downstairs, always under Lee's watchful eye. They walked around back and continued in silence to the pink castle, now surrounded by a dense mat of dry leaves.

Behind the castle there was, in fact, a path leading into the woods.

"Here it is," Ted announced gravely. His eyes had hardened and he seemed to be issuing this narrow footpath a challenge.

"Let's go, then," said Laura. There was anxiety in her voice.

62

1994

TO GET to the party, they had to walk almost a mile through an unfamiliar section of the sprawling campus. Luckily Ted had the whole map in his head; moreover, his sense of direction was infallible. He assured Justin that the winding path they were on was the most direct route to the frat, and he was correct. The blaring music confirmed that they were headed in the right direction, and before long they came to the wood fence surrounding the backyard of Delta Tau House.

It was past ten and the party was just getting started. The large Greek letters above the front door were conveniently illuminated. Two guys, bigger than Ted and Justin in every sense of the word, greeted them with snarls. Ted turned to one of them and gave their names. Just then a car pulled into the parking lot in front of the house. Three girls jumped out and walked into the house without a word to the bouncers; the girls merely nodded at them without interrupting their giggling conversation. Ted looked at his leather jacket and at Justin's coat—Justin was in his long black trench coat, which was a bit too much for a spring night by anyone's standard—and then at the girls' tiny tops and skirts, and he felt out of place. The guy holding the list found their names and gave his okay to the other bouncer, who seemed unconvinced and asked for ID. Justin pulled his university ID from his wallet and unwillingly showed it to them.

"Not you," the other bouncer said without looking at him. "Your friend."

Another second and Ted would have turned around and left. Justin would have followed him, of course. Seeing how things turned out, it would have been the smartest decision of his life.

But Ted took out his ID, and they went into the yard.

Most of the partygoers were inside, though others were scattered in groups through the yard, drinking and shouting to be heard over the music. A droning, pulsating bass line invited them to stay away. Justin and Ted crossed the yard and forced themselves to take a peek inside. A fairly large crowd was jumping and shaking—to call it dancing would be too generous—while the rest milled about with big red plastic cups in their hands. A DJ stood on a small platform, working twin turntables. There were a couple of tables covered with strategically arranged drinks. Ted counted five coolers of ice and many cans of Keystone beer. It was hot inside, so they took off their coats and didn't know exactly what to do next. There were hardly any other freshmen at the party—that was obvious.

Ted recognized Dan Norris in the group standing around the drink tables. Norris, who at that moment was drinking tequila with his frat brothers, was the idiot who had invited him. Fortunately, he didn't notice Ted, who suggested to Justin that they keep moving. They each grabbed a beer and went out a side door and onto a porch, where things were much quieter. A couple was kissing frantically in one corner; another couple was making out in a hammock. This side of the house was lit by a single low-wattage bulb.

A cooler with more cans sat on a corner of the porch. They headed toward it and perched on the railing, where they could see inside the house through an open window. They each finished their first beer and grabbed another. Then another. Neither was used to drinking heavily, so three beers was plenty to get them dizzy.

"We should have gotten something to eat first," Ted observed.

Justin agreed.

"How are things going with Denise from creative writing?"

Ted jumped down from the railing, but when he headed off to get another beer from the cooler, he lost his balance. He spread his arms to recover, moving like a surfer on his board. After the porch stopped swaying, he continued toward the cooler. He picked up two cans and tossed one to Justin, who of course missed it. The can bounced off his chest and fell to the floor. That made them laugh so hard that for more than a minute they couldn't do anything but hold their stomachs.

Ted picked up the fallen can and handed it to Justin. When Justin opened it, a yellow jet shot straight into his face, and for a second his attempts to catch it in his mouth were in vain. This unleashed another fit of laughter.

"So?" Ted sat down again on the railing, paying special attention to not falling over backward.

"Nothing's going to happen with Denise, fortunately," Justin said. "She's *taken*."

"I thought you said she didn't have a boyfriend."

"She does now. An arrogant prick who looks like he'll be the next Michael Jordan. She told me so herself, so you can imagine why I say it's lucky I didn't get mixed up with her."

Justin's face suddenly darkened. He was about to ask his friend about his own girlfriend, Georgia. That's what good manners dictated he should do, wasn't it? But Justin was afraid he wouldn't be able to hide what he had found out about her a couple of weeks earlier. Now he was wondering if his silence wasn't worse. Ted was intelligence personified, and he might realize something was wrong. It wasn't as if they talked about their romantic lives all the time, but Justin's lack of interest in Ted's could look suspicious. He knew it.

Justin hadn't given up his nocturnal habits; he was familiar with the campus routine of lights going out in the dorm windows one at a time. As an invisible observer, he could see boyfriends climbing out through back windows and slipping away through the shadows, thinking they hadn't been seen, as well as couples looking for a bit of privacy in the bushes, while others simply strolled hand in hand. It wasn't that Justin was particularly nosy about other people's business. These rituals were part of the night, like the hooting of owls or the prowling of raccoons.

It was on one of these nights, back behind the library, that he saw Georgia McKenzie with another guy. She stood waiting for him by a corner of the building, where it was so dark that at first Justin didn't see her. The guy showed up a few minutes later, walking briskly. He was wearing a varsity hoodie and baseball cap, making him almost impossible to identify. Justin didn't even realize that the girl was Georgia that first time. The same scene repeated a few days later, except that this time it was the girl who showed up later. They did the usual: indulge in a long kiss, talk for a short time, and go their separate ways. Neither of these encounters went on for more than ten minutes, and they showed no signs of the frenzied lovemaking typical of students.

The third time he saw them, Justin had pretty much decided that he would follow the guy afterward to find out who he was. Then he'd tell Ted. He didn't worry much about it; after all, his friend didn't seem that interested in the girl. And from what Justin had seen behind the library, the feeling was mutual with Georgia, who seemed to have a real connection with the mystery fellow. So it was that Justin trailed him at a distance, watching him as he rounded the library and walked along a footpath that led to the parking lot by the central administration building. As he walked, the young man did something odd: he took off his hoodie, folded it up, and put it away in his shoulder bag. Then he took off his cap, and a thinner head of hair than the campus norm gave Justin his first hunch. This hunch was confirmed when the man went to the professors' parking area, where the sodium lights revealed him to be quite a bit older than Georgia, though his athletic body might have fooled a casual observer. He got into a car and drove away.

Justin recognized him immediately. It was Thomas Tyler, his creative writing professor.

Four weeks had passed since that regrettable first discovery. Justin had seen them several more times, and he was sure there was something real between them. Otherwise, why take such a risk? All that time he had been hoping that Ted would tell him he had broken up with Georgia, and then Justin would silently nod and that would be that. Why hadn't he done so yet? Justin knew he couldn't keep avoiding the issue. Why hide something like this? Why didn't Georgia tell Ted herself?

Now Ted was watching him with a comically drunken perceptiveness, which was luckily cut short by a woman's voice calling out to them from the window. Turning around, they saw two girls lifting their plastic cups and waving at them, as if they knew them. Ted and Justin exchanged a confused glance—neither of them knew these girls—and a second later they saw the pair run out the door and straight toward them. One was dragging the other along. A short girl, the leader moved at just the right speed to make her ample bosom swing from side to side. She was pretty, wore her hair short, and smiled constantly. The red plastic cup looked enormous in her hand.

"Hey, guys!"

Her friend was also pretty and apparently not as uninhibited as the first girl, because she blushed like a tomato when her friend greeted these strangers. She was a head taller, very thin, and wore a discreetly low-cut top.

"I'm Tessa. And this is Maria. My cousin."

Ted and Justin introduced themselves and shook hands with the girls.

Tessa went up to Justin, still sitting on the railing, and stood in front of him, her left leg out to the side.

"Are you a first-year student?"

"Yeah."

"Great! So's Maria."

Maria nodded to confirm this information. They still hadn't heard her voice.

"So, Justin," Tessa said as if they were old friends, "I was telling my cousin you're kind of hot. Right, Maria?" Tessa shifted her weight to her left and now stood between Justin's legs, subtly rubbing her boobs against his crotch.

Maria, for her part, was keeping a prudent distance from Ted.

"Shit," Tessa observed, seeing that her cup was empty. She crushed it and tossed it in the bushes. Turning away, in two hops she was at the cooler. She came back with a pair of cans and handed one to Justin.

Your fifth...

"Tessa, are you sure..." Maria began.

"Of course! Don't worry about it. Your cousin knows what she's doing."

They continued drinking for quite a while, talking about college, their hometowns, and not a word about any girlfriends or boyfriends. Every now and then Tessa would hop over to the cooler and come back with more beers, handing them around without asking. She must have done this a couple hundred times. At some point she pulled Justin, still perched on the railing, by the arm, and he barely had time to stretch his legs and land on his feet. The porch swayed dangerously for several seconds, like a ship on the high seas. Justin took a swig from his can as a kind of reflex action. He was barely aware of the liquid sliding down his throat, and then immediately took another swig, this time longer than the one before. Tessa was dragging him toward the stairs down to the yard. How many steps were there? Three? Four? Eighty? Justin tried to put his foot on the second step, but the little fucker ducked down a couple of inches and he nearly fell. Tessa held him up by the arm. One of her breasts squeezed against his ribs. Even in his drunken daze, he was fully conscious of the delicious sensation.

They headed off across the yard, far from the lamplight.

"Where're you taking me?" he asked. He felt that he was literally being taken away against his will, though that was impossible. This girl couldn't be taller than five foot two.

Tessa laughed and didn't let go of him.

"Don't worry. I'm not gonna rape you," she said, giggling.

They went maybe twenty yards from the house, far enough that the music was muffled by the trees. All that came through was the raucous, pulsing beat. They slipped behind some bushes and Tessa handed Justin her beer can. He stood there, confused, with both of their beers in his hands. They were standing at what looked like the foot of a small hill. Tessa squatted and lifted her skirt above her hips. Acting natural as could be, she pulled down her panties, spread her legs ninety degrees, and let loose a thick yellow stream in a perfect arc.

"The line for the bathroom goes all the way down the stairs. It's incredible," Tessa said. She sighed as the stream of liquid lost pressure.

Justin also felt an urgent need to pee, but at that moment a powerful erection radically rearranged his little buddy's priorities. There was something about Tessa's uninhibited attitude that sent his hormones skyrocketing. When at last she had almost emptied her bladder, Tessa shook her pelvis with a rhythm that drove Justin wild.

Tessa smoothed her skirt and lay back on a blanket of pine needles. Her pee flowed downhill in a silvery rivulet. Again she emitted that sigh of relaxation, like a long, low moan, and Justin couldn't resist. He sat beside her and handed her a beer, knowing perfectly well what would happen next.

"Can I tell you something sick?" he said.

"Mmmmm...sick." She immediately sounded interested. "Let's hear it."

"That was very sexy."

Tessa laughed. Now that they were sitting side by side, their faces were closer than ever.

"That isn't sick, silly. Sick would be if we did it on top of *that,*" she said, pointing at the steaming liquid that was disappearing into the earth.

Justin was left speechless. Lila had never talked to him like this. Lila would have been horrified by the very thought of peeing in front of him.

"You're really handsome," Tessa said, caressing his face. She had drunk more than the rest of them put together, yet she seemed to be in complete control.

Justin sensed a hint of acidity on her fingers that excited him even more. It was the pine needles, the discomfort of the setting; there was something primitive and potentially violent about all this that had put him in a state he'd never known.

"You're beautiful," Justin said. And, no longer able to restrain himself, he grabbed one of those huge breasts. He had to spread his hand wide, all the way, and even so, he couldn't encompass it all. His mind was about to explode.

63

1994

TED HAD a nice conversation with Maria, who, it turned out, was in one of his classes and had even heard a few things about him. She knew about his academic abilities and was surprised to find him at the party, which she had gone to only because her cousin had insisted. Ted replied almost robotically. He promised himself that the beer he was holding would be his last, and he took short sips while Maria told him how hard she had worked at school, only to get Bs, and so on about other things that Ted would be hard-pressed to recall a few hours later in spite of his prodigious memory. They were interrupted a couple of times by Tessa, who would come running back from the bushes in search of more beer and disappear again in a flutter of giggles and bouncing breasts.

The party was in full swing around one in the morning. Ted felt ready to start walking back to the Box and the calm of night, far from this jarring racket, but he didn't want to abandon Justin.

"My cousin's a little forward," Maria said, almost in apology.

"Justin can take care of himself."

"Oh, sure, but that's not what I meant." Maria blushed. Poor kid. Her face was an open book.

The porch was a lot more crowded now than at first. Suddenly the bodies parted and two muscular students strode through like a couple of gunslingers. One of them was Dan Norris.

"Hey, McKay!" he barked.

He walked over to Ted, smiling broadly. He slapped him on the back and gave him a sort of quick hug, or rather a simultaneous pat on his chest and back.

"Great you came!" said Norris. Turning to his buddy, he added, "Get this, Tim: this guy's a wiz at poker."

Tim kept a neutral expression. He was thick-necked and had a buzz cut.

"I came to pass the time," Ted forced himself to say. He thought of thanking Dan for the invitation, but he kept his mouth shut. He had already figured out that these upperclassmen weren't there to act friendly, and he hoped to get out of this with a modicum of dignity.

Maria had turned white as a sheet. Dan and Tim were juniors. What were they doing here? Several faces had turned to watch. Something was about to happen...

"Really, Tim," Dan barked. "You shoulda seen it. Almost seemed like he was cheating!"

"Oh, really?" Tim sounded interested.

"I've never seen anybody win so many hands in a row. Dude won thirty bucks offa me!"

Ted was holding himself together, trying to keep his cool. Maria looked as though she were about to cry.

"What's your trick, McKay?"

"No trick," Ted said, shrugging. "Practice, I guess."

Dan exploded with laughter. Tim nodded, and then nodded again.

"Tell you what we're gonna do, McKay," Dan said. "Later we'll head upstairs and play us a little poker. Whatcha say?"

"Oh, I don't know. It's kind of late."

"Late? C'mon, man! You owe me a chance to get my money back."

Dan gave him another frat hug with his powerful arms. The alcohol on his breath was unbearable, though the man-mountain didn't seem very drunk, at least not from the way he talked. Ted, for his part, had regained total control of his senses as if by magic; his dizziness and his piercing headache were gone, and his usual mental acuity was back. The healing power of fear, he thought with a touch of amusement. Better play along with Dan, he reflected. If he was forced to play poker, he wouldn't have any problem with letting himself lose a few hands. If need be, he could even give Dan back his stupid thirty bucks. It would be a good lesson for next time: don't make it look so easy to fleece upperclassmen.

"Sure, Dan."

"Excellent!" Dan gave him a thump on the shoulder that he made look gentle. "See ya soon, then."

Tim threw Ted a threatening glance as they left. Through the window Dan and Tim could be seen joining up with another group and heading over to a table for shots of vodka. The impromptu group formed a semicircle. They shouted in unison at every shot and then pounded their shot glasses on the wooden table. Dan downed three in less than a minute. Ted told himself he had nothing to worry about: Dan Norris would be under the table in no time if he kept this up. There would be no poker party that night.

"Those guys seemed a little crazy," remarked Maria, still reeling with fear.

"A little," Ted agreed.

Half an hour later Ted managed to get rid of Maria. There was still no sign of Justin and Tessa, and he began to weigh the idea of taking off without his friend. For the time being, however, Dan and company still occupied the middle of the living room, so it seemed impossible to leave without their noticing. Ted thought about walking around the house, but a quick glance showed that wouldn't work: a fence completely surrounded the backyard, and the only gate was padlocked. Some guys were peeing by the fence. He didn't hesitate to join them. As the stream splashed against the wooden boards, he decided that if the only way out was to walk past Dan and friends, then he should wait until the coast was a little more clear.

The wait seemed endless. At last he gave in to the temptation to have another beer. He sat on one of the porch steps and drank alone. The dizziness returned, but now it brought a pleasant sensation of weightlessness and light-headedness that induced him to keep drinking. At some point he stuck his hand in the cooler and fished through ten inches of ice water without finding a single can. They were all gone and nobody had bothered to refill the cooler. He stood up. His movements were clumsy, spasmodic. Completely forgetting about Dan, he went inside. He'd be sure to find more beer at one of the tables, he sluggishly reasoned. He had never drunk more than a couple of beers before, yet now all he could think about was putting more of the stuff into his body.

The living room was packed and everyone seemed intent on bumping into him. Hands holding drinks jumped into the air to avoid collisions. He went over to a table where two girls were pouring some green liquid. Ted randomly grabbed a cup off the table and held it out to them. The girls must have thought he was hilarious, because they started laughing while one of them poured him a quarter of a cup. Ted took a sip and scrunched his face. It was the most god-awful stuff he'd ever tasted, but what the hell?

He wandered aimlessly around the room. The music hit his head like a jackhammer, and in a sudden fit of lucidity he wondered what he was doing there, why he didn't leave, why he was drinking that nauseating beverage...But the moment passed, and he drank more and more of the green liquid. At one point he doubled over, feeling a need to retch. Everyone passing by gave him a wide berth, but he didn't vomit. He slowly stood up again and smiled at no one in particular.

"McKay!"

He turned around. The shout had been so loud he'd been able to hear it over the pounding music. Dan was by his side, with Tim and another guy behind him, in perfect formation.

"Hey!" said Ted, and he tried slapping Dan on the shoulder but missed. His hand continued the circle and ended up on his own knee. He tried again and barely grazed Dan's T-shirt.

"Enjoying the party?"

Ted nodded.

"Why's he so serious?" Ted asked, pointing at Tim.

"Listen, McKay." Dan's voice was slurred, but only slightly. Ted's attention wandered to the cleavage of a girl dancing near him. "McKay! Up here, eyes on me. Me and the boys are gonna go play a couple games. You're coming."

Ted found the idea hilarious. He started laughing uproariously.

"Poker?" he asked half a dozen times, as if the word itself were a joke.

"Right: poker. You owe me. Let's go." Dan grabbed him under one arm and Tim seized the other. The two of them lifted Ted off the floor and carried him upstairs. Ted didn't feel as though this were a hostile action at all.

"Thanks, guys. I can take it from here."

But the fact was, he couldn't. A few more joined the group, so now there were six, including Ted, making their way up the stairs. How many people were there?

"Hey, we're a choo-choo train!" Ted said, laughing at his own joke.

They looked at him as if he were a survivor of some natural disaster being rescued by a bunch of firefighters. Ted was starting to feel more and more lost.

The second floor was as crowded as the first. When they got to the third floor, the sudden calm came as a shock.

"You owe me this one, McKay," Dan said. Now his voice was slow and perfectly audible. The music had been reduced to a distant, guttural groan. They went to the far end of the corridor. Tim unlocked a door and Dan shoved Ted inside. The other three crowded in behind them.

There was no poker table in the room.

Ted took a terrific blow to the ribs and fell to the floor. Then the kicks rained down.

64

1994

A MERCIFUL fraternity brother drove Ted back to the Box. Ted remembered snippets: coming out of the house, being loaded into the tiny red car. He remembered nothing about the drive itself. He woke up in bed as if by magic, fully dressed and aching all over.

Justin, for his part, decided to leave the party when the possibility of his throwing up on Tessa began to feel more like a certainty. She made him promise they'd get together again soon (Justin was happy to give his word on this), and in an outbreak of drunken sincerity he told her that he'd never had such a good time with a woman before, which was the truth. Before he left, he searched high and low for Ted, unaware that his friend was getting beaten up at that very moment by five brothers of the prestigious Delta Tau fraternity. Justin assumed that Ted had already walked back to the Box by himself. He vomited once along the way and again when he reached the dorm. His roommate wasn't in bed, but that didn't worry him.

When Justin woke up and saw Ted lying on the bed next to his, he did get worried. At first he thought Ted was dead. His face was red, swollen, and covered with blood. Once he was sure Ted was breathing, he calmed down a little.

Ted refused to go to the infirmary. He remained shut up in the dorm room for three days, hardly leaving his bed. During that time most of the swelling in his face went down, and with the help of a pair of mirrored sunglasses he was able to return to his studies. The slight limp he was left with wore off over time. Nobody but his roommate (and, of course, the five cowards who beat him up) ever found out what had happened that night on the third floor of Delta Tau.

65

1994

THE BEATING led to a series of dreadful events, some of them direct consequences, others indirect. Ted gradually became less communicative and more apathetic than before. This change affected his luck at the gambling tables, where charisma and manipulation were essential weapons. The change also damaged Ted's relationship with Georgia, from whom he slowly began to distance himself. Neither of them did anything to try to make things better. Justin was perceptive enough to know better than to torture him with questions; he had begun to know Ted's moods, which meant knowing when it was better not to pester him with pointless interrogations.

The worst came five days later, when he got a call from his aunt Audrey, his father's sister. She was the only one on his father's side of the family with whom Ted kept up a sporadic relationship, and even so, she had never called him on campus. When he heard her voice on the other end of the line, his first thought was that something must have happened to his father. And the fact was that Ted couldn't help feeling happy about this; he hadn't seen his father in five years, and it wouldn't bother him if they never saw each other again. But it turned out that Frank McKay hadn't died or been injured in a gruesome accident; he simply wanted to speak to Ted, so he had turned to Audrey. Over the past decade Frank had become a prosperous farm equipment salesman, and he was apparently back to his pathetic efforts at making contact with his son.

For some stupid reason Ted called him.

It turned out that his father was going to be in the area for a convention and he had every intention of coming to campus and paying Ted a visit. Ted refused categorically, of course, and told his father he'd go see him at his motel. The very idea of seeing his father on campus turned his stomach. He'd go find him and put an end, once and for all, to these pitiful attempts to remake himself as Father of the Year.

He parked his car in front of the modest Lonesome Pine Motel and didn't bother going to the office. He recognized his father's silhouette against the curtains of room 108, moving back and forth with packages he was piling up somewhere. Ted stood facing the window for a while, the twitter of starlings at dusk a prelude to the mistake he was about to make. The door suddenly swung open.

"Ted! Son! Great to see you."

"Hey."

His father's hair was gray—not entirely, but much grayer than the last time Ted had seen him. Even so, he looked a good ten years younger than his age. His features were still sharp, and he hadn't put on an ounce of fat. His skin was as tanned as in his door-to-door salesman days. But beyond his physical appearance, Ted paid special attention to his eyes, because if there was anything he had learned as a teenager, it was that no matter what his father said or did, those two tiny, brilliant blue irises were the only part of him that told the truth. And right now, what they were telling him was very simple: *I'm smarter than you.*

Frank walked over, clearly intending to give Ted a hug. Ted held up a hand to stop him and took a step back.

"Please, Dad."

He put up his hands in surrender and silently gave up.

"Come in."

Ted was planning to make this a short visit.

The room was small. What Ted had seen through the window was his father unpacking his suitcase, which lay almost empty in the center of the bed. Under the TV set attached to the wall there was a tiny table and two chairs. Frank sat on one and gestured to his son to take the other.

"Come on, Ted. We've got to talk sometime."

That at least was true.

Ted stood looking at a horrid painting.

"I don't want you coming to campus to look for me. Ever."

Frank didn't respond right away.

"If you don't want me to come, I won't come."

"Perfect."

Another uncomfortable silence settled on them. Ted didn't want to ask his father what he wanted to tell him; he wanted him to talk on his own initiative. It drove him crazy to feel that every word coming out of his mouth was a kind of competition. But it was.

"What happened to your face? Fistfight with some college boys?"

Ted instinctively raised his hand to his cheek. No sign of the beating remained on his face other than an almost imperceptible bruise on his left cheek. He tried to remember if he had mentioned the incident to his aunt Audrey, but he didn't think so.

"No fights," Ted replied drily.

"Aunt Audrey told me your grades are very good. She also showed me a photo of your girlfriend, Georgia..."

Frank stopped talking when he saw Ted's reaction. He tried another approach.

"I'm your father. Naturally I want to—"

"If you keep asking my aunt about me, the only thing you're going to accomplish is that I'll never talk to her again."

Frank sighed in resignation.

"What happened to us, Ted?" he said, leaning slightly forward. His hand reached out and stopped, halfway to Ted's. "We were a team, remember?"

Ted felt like laughing in his face. He shook his head.

"Remember when we used to go around to those chess tourna—"

"That's enough. I refuse to talk about the past with you. I know perfectly well what was going on and what you've done. And I'm not talking about your cheating on Mom with that woman. Even though that was what broke her heart in the end, I think you did us a favor."

"I think we do have to talk about the past, because otherwise we won't be able to piece together the present."

"Great. Did you get that from a fortune cookie? There is no 'present' for us to piece together. There's only one thing that you and I need to clear up: that we're never going to talk to each other again. Is that clear?"

Frank bowed his head.

"You have to leave the past behind someday," he said, staring at the floor. "You're grown-up now. I'm not going to try giving you advice. But I know what I'm talking about."

"You don't get it, do you? It isn't a question of whether I'll forgive you or not. What do you want me to forgive you for? How you beat Mommy, or how you beat me? Which of those two should I forgive you for?"

"Don't say it like that."

"There's no other way to say it. So it isn't a matter of forgiving you. It's just that I don't fucking feel like seeing the guy who used to beat my mother for spilling the salt in the kitchen or for putting her shoes in the refrigerator when her illness made it so she didn't know what she was doing."

"You know it was a lot more than that," Frank muttered, looking up. There was a mixture of pleading and suppressed rage in his eyes.

"Well, of course there was a lot more. She was ill!"

Frank bit his lips. He raised his hand to his mouth and started biting his nail.

"I asked you to forgive me for that. That's all I can do. She was ill, and I...I didn't know how to handle her. Obviously I did a terrible job. That's what things were like when I was growing up, and that's what I learned at home. I didn't know any other way to fix the situation."

Ted shook his head. His father always tried to put himself in the victim's role.

"Dad, I don't care why things happened the way they did. I also don't care about your side of things. I was the one who had to live with Mom all those years, watching her getting worse and worse, day after day, while you were off running around somewhere. And if you want to believe that abandoning her didn't affect her, you're wrong: it did. And if you want to believe that every time you hit her and every time you yelled at her it didn't make her worse, I'm sorry, but that's not how it was."

Frank swallowed.

"No doubt you're right."

"No doubt at all."

A glimmer of hope appeared in Frank's eyes.

"But with you...with you, I always tried..."

"I was seven years old the first time I heard you beating her!" Ted exploded. "You know something? I never told you this, but maybe it's good for you to know." He pointed an accusing finger at his father. "Maybe it'll help if I tell you all the good you did me. If I tell you that after you left home, I could hardly sleep because of the nightmares. Nightmares I still get now. You want to know what happens in them?"

"Ted, please. I don't think this will help to—"

"Of course it helps. Of course it helps!"

Frank was watching him now with the pitiless gaze that Ted had come to know so well as a child. Because deep down, Frank McKay hated to be contradicted. He could wrap himself in sheep's clothing for a while and beg forgiveness, but nothing bothered him so much as when things weren't done his way, when *he* wasn't the one dictating what should be done and what shouldn't.

"When I get these nightmares, there you are, sitting like you're sitting now, and you're calmly smoking a cigarette. And you're telling me I should go to your red Mustang. Remember that car?"

Something shifted in Frank's face.

"Of course I remember my red Mustang."

"I don't want to get near the trunk because I know what I'll find in there. But you insist and insist that I have to see. And finally I go over, and before I get there, the trunk opens like magic. And there's Mommy, with her wrists tied and her face disfigured, covered with insects."

"Ted," Frank muttered.

"In my dreams, I can't pull my eyes away from the corpse until I wake up. And what I hear in the background is you laughing, because you're getting a kick out of it."

Ted spoke without taking his eyes off Frank for one second. As soon as he finished he felt worn down from having told it all. He'd never spoken about this to anyone, and could never have imagined telling his father, yet now he felt much better—not only relieved of a heavy burden but satisfied, because his son of a bitch father deserved to learn how he had made his little son suffer.

"Sometimes the woman isn't Mom but some girl I like, or a woman I happen to know. They lie there, scrunched up inside the trunk, and suddenly they come back to life and grab me by the arm, staring at me with their eyes pleading, like they want to tell me something. The rest is always the same: the red Mustang, you smoking and laughing. Always the same."

Ted stood up abruptly, kicked the chair aside, and swore under his breath.

"I can't look at a woman without thinking about what you did to Mom," he said, near tears. "Now can you understand why I don't want you in my life?"

Frank looked unflappable. He didn't seem inclined to continue arguing. He went to the nightstand and picked up a book with a photo sticking out of it. He took out the photo and set it on the table.

Ted was still standing; he had to come closer to see what the photo showed: a boy, maybe twelve years old. The features, which he recognized from his own face, plus the tiny blue eyes told him everything.

"That's your brother," Frank said. Not a trace remained of his earlier pleading tone.

Ted looked up and stared at Frank with a wild expression. Then he turned back to study the boy, handsome and smiling. Ted was speechless.

"That's your brother," Frank repeated. "Edward. He's got his mother's last name: Blaine. It doesn't matter what you think of me. You ought to get to know him. That's why I wanted to see you today."

Ted never met Blaine, but years later he recognized his face on the news when he was accused of killing his girlfriend, Amanda Herdman.

66

Present day

TED STOOD in silence at the entrance to the footpath, like a gunman about to fight a duel. Laura and Lee were behind him.

"I've walked this path many times," he said in a low voice.

Lee kept a couple of yards back. The doctor had assured him that McKay wasn't dangerous, but Lee knew he'd left a man in a coma, and though he'd been having a nervous breakdown or some such at the time, Lee didn't care. If it happened once, it could happen again, right? The prisoner was his responsibility as long as he was outside the hospital, and Lee wasn't about to trust the guy. If he tried to attack Dr. Hill, Lee would just have to run forward a couple of yards and Tase him. If instead he tried to make a run for it, that would be even easier, because he wouldn't get far with those chains on his legs.

A hundred yards on, Ted was still in some sort of dream state, suddenly bowing his head and apparently following invisible tracks. Laura tried talking to him, but she got only monosyllabic answers and decided to leave it. One thing was clear: this path possessed some special importance for Ted, and walking along it appeared to be helping him understand why. Laura took advantage of the situation and pulled out her cell phone to check for a signal.

Only one bar.

At times Ted looked like one of those mediums on TV. He would stop, look around, look down, as if he were expecting a revelation that would show him the right way.

"Is something wrong?"

Ted had stopped. He was chewing his thumbnail, staring at the trees.

"I remember a bicycle," he said cryptically.

"You used to ride a bike on this path?"

"No, not me. I don't even own one."

Laura asked no more questions. She was thrilled, however, because this recollection of a bicycle, however insignificant or unimportant it might turn out to be, was something *new*. The first thing filtering through. It could be the start of everything.

"What color is the bike, Ted?"

"Red," he said, almost without thinking.

As soon as he said it out loud, he weighed the new information.

"A red bicycle," he said, nodding slowly again and again.

He looked down. Then he moved off in silence.

All three of them walked along a narrow path that at this point had all but disappeared. They had to push branches aside and dodge fallen trees until they came across an abandoned dirt road. It was overgrown with weeds. And there they saw it, to one side, barely visible through the yellow weeds. The ruins of a red bicycle. It was missing a wheel, and rust had attacked it mercilessly, but here and there the original paint was visible.

"The abandoned bike," Ted said as he drew near. He stared at it.

"Ted, this is fantastic!"

"So it seems," he said without enthusiasm.

"Cheer up." Laura put her hand on his shoulder to comfort him. Lee looked on disapprovingly but didn't stop her; he walked over to the bicycle and looked at it with one raised eyebrow.

"The bike's here because it had an accident. The frame is bent. The missing wheel must be around somewhere."

The word "accident" floated around them.

"Do you know anything about this, Ted?" Laura asked.

"I don't think so. I—I only saw it lying here."

On the other side of the road was more wooded land. Ted hesitated for a second.

"We can take a shortcut through the woods," he said robotically. "Or keep to the road and go around the long way. Either way will work, and we'll come to the same place."

Filtrations.

"Where will we come to, Ted?" Laura asked, her voice trembling.

"To the truth," he said.

And he started walking along that dusty road, dragging his feet and the chain that linked them. He kept his hands against his thighs. Laura and Lee couldn't see his face, which was lucky, because at this moment it was beginning to transform under the weight of a new revelation.

They had walked nearly a mile and a half by the time they arrived.

67

Present day

MARCUS COULDN'T remember ever feeling as happy as he did that Saturday. He even thought about going jogging. On that day he felt capable of anything.

When he was heading to pick up the newspaper from his front stoop, he stopped and held the doorknob for a second, smiling like a fool, reminding himself that in just a few hours he would open this door and find Laura on the other side.

And remember what you have to do...

At lunch he felt an urge to call her, but he restrained himself. He had talked to Bob, his friend on the Boston police force, who had assured him that he'd take a look that very day at the murder cases starting in 1993.

He spent the morning shopping. First he took off for the supermarket to buy everything he'd need for his special sauce. Marcus wasn't a great cook; his diet consisted mainly of frozen microwave meals, pizza, and Chinese takeout, though he had a few dishes that he'd learned to make passably well. Linguini with wild mushrooms and onions was his specialty. But before hitting the grocery store, he stopped by the mall and spent a small fortune on new clothes. He'd been postponing this shopping trip for weeks, but if ever there was a perfect day for sprucing up his wardrobe, this was it.

Marcus got back home around midday, carrying a dozen shopping bags. He had everything he'd need. When he shut the door, again he got that sensation of vertigo. Marcus smiled. He had a few hours to fill before he started making the sauce, so he decided to go to his home theater and watch a couple of the films on his list. He set a bag of popcorn in the microwave. Before the first kernel had time to pop, he was interrupted by the insistently ringing doorbell.

He went to the window and saw Bob at the front door. He was holding a folder in his right hand. Why hadn't he called first?

He opened the door. Fate was pulling another fast one on him. When he opened this door, the woman of his life was supposed to be standing there, not a cop with an actor's name.

"Bob. What a surprise. Did you find something?"

"Yes."

Something that disturbed him—that much was clear from his face.

"Come on in, please."

They turned into the living room. A barrage of popping corn could be heard in the kitchen.

As they were about to sit, Bob turned and looked his friend in the eye.

"Did you know that McKay is the brother of Edward Blaine, the guy they accused of killing his girlfriend?"

Marcus froze.

"I did not know that."

"Same father. Different mother," Bob said as he took a seat. "But that's not why I came here. I could have told you that much over the phone."

Marcus sat down.

68

1994

THE MSU campus awoke to the news of the murder. A student, it was rumored at first, had been found dead near the library. University authorities asked students to remain in their dorms and apartments if possible, and all academic activities were suspended. The news dominated the local media. Every television set in the Box was turned on, though the most current information came from the campus itself. When the TV news was still reporting that the victim was a student whose name had not yet been revealed, students already knew this wasn't so. The dead man was Thomas Tyler, a prominent professor of English literature who had taught at MSU for nearly a decade. His identification was delayed by the fact that he was inexplicably wearing a varsity hoodie and cap over his usual clothes, confusing the two young women who discovered his body that Friday morning.

Contradictory rumors flew around the Box. A guy on the fifth floor, Mark Manganiello, known to all as Marman, became the principal source of reliable facts. His girlfriend lived just a couple of doors down from Jules Loughlin, one of the girls who found the body. According to Marman, the professor's body was lying facedown, which was why they didn't recognize him. At first they thought he was a student sleeping off a binge or whatever, but when they got closer they saw the puddle of blood around the body. His throat had been slit. During those anxious early hours, it was also rumored that the motive for the murder had been to steal an expensive gold cigarette lighter that Tyler always carried.

When the victim's identity was revealed at last, the news programs focused on the mystery that was attracting everybody's interest: Why had the professor been hiding his professorial clothes under a student hoodie? Thomas Tyler was fifty-one, married, with two teenage daughters. Production crews staked out his house, hoping to get a glimpse of his family.

MSU attracted a considerable amount of national media attention. The hoodie was what didn't fit. But there was something else, a rumor that was already running wild through all the dorms and that the police had possibly already heard. And if the police knew, it was reasonable to assume that some reporter had heard it, too. It seemed that Tyler was having an affair with a student. This was the sort of detail that would add an irresistible pinch of spice to the story as it came before a national audience.

Ted was returning from the sixth floor, where the poker party had become a favorite way for many students to kill time, when Justin approached him with a wild, stunned look in his eyes. Ted became alarmed and all but shoved him into 503 and shut the door to their room behind them.

"What's wrong, Justin? You can't walk around campus looking like that. Not on a day like this."

"Sorry, sorry, but I can't take it anymore, Ted." Justin was pacing back and forth.

"Sit down for a second."

Justin sat on his bed.

"You haven't done anything," Ted said, looking at him closely. "Have you?"

"Of course not!"

"So why do you look so worried? There's no reason to walk around looking like that."

"You haven't talked to Marman, have you?"

"No. I just came from the sixth floor."

"The girl that Tyler was having an affair with...was Georgia."

Ted raised an eyebrow, but didn't lose his cool.

"Where'd you hear that?"

"I just told you: Marman. You don't look too surprised."

Ted sat on his bed.

"I'm thinking it through," he admitted. "The police will come and question me. Don't sweat it. Everything'll be okay."

"Did you...know about this? The affair, I mean."

"No. Things weren't going well between us. Maybe we had technically broken off—I don't know. But that doesn't make much difference. The police will still want to question me. Chill, Justin. And stop looking like that. We have to act normal."

"The thing is...Ted, I've got to tell you something."

"Go ahead."

Justin glanced at the closed door as if someone might barge in at any moment and catch him in the middle of talking. He swallowed.

"I knew about Georgia and the professor, Ted. I saw them together behind the library. More than once. Several times. If I didn't say anything to you, it was because—"

"Justin, stop right there. I understand why you didn't want to tell me. The problem is whether the police will think you told me."

"They shouldn't."

"And you shouldn't tell them, either." Ted was looking hard at his friend.

"I wasn't planning to tell them, Ted. But tons of students have seen me hanging out in back of the library at night. And if I keep my mouth shut, it could look worse."

Ted stood up and strode around the room. Thinking out loud, he said, "Your seeing them certainly does complicate things."

He then fell silent for some time.

"Where were you yesterday?" Ted suddenly asked his roommate.

"Studying in the commons until ten thirty."

"So you have an alibi."

"I don't know. How can we be sure when he was killed?"

"The guy was wearing his hoodie and cap, and the only reason for that was if he was with...Georgia. When did you see them together?"

"Never after eight."

"There you go. Besides, she can confirm it."

"What if they also hooked up later but I just never saw them?"

"Justin, I can't see Georgia walking around campus by herself so late at night. Most likely this was just like the other times. She left and the guy stayed there awhile, walking around a little to throw off anybody who might have seen them, before getting in his car and leaving. That's what happened. But before he reached his car, he was assaulted and killed. And you were studying in the commons, with lots of witnesses. You didn't leave at any time?"

"No."

"Perfect. That's what you'll tell the police if they ask you. You often hung around the library but you never saw them there. Therefore, you never told me about them, because you didn't know."

Ted put a special emphasis on those final words, pronouncing them slowly and clearly. Justin nodded. His face began to relax, but only a bit.

"I'm not so sure. Don't the police have lie detectors and stuff?"

"Hey, Justin, look at me." Ted grabbed him by the shoulders. "You will simply keep quiet about what you saw a couple of times, and you will do that only so the investigation doesn't get diverted toward you and toward me, and they can concentrate on finding the real killer." Justin was shaking his head. "Listen. We're planning for a worst-case scenario. Most likely, the police already have a suspect or a solid lead, and you're just worrying yourself unnecessarily."

"Yeah, maybe."

"Of course. And remember, you have a solid alibi. As little time as you've spent studying lately, it was lucky for you that you decided to have a study session just then, don't you think?"

For the first time, Justin showed a nervous smile.

"Yeah, really. If I'd been wandering around campus last night, I'd be pissing myself right now."

"Exactly. Now you have no cause for worry. If anybody squeals to the police that you enjoy skulking around the library at night, just tell them it's true, but you never saw them or found out about their affair. And as for last night, just describe what you did. Everything will be all right."

When Ted put it that way, everything seemed so easy. And why shouldn't it be? Justin hadn't killed Professor Tyler. Plus, he hadn't told his roommate anything, so Ted couldn't have done it, either.

"How about you, Ted? Where were you last night? On the sixth floor, I suppose?"

Ted's expression changed.

"Yeah, I was up on six. But I left around six o'clock."

A heavy silence fell over them.

"And after that?" Justin asked in a worried tone.

"I came down here to study. No solid alibi for me, I'm afraid."

Ted started laughing.

69

1994

THE FOLLOWING day it was officially acknowledged that Tyler had been having an affair with a student named Georgia McKenzie, and the attention being paid to the case went up exponentially. Coverage was constant. Two helicopters flew over the campus taking aerial footage. The university suspended classes for three days (which turned into five). The story of a married professor with a respectable family having an affair with a student was just too juicy. The most daring and least ethical journalists bandied about the theory that Georgia killed her lover in a fit of jealousy. *Girl hopelessly in love with her professor loses her head when he tries to dump her.*

Attention soon enough focused on Ted.

70

1994

RUMORS OUTPACED facts around campus. Ted went to Georgia's dorm to see her as soon as he learned that her fling with the professor had become common knowledge. She was holed up in her room, overcome by panic attacks. Ted skipped the formalities and got straight to the point: he wanted to know what she had seen that night, if anything. Georgia told him her parents were on their way with a lawyer in tow, so she didn't have much time. He was stunned to hear her reveal, trembling and with tears in her eyes, not only that she had been with Tyler that night, but that she had witnessed the precise moment when he was killed. Ted froze. The story she falteringly told confirmed that she had been sitting with the professor on one of the benches behind the library.

She had only agreed to meet him that one last time (she swore it was to be their last time together) in order to break up with him. The conversation hadn't been pleasant. They got into an argument: the professor insulted her with a cutting remark (which Georgia refused to repeat to Ted) and she started crying. Tyler tried to hug her but Georgia pushed him away. After a while she stood up and threatened to do something that, according to her, she had no intention of carrying out: if he didn't leave her alone, she told the professor, she would tell his wife everything. Then she turned and walked away. But after a few steps she started feeling guilty, so she turned back, not to beg for his forgiveness but simply because she felt she shouldn't have threatened Tyler like that. And that was when, from several yards away, she saw everything. A shadow jumped out of the bushes and slit the man's throat with astonishing swiftness. Tyler fell like a stone. He didn't even have time to scream. The murderer stood stock-still for a moment, barely an outline among the shadows, and before he left he did something odd: he bent down and searched the professor's body. Georgia couldn't see what it was he found, but he pocketed something. Immediately afterward he disappeared like a ghost.

Ted followed her story in complete silence. She sat on her bed; he sat on a chair. He never tried to console her. He thought it would be a bad idea.

"Could you see who it was?" he asked instead.

"When he bent down, the light from the streetlamp nearly fell on his face, but no, I couldn't tell."

"Are you going to let the police know about this?"

"I don't know, Ted. I'm so scared. Last night I came here and took a whole bunch of pills to sleep. I didn't think Tyler could have survived—that's why I ran off. I thought it was for the best. You can't imagine how the blood flowed from his neck and how he fell to the ground. It was like..."

Georgia wept convulsively. Frail and trembling, she was begging for a redemptive embrace that never came.

"Like the killer knew what he was doing," she concluded.

Ted nodded.

"I need you to forgive me."

But before Ted could respond, the door to her room swung open, and there stood none other than the detective in charge of the case, Detective Segarra, and two other cops.

Georgia made a statement to the police the next day, followed by Ted's statement. They weren't allowed to meet again. As for Ted, he stuck to what he had told Justin in their room: on the afternoon before the crime took place, he had been playing poker on the sixth floor of his dorm and then had gone to his room to study. They asked him all sorts of questions, not only about that day but about previous days, jumping from one point in time to another in a clear attempt to confuse him. Ted never contradicted himself.

Journalists working the story somehow got hold of Georgia's statement, and her version of the facts became the official story. Dozens of reporters, some of them planted in front of the murder scene from just outside the restricted area, narrated the tryst between student and professor and how she had turned back seconds after leaving him and watched him die. Many people (including Ted) believed that Detective Segarra had carefully orchestrated the leak. Though the young woman couldn't identify the killer, she insisted it couldn't have been her boyfriend, Ted, who she said she would have been able to identify despite the lack of light. Speculation ran amok. All sorts of theories were advanced. Some people doubted Georgia's whole story, accusing her of committing the murder herself. Others speculated about a possible conspiracy between Georgia and her boyfriend. Still others suggested that Tyler's wife was the vengeful killer.

Ted's situation worsened when Georgia's lawyers suggested that she elaborate on her statement. She was already implicated, she had a motive for killing the professor, she had left the scene of the crime, and she hadn't immediately called the police. In her favor, of course, was the fact that everything known about the murder came from her own statement. But was that good enough? At least two of her girlfriends knew about her secret affair, and anybody else might have seen her with Tyler as well, so the fact that she was the first to reveal it publicly could have been just a smoke screen. Indeed, more and more suspicion fell on Georgia as the days went by. Her lawyers recommended that she correct her statement as to what she had seen that night. The truth was that there was so little light that she couldn't rule anyone out, not even Ted. The lawyers claimed that McKay had intimidated Georgia when (as witnessed by

Segarra himself) he had visited her in her room the following day. She couldn't believe that her boyfriend was capable of doing such a thing, and had therefore ruled him out in the first place, but the fact was that she couldn't say anything about who had or hadn't killed Tyler. She couldn't even swear that it had been a man.

71

Present day

LAURA, TED, and Lee stood before a long perimeter wall whose original color was indiscernible. A yard or so of gray concrete blocks had been added on top to bring the wall to the imposing height of ten feet. Paint was peeling off the bottom third of the wall in large patches, revealing the original bricks. The rest was faded or covered in graffiti. The wall was topped by a double row of barbed wire. At the center of the wall stood a gate, padlocked with a heavy chain.

"It's the abandoned typewriter factory," Laura said. It wasn't a question.

"That's right." Ted walked up to the wall and placed both of his hands on it, as if he expected to receive some sort of vibration. In a way, he did. "My company acquired it ten years ago."

"In one of our sessions, you told me that Wendell had bought it," Laura said, wondering how he would react.

It seemed to take Ted a while to figure out who she was talking about.

"I acquired it, through my company," he repeated, walking along the wall now without lifting his hand from its surface. "The keys are right there."

He was pointing at one of the bricks, practically at ground level, hidden behind weeds and an odd, prickly bush.

Lee went immediately to the spot where he was pointing, telling Ted to stand back. With some difficulty, the guard squatted and stretched his arm through the weeds until he touched the wall. One of the bricks moved a little when he pushed it. He had to use both hands to grip it and pull it out. A key ring rested in the cavity.

"We have to go inside," Ted said. "But only Laura and me."

"No way," Lee said.

"Ted," Laura interceded, "you know we can't do it like that. Is there something you need to tell me? Lee can give us a little privacy, but he can't leave us completely alone. You understand that, don't you?"

Ted rubbed his temples. He wasn't convinced. Lee and Laura waited.

"It's simple, McKay," Lee said. "Either we all three go in together, or we all three turn around and go back. No other alternative."

"All right."

Lee went to open the gate.

"It's the biggest key on the ring."

Laura stood by Ted.

"You're doing great. I'll ask Lee to let us talk in private a little. Do you know what we'll find in here? Something you've remembered?"

Ted didn't speak. There was a strange look in his eyes.

"No, I don't know."

But he did.

Passing through the gate, they entered a large parking lot that looked as abandoned as the perimeter wall. Weeds and bushes had grown unchecked. The crumbling concrete sidewalks were the only areas where they could walk. On the right was a two-story building, its windows and most of its doors shuttered with sheets of plywood. The exception was a single door on one corner. The three of them headed for it.

On their walk through the woods they had scarcely noticed that the winds from the south had covered the sky in a layer of clouds—not threatening, but thick enough to block the sun.

Lee used one of the keys to unfasten another padlock, and a smaller key to unlock the door, which closed behind them with a soft *click*. They had walked into a tiny room, completely empty and falling apart; after all, this wasn't the main entrance. Ted guided them through a side door to a hallway that led to an area with offices. Lee had turned on his flashlight to make up for the dim light filtering through cracks in the plywood sheets nailed over the windows. The offices weren't completely empty: there were a few desks, filing cabinets, and so forth. Halfway down the hall, Ted stopped and contemplated a side door, as if he couldn't recall it—or perhaps to the contrary: as if it held some special significance. At last he walked on, until he came to a double door at the end of this office area. They entered an enormous space that had once held workshops and assembly lines. Some of the machinery was still standing. The ceiling here reached up to the full height of the building. It was outfitted with skylights that, though grimy with years of dirt, allowed some light through.

Lee put away his flashlight. What he needed to have at hand was his Taser, or even the Beretta. He didn't like this place. Too little light, too many places to hide.

That was when Laura's cell phone rang, and all three of them jumped.

"Marcus?"

The reception sucked.

"...lo...gency...ospital."

Laura instinctively stepped away. She asked Lee for the key ring and he gave it to her without objection.

"Marcus, I can't make out anything you're saying. An emergency at Lavender?"

"...listen...way..."

It was pointless. Laura ran through the labyrinth that had brought them there, but in reverse. She had to try three of the small keys before she managed to get outside. She tested the phone again.

"Can you hear me now?"

"Yes. And you can hear me?"

"Now I can. I'm outside the building."

"What building?"

Marcus sounded alarmed.

"The footpath behind Ted's house led to an old factory. It's the one that—"

"Laura, listen closely. Is McKay with Lee?"

"Yes."

"Is he shackled hand and foot? Is he being closely guarded?"

"Yes. Why?"

"Are you sure he can't hear you?"

"Yes, I'm sure! Marcus, you're getting me worried. What happened?"

"I need you to listen to me very closely. I'm with Bob Duvall right now. Bob checked up on the things I asked him to look into. There really was a murder at MSU in nineteen ninety-four, when Ted was a freshman. A professor named Thomas Tyler had his throat slit. A pretty high-profile case. The police investigated several students, including Ted McKay and Justin Lynch, but they came up empty. The case went cold and was left unsolved. I have the file in my hands. And guess what?"

Laura couldn't guess anything. Processing this new information was as much as she could manage. A professor murdered? Marcus's urgency could mean only one thing...

"Tell me the rest—please."

Her legs went wobbly and almost gave way. She knelt on the ground and listened.

72

1994

FIVE DAYS after the murder of Thomas Tyler, the campus was still shaken. Classes were running normally again, yet the crime against the professor seemed to be the only possible topic of conversation. Television production trucks were no longer stationed at MSU around the clock, and helicopters no longer buzzed above the campus every few hours, but the media hadn't forgotten the case. Not at all. The love triangle was the new focus of attention. Reports carried photos of Tyler and his family, of Georgia McKenzie, and two or three of Ted (including his high school yearbook photo). Georgia had returned home on her doctor's advice, but the police issued a press release stating that she was not under investigation for Tyler's murder. Hardly anyone believed it.

It was seven in the morning when three short blasts of a siren sounded in the Box. Then a voice crackled over the dorm's old intercom system, a rarely used relic from the days of civil defense drills. Doors opened throughout every corridor. Sleepy-eyed students, most still in pajamas, looked at one another and tried to take in what the voice was saying. The speaker was the dean of students. He was asking everybody to gather downstairs in the first-floor assembly hall. An important announcement would be made there in fifteen minutes.

The situation was beyond unusual. Who had ever heard of an unscheduled all-dorm assembly? And what kind of announcement justified waking students up at seven in the morning?

Ted was the first out of bed in room 503. His roommate was the heaviest sleeper Ted had ever known, and it was a couple of minutes before Justin's brain began functioning minimally. When it dawned on him that the announcement might be about the murder, he went on the alert.

"Don't rush things, Justin. Please. Take your time, get dressed, and then we'll go downstairs."

The other fifth-floor residents were stumbling down the corridor, half asleep.

When they reached the first floor, any doubts as to whether the announcement concerned the murder were dispelled. A group of ten police officers ran upstairs while some students were still on their way down. The assembly hall was packed. Next to the door stood the dean and Detective Segarra, who everyone recognized from his brief televised press conferences about the case. With them were more police officers and two assistants to the dean.

"What is all this shit?" Justin muttered.

"Some routine procedure, no doubt," Ted said, sounding unconcerned.

"Good morning," the dean began. "I will be brief. As you can imagine, we require your cooperation in the police investigation that is being conducted at this time. Detective Segarra and his officers will be searching this building. What we ask of you is to remain here while the search is ongoing."

Murmurs and protests spread through the hall. Segarra took the floor.

"If any of you require any indispensable items over the course of the next two to three hours, raise your hand and an officer will accompany you to your room to retrieve them." He paused. "By 'indispensable,' I mean medicine."

"Can they do this?" someone asked.

The dean responded.

"University lawyers are present and will ensure that the search is conducted according to the letter of the law."

Nobody else raised any further objections. Segarra and a few of his officers went upstairs, leaving two behind on the first floor to watch the doors.

What was going on?

Of all the dorms on campus, the Box was the only one in which a search like this had been carried out so far. Perhaps it was a coincidence, but logic indicated that the dorm hadn't been chosen at random. As soon as one building was searched, of course, every student on campus would be on the alert, so if anybody was concealing objects relevant to the investigation in his or her room, he or she would have plenty of time to get rid of the evidence before a second dorm was searched. Obviously, then, the other dorms weren't going to get searched; whatever the police were interested in, it must be here in the Box.

Justin, Ted, and a couple of other students huddled in a group. Among them were Marman and Irving Prosser, as well as a kid named Joe Stilwell, who had gone pale as a sheet and seemed to have forgotten how to blink. Ted was glad Stilwell was with them; he made Justin's terror that much less obvious.

"Do you guys think they're searching for the lighter?" Marman suggested.

Ted had forgotten about the lighter, an urban myth that had grown from the fact that a few students had once seen the professor holding an expensive-looking gold cigarette lighter.

"There isn't any lighter," Irving observed.

"So what are they looking for?"

Ted wasn't really interested in what they were looking for, only in why. Searching an entire six-story university dorm wasn't a measure to be taken lightly, not even in a high-profile murder case. Though the dean had sounded cooperative when he made the announcement a few minutes ago, he and the university lawyers must have raised massive objections. A judge would first have to grant a warrant. But a warrant to search an entire dorm? It was too big an operation for it not to be based on a concrete piece of information. What could it be?

A little more than an hour later, Segarra and his team were headed back down to the assembly hall. Ted counted them. Fifteen altogether, plus Segarra. The first conclusion he drew was that they were all regular cops or detectives, not forensic police, which meant that the judge's warrant must have authorized only a limited search for some particular object, not a general fishing expedition for fingerprints or DNA evidence. This said something about the likely progress of the investigation, he reasoned. The second and more important conclusion was that it would be impossible for a mere fifteen officers to search every room in the dorm with any degree of thoroughness in such a short time.

Ted ran upstairs as soon as students were allowed back on their floors. He took a few seconds to peek into some rooms along the way; he saw signs that many of them had been combed through. But that was impossible given the time allotted, of course. He immediately knew what had happened: two or three members of the team had been tasked with ransacking all the rooms a little, some more than others, while the bulk of the team undertook a detailed inspection of the room they were really interested in. There was no other possibility. Fifteen officers could not possibly have searched the entire Box in just an hour and done a decent job of it. And otherwise, why bother?

When he got back to room 503 his suspicions were confirmed. Everything was in disarray: the mattresses dumped on the floor, clothing scattered everywhere. They hadn't made the slightest effort to hide their tracks. Of course, even this mess could have been made by one person. Ted hunted for more subtle clues, and it took only a glance at the bookshelf to determine that the genuine painstaking search had been carried out there. Ted's photographic memory told him that the books were in the correct order but had been replaced farther back on the shelf than he had left them. Someone had taken the time to look through them one by one.

"What's got your attention?" Justin asked.

"Nothing," Ted said, still looking at the books. "Pretty soon we'll be hearing from Segarra."

"What are you talking about?"

"This," he said, completely serious. "You have to control yourself, Justin. Remember what I told you. That detective is going to want to talk to you. Maybe with me again, too, though he knows he won't get anything new out of me."

Ted knew that Segarra hadn't discovered anything. The detective would now be regretting this false move.

73

1994

IT WAS Marman who brought the news to the Box. In recent days he'd done nothing but roam the campus in search of information. He really seemed to be enjoying his new role as the unofficial campus news anchor. Not only did he hasten to spread rumors, even the most unlikely ones; he also kept on top of the latest developments, so any student who wanted to find out what was going on would unfailingly turn to him.

"Have I got news for you guys!" Marman announced in the fifth-floor corridor. "And this is no rumor."

Irving Prosser and Justin were all ears.

"Let's go into a room to talk," Ted urged them. He was the fourth member of the tiny group.

Marman was unsure. More people could hear him out in the corridor.

"Come on, Marman," Ted insisted. "It's better to tell people the news individually, don't you think?"

"Oh, sure."

They went into 504, the room next door to Ted and Justin's, and sat on the beds, two on each.

"This is incredible. I've got three different sources that confirm it," Marman said, playing his new role of investigative journalist. "Fiona Smith, my girlfriend's study partner, got it from her father, who heard it last night from his own father, a police officer who's working the case. I also got it from Meredith Malone, the sister of the dean's secretary, who heard the dean talking over the phone with Segarra. And finally—"

"Skip the sources. Just tell us what it is, already," Ted broke in.

"Yeah," Irving said. "Let's get to the good stuff."

"Fine. The police have an eyewitness," Marman said, pausing to gauge the reactions of the other three.

"Someone who saw what happened?" Justin asked.

"What part of 'eyewitness' don't you understand?" Irving said.

If anyone else was in the habit of walking around the library area at night, Justin thought, they might have noticed him there at some point and told the police about it.

"Yes, someone who saw what happened," Marman corroborated. "I even know the guy's name: Wendell."

"What else?" Irving didn't seem very impressed.

"Fiona says her father was talking about Wendell as if he were the key to everything. She said he was providing key information: not only was he there when the murder took place, but he can also lead them to the murderer. Segarra promised the dean that the case would be solved in less than a week."

"Wow. And who is this Wendell guy? A student?"

"I have a friend who works in the student office, and he's checking it out right now. For the time being, nobody seems to know anyone by that name."

"If it isn't a student, it's got to be somebody on the grounds crew, or a security guard, or something like that."

Ted spoke calmly. "We need to find out who Wendell is. Can you?"

"If he's a student, probably," Marman said. "Though I doubt he is, to be honest. We would have heard about him by now."

"That's what I think, too," Justin said.

Ted went back to room 503. He had some thinking to do.

74

1994

THE MURDER of Thomas Tyler was never solved. His dossier ended up in the police department's cold case files, along with what little evidence had been collected. There it remained for years. Nobody in the Box ever learned who Wendell was or what kind of key information he had provided that might have thrown light on the subject.

Tyler's killer went on to kill again. Not once, but many times.

75

Present day

LAURA WAS still on the ground, her back propped against the grimy building. Over the perimeter wall she saw treetops swaying rhythmically. The clouds had darkened and the breeze had turned into a stiff wind. Dry leaves skated across the asphalt parking lot before her. Marcus's voice, emerging metallic from the tiny speaker of her phone, was all that kept her halfway focused.

"Laura, are you there?"

"Yes. The signal is weak. I'm shaking, Marcus."

"You'll be all right. If McKay is shackled—and doesn't remember anything—there's no reason for worry. But if he does remember, why did he lead you two there?"

"I don't know. Anyway, there's still one other thing I can't figure out. You said there's a witness in the police file named Wendell."

"Precisely, but he wasn't a real person. The police made him up and spread the rumor that they'd found an eyewitness. It made sense if they were guessing that the killer was a college student who'd get jumpy and make a mistake. As soon as I saw that name in the file, I understood everything..."

"I fail to see it."

"Listen to me, Laura—please. McKay killed the professor over his girlfriend, who was cheating on him. Wendell was the only person who could expose him, so McKay needed him dead, too, like in the cycles. See?"

"I'm trying to think."

"Laura, Bob and I are heading up to meet you there. I need the exact coordinates from you. Bob has contacted the FBI, and they've got a team on the way. I realize it can't be easy to think clearly while you're in the situation, but you can trust me. Think about what I first told you. McKay and Blaine are brothers. Blaine had an airtight alibi when his girlfriend was killed, but what about McKay? He could have done it, easily. We don't know anything about the relationship between the two brothers."

Laura was having a hard time getting used to the idea that Ted and Blaine were brothers. How did that piece fit the puzzle?

"Marcus, I'm going to hang up. They'll suspect something's up if I'm not back soon. I'll text you the coordinates."

"Okay, Laura. Be very careful. If McKay did kill the professor, and probably his brother's girlfriend as well, then there's another reality we have to deal with. A lot of time passed between those two deaths. Bob thinks there might be more."

She said nothing.

"I'm telling you this because I need you to promise me you'll be careful."

"I will. Good-bye."

Laura hung up but continued to press the phone to her ear. Shock and surprise began to recede, while fear gained ground. The factory looked suddenly menacing. She hardly knew Lee Stillwell, a guard who didn't even work on her wing. But her need to feel that someone was on her side was so strong that she could think about nothing but going back in and joining him.

She turned on her phone's GPS and texted Marcus the coordinates.

There might be more.

She reentered the factory, mulling over everything she knew about the case. She was still shaken by Marcus's new revelations, but she was starting to see beyond them and to understand the invisible strings that had been manipulating Ted the whole time. The main challenge was figuring out how much of it Ted was now aware of.

Laura walked past the offices and stopped in front of the side door where Ted had paused minutes ago. Why was this inner door padlocked? Without thinking twice, she tried the largest keys on the ring until she landed on the one that opened the lock. She found herself in a furnished office in complete disorder. She tried the light switch, with no luck. She turned on her cell phone's flashlight and explored the room. It held a wooden desk, a broken chair, and several filing cabinets. In spite of the general filth and decay, it was obvious that this office had been visited with some regularity. Laura tried one of the desk drawers. Against all her expectations, it opened easily. Inside was a series of sturdy document folders, which she didn't dare touch. She opened the other drawer, the one on the left, and found more folders. She knew what was in them. She was sure of it.

She pulled out the first folder and opened it. It contained a handful of pages, which she flipped through with one hand while holding her phone in the other. She'd been right. She was looking at a series of newspaper clippings about the murder of a woman named Elizabeth Garth.

Who had her throat slit.

Unable to restrain herself, Laura read three or four articles about the case.

Then she leafed through the other folders in the drawer. Ten of them, all told. All women.

There might be more.

76

Present day

LAURA HADN'T been gone for five minutes when Lee began getting uncomfortable. McKay observed him with a calm, enigmatic smile.

"What is this place?" the guard asked.

Ted looked up, and to the left, and to the right, as if he might find an answer floating in the air.

"A sort of refuge, I guess. A getaway."

Lee wasn't too surprised. He'd heard about much creepier things at Lavender than some rich guy who liked to hang out in an abandoned factory.

"So you remember now," Lee said unenthusiastically. "When the doctor comes back we can go ahead and get out of here."

"I don't think she'll be coming back."

Lee narrowed his eyes.

"I don't think she'll be coming back very soon," Ted went on. "It sounded like a pretty serious emergency."

"She only said a few words before she left."

"Maybe so."

Ted sat on the edge of a steel desk. Pieces of rusted metal, paint cans, and other junk lay scattered on the desktop. His hands were shackled in front of him, but even so, Lee was on the alert. This guy might have gotten word to somebody on the outside to come help him escape. Dr. Hill trusted him, but in Lee's opinion she was acting in a very unsafe manner.

"Before I got locked up at Lavender, I was planning to commit suicide." The sudden change of topic was accompanied by a remarkable transformation in Ted's face.

"Are you sick or something?"

"No."

Once more, that dreamy expression...

"I still want to kill myself, Lee." Ted opened his eyes very wide. Mad eyes. Imploring eyes. "I want to do that more than anything in the world."

Lee immediately went on the alert. He inched his hand toward his gun but didn't unholster it.

Ted smiled, not stirring a hairsbreadth where he sat.

"Keep your cool, Lee. I want to make you a proposition."

"Like what?"

"When the doctor gets back, I'm going to try and escape. You give me my fair warning, everything to the rule book, tell me to stop or you'll shoot, all that. I'll simply disobey. Bam bam, case closed."

"I'm not going to kill you, McKay. If you step out of line, you'll get a bullet in the leg."

"Come on, Lee. Play along with me for a minute, okay? Dr. Hill will be a perfect witness. Nobody will care whether you aim at my leg or my head, and nobody could prove it if they did care. I can run pretty fast—these chains aren't all that tight. It won't be a simple shot."

"I'm not going to kill you," Lee repeated. "All I want is to get back to Lavender before three and go home to my wife."

"Now that you mention it, about your wife—Martha, wasn't that her name? Imagine: What if you really could have your dream cabin by the lake? Wouldn't that be something?"

Lee wrinkled his brow and kept his mouth shut.

"Imagine, Lee, if you could also buy a four-wheel-drive pickup, and you and Martha could drive to your house in the middle of nowhere, buy all the supplies you need, and spend two or three days there together.

Imagine if, after you retire, you and Martha could take two or three months and travel around Europe. Have you and your wife been to Europe? Imagine: seeing it all without worrying about how much it costs..."

"'Imagine,' 'imagine.' Okay, John Lennon, what's your point?"

"My point, Lee, is that we can make all this a reality right now."

"How?"

"There's a huge basement underneath this factory. A million bucks are hidden there. In cash. All yours."

Lee smiled.

"A million bucks, in the basement?"

"Come on, Lee. You just saw my weekend house. I own this property, and plenty more. Do you really doubt I'd keep a little stash like that tucked away for an emergency?"

"No, I don't doubt it at all. What I doubt is that you'd have it conveniently tucked away here in the basement."

"So why do you think I brought you here?"

Lee studied Ted for several moments. Then he looked at the door to make sure they were still alone. The last thing he wanted was Dr. Hill overhearing this conversation.

"I thought you couldn't remember anything."

"Which was true. But things are starting to come back. Look, Lee. The million bucks are sitting there. All we have to do is take a peek in the basement and you'll see. It's that easy. Who cares what it's doing there or where it came from?"

The guard had his doubts, Ted could clearly see.

"We all come out ahead on this, Lee. I'm not asking you to kill somebody else—just me. Believe me, it'll be better for everyone all around if I get a bullet through my forehead."

"I can't shoot you just because you're trying to escape."

Ted understood what the guard was hinting at.

"Maybe...maybe I could do a little more than just escape. I could attack Dr. Hill. Make a grab for her throat, like this." He mimed the action. "Then you shout for me to let go, I step away, try to pick up something to clobber her with. Anything on this table would do."

"I'm not saying I'd go through with it."

"I understand. We're just speculating. You shoot me in front of Laura, she'll see that you were just reacting, defending her, and the shooting is perfectly justified. I'm sure there'll be questions from the police for you to answer, maybe a form to fill out. But that's all. Later, you come back here and get the money."

"Where is it? I want to see it."

Ted smiled.

"Through that basement door. The key isn't on the ring with the others. It's hidden in that hole over there."

The door to the basement was metal and looked like solid steel. Lee felt around in the hole Ted pointed out and found the key.

"If Dr. Hill comes back, I'll tell her I heard a noise down there. Don't do anything dumb."

Before he fit the key into the lock, Lee turned.

"Wait. Before I see the money and make a decision, I have to know what you did."

"It would be better if that died with me."

"The money..."

"The money was a precaution. It's mine, if that's what you're worried about."

"Well, then, let's go."

They climbed down a narrow staircase to a landing, where they found an electrical panel.

"The breaker board for upstairs."

Lee looked at him in disbelief and, after a second's hesitation, flipped the main switch. The lights went on. They continued down the stairs, Ted going first and stepping carefully so as not to trip over his chains. Lee followed at a prudent distance.

Downstairs everything was a mess. There were old machines, huge wooden crates, filing cabinets, desks, chairs. Whatever hadn't been taken in the final move out seemed to have ended up in this forgotten underworld. There were plenty of hiding places upstairs, but the situation was much worse in this labyrinth of junk and discarded debris. The windows high up on the walls had been bricked over, and the electrical lighting was too dim. A city of outstretched shadows seemed to arise at every turn.

Ted moved easily through the byways of this labyrinth. Lee followed in silence. What sense would it make to give him a warning? The bastard wanted to be shot.

Or did he?

On two or three occasions they heard the unmistakable scurrying of rodents. Lee had a deep aversion to rats, but he didn't say anything. He and Ted stopped in front of a tall shelf lined with ancient typewriters and covered with a film of dust. Next to it, in a lobby with pretensions to opulence, was a decrepit green corduroy sofa long past its glory days. Ted pushed it aside. Lee was observing from a cautious few yards back when from the corner of his eye he glimpsed a rat racing across the floor. At least he'd have a good excuse to give to Dr. Hill, Lee thought. There really were weird noises down here.

Under the sofa was a trapdoor with no handle. Ted told the guard he'd need something sharp to get it open. Lee had to keep himself from laughing.

"I'm not going to give you anything sharp," he scoffed. "Stay back and keep still."

Lee used one of his keys to lift the trapdoor. He was suddenly feeling a little excited, no denying. What if he really could get hold of the money? A plan began to form in his mind. He had no reason to shoot McKay; as soon as Dr. Hill got back, he'd insist on getting out of there immediately. He was responsible for the patient's safety, and she couldn't contradict him. McKay would keep his mouth shut, because now Lee knew too much. Then he could come back later on and pick up the money. He smiled.

If there is any money.

In the space under the trapdoor he found a large metal box. Lee slid apart the two locking clasps with his thumbs. The box opened with a soft *click*. When he lifted the lid, there they were, wrapped in clear plastic bags: ten perfectly formed blocks of hundred-dollar bills. Lee had never seen so much money at one time. He could take a trip with Martha, he thought excitedly. McKay must have some sort of telepathic power, because he had suggested the perfect plan: Martha had always regretted not having seen other countries. The farthest she had ever traveled was to North Carolina, to visit her sister. Now she could...

Then something crawled from below and leaped out from beneath the metal box with astonishing speed. It was big and gray, with enormous toothy jaws. Its eyes shone when the light hit them, and Lee, who had been squatting by the trapdoor the whole time, jumped back and lost his balance. The animal stuck its head up through the hole in the floor, and that, together with a quick movement on Ted's part, was the last thing Lee saw. Then a shadow embraced him and it was as if his head exploded.

He gave a stifled scream.

Typewriters rained down on him as the whole shelf toppled over.

77

Present day

ON HER way back to the assembly floor, Laura imagined many things, but the last thing she imagined was that the guard wouldn't be there.

Ted was waiting for her in the middle of the vast room, his arms loose on either side of him. His chains were gone.

"Where is Lee?"

"In the basement."

Laura wondered if that implied he was still alive. She didn't dare ask.

Stay calm.

"I chained him up," Ted said, displaying his wrists. "I'll let him go later. You, however, should leave now, Laura."

"Leave? Why? I thought we were making progress. Let me take you back to Lavender. Whatever is disturbing you now, we can get you past it. Think about your family, think about—"

"Laura, I appreciate everything you've done for me. But therapy can't solve everything. Some facts are *irreversible*."

Laura kept her distance.

"Go on," he snapped. "Get out, go back the same way we came, back to my house. And don't tell anyone."

"What are you going to do?"

For a moment he hesitated. A conflicted expression flitted across his face and disappeared.

"Nothing bad."

Laura was beginning to understand what was going through Ted's mind. She saw that he was confused and that she should use what she knew to help.

"Who called you?" Ted suddenly asked. He took a few steps forward.

"Marcus Grant, the head of C wing. There was an emergency with one of the patients."

"Uh-huh."

"That's all."

"What sort of emergency? You were talking to him for a long time."

They were close enough now that he could reach her in two or three strides.

"They know, don't they, Laura?"

She frowned. She had to regain control somehow.

"I stopped in the room where you keep the folders. I've been looking at them. That's what took me so long."

"So you know what I've done," he muttered.

Ted looked up, as if alarmed by a noise. Then he lowered his eyes and stared for a long time at a corner of the room. He seemed to have forgotten where he was.

"Ted, please. I'm afraid things are a little more complicated than you think they are."

"Get out," he said. He turned around and headed for the basement.

"I'm going with you," she announced.

He replied without turning around.

"You know very well what will happen if you do."

Even so, she went after him. Halfway down the basement stairs, she smelled the unmistakable odor of gasoline.

78

Present day

LAURA SAW at least five jerricans lying around the bottom of the stairs. She and Ted made their way along a junk-lined corridor until they got to an old sofa next to a trapdoor and a jumble of antique typewriters. The empty shelf gave Laura a fairly exact idea of what had happened here. Looking more attentively, she noticed fresh blood by the open hole in the floor, but no guard.

"Where is Lee?"

"Back there," Ted replied listlessly. He pointed at a piece of office furniture a few yards from where they stood. It was three or four feet tall and had sliding doors in front. Like everything else in the basement, it was utterly devoid of modern design sense, and it must have weighed a ton. The guard's boots stuck out one end of it.

Ted knelt down to fish something out of the hole. Laura caught sight of a metal box.

"What are you planning to do, Ted?"

He didn't reply. Laura took advantage of this reflective pause to pull two dusty chairs closer and sit in one of them.

"I want us to have our last session," she announced.

Ted turned around and looked at the empty chair, and then at Laura.

"Are they on their way?"

She nodded.

"How much time do we have?"

"I don't know. Maybe an hour."

Ted sat.

"This is a good idea. I want you to talk to Holly. People are going to say lots of awful things, most of them true, and I wouldn't blame her if she chose to hate me..."

"I will talk to her, I promise you."

"And if you want to write about this, you have my permission. Not that you need it, I know."

Laura didn't think she had mentioned that possibility to Ted.

"I realize my case has been important to you," Ted said, smiling sadly. "You've done your work well. Otherwise we wouldn't be here, and my whole filthy past would still be buried."

"Ted, as I told you earlier, I don't think things are that simple."

"Yes, they are. I killed those women." Ted fell into a sort of dream state.

A rat ran swiftly past them, making Laura jump. Rats were everywhere; apparently the smell of gas alarmed them.

"Ted, I want us to talk about Blaine."

He nodded.

"Do you remember him now?"

"Blaine is my brother. But I hadn't thought about him until you mentioned him. Everything's coming back, Laura. It's as if I could look inside my head with a flashlight...It was all dark before, and now I can see."

"That is very good."

Ted didn't agree at all.

"Did you know all this time? That Blaine was my brother, I mean."

"No. The police just made the connection."

"The police..." Ted said to himself.

Laura was sorry she had said it. She needed to keep Ted focused on the therapy; she had enough trouble with this unconventional setting without having to struggle with discussing the authorities and the future of his case.

"I found out when I was a freshman in college," Ted said. "At the time, my father was making sporadic attempts to get closer to me. He'd try to reconnect through my aunt Audrey, who always cared for me and deserved better than the brother she got. I met with him reluctantly and he told me about Blaine. He even showed me a photograph of him."

"Why did he do that? At that particular moment, I mean."

Ted shrugged.

"He told me some nonsense about how I should really get to know Blaine and that Blaine shouldn't have to pay for the bad relationship between him and me."

"That sounds sensible enough."

"Of course it does. My father always sounded like the most sensible bastard in the world. But you're right: Why exactly then? I was at college and Blaine was in high school. The truth is, Laura, that my father decided to fuck me up, and he latched on to the first thing that occurred to him. It's that simple. The only thing that bastard cared about was covering his own ass. He didn't care if his sons got to build a relationship with each other. You can be sure of that."

"And did you?"

"Build a relationship with Blaine? Of course not. I got into an argument with my father that day, like always, and I left. I didn't have the slightest intention of meeting my brother."

"But you thought about it? Your father was right, in that it wasn't the boy's fault. Or yours, either. Why deny yourself the chance to meet him?"

"I didn't really analyze it. That was a messed-up year at college. I guess getting to know Blaine would have meant never really breaking ties with my father. It would have been one more way of letting him into my life. Seeing how things turned out, I was better off not meeting him. Blaine was as big a son of a bitch as our father."

Ted fell silent and looked down. Laura knew what he was thinking. She reached out and grasped him under his chin.

"Look at me, Ted."

"I guess I couldn't escape it, either," he said.

Laura didn't let go of his chin.

"I don't want us to talk about you—not yet. And not about your father, either. I want us to talk about Blaine."

Laura pulled her hand away and settled back gently in her chair.

"What do you want to know?" Ted asked.

"We know you were at his house. Can you remember why?"

Ted seemed not to remember very clearly.

"When I saw the news about his girlfriend's murder, I knew he was my brother. All I had ever seen was that one photo of him, years before, but his face was etched in my mind. He had some of my father's features, especially around here." Ted pointed to his forehead. "But I was absolutely certain when I saw footage of him out in the street, trying to get away from a reporter. His walk was exactly like my father's, bent slightly forward, with his arms straight by his sides. I've never seen anyone else walk like that—not swinging his arms."

"What did you think when you saw him?"

"I don't know. That he was guilty, I guess. I really can't remember."

"Tell me what you think now. About Blaine."

"Do I have to?"

Laura nodded.

"Blaine is my brother. I guess there's something in our DNA. Something wrong with us inside."

"And thinking that makes you feel better?"

"To tell you the truth, yes, it does."

"You told me before that you learned about Blaine during your first year at college, but you hardly had time to think about him because it was a messed-up year. What did you mean by that?"

Laura already knew, but she wanted Ted to be the one to tell her.

"That year, I killed a man. His name was Thomas Tyler. He was a professor at MSU. The guy was having an affair with my girlfriend at the time, Georgia. He's the man I saw in the yard at Lavender."

A rat's shrill screech lent emphasis to his words. Another rat responded from across the room.

"How did you do it?" Laura asked.

"They used to meet at night behind the library. I waited until Georgia left and I snuck up on him from behind. I slit his throat and ran away. There was an investigation but it never amounted to anything."

It was odd how mechanically Ted retold the events from that year.

"It's strange. In the folders you have upstairs, I only saw women."

"This was a...personal matter."

"Were you very close to Georgia?"

The question took Ted by surprise. He'd often thought of Georgia over the years, but always as a bit player, never as someone important in her own right. The fact was, he could barely recall her face.

"We didn't have much in common. I think we had drifted apart a little, and afterwards we really never saw each other again."

"But even so, you killed the professor."

"Laura, what's the point of all this?"

"We've been trying all along to undo a complicated knot. Every time we managed to loosen it a little, we've pulled too hard and taken a big step backwards. It's time to pull on all the loose ends, Ted. Your brother, Blaine, is one loose end. Tyler's murder is another. And all those dead women, the same. There's something we've been missing all along: the connecting thread. And the only way we'll see it is by looking deeper into your past and bringing it out into the light."

"I understand what you mean, but does it really matter? The result will still be the same."

"It might make a huge difference to Holly and the girls."

"What else did you want to know?"

"I want you to tell me how you killed the first woman, Ted," Laura said, looking him straight in the eyes. "And I want you to tell me all the details, everything you can remember. Her name was Elizabeth Garth, right?"

"If that's what you want."

Ted thought it over for a second; his eyes went glassy. His voice sounded as monotone as before.

"Elizabeth Garth was a young single mother. She was barely twenty and worked at the movie theater in Harperfield, a small town not far from where I grew up. Her son was two. He lived with his grandparents somewhere in New Hampshire, though I only learned that later. She wasn't a bad mother; she hoped to get ahead and start raising her son herself. It wasn't that her parents didn't let her see him or anything like that, just that they didn't think she was in a position to raise him properly, so they took him in. The boy's father was the most opposed to this arrangement. He and the mother were hardly on speaking terms. The guy always blamed her for getting pregnant, and even after the murder, when they were still looking for the killer, there was a sense that he was pointing fingers at her, like Elizabeth had been asking for it. Or, worse, like she deserved it."

Ted shook his head.

"But she hadn't asked for it. She was blond, very thin. Frail. Like the others. She was in the wrong place at the wrong time. She shared an apartment with two other girls who worked at the same theater. They weren't friends and weren't on very good terms with each other. She couldn't have imagined bringing the boy to live in that tiny apartment, so at the time all she ever thought about was moving. She had posted little handwritten flyers in the theater and in the stores around there: 'Mature, responsible woman available to do housecleaning and chores, also elder care, in exchange for an acceptable wage and a room for myself and my young son.' It was signed 'Elly.'"

"So you called and offered her a place to live."

"Exactly. It was too easy. Because the girl was desperate to get out of that apartment and bring her kid with her. Under other circumstances, she probably wouldn't have agreed to meet a stranger in such an out-of-the-way place. I picked out a practically deserted road outside of town where the horsey crowd have their mansions and told her to meet me there. I parked my car by the side of the road. She showed up driving an old rust bucket just after the sun had set. The route got complicated after that, so we had to go together. That wasn't really true, of course; there wasn't anything at all there for her to see. She left her car and we went in mine. She had just finished a double shift at work and was exhausted. I told her I was a widower with a seven-year-old son and a big, empty house. She talked to me about the father of her boy. Some young slacker who was never there for her. I quickly won her confidence.

"But at some point Elizabeth realized that there were no houses in the direction we were going, and no opportunities for her or her son. She jumped from the car and ran for the woods as fast as she could. I followed her easily enough to a clearing. She was weak and hardly put up any resistance."

"Did you kill her with a knife?" Laura asked, as if it were the most natural question in the world. "Did you slit her throat, like you did Tyler's?"

Ted seemed genuinely repentant; in fact, he was about to cry.

He silently nodded.

"In the clippings I saw before I came here, it said she was also stabbed in the chest about ten times," Laura said. "Did you also stab her ten times in the chest, Ted?"

Again, Ted nodded.

"Can I ask you one more question?" Laura continued without the slightest hesitation. "If you made all those arrangements with her after reading her flyer and talking to her in one phone call, how did you know what she looked like? How did you know she would serve your purposes?"

Ted shook his head, more and more upset.

"I don't know, Laura—maybe I saw her putting up one of her flyers? Do you think it matters?"

"Yes, Ted, it does matter. Because most of the facts you've told me about Elizabeth Garth come straight from the clippings I read upstairs just now."

"It really happened."

"What I saw in that room," Laura said, pointing upstairs, "was no collection of ghastly mementos, Ted. It was an investigation."

Ted looked at her, flustered. Laura went on.

"Elizabeth Garth died in nineteen eighty-three. You were seven years old, Ted. Seven."

Even the rats stopped skittering as she spoke.

"You didn't kill Elizabeth Garth, or any of those other women. You didn't kill Thomas Tyler, either. You didn't kill anyone! Can't you see the connecting thread now?"

79

1983

TED WAS lying on the worn carpet in his bedroom and studying a small portable chessboard the first time he heard his mother scream. He remained very quiet, waiting to see if another shout would follow, and almost without thinking about it he slid into the space under his bed, which offered him, through the crack under the door, a view of the light in the hallway. If Mommy came, he'd be able to see her. Daddy wasn't home.

Next to the chessboard was an old pamphlet of Bobby Fischer games, a gift from a neighbor that had become his only source of knowledge. Soon enough he would learn all these games by heart, but for now this pamphlet was his great treasure. The chessboard with its thirty-one pieces was also a gift, from an unknown congregant at church. Mommy had made a pawn of aluminum foil to replace the missing piece. Mommy could do the most amazing things—so long as she took her medicine.

And today she hadn't taken it—Ted was sure. Lately Daddy had to force her to take her pills. If he wasn't home, she'd forget, or choose not to, and then her head would start playing tricks on her. Like Bobby Fischer when he made moves to trick his opponents and hide his real plans.

Ted was scared. He'd stayed inside all day, shut up in his room, passing the time with Bobby's games, and now he realized he might have made a serious mistake. Mommy hadn't made dinner, hadn't said one word to him all day, and he himself hadn't even gone downstairs for a glass of water. He hadn't gone to the bathroom all day! And if Mommy wasn't worried about him, it meant her head was playing tricks on her. Maybe if he had tried talking to her earlier, he could have convinced her to take her pills. But now he knew it would be impossible. Worst of all, the only person who could fix things was Daddy. As Daddy had explained to Ted so often. The problem was that lately their fights had been getting worse and worse. Daddy even had to hit her to get her to understand.

"Teddy!"

Mommy's unmistakable scream.

What should he do? What if something really had happened to her? His friend Richie's grandmother once slipped in the bathtub and they didn't find her till two days later. Mommy wasn't an old lady, but she could still trip over something, Ted thought. He was upset with himself for not going to help right away.

He came out from under his bed with all the resolve he could muster, unsure whether he wanted his mother to call him again or not. He didn't want her to break her head like his friend Richie's grandmother, of course, but he also knew how confused Mommy got sometimes. He grabbed the doorknob and softly turned it.

No more shouts came, and in the hush of the upstairs hallway, the silence was definitely worse.

Ted crept down the first steps and peered over the landing. He could see the living room between the slats in the wooden railing, and he immediately spotted the graying hair of Kristen McKay behind the sofa. This wasn't the first time Ted had seen her sitting on the floor, leaning against the back of the sofa, stretching her feet until they touched the wall; for some reason she found this space comforting. He came down and slowly approached her.

"Mommy?"

Kristen turned. In her eyes, Ted saw all he needed to know. They were filled with confusion and desperation.

"Hide!" Kristen grabbed him by the hand and yanked him to the floor. Ted plunked down beside her.

"What's wrong, Mommy?"

"Strangers in the house," she whispered.

Months ago, Ted would have tried his hardest to believe her. *It's Mommy*—something inside him told him he *had* to believe her. But deep down he knew they were alone.

"Did you take your pills, Mommy?"

She looked at him with one eyebrow raised. She petted his hair.

"You have to be very quiet, Teddy."

"Who's in the house?" he asked, keeping his voice low. "Did you see them?"

Kristen nodded.

"The antenna men."

Ted had never heard of them before. And their name certainly scared him. Kristen turned around and pointed over the top of the sofa.

"One's in the kitchen. He walked through the living room a minute ago and I could see him from here. They're very tall, Teddy. They have to crouch down to keep from banging their heads on the doorframes. They're skinny, with heads like ants and long antennas."

"Maybe they left already. I'll go check—"

"No!" Kristen dug her sharp nails into Ted's little forearm. "It's too dangerous. I told you, I just saw them."

"But what are they here for, Mommy?"

She hesitated for a moment.

"You're a smart boy, Teddy. Those pills you asked about—they aren't medicine. They aren't helping me. Your father forces me to take them because he wants me out of the way. He wants me lying in bed all day, doped up."

"Daddy loves us," Ted said, though even at the age of seven he was beginning to have his doubts.

"I washed the pills down the kitchen sink. That's why the antenna men came."

"*All* your pills?"

The pills were very expensive. His father was always complaining about how much they cost. Sometimes Kristen would flush one or two down the toilet, and that was enough to launch an endless fight. Now it had been... *all* the pills.

"The antenna men know—they picked up on it with their antennas. That's why they came."

Ted couldn't take it anymore. He jumped up to run into the kitchen. Mommy tried to grab him, but he was too fast for her.

"No!" Kristen screamed. She turned and, on her knees, watched her only child race into the kitchen.

"There's nothing here!" Ted ran to the sink. Next to it was a pile of cardboard boxes and blister packs, all empty. Mommy hadn't been lying: all the pills had gone down the drain. He felt a chill. He couldn't even imagine the consequences that this massive destruction of medicine might provoke. Just thinking about it...

He ran back to the living room just as fast. Mommy was still hiding behind the sofa.

"There aren't any antenna men in the kitchen, Mommy! There's no such thing as antenna men. You threw away all your pills!"

She crawled over and tried to catch him by the arm. Ted freed himself from her grasp and shrank back.

"Daddy will get mad!"

"Your father hates us, Teddy. He has another woman. That's why he wants to get rid of me, and then it will be your turn. He'll put you in an orphanage and—"

"Shut up!"

Kristen ignored her son's rising anger and again crawled over, now beyond the protection of the sofa, and once more tried to catch his arm. Still no luck.

"This is all your fault!" he said. "I hate you!"

Something changed in Kristen's expression. She retreated to the safety of the sofa. She lowered her voice.

"You're not my Teddy—you're one of them." Kristen pointed at the kitchen. "You've got him in there, don't you?"

Ted whimpered. He couldn't help it.

"Don't you try to fool me," she said. "Out of my sight!"

"Mommy..."

She kept shaking her head as she peered wide-eyed over the sofa. Ted knew there wasn't any more he could do there, just as he knew that things would get worse somehow. He ran to his room in a flash, shut the door behind him, and ducked under the bed. The chessboard and the Bobby Fischer book were still there. He pushed them aside with a swipe of the hand and buried his face in his arms. He wept inconsolably.

After an endless half hour, he heard what he feared the most. Frank McKay's car pulled up in front of their house. Ted sprang from his hiding spot. His reddened eyes slowly adjusted to the light in the room. He went to the window, and indeed, there was his father getting out of the car. Ted paid no particular attention to the fact that the driver's window was down. Daddy always left his window down when he intended to go back out.

Frank's booming voice thundered through the house. Ted might have chosen to hide under his bed again. Of course, hiding there wouldn't keep him from hearing everything that happened on the first floor. But for some reason he opened his door and crept to the top of the stairs instead. Something bad might happen. Ted was scared.

Soon enough Frank discovered the trash by the kitchen sink, and that's when he blew his top.

"I can't believe it!" he shouted over and over. "Goddamn worthless bitch!"

Insults were Frank's specialty.

Kristen didn't say anything. Ted didn't dare look, but he could imagine her sitting behind the sofa. Something shattered on the floor—a pitcher or a flowerpot, maybe one of the living room lamps.

"I'm leaving this house, do you hear me? The only thing you had to do was take two fucking pills. And you can't even do that right! That's how worthless you are."

Kristen spoke for the first time. "Get away from me!"

"I'm not moving one fucking inch."

"Don't touch me!"

"Shut your damn mouth, bitch."

"Where—"

A resounding blow stopped Kristen from talking. Then two more blows. Apart from his creativity with insults, Frank was generous with his beatings.

"Swallow it, stupid!"

"Where..." Kristen could barely speak.

"Where'd I get 'em? Where'd I get 'em? I kept 'em hidden, because I knew you'd do this someday. That's how well I know you, slut. Always looking for new ways to fuck me over. Swallow it now, bitch! Let me see—move your tongue out of the way! Don't bite me, you fucking whore!"

Another blow. It must have been his open palm against her cheek, because it sounded like the crack of a bullwhip.

"You're gonna take one more, and don't you dare spit it out—I'm warning you."

Mommy never took two of her pills at once. She took one every eight hours, Ted knew.

"And this time, it'll be three," Frank said furiously, gloating over each word.

Three! Ted was horrified. It might work to take two if she had skipped one. But three? What sense did it make to force Mommy to swallow three gigantic pills?

"I'm leaving, Kristen. Do you hear me? Maybe I'll never come back, and the state will have to deal with you. That'd be great, wouldn't it?"

No more replies from Mommy. Maybe she had fallen asleep faster than usual. Maybe three pills could do that. Couldn't they?

The state will have to deal with you.

Ted jumped when he heard Frank at the bottom of the stairs. He ran into his room and quietly shut the door behind him. He got into bed and pretended to be asleep. After a few seconds he heard the door to his room open and then close. He hoped his father really thought he hadn't heard any of that, though it was hard to believe.

Then he heard the shower running, and he snuck out of bed.

His father usually showered in the morning. If he was repeating the ritual now, it was because he meant to go out. And then Ted understood. Frank was going to leave them! Wasn't that what he had said?

I'm leaving, Kristen.

At that instant, Ted decided what he would do next. He arranged pillows in his bed to make it look as though he were still there, grabbed a bag, and stuffed a few clothes in it. He set it on the bed and weighed whether it would be smart to go downstairs. He knew he'd have to. Daddy was still taking a shower, and that calmed him. Ted reached the first floor and found Mommy sitting behind the sofa, her legs spread and her head lolling to one side, dozing.

"Teddy..." she murmured, barely opening an eye.

Ted kissed her on the forehead.

"I don't hate you, Mommy."

The state will have to deal with you.

A gentle smile bloomed on Kristen McKay's lips.

Ted went back to his room. He retrieved his chessboard and his Bobby Fischer book. He climbed out the window and slid down the roof to the sidewall that he had scaled a million times. Frank's Mustang was waiting for him. Ted didn't have the keys to the trunk, but he knew the trick for getting in anyway. He easily squeezed through the open window and clambered into the backseat. He pulled it down, and voilà!

He would run away with Daddy. Daddy was furious now, but when he got over it he would understand.

And Mommy would be better off without them. Ted still didn't understand what the state was or how it was supposed to take care of Mommy, but he was sure it would do a better job of it than Frank McKay.

He huddled in the trunk and waited.

80

1983

THE TRUNK was comfortable for a seven-year-old—so comfortable that Ted miraculously fell asleep. Which was lucky, because it meant he didn't think about the possibility that Daddy might bring a suitcase. Wouldn't it have been perfectly reasonable for him to bring one, after all? The idea only crossed Ted's mind after the car started moving, and by then it made no sense to worry. Daddy had money and could buy whatever they needed.

Ted couldn't imagine where they might be going. After traveling for a while, he discovered that if he pushed up on the rear window shelf, a slit appeared through which he could peek into the car's interior. This gave him a view of Frank's silent and unmoving silhouette, and of the highway beyond. They had left the city behind.

They drove for more than an hour, or so it seemed to Ted, who at some point found himself holding his chessboard against his body like a protective shield and was about to fall asleep. He was just becoming accustomed to the idea that they might be going on a very long trip when the Mustang slowed down and rolled to a stop. Ted waited a few moments with his eyes wide-open in that impenetrable darkness and then turned around, set his chessboard aside, and lifted the window shelf very cautiously. A beam of light hit him full in the face and forced him to close his eyes. He couldn't see Frank get out of the car, but he heard the door open and close.

Outside he heard voices. One was Frank's, of course. The other was a woman's. Then the doors opened and the car rocked back and forth the way cars do when two people get in at the same time. Ted tried his special peephole again, but it didn't give him a view of the passenger seat.

What if he tried pushing up on the other side? He did his best, but no luck. The shelf held tight on that end.

"Sorry I couldn't come earlier," the woman said. "I pulled a double shift at the theater today."

Ted froze. He hadn't been expecting company. Daddy always said he didn't like hitchhikers, and as a traveling salesman he saw them all the time and knew them better than anybody. This young woman (Ted pictured her much younger than Daddy) wasn't a hitchhiker. *Sorry I couldn't come earlier.*

"Don't sweat it," Frank said. "I had a busy day at the office myself."

At the office?

"Is it far from here?"

"Not too far. But it doesn't make sense to take two cars. And this way, we can get to know each other a little."

Ted had given up on peeking but was listening with one ear pressed against the backseat.

What if Mommy was right? This might be the other woman she had been talking about that afternoon. And thinking of Mommy, sitting in the living room behind the sofa, made Ted feel a twinge of distress. Mommy had taken three pills...

She hadn't taken them. Daddy had forced her to take them.

However it happened, she would most likely keep sitting wherever she had been left, even after night fell. She would wake up there, confused and surrounded by darkness—confused and alone. The state might not find her in time.

Ted shivered. His mind's eye showed him the living room in almost total darkness, with Mommy sitting unconscious on the floor, her head lolling to the side, and four antenna men standing around her, examining her like a bunch of doctors and looking at one another with their ant-like faces.

In the car, Frank started calling the young woman Elizabeth. They talked about her young son, who was living with her parents somewhere. But Ted was too caught up in his own thoughts to pay much attention to them. He wasn't ready to admit it, but he might have made a mistake when he left his mother alone.

A big mistake.

"...his father has never seen him," Elizabeth said. "He knows he has a son, of course—I told him. But he never cared. How about you?"

"My wife died and now the house seems too big for me," Frank McKay said. "Teddy is seven, and sometimes I think he's growing up too much on his own..."

His wife died? *"Teddy"?* His father never called him Teddy.

What was going on?

Ted felt an urge to lift the shelf and watch. He didn't doubt he had heard what he heard, but he could barely believe it. Ted wasn't growing up on his own! He had his mother! And the house where they lived was kind of small for their neighborhood. Nothing Daddy was saying made sense. He tried lying on his side to see Elizabeth but he couldn't. The farthest he could see in that direction was the rearview mirror—and when he looked into it, he saw Daddy's eyes staring back at his. Daddy was watching him!

He dropped the shelf, which hit the backseat with a thump, and lay on the floor of the trunk.

Daddy didn't see you. He was just looking back at the road. That's what rearview mirrors are for, isn't it?

"What was that?" Elizabeth asked.

"What was what?"

"I thought I heard something—on the roof, maybe."

"It was nothing."

"Is there far to go?"

"Not too far."

Nobody said another word for some time. Ted had lost all sense of time; he couldn't have said how long they'd been driving.

"Can we stop for a second?" Elizabeth suddenly asked. "I have an emergency."

"We're almost there. A quarter of a mile and you'll have a nice bathroom just for you."

"I can't hold it in."

"Of course you can," Frank snapped. Ted knew that tone well. It was a tone that admitted no questions.

The Mustang was speeding faster and faster.

"And don't even think of opening the door. Hear me?"

Elizabeth let out a bloodcurdling scream.

"Let me go!"

Ted held his breath.

A few seconds later the car stopped somewhere.

"See this?" Frank said calmly. "If you open the door, I'll stick it in your leg."

Ted didn't watch. He couldn't understand what was happening, but he knew this inflexible, authoritarian side of his father all too well.

"Don't hurt me," Elizabeth implored. "I have a son."

"No, you don't."

Frank removed the keys from the ignition and for some reason he jingled them. He opened his door and got out. Moments later he was opening the passenger door.

"I don't want to mess up the car. You understand, don't you?"

"Don't hurt me." The girl was broken. Her quivering plea turned into a ceaseless wail.

"Out."

"No. Please."

"Are you afraid?"

Elizabeth was sobbing uncontrollably. Frank was doing something to her, and Ted didn't dare look.

"Okay, okay, I'll go with you," Elizabeth said in the midst of a hysterical fit.

She left the car and, seconds later, let out a heartrending scream. Ted had never heard anything so disturbing in his short life. The screams would not cease, and he could do nothing but cover his ears. Even that was not enough.

A while later, Frank got back in the car, put it in drive, and started whistling his favorite melody.

81

Present day

IN THE basement of the abandoned typewriter factory, the rats had become extremely disoriented. Unsettled by the gasoline fumes, they paid no attention to where they scurried, crossing the basement floor only inches from Laura and Ted. Sometimes they walked right up to them and watched.

"You didn't kill those women," Laura said. "Your father did."

Ted stared, confused.

"Most likely you always suspected," she went on, "and when Frank died, your suspicions became certainties."

"The dream of the girl in the car trunk," Ted said, more to himself than to Laura. And as he thought it over, a hard truth hit him. He looked up, his eyes wide-open.

"What is it?"

"My father tried to kill me," Ted said, astonished.

Laura had reached the same conclusion.

"One of the last times I talked to him," Ted explained, "was at the university, when he told me Blaine was my brother. I was so angry at the way he'd treated my mother and me, I told him for the first time about the dreams where I saw the woman in the trunk of his Mustang."

Ted paused.

Ted tried his special peephole again, but it didn't give him a view of the passenger seat.

"When I told him my dream, he must have realized that I'd remember everything sooner or later. The son of a bitch went looking for me at the university that very night."

Laura completed the thought: "Tyler was with your girlfriend. But he was wearing a varsity hoodie."

Ted jumped to his feet. A rat that had been watching him from the hole in the floor turned and hid.

"The bastard was even lucky about dying. If only I'd remembered earlier. It won't do anybody any good now."

"Ted, please, sit down. And don't say that. A lot of families will get answers."

Ted slumped into his seat. "Yeah, sure. That a homicidal maniac terrorized and dismembered their daughters. A lovely answer. The guy's dead, Laura. Cancer took him. He died at home in bed, in his sleep. Can you imagine anything more unfair?"

"I really can't. But none of this is your fault."

Silence.

"If I'd only remembered earlier..."

"We've had to work very hard to get to this point, Ted. The treatment and the medication have helped a lot, but in the end you did it yourself. You did it for Holly, for the girls."

He nodded. His family seemed to belong to some galaxy far away.

"Do you remember how you found out, Ted? Was it through your dreams?"

"I don't think so." Ted didn't seem completely convinced. "The dreams had always been there. I think it was because of Blaine. When I saw him on TV and recognized him as my brother, I thought that maybe my father had murdered his girlfriend, that he'd done it as a favor or something. It was a thought. Unconscious, I guess. I don't know. I thought, *My father's been diagnosed with terminal cancer. Maybe he did it.*"

"I see. And that raised your suspicions—that thought."

"Yes, I think so. That's why I followed Blaine. I needed to investigate him, find out if he'd played any part in it. But by then, I already knew my father had done it. It was the chess tournaments, Laura—that's how I discovered all the murders from back then. He took advantage of our trips to kill defenseless women."

"Look at me, Ted. We know everything now. Your father is dead, and your family needs you. Look at me."

"You know it isn't that easy. I've hurt them." Ted's eyes filled with tears. "How is Justin?"

"I'm afraid he's still in a coma. But the doctors are optimistic."

"I assaulted my friend, almost killed him."

"You were in a fog, Ted. The burden of guilt for those murders had overwhelmed you. You felt responsible and you reacted irrationally. Because Justin found out somehow, didn't he?"

"Yes, I think so. I learned he was following me. I saw him one night when I slipped into Blaine's house; he was outside, in his car. I hired a detective to follow him, and that's how I learned that he and Holly were seeing each other." Ted smiled with resignation. "The poor detective must have thought that he'd blown the lid off something big, but their affair was no big deal for me. My problem was that Justin had also followed me here, and he may have seen what I had in the room upstairs that you got into."

"Did Justin call you to his office to talk about the murders?"

"I really don't know. Maybe he wanted to talk about something else. But it was too late. Me, I wasn't seeing things clearly. Now I understand."

"Justin will get better, and he will understand—I'm sure of it. Your illness was severe at that time, Ted."

"Yes, I know. I had already decided to kill myself. I'd gone to see Robichaud about the will, and I thought a brain tumor was going to kill me."

"Don't you think things are much better now?"

Ted knew things would get better only if his friend recovered.

"I guess so."

Laura stood up. Ted watched her incredulously, unable to comprehend what the doctor meant to do. Even when she held out her hand to him, he wasn't exactly sure what he was supposed to do with it.

"You've done very well, Ted."

He clumsily got to his feet and shook her hand.

"Thanks for everything, Laura." He was speaking in a whisper. His voice was about to break.

Just then they heard a loud noise in the back, too loud for rats to have made it. Laura jumped. Ted, for his part, felt a chill as he recalled that he had left the guard tied up back there. My God, he had allowed a heap of typewriters to fall on him! Before leaving him there, Ted had made sure he was still breathing, but he might have suffered internal injuries or something of the sort. These thoughts were going through his mind when the figure of Lee Stillwell rose up like a gray effigy, beyond the cone of light that illuminated only Ted and Laura.

A gruff voice emerged from the shadows. Laura turned and got the fright of her life when she saw Lee standing there. She had all but forgotten about him.

"Let us out of here right now, you goddamn bastard," Lee said.

The guard had his fettered hands at chest level and was holding a small object. There was no way to tell what it was at that distance, until a tiny flame emerged with a soft *click*.

82

Present day

MARCUS TOOK the passenger seat. Bob drove. They talked for the first half hour; afterward the drive passed in silence, interrupted only by calls from the FBI team that had set out from Albany at the same time and would reach the factory first.

When they were half an hour away they got the last call. Bob listened to what they were saying on the other end of the line; it didn't sound good to Marcus.

"There was a fire, apparently intentional," Bob said after he hung up. "An accelerant was used. The flames propagated very rapidly."

"A fire?" Marcus couldn't understand. He didn't want to ask the question whose answer he most feared.

"The Albany team arrived and found the firefighters at work. Somebody noticed the smoke and called it in, but they got there too late."

"What do you mean, 'too late'?" Marcus couldn't restrain himself. "What's that supposed to mean?"

"They recovered two bodies. There was only one survivor."

Marcus covered his face.

"Who?" he asked in the darkness of his own hands.

83

Present day

FOR SOME reason, Lee thought that threatening Ted with his cigarette lighter would be a good idea. Either the blow to his head kept him from thinking clearly or he had never heard that gasoline fumes are explosive. When the small blue flame from the lighter ignited a huge fireball, he seemed taken aback. Staring first in surprise at what he had caused, the guard dropped the lighter and began dancing frenetically, screaming in pain and unable to escape the circle of flames.

Laura and Ted had little time to react. A wall of fire was heading toward them, its blue tentacles of flame racing ahead. They quickly got as far from the fire as they could, running in opposite directions. Lee's screams grew more bloodcurdling. The smell of burning flesh filled the air.

The basement was divided in two, and Laura was trapped on the side opposite the door. As the guard let out his dying screams, she tried to find a way to cross to the other side, but the fire had formed a barrier that was advancing toward her; the smoke was growing dense. Lightbulbs exploded one by one, their light replaced by the new reality painted in pulsing orange. The rats shrieked.

Ted shouted at Laura to get back while he tried to move the green sofa, which the flames had not yet reached, to form a bridge between a table and a pile of rusty furniture. It didn't work. The flames nearly caught his shirt, and he had to take it off and cover his mouth with it in order to breathe. He shouted something unintelligible.

"What?" Laura was a good ten yards away, but instead of moving closer, she was forced to retreat. She also removed her shirt and breathed through it, but even so, she felt her thoughts growing sluggish.

Ted shouted again, this time taking the shirt from his mouth. "The trapdoor, Laura! Get in and close the top."

This time Laura understood. But she saw that it would be impossible for her to do this under these conditions. The flames stood between her and the opening in the floor.

"Ted, I can't reach it!"

He shouted something else, but his voice was muffled by the crackling flames. The smoke had become too thick, and it was all but impossible to breathe even through the filter of her blouse; Laura took it from her mouth. A fit of coughing brought her to her knees. She hadn't been conscious of the stinging in her eyes until she discovered that the air was somewhat more breathable close to the floor. She again covered her face with the fabric and crawled toward the side door. She told herself that her only chance of making it out alive would be by creeping along the base of the wall. A series of steel tables formed a sort of tunnel through which she could move relatively easily. The fire impeded her progress two or three times, forcing her to squeeze as close to the wall as she could get or even to exit her improvised tunnel. The closer to the door she got, the thicker the smoke grew, even at floor level.

Altogether she had another twenty-five feet or so to go. It seemed simple, but halfway there she started thinking she would never make it. A curtain of red flames blocked her way completely. If she wanted to keep going, she would have to leave her tunnel, but the situation wasn't much better out there. When she looked behind her, she saw she couldn't even go back.

She shouted to Ted but got no answer. Had he left the basement, or was he unconscious? The police were on their way; they might arrive at any moment. If she could get to the trapdoor, she might be able to hold out in there and yell long enough to be heard by anybody who was outside.

But first she'd have to reach the trapdoor; she didn't have much time. Either she tried leaving the tunnel and circling back to it, or she kept going straight ahead and jumped through the wall of fire. She had to try to break through, for Walter's sake.

She wrapped her head in her blouse, held up her arm to shield her face, and raced forward as fast as she could.

EPILOGUE

Two years later

RANDALL FORSTER was greeted with warm applause. For the past three years he had been the public face of crime reporting on Channel 4, and the exposure had made him immensely popular. The Frank McKay case had been key to his meteoric ascent: as a young, charismatic reporter, he had straddled the thin line between popular interest in the morbid details and the forensic technicalities of that salacious story.

Projected onto the screen dominating one side of the stage were the penetrating eyes that everyone had come to know. Underneath them, the title:

THE BUTCHER OF BARSTON FALLS
Frank Edmund McKay
1951–2011

The auditorium fell silent. The reporter's voice came solemnly over the address system.

"A middle-class home in the small hamlet of Barston Falls. A father who worked long hours at the machine tool factory. A mother who was cook, seamstress, shop assistant, and maid. Young Frank, growing up almost unsupervised to the age of twelve, when his baby sister, Audrey, came along."

Randall moved around the stage with the conviction of a practiced speaker. Gazing alternately at the audience and at the air above their heads, one hand in his pocket, he seemed to be peering into a distant, revealing past.

"That is as much as we know about his early years. What happened in the heart of the McKay family is, and perhaps will always remain, a mystery. In nineteen sixty-four, Ralph and Tess McKay moved to Boston with their two children, leaving little behind to be reconstructed years later."

A black-and-white photograph of a group of schoolchildren appeared on-screen. Two faces were circled, one of them with those unmistakable large, deep eyes.

"Frank learned early on to hide his true nature and to manipulate those around him. He was a model student, far above average in intelligence, and he never started any trouble. He knew how to go unnoticed. Andrew Dobbins, perhaps his only friend during his years in Barston Falls, has provided what is almost certainly the only characterization of Frank McKay that reflects the true essence of this prolific serial killer."

Randall paused purposefully. He had given this talk a handful of times before, though under different circumstances, and he knew how to rouse his audience's interest.

"When the truth came to light, everyone who had known Frank McKay over the course of his lifetime seemed shocked and horrified, including his sister, his former wife, his neighbors, his business partner. Everyone except Andrew Dobbins. Andrew Dobbins, who had not seen Frank McKay since he moved away from Barston Falls with his family at the age of thirteen, was the only one who immediately believed the news that was beginning to spread across the country. When others were unsure what to think, Andrew Dobbins knew—in his heart, he *knew*—that Frank McKay was guilty. Because Andrew Dobbins was the first and, as I have suggested, perhaps the only person ever to have peered into the abyss and seen this man's true face."

At some point the image on the screen had changed. It now showed a young Frank posing next to a red car. He looked about twenty, and at first sight there was nothing particularly remarkable about his smiling face. As the image drew closer, however, something about his eyes seemed to cross the barrier of time and space and to rest on each one of those present, revealing his genuine intentions.

"Frank McKay was not a perfect husband or a model neighbor, much less a good father. But in the view of those who knew him, he wasn't a murderer. He *couldn't* be a murderer. He was a temperamental man, certainly. An impulsive man, perhaps. But a murderer? Not at all. How many times have we heard this about others like him? Because when people such as McKay learn to hide behind the mask of sanity, they become undetectable. They walk among us with impunity. And it is this, it is precisely this ability to get away with things over and over again, to feel superior to everyone else, that drives them to go farther and farther. It is not only the unstoppable desire to harm and kill, but also the ego of a man who thinks he is above everyone else.

"Andrew Dobbins lived a few houses down from Frank. They walked to school together, came home together, became friends. One day Frank invited Andrew over to his house. It was summertime and his parents were both at work, so the boys were home alone. Frank told Andrew he didn't want to ride bikes that day or do any of the things they normally did. He led him to the backyard and showed him a number of jars that held spiders, beetles, and other large bugs. Frank had his pocketknife with him; he had bought it from an older boy, and no one knew about it except for Andrew. It was their shared secret. On that day, in that backyard, Frank asked his friend to pick out one of the trapped bugs. Andrew chose a medium-sized spider that seemed a little sluggish. He figured Frank was planning to kill the spider with his pocketknife—by then, he knew Frank was capable of such a thing, and the truth was that it didn't really bother him. Who hasn't killed a spider at one time or another?

Andrew was willing to join in the game, never imagining that he was actually being put to the test."

Though the case of the butcher of Barston Falls had been the subject of exhaustive reporting and analysis, most commenters focused on the killings that would come later. Journalists loved portraying the monster, but they often forgot the person. Randall had discovered that certain details, such as those he was about to reveal, could have a much deeper impact than even the most aberrant murder. The audience had fallen completely silent.

"Frank didn't kill the spider with his knife. Not right away. He cut off four of its legs. Then he and Andrew watched as it tried to run away, laughing to see how it could only crawl in circles. Then Frank cut off another leg, and then another, all the while explaining that he shouldn't cut them off too close to the body because then the spider would die too fast. At last the poor spider had only one stub of a leg left, with which it could barely scratch the ground and spin in circles until it died. It was not merely a wicked game but, as I have said, a test.

"Late that summer, Frank asked Andrew to come over to his house. He told him he was planning to do some 'special tests'—that was what Frank called the bug mutilations that they had both taken part in three or four times by then. Andrew was delighted. He was beginning to feel a sort of worshipful fascination with his friend. Frank led him back to the yard, but this time there were no jars of bugs. Instead, there was a basket with a tiny kitten of about three or four months, as Andrew Dobbins would recall many years later when he recognized with some guilt that, though he guessed at Frank's intentions at the time, they didn't especially trouble him. He had never been especially fond of cats.

"Frank spread the kitten's legs using four slender ropes. When he had it immobilized, and as the animal yowled in desperation, he gouged out its eyes with his pocketknife, then used a cigarette lighter to burn it on the stomach, the ears, the nose, until the kitten could no longer resist, and it died. Andrew stopped playing with Frank almost immediately thereafter, and his reaction may have served young Frank as a warning. A warning as to what could happen if he let others see his true nature."

There was no photograph now on the screen. Randall waited a few seconds, until the face of a twenty-year-old woman appeared.

"It is unlikely that Elizabeth Garth was his first victim, but she was undoubtedly one of the first, because McKay never again committed his murders so close to Boston."

Randall paused thoughtfully, slowly shook his head, and added, "What I just stated is not the absolute truth, of course. But we'll get to that. After all, it is the main reason we're gathered here today.

"The way in which Frank McKay killed Elizabeth Garth, a young single mother, shows that he was still on a learning curve. It is even likely that he was acting rashly. Not only did he kill her relatively close to home, but he had also made contact with her in a way that could have led to his capture. In addition, though Elizabeth's body revealed a few knife wounds on her arms and legs, a deep gash in her throat was sufficient to cause her death in a matter of seconds—a very different pattern from the type of sadistic torture found in his later murders.

"What was McKay thinking after he killed Elizabeth Garth? I would wager it was something along these lines. First, he had experienced tremendous pleasure from torturing and ultimately killing a defenseless young woman, so he knew he would want to do it again and again. Second, he realized that if he continued acting as recklessly as he had done on that day, he would ultimately be caught. He needed to come up with a system to guarantee his ability to continue indefinitely.

"There were at least seven killings between nineteen eighty-three and nineteen eighty-nine, and every one of them was committed out of state. The victims were young women, but that is where the commonalities end. Frank killed with a knife, with a hammer, even with his own hands. He selected his victims at random, keeping his contact with them to a minimum. During those years he took advantage of his son Ted's chess tournaments to justify his absences. He would travel more than an hour's drive from the tournament site, pick out a victim, and torture and mutilate her over the course of two to three hours. Few killings display such a level of cruelty, and yet discovering a pattern to connect these crimes would have been all but impossible."

The victims' faces appeared in sequence on the screen.

"Frank McKay died before he could be unmasked. He killed nineteen women and two men, and is a suspect in fifteen other murders. Not even a modern tracking program such as ViCAP could have established a common pattern."

A circular maze was projected on-screen.

"I told you earlier that perhaps no one saw the real Frank McKay other than his childhood friend Andrew Dobbins. But that may not be entirely true. It is possible that his first wife, Kristen McKay, who had to put up with his beatings and abuse for years, had glimpsed the evil that dwelt in her husband's inner being. But Kristen had psychiatric problems, and her condition became severe during the years they lived together. McKay's child Ted, however, also witnessed his father's erratic behavior. Young Ted, a chess prodigy who became a successful businessman, held the key to the mystery."

Randall pointed to the center of the labyrinth.

"A key that would remain hidden for years, and whose fascinating trajectory you will have the opportunity to learn at first hand."

The image of the labyrinth receded slowly, until it was revealed to be the image on the cover of a book. *The Only Way Out* was the title. Underneath, in large red letters, was the author's name.

"Ladies and gentlemen, without any further ado, I present to you the woman who finally brought these facts into the light of day. I give you Dr. Laura Hill."

Loud applause greeted Laura, who dashed to the front of the room and took her place at a table beside the screen. It was her third book presentation, but she was still as nervous as she'd been the first time. She sought out Deedee in the front row, and the mere sight of her sister there, clapping effusively, gave her strength. Her sister had always been important in her life, but in recent months, since her dismissal from Lavender and her subsequent breakup with Marcus, Deedee had become her main support. Deedee and Walter, of course. But Deedee was the only one who had encouraged her to finish her book when things got rough at Lavender. "The manuscript is excellent. If your bosses at the hospital gave you an ultimatum, I say the hell with them. And as for that boyfriend of yours, it wouldn't surprise me if he washed his hands of it all. You know I never did like him."

Deedee was not mistaken.

"Welcome!"

"Thank you, Randall."

For this night, Laura had picked out a mustard-yellow skirt and a long-sleeve white blouse. *Always long-sleeve*. It hugged her figure, and when she sat down and laid her hands in her lap, she made sure her right wrist was not exposed. Only a thin strip of burnt skin could be seen peeking out from the cuff.

"First off," Randall said, "let me say what a tremendous pleasure it is for me to have been invited here tonight."

Laura nodded.

"Thank you for your wonderful introduction."

"You're very welcome."

The reporter turned to look at the screen, on which the cover of Laura's book was still projected. As if the question had just occurred to him, he asked, "Tell us: why a labyrinth, Laura?"

"Oh, I've always found labyrinths fascinating. I grew up in Hawks Nest, North Carolina, and there was a little amusement park there. The owner, Mr. Adams—a charming man—kept the park running for years, in spite of everyone's predictions that a small local attraction was doomed to fail. Its main feature was a huge circular labyrinth."

"Like a corn maze?"

"No, not corn. It was a labyrinth of stone and wood, and what made it special was that it could be reconfigured on the go. It had a series of doors that opened and closed, and every time you entered it, the maze had changed. Mr. Adams said there were more than a thousand configurations, but perhaps he was exaggerating. A guy in a Minotaur costume roamed around inside, making it even harder to escape. When we were little we were terrified to go in. And the fact is, I rarely saw anybody discover the way out. I used to go there with my sister—who is here in the audience tonight—almost every day during the summer. A boy we liked worked there."

Deedee pointed at her from the first row and mouthed the words, "A boy *you* liked..."

Laura couldn't help smiling.

"I've always been attracted to labyrinths," she went on. "There's something about the way we think that is like escaping from a labyrinth."

"Or like being trapped inside one, I suppose," said Randall.

"Exactly! For example, you entered the Hawks Nest labyrinth through a passageway that took you directly to the center of the maze. And for some reason, I always thought that if I chose the path that took me away from the center, I'd be able to get out. And of course I never succeeded."

"Because sometimes we have to backtrack in order to get out. Is that why?"

"Yes, exactly. When Ted McKay was sent to Lavender Memorial, it was as if he were trapped in a labyrinth created by his own mind."

"Being the brilliant man he was, I imagine his maze was quite complex."

"Definitely. He spent weeks trapped in cycles, spinning round and round and never getting anywhere. When I tried to force things, tried to lead him outside the labyrinth in the wrong direction, the way I did as a young girl trying to escape the Hawks Nest labyrinth, he'd end up lost again. It was like starting all over."

"Ted McKay perished in the fire in the abandoned factory," Randall said, imbuing his voice with a certain gravitas. "A fire which you, Laura, were lucky to survive. In a sense, this story has been your own labyrinth. Is that how you see it?"

"Perhaps. But it was Ted McKay who bore the brunt of it, not only because he lost his life, but because he had to struggle with such a heavy burden for so many years. This book, Randall, deals with that traumatic experience and tells the story of how he escaped from a trap set by his own mind. If it hadn't been for his strength, I wouldn't be here today, and none of these terrible crimes would ever have been cleared up."

A scattering of applause spread through the auditorium and grew into an ovation. Laura and Randall joined in.

"One of the last things Ted told me before he died," Laura said, "was that for him, none of this made sense now that his father was dead. But you and I have seen how important it is to know the truth."

"Oh, absolutely. I've had the opportunity to talk with members of the victims' families, and for many of them, knowing that the person responsible for these crimes no longer walks among us has been a great relief."

"And also for Ted's former wife and his daughters, who've had to face the loss of a loved one. I can't even imagine what that must be like. But at least they've been able to see him as he really was: a man with a great heart, who was forced to bear up under a burden not his own."

The presentation continued for another half hour. Randall was an excellent interviewer, and their exchange sounded like two friends having a deep conversation.

Afterward came the book signing, when Laura could finally relax and enjoy the affections of her readers. Some sneaked a look at the hint of a scar around the cuff of her right sleeve; others made comments about the book or asked questions. The most frequently asked questions were about Justin Lynch. Laura knew from news reports that he had woken from his coma but not much more. She politely replied that she wasn't in contact with Lynch and that the permission she had been granted by

Lynch's family to reveal information had ended with the last page of the book.

At some point Laura glimpsed a short man in thick horn-rimmed glasses lingering at the back of the room; he wasn't waiting in the line for books to be signed. He looked to be about fifty, or maybe a bit younger, and he had her book under his arm and a half smile on his face.

With every book she signed and handed back, Laura stole a glance and found the stranger in horn-rims still standing there, always in the same place. The auditorium was emptying out when one of the organizers, a tall fellow named Matthews, returned to the table where Laura sat. She asked him if he wouldn't mind sitting there with her. He agreed, of course. That was when Horn-rims left his spot and got in line. At the end of the line.

A colossal woman planted herself in front of the table, and Laura lost visual contact with Horn-rims. She was one of those people who are always smiling and brimming over with energy: *"I'm sooooooo glad to meet you. I loved your book sooooooo much."* Laura made an effort to focus on the woman, who really was charming and had obviously gone to some lengths to be present that night. *"I drove here from Vermont—I have family here, but I came especially to see you, Dr. Hill. You have so much talent."* Laura nodded and wrote a few words on the title page. She looked up to see if the man was still there, but she couldn't see past the woman's stomach. *"Thank you sooooooo, sooooooo much. Keep writing, please. Can I tell you something?"* Laura kept smiling, but she was afraid her smile might be turning into an uneasy grimace. Where was Horn-rims? She pictured him jumping out from behind the woman, knife in hand. Why was she thinking that such a thing might happen? It wasn't as if serial killers had a club and they were all angry with her. Yet it wasn't the first time the thought had crossed her mind. *"I've fallen in love with Ted, a little bit."* The woman was talking, and her cheeks blushed as red as glowing coals. *"Oh, you must think I'm silly. I don't really mean 'in love'—only the way one falls in love with good characters."* Laura told her she understood perfectly what she meant and thanked her for coming. She handed the woman her signed book, and at last the woman left. Horn-rims was still waiting at the end of the line.

Ten minutes later, Laura signed two copies for one couple, and then it was the little man's turn.

"Don't you recognize me?"

His voice was musical and measured. If this man was a serial killer, he was the world's most charming one. Laura relaxed.

"I'm sorry. I don't," she said. But no sooner had she said it than her mind made the connection.

"My name is Arthur Robichaud," the man in the horn-rimmed glasses confirmed.

Laura had found a photograph of the lawyer on the Internet but had never met him. They had talked briefly over the phone, and the conversation had not been exactly pleasant.

Robichaud looked in both directions. A few people remained in the auditorium, conversing in small groups, but they were all far from them. The only one who could hear them was Matthews, and Laura asked him to step away for just a moment.

"Thank you for changing my name," the lawyer said.

"You asked me to."

"Yes, of course, but even so, you might have refused. I apologize if I was a little rude when we talked by phone that time, but you must understand how something like this could affect my practice."

"No worries."

Robichaud seemed uneasy. He still hadn't handed her the book he was carrying under his arm.

"I didn't want to interrupt you earlier. I've read your book, and I think it's very good. Congratulations."

He set the book on the table.

"Thank you. I get the sense, though, that something else has brought you here. Am I mistaken?"

Robichaud shook his head in silence. He looked up at the ceiling as if the words he was looking for might be written there.

"I've been thinking over what I'm going to tell you, and still I find it so hard..."

Laura didn't understand. She had reduced Robichaud's role in the book to the minimum, partly at his own request. What might he have to tell her that could be so important?

"I haven't even told my wife," the lawyer now said with genuine regret. "I haven't told anyone, but you'll understand me, or I hope you will."

"I'm listening."

"Ted came to my house one afternoon, just as you describe it in the book. It was my birthday, though of course he was unaware. It isn't true that all our old schoolmates were there, but some of them were. I mean, what you describe in the book is pretty close to what really happened that day. He and I...We met in my office to discuss topics related to his will."

Laura studied him.

"All of his cycles had their basis in actual episodes," she said. "I was able to talk with other people and confirm it."

Robichaud nodded.

"I'm sorry I didn't talk with you before. I...If I'd only known." Robichaud placed his hand on the book, as if he were going to swear an oath.

"Don't worry about it."

"In the book, you write about a possum. What exactly does it signify?"

Laura leaned back in her chair, taken by surprise. She hadn't really delved into the theme of the possum. Ted had barely talked about it, and most of her references to it came from speaking with Mike Dawson, who hadn't been very generous with details when he spoke with her, either.

"For some reason Ted was afraid of it," Laura said with an understanding smile. "He must have gone through some traumatic incident, or so I infer. I never asked him."

Robichaud nodded.

"But in those 'cycles,' what role did the possum play, exactly?"

"Mr. Robichaud, is this important to you somehow?"

"Yes."

"May I ask why?"

"On that day, in my backyard, Ted thought he saw a possum, just as you describe it in your book. Well, not exactly: he didn't see it inside an old tire, but hiding among some flowerpots my wife keeps."

Laura couldn't hide her bewilderment. She had assumed that the part of the story in which the possum appeared hadn't been real but only part of the cycles.

"I'm surprised."

"I can imagine. So, what is the role of the possum?"

"I can't be certain, Mr. Robichaud, but I think it was Ted's way of staying inside his cycles. Whenever things began to spin out of control, the possum was there. I know that Ted dreamed of it at times, and it's possible that its representation in the cycles was as a kind of guardian."

Robichaud paused in thought.

"Like the Minotaur in the labyrinth in your hometown..."

Not bad for a lawyer.

"Something like that, I suppose."

Now the auditorium was empty.

"I saw the possum that day," Robichaud suddenly said.

Laura kept silent.

"Ted started shouting that there was a possum in the backyard, and some of my friends ran out to try and catch it. They couldn't find anything. But I was in my office, watching out my window—and I did see it. I saw the exact moment when it ducked in among the flowerpots."

"I don't know what to tell you. Possums really do exist. It must have escaped."

"There must have been thirty people there, and nobody saw the possum leave. The flowerpots sit on a brick porch in the middle of the yard, and there was no way it could have run out without being seen. Ted saw it. I saw it. Nobody else."

All Laura could do was stare at him. He held out his hand and Laura shook it.

"Now you understand why I couldn't talk to you earlier, don't you?"

Arthur Robichaud didn't wait for an answer. He picked up the book he had set on the table, smiled, and sauntered away, as if a great weight had been removed from his shoulders.

ACKNOWLEDGMENTS

This book was not written overnight. Ted McKay remained in his study for a long time, waiting for the author to grasp the true reasons behind his decision. Fortunately I was able to rely on a number of people for help.

To my mother, Luz, who listened attentively to the early ideas for this book, absurd as many of them were. She and my father, Raúl Axat, have always been by my side throughout my writing career.

To Patricia Sánchez, who heard about this story when it was just starting to take shape and who, in trust and friendship, built the bridges that have made it a reality today.

To Maria Cardona, my agent at Pontas Agency, who read the original manuscript and suggested some important changes to the plot. Thanks, Maria, for pushing me in the right direction!

To Anna Soler-Pont, the captain of the most incredible literary ship, and to her whole crew, for achieving the impossible with this book.

To Anna Soldevila and to the editorial team at Destino, for working tirelessly on the original manuscript.

To my sister and brother, Ana Laura Axat and Gerónimo Axat, and to my nephew, Ezequiel Sánchez Axat.

To Ariel Bosi and María Pïa Garavaglia, for reading the original manuscript and sharing their thoughts.

To the colleagues I admire and respect who have helped me with their advice and their example: Raúl Ansola, Paul Pen, Montse de Paz, and Dolores Redondo.

ABOUT THE AUTHOR

FEDERICO AXAT was born in Buenos Aires, Argentina, in 1975. He is the author of the novel *Benjamin,* which was published in Spain, and *El pantano de las mariposas* (*The Meadow of the Butterflies*), which was translated into German, Portuguese, French, and Chinese. *Kill the Next One* (*La última salida*), an international phenomenon, is Axat's U.S. debut; translation rights have been sold in twenty-nine countries.